MW01138151

COMMISSAR

COMMISSAR

A NOVEL OF CIVIL WAR RUSSIA

D.V. Chernov

Copyright © 2022 D. V. Chernov

The moral right of the author has been asserted.

Apart from any fair dealing for the purposes of research or private study,
or criticism or review, as permitted under the Copyright, Designs and Patents
Act 1988, this publication may only be reproduced, stored or transmitted, in
any form or by any means, with the prior permission in writing of the
publishers, or in the case of reprographic reproduction in accordance with
the terms of licences issued by the Copyright Licensing Agency. Enquiries
concerning reproduction outside those terms should be sent to the publishers.

This is a work of fiction. Names, characters, businesses, places, events
and incidents are either the products of the author's imagination
or used in a fictitious manner. Any resemblance to actual persons,
living or dead, or actual events is purely coincidental.

Matador
9 Priory Business Park,
Wistow Road, Kibworth Beauchamp,
Leicestershire. LE8 0RX
Tel: 0116 279 2299
Email: books@troubador.co.uk
Web: www.troubador.co.uk/matador
Twitter: @matadorbooks

ISBN 978 1800465 596

British Library Cataloguing in Publication Data.
A catalogue record for this book is available from the British Library.

Printed and bound in Great Britain by 4edge Limited
Typeset in 14pt Baskerville by Troubador Publishing Ltd, Leicester, UK

Matador is an imprint of Troubador Publishing Ltd

To my wife and daughter –
two of the most amazing women in my life.

RUSSIA
1918

A HISTORICAL NOTE

This novel is based largely on real historical events and people. For more information about this fascinating period in world history and about the characters in this novel, both real and fictional, please visit the author's official website dvchernov.com.

A NOTE ON RUSSIAN NAMES

Russian first names can have a number of commonly used nickname forms. For example, Anna may also be called *Annochka* and *Annushka* by her friends and family. Additionally, Russian last names have both feminine and masculine forms. So, while Anna's last name is *Sokolova*, her brother's last name is *Sokolov*.

JULY 12, 1918

The first shipment of dynamite arrived in Moscow last night. Ninety pounds is not nearly enough, but it is a start. V. promised more next week. If he is unable to deliver, we will have to manufacture the rest. Let's hope it does not come to that – sourcing the materials is risky enough, never mind the process. For now, we stored it in the basement under G.'s office. I've forgotten the sweet smell nitroglycerin gives it. And the headaches that come with it. Tomorrow, N. will have an update about the guns.

– Boris Savinkov's Journal

BLOODLINES

"Are we going home?" a girl's voice asked.

Anna gasped, jolted awake into the darkness of the room. The awakening felt like a fall, and her first sketchy flash of awareness was the voices and the heavy steps of the soldiers' boots approaching in the hallway. The second was her fingers clutched around the checkered grip of the revolver. She held her breath, her pulse thumping furiously at the temples. This wasn't her room. The steps grew closer and passed, stomping through the slit of light under her door and then down the creaky stairs, growing muffled and fading into the depths of the house.

The memories of the last two days reassembled in her mind. She put the heavy pistol on the bed and lay there in the dark, listening and letting the galloping heartbeat subside. The house was quiet again. In the open window, a warm breeze rustled the leaves in the humid July night. Far off, thunder rumbled – artillery shells detonating in the distance. The frontline was edging closer.

2

The *errand* was simple enough in its essence but there was nothing simple about it. Delivering an urgent dispatch from Central a thousand miles away from Moscow was no trivial feat in times of war. But she managed to make it. She made it in just under two sleepless days – by trains and by cars, edging further and further east on the map, and not knowing if each next town had already fallen into the enemy's hands. She remembered getting in last night and finding the house with a makeshift fence and a guard posted outside. She had spoken with the commandant, and then crashed here, exhausted, still in her uniform, on top of the covers.

Her eyes adjusted to the dark, but remnants of interrupted sleep still lingered in her head like a fog. Somewhere in the depths of the house, another burst of muffled voices rumbled. How long had she been asleep? She squinted at the white face of Alexei's watch on her wrist. The hands shimmered semi-opaque in the pale light of the window – just past one. What could be going on at this hour? With a sigh, she resolved that sleep was not going to happen now.

Let's go – she gave a mental mandate to self and sat on the edge of the bed. After the countless short nights, the act of pulling on her boots and standing up – dizzy with half-sleep – no longer took conscious effort. It was just the first step of the now mechanical routine: slipping the revolver into the holster, tugging the heavy belt into place on her waist, and checking for the escaped strands of hair from the dark ball pinned tightly at the nape of her neck.

And yet, there was something not routine about this place. She did not feel it last night, maybe because of the exhaustion, but she felt it now, tugging at the back of her heart like a forgotten warning from a dream. She turned the door handle.

The blinding lights outside the room illuminated a mystery: there were no people in sight. Last night, *the guests* were here. But now, the rooms stood empty, with the lights on and the doors ajar. The only sound and the only movement in this side of the house came from the empty dining room, where a large clock was still

3

measuring out time with indifference, its brass pendulum aglow with the light from the crystal chandelier.

She followed the thin scent of cigarette smoke toward the murmur of voices coming from somewhere deep in the meander of corners, doors and hallways. The lights were on and the curtains were drawn in every room.

She glanced down the stairway leading to the cellar. The carved handrail curved elegantly in its downward swoop towards the closed double doors. The cool, lacquered touch of the wood echoed a childhood memory: the summers at the family manor. It was much like this one – all parlors, stairs, heavy drapes and crystal chandeliers. *Our modest mansion*, as her father used to say.

Except this one was worn to the bone. The parquet floors were scuffed and marred, the gilded paint was chipping away from the trim. *Elegant, delicate, intricate* – all the words that used to describe things in their lives then – now and here were grotesquely out of place. And out of time. Vestiges of an over-turned era. Elegance was now just a specter, like this house – a flaking veneer of opulence revealing the decaying empire underneath – shabby, barren, dirty.

The voices were coming from the drawing room – the front parlor where half a dozen soldiers were congregated, discussing something in half-voices and smoking. They hushed down, seeing her enter. She scanned them with a momentary glance, but the man she was looking for wasn't among them. They watched her glumly from the smoke. A couple of them looked like they had been digging in the dirt. There was a nervous air of anticipation laced into the cigarette smoke in this room. She wondered what they were waiting for, at this hour.

"Yurovsky?" she inquired and cleared her voice. One of them pointed towards the door to the kitchen. Walking through the parlor, she felt their eyes on her. Was it her uniform or her looks that made them hush? A woman in uniform was still an uncommon sight this far from Moscow. Especially a pretty woman. She knew she was pretty but, but unlike some girls, never liked to draw attention to that fact, learning from a young age to be judicious with her glances and her words when she did not care to invite attention. As she did not care to now.

"Did we wake you?" Yurovsky's raspy baritone rolled towards her as she crossed the threshold to the kitchen.

The commandant sat stooped at the old oak table meant for the servants, cleaning his Nagant revolver. His eyes studied her over the rims of his small glasses. The strapping Cheka officer she met last night now reminded her of some dark creature from an old painting – a Rembrandt or a Bruegel, half-emerged from the semi-shadows, with his army trench coat draped on the back of his chair, falling behind him like a pair of dark folded wings. The seven rounds from his gun stood lined up on the table before him like a formation of toy soldiers awaiting orders, gleaming in the dull yellow light of the kerosene lamp.

His glasses glinted downward as he refocused on his task.

Did he really care if his men woke her? His face was hard to read – thin, with sunken cheeks and sunken, sleepless eyes under a heavy brow. A full, dark beard concealed his lips. Yurovsky was what they called a *Starík* – an Old Man – a career revolutionary hardened not by his age but by the many years spent in the underground and often many more in the imperial prisons and labor camps. He was older than her, but she could not guess by how much – as it often was with someone who had lived an uneasy life. His appearance was impenetrable and composed, except for the single rebellious dark curl hanging out of place from his deeply creased forehead.

"Where are *the guests*?"

He glanced at her over his glasses again, without interrupting his task. His fingers pulled out the center pin and removed the cylinder. "The cellar," he finally uttered. His face now looked even more sunken and sleepless than yesterday. Maybe it was just the uneven light of the kerosene lamp.

"Why?" Why would a family of seven need to be moved to the cellar in the middle of the night?

He did not answer immediately, appearing wholly consumed with his task. He ran the brush through the barrel a few times, blew through it, checked, and then repeated.

At last, his voice measured out the words: "Tell me, Commissar, why are you here?"

"What do you mean?" She felt on guard.

"I am not trying to pry," he shook his head. "You just don't seem the usual Cheka type. You are what – twenty-two? Twenty-three? Well educated. There must be things more suitable to your level for you to do in Moscow, instead of the grunt agency work."

"They said this was highly important and top secret... the telegraph was down, and Central needed confirmation."

He nodded, focusing his attention on cleaning each chamber of the cylinder. "Yes, but why *you*? Why the Cheka? Wouldn't you rather be organizing party meetings, running committees, socializing with other young, educated people? Instead, you are *here*."

His line of probing was irksome to her, as this wasn't the first time someone – usually a man – had questioned her choice of occupation. And yet, his tone was different – disarming with a rough-edged softness, showing no intent to judge or antagonize.

"I am *here* because a war is going on," she obliged. "I can't sit in Moscow and wait to hear about it in a party meeting. I am here because the fight is here."

He nodded again. "The *fight*." He weighed the word pensively, wrinkling the mustached corner of his lip while his practiced soldier's hand snapped the drum back into place and locked the center pin. "Now, there is a passionate term." The dark circles of his glasses caught the light as he glanced up at her. "So, you have a score to settle with the old regime?"

She shook her head, but her mind was already back in front of the Winter Palace, watching helplessly as the thin red lines of blood spread through the cracks between the snow-swept pavestones. And in the cold air, the smell – metallic, sickening, mixed with gunpowder and frost.

"No. I just have something to fight for." She disliked being probed. "And *you*? Why are *you* here?"

He cocked the hammer, spun the drum like a roulette wheel, and tested the trigger with a hollow click of the firing pin in the empty chamber.

"Because a long time ago, I chose a certain path. Or maybe it chose me. I don't know anymore. It was the fight, as you said." He produced a handkerchief from his pocket and carefully cleaned the lenses of his glasses. His face looked even thinner without them. "Much has changed over the years, but much has remained the same. The fight still rages on, but now I have new reasons. Right now, my wife and children are sleeping in a house down the street. I am *here* for them, for their future. I am here because someone must be."

He put the glasses back on and took the gun in his hand again. He snapped the drum open, picked up the first round off the table, examined it and lowered it into its chamber. His face was solemn, as if he took no pleasure in the task.

"Russia is like a house," his finger circled the air. "Generations come and go, like families moving in and out. People dream, suffer, grow old, die. New generations are born. But it does not mean the house itself can't change. This house was somebody's mansion last year. Today it is a prison. If we do the right things, maybe next year it will be a school." He loaded more rounds, until only one remained. "But doing the right thing – sometimes that's the hard part. If you stay in the Cheka, you'll find that the right things are not always black and white."

"I don't see it that way," she shook her head. "I think in the end, things are always either black or white."

He paused and regarded her words with a light nod and then took the last bullet from the table. He wiped it with his handkerchief and slotted it into the drum. The center pin locked into place.

"Perhaps you are right. Perhaps in the end, we'll know." He rose from his chair and holstered the loaded gun. "Do you know what is in the orders you brought from Moscow?" He picked up the folded papers from the table and pushed them into the pocket of his uniform.

She shook her head, as the unease she had felt earlier twisted into a tight pit in her stomach.

"Stay here, then. It's an order."

"Why? What is going on?"

He looked at her without seeing her, his mind already preoccupied with something else. "Just stay here. No matter what you hear."

He walked past her, his boots driving heavily into the floorboards. "*It's time,*" she heard him say to the soldiers waiting in the parlor, and no one said another word – just more heavy footsteps in silence, lumbering down the hallway and down the stairs to the cellar. A door creaked shut.

She darted back to the top of the staircase above the closed double doors and listened intently but heard only her own frantic heartbeat over the muffled movement and voices below. And then, Yurovsky's words cut through. Raspy. Cracked and forceful.

"Citizen Nikolai Romanov," *(had anyone ever called him that before in his life?),* "it is my duty to inform you that, in the face of imminent risk of you being recaptured by the enemy, your trial has been expedited. You have been found guilty of grave crimes against the Russian people. For these crimes, by the order of the Ural Regional Soviet of the Worker's Government and the Central Committee of the Communist Party of the Soviet Republic, you and your family have been sentenced to death. The sentence is to be carried out immediately."

The family? She froze, mortified. *All of them!?* Certainly, *not all* of them were in that room right now. And yet, in the same moment, she knew that they were.

Behind the closed doors, there was a pause of stunned silence, and then several voices burst out in an escalating protest, Nicholas' probably among them. But they were cut short by an eruption.

She had never before heard gunfire inside a house. The blasts detonated in the enclosed cellar in a deafening, ringing assault on her eardrums like a battery of sledgehammers pounding iron into the rock. There must have been screams in the room, but she did not hear them. She did not need to hear them. She had heard them before – the blasts and the screams. Each blast a bullet hole – a rough, seeping puncture. And now, gripping onto the railing at the top of the stairs, she was in front of the Winter Palace again, surrounded with blasts and screams, and people running and the hooves clattering, and she watched helplessly again as the blood spread in a red tide through Alexei's shirt, steaming in the frozen air, seeping into the white snow. The thin red lines were drawing themselves again, spreading through the cracks between the frozen pavestones. She smelled blood – sharp and sickening… She tried to breathe, but her breath choked at the back of her throat. All she could hear now was her own heartbeat racing faster and faster in a freefall, and all she could do was to keep holding on to the railing, gripping it tighter and tighter with her bone-white fingers.

How long did the execution last? It must have been mere seconds. But for a while, she stood there, unsure if it was over. Was she still hearing the gunshots ringing in her ears? Were the blasts still reverberating through the floorboards? She breathed in, and an uncontrollable tremor shuddered at her core. A single shot rang out. Silence. Two more. Silence.

The double doors creaked open, and a young soldier stumbled out, coughing. A thick billow of gunpowder smoke crept after him like bluish fog. It spread, rolling and churning slowly through the doorway, until it thinned enough for her to see shapes and to fix her gaze on a white blotch on the floor. She soon recognized it, as the gun smoke thinned more – the lacy arm of a dress, partially covered by another body.

The blast of another gunshot made her recoil. A soldier knelt next to the body and took the white-sleeved arm in his hand. This was a gesture someone could mistake for compassion, but she knew he was checking for a pulse.

Yurovsky emerged with his glasses in one hand and his revolver in another. He staggered up the steps heavily, like an overburdened man; his shell-shocked stare fixed blankly ahead. The nauseating metallic smell of singed gunpowder and blood followed him.

"How could you?!" she managed a hoarse whisper. "Their boy was just a child!"

She searched his face, but there was nothing left. When his eyes rose to meet hers, he looked ill.

"That was the order," his voice cracked. "The entire bloodline."

He cut gloomily towards the kitchen and then half-turned in the doorway, looking at the floor. "The army has been ordered to retreat. The Whites are advancing. You should get yourself back to Moscow." He put on his trench coat and went outside.

MOSCOW

The new Cheka headquarters on Lubyanka Square was a big, fanciful city block of yellow brick in the center of Moscow, just a few minutes' walk from the Kremlin. It was like a small-scale baroque palace that rose above the pavement in layers of stone, windows and iron, trimmed with turreted corners, pointed rooftops, decorative pediments and a large clock inset like a crown jewel into the façade above the top-floor portico.

This building was designed with grandeur and class unintended for its current occupants – the small contingent of former soldiers and sailors who constituted the new Moscow Cheka and whose boots now treaded the miles of golden parquet on all five floors, whose fingers rattled with the typewriter keys, and whose loud laughter and swearing now rang through the hallways. And yet much of the building remained vacant – entire hallways preserved as dusty, ghostly, still-life reminders of the insurance underwriters, bankers and lawyers who had inhabited this edifice before the revolution.

It had now been two weeks since Ekaterinburg, and she was still acutely aware of its looming gravity in the recent past. She wasn't ready for that level of violence. Maybe she had been naïve, but when she returned, she never wanted to be ready for that. That's why she transferred to a new department, and then they had moved into a new building. And with each day, she deflected her mind to think of Ekaterinburg less and to think of it less viscerally. She had a new office now, new cases and new co-workers, and Ekaterinburg had become an abstract form – sorrowful but un-referenceable and unusable. It was like the odd inner courtyard at the new HQ: a gloomy, treeless, blunted wedge of pavement – the bottom of a deep well of four walls and countless watching windows, where the sun never seemed to reach. To her, it was a space of claustrophobic doom. She preferred to not even look down there.

Luckily, her department's windows faced outward. Their office was a medium-sized room fitted with six desks and a permanent cloud of cigarette smoke floating just below the ceiling. Anna zigzagged to her desk, plopped into the chair and kicked up her boots. The office was empty except for Anton Egorov, a burly, rosy-cheeked farmer's son with a shrapnel scar across his temple. He was dutifully suffering through typing up a report, his fingers frustrated with the multitude of keys.

"Ah – there you are!" Sergei popped into the door. "Where the heck have you been? You left me a note this morning and then disappeared."

"Sorry – Egorov and I did not get back till noon, and I had to debrief with Surveillance."

He sat on the corner of her desk, his black army boots polished to a shine and his smooth, cleanly shaven face beaming with a smile.

"So, you had some news? What is it?" He got out a pack of cigarettes from his shirt pocket.

"It's big," Anna said, relishing his suspense. "Huge."

He raised an eyebrow, his hands busy with lighting a cigarette.

"Since we've had no new leads on Savinkov, I had the surveillance team check up on several of his old associates. Really old – before the war."

"Where did you find their information?"

"The Okhrana archives."

He smirked. "Guess we can always count on the good old imperial secret police to have kept impeccable records. So... what did you find?"

She could tell he was hanging on to her words, but she was enjoying torturing him a bit. "One of his old pals had a *very* interesting meeting last night."

"With Savinkov?!" His jaw hovered open in anticipation, cigarette hanging between his fingers.

"No," she dropped casually and probably a bit cruelly, knowing exactly the effect it would have.

He visibly deflated. "Who, then?"

She paused for a dramatic effect. "Robert Hamilton Bruce Lockhart."

His eyebrows shot up: "The British consul?!"

She gave him a nod and watched the wheels frantically ratchet up in his head.

"Where?"

"At Lockhart's residence."

"Who was it?"

"Natalia Goncharova." She dug a key out of her pocket, unlocked her desk and pulled out a file. "The Okhrana had a hefty volume on her," she said, flipping it open. "Are you ready for this? Not only was she a known member of SR Combat Operations, she and Savinkov were both active in the group during the assassinations of the Grand Duke of Moscow and the Governor of Ufa."

"That was what... thirteen years ago? So, they go way back. Before he headed the organization. Is there anything more recent on her?"

"Nothing. It looks like she deactivated shortly after. That's why she did not come up in our earlier searches. Maybe she decided she did not have the stomach for it?"

He gave her a sideways nod. "It's not uncommon for those types of organizations. They start out young and idealistic, and then decide they don't agree with the methods or the objectives. What is she doing now?"

"She works at the textile factory and lives with her son, age four, and her elderly mother."

Sergei stared into the smoky corner of the ceiling, trying to assemble the pieces into a plausible scenario. "So, she is a nobody. But the British would not talk to a nobody, so she must be speaking for Savinkov. Maybe that's why he chose her – she's been inactive for so long, he figured she would be less likely to be watched." He looked back to Anna. "Tell me exactly what she did."

"The surveillance team tracked her last night. She met with Lockhart from seven to seven-forty and then went home. Egorov and I followed her this morning. According to the factory foreman, she had the day off today. She took her son to a doctor's office in Molochny Alley at eleven and then back home. Nothing out of the ordinary. Nikolaev and Borovsky are on her now. She is back on the shift at the factory tomorrow. Why do you suppose Savinkov is talking to the British? Maybe he is seeking asylum?"

He raked his fingers through his hair and sighed. "As much as I would like that, I doubt it. If he wanted to leave, he would have done so already – of all people, he does not need help crossing the border illegally. If the reports are true and he is back in Moscow, then he is here to fight, and whatever he needs from the British has to do with that. Now, the good thing is that Lockhart is easy to follow. I will get Dzerzhinsky to sign off on full-time surveillance. I'll also see if we can intercept the diplomatic cables and find out what the British want with our most wanted terrorist." He looked around for an ashtray and pulled one from a nearby desk. "This is really good, Anna. This can lead us right to Savinkov."

She tapped the pencil on her lips. "But all of this will take time. Can't we just pick her up and question her?"

He shook his head firmly. "No. She won't give him up."

"Why not? She's been out for almost a decade. She has a son now... different priorities."

"If she had different priorities, she would not have gotten pulled back in. People from the Combat Organization are fanatical. They are willing to become martyrs for the cause. I'd bet she would be willing to sacrifice both herself and her son, if needed."

"You don't think it's worth a try?"

"No. Not now. If we pick her up and she calls our bluff, we end up with nothing, and we spook Savinkov in the process. Let's just see if she leads us to him. I can help with the tail tomorrow."

"*You* want to go out *in the field* with *us*?" She squinted at him – a mischievous smirk playing on her lips. "Are you sure your busy lecturing schedule will allow it?"

"Oh!" Egorov leaned back and erupted in laughter, his thumbs stuck in the straps of his suspenders and his chair creaking precariously under his hulking weight.

"Well, now you two clowns are definitely stuck with me tomorrow," Sergei chuckled. "I've been trying to nail Savinkov for the last five months. The last thing I want is for you two to fumble it up." He checked his watch and walked to his desk to grab a file. "But, speaking of lecturing, I do have a new class of recruits waiting."

*

"*How does one go about creating a better Man?*

"Consider how much our civilization has evolved over the ages. It is 1918 – some say the golden age of industry. We now have the knowledge to make everything in this world better. We can build machines that fly us through the sky, that take us under the sea, and even do our backbreaking work for us. Yet none of this has really made *mankind* better."

Standing in front of a makeshift classroom, Sergei scrutinized the motley congregation before him: two dozen men and women, some in civilian, and others in uniforms of various ranks and branches, all listening intently from the mismatched assembly of chairs liberated from the nearby rooms. To his side was Director Latsis, a stately-bearded Chekist, cross-armed, and nodding along weightily from behind a table with a stack of papers and a munitions crate. Sergei took a few steps along the front of the room. The crisp lines of his uniform accentuated his tall, broad-shouldered frame.

"It's true – we've reached a great level of industry. We can now produce more of everything. More food. More clothes. More books. If we wanted to, we could feed, clothe, and teach every single person on this Earth to read…"

He paused just long enough to let the quiet tension build up.

"Yet, we don't want to. Instead, we make better bombs. Better guns. And that's what we've done since the beginning of time. Frankly, I am surprised we have made it to the twentieth century. But we have, and how did we mark this milestone? By starting the worst war the world has ever seen. We took thousands of years of human knowledge and used it to invent more ways to kill our own kind, faster. They say this is *the war to end all wars*, but you know what – I don't believe them. If something doesn't change, there will be others. Why *is* that?"

He stopped and scanned the room, in a deft bid to elicit response. A black-haired sailor with a mustache and a dusty peacoat leaned back in his chair and cleared his throat. "Because the imperialists are in control," he said with solemn conviction and smoothed his mustache.

"That's exactly right!" Sergei got visibly charged by the response drawn from his audience. "The world today is still driven by the same impulse that drove thousands of generations before us: *greed*. It tells our brains to take and to keep taking. It drives us to wars, to murder, to the enslavement of others."

He paused and lowered his voice for insight.

"But greed is a vicious circle. It is an evolutionary dead end. It is like opium – it only makes you crave more. No amount of gold is ever enough, no amount of power or land. And so, it repeats, generation after generation, century after century. And as the rich and the powerful squabble for wealth and control, all they give back to this world is oppression, suffering and death. And no amount of religion or science or industry has changed this since the beginning of human history. When will this finally stop? How do we get Man to evolve and think of what's good for the whole mankind instead of what's good for *me*?"

Anna liked watching Sergei speak. Standing just outside the doorway, she admired the quiet power of his figure and the polished passion of his words. His audience was enthralled. They always were. He raked his hand through his hair.

"The only way to elevate Man above greed and self-interest is to remove the social order that rewards greed – *capitalism*. And to do this, we must create a completely new social order in Russia. A type of government that's never existed before. A government that will never leave its citizens hungry, sick, unemployed or homeless. A government whose citizens are driven by a higher social consciousness." He scanned the room, to make sure his words had sunk in.

"But our enemies are determined to stop us. They are afraid of us and what we stand for. They are afraid that other countries will follow our lead. They want Russia to return to being a land where greed thrives. They will stop at nothing, and it is your job to stop them. This is why the Cheka was created – the first and only state security agency of the Soviet republic." He looked around the room. "Does anyone know what *Cheka* means?"

A young woman with short blonde hair in the second row adjusted her glasses. "*Che-Ka* stands for *Emergency Commission.*"

"Correct! Our country is in a state of emergency and the Cheka has been granted emergency powers to protect it. While the Red Army is defending our country from military enemies, today, you are given a gun and a badge to defend it against the political ones."

He resumed his measured pace across the front. "You'll all have important jobs. Some of you may be assigned to gangs, others to counterfeiting or profiteering. These criminals are rotting Russia from within, thanks to the decades of hardships, wars and inept governments. They infest our cities, and, like parasites, they feed on our people. Greed is all they know, and, if left unchecked, they will corrupt Russia's future. Winning the war at the front won't matter if we lose it in our streets.

"But there is also another enemy lurking in the shadows, and this enemy is more sophisticated and more cunning. These are proficient counter-revolutionary organizations who want to see our government fail. They do not want this country ruled by common people. They want to reinstate the old structures of power and regain control of Russia's land and industry. And they use terrorism and sabotage to wage war against us."

He counted out on his fingers: "The SR coup in Moscow last month; the assassination of the German ambassador; the coup in Yaroslavl; the explosion at the Yakimanka power plant; the assassination of Commissar Volodarsky in Petrograd – and these were just in the last two months."

He picked up an enlarged photo from the table – a man with a thin face and bowler hat staring coldly past the camera. "This is Boris Savinkov – the head of the SR Combat Organization. Before the revolution, he fought the monarchy and assassinated tsarist officials. Now he is fighting our government. Savinkov is calculating and persistent. He has been on our most wanted list for many months. Now we have reports that he is back in Moscow."

He put down the photo. "There are many others, and they are relentless. My department deals specifically with terrorism and sabotage. We work to uncover and prevent future attacks, but there are just six of us, and there are two million people in this city. That's why we need your help. As you do your jobs, we need you to also be our eyes and our ears. Terrorist organizations often rely on the criminal world to obtain information, procure supplies, or recruit sympathizers. Look for anything out of the ordinary: large sums of cash, gold, diamonds, foreign currency, weapons, explosives, forged IDs, classified documents. If you come across anything suspicious, talk to your supervisor or come directly to my department. Always question what you see and hear. The smallest clue could help prevent the next attack."

He stopped and surveyed the faces before him.

"Today you are getting not only a badge, but also a gun. Yes, your jobs will be dangerous, and many of you may have to use it in the line of duty. But don't think of it as just a weapon for defending yourself. Think of it as a weapon for defending our future. Think of it as a tool of your trade, just as a farmer uses tools to clear the field from weeds and to defend his crop from vermin. This gun is there to protect something greater than you; greater than all of us. Mankind will never evolve by doing the same things it has always done. Today, Russia is a spark of hope in a world gripped by war, greed and injustice. If we succeed, our spark will spread throughout the world. And if we fail, we will condemn our children to a future of oppression and more wars like the one raging in Europe right now. Their future depends on *you*."

He scanned the room. "Do you have any questions, comrades?" Heads shook.

"In that case, welcome to the Cheka. I look forward to working with all of you. Be safe and vigilant out there."

A round of spontaneous applause burst in the room.

Latsis stood up, his hand outstretched to shake Sergei's. "Thank you, Comrade Zaverin. Inspiring as always." He patted Sergei on the shoulder and turned to the group: "You will now be assigned your sidearm. When your name is called, come up and sign the register."

The clerk began reading out the names, and Sergei took his jacket from the chair and walked out of the room, just now noticing Anna in the doorway. He grinned. "What are you doing here?"

"Just wanted to come hear you speak. You are getting quite good at this," she smiled. "I don't think I've ever heard anyone deliver the orientation speech like this. A very compelling sermon."

"What can I say? We don't want thugs with badges. We need believers."

"Well, I think you definitely got through to the little blonde. I don't think she blinked once."

"She *was* kind of cute," he contemplated out loud and winked at Anna.

She shook her head and jabbed him playfully with her elbow.

He laughed heartily and put on his jacket, dodging a group of Chekists in the corridor. "Are we all set for tomorrow? I *am* looking forward to getting to know this terrorist of yours."

NATALIA

The girl was late. Anna watched from the park across the street as the tin roofline above the four-story façade caught the first glow of the morning sun. The doors of the building squeaked and slammed as people came and went, but there was no girl.

The rainy night had dissolved into a cool, misty morning. Anna drew tighter the pockets of her coat, trying to keep out the chill. The coat smelled of old cigarette smoke. It was a shabby trench coat with ripped lapels that she had dug out of the coat room at the office – perfect because it was like hundreds or thousands of others in the streets of Moscow. It was the smallest one she could find and still too big for her slight frame. But big enough to hide the angular steel of her Mauser pistol tucked at her side. She lit a cigarette, keeping the corner of her eye on the building. She did not smoke much, but the chill and the scent on the coat had coaxed her to light up.

At last, another squeak of the door, and then the familiar short black overcoat and the red scarf. The girl stopped in the doorway, pulling the scarf over her head and raising her collar to protect from the chill.

Anna watched. The girl descended the few steps from the doorway and proceeded down the street, her feet hurriedly picking the way between puddles. Anna checked her watch – twenty past seven. Her shift at the factory had already started, and she was not headed towards work. This was shaping up to be a promising day.

Anna followed at a distance on the opposite side, tracking the red swatch of the scarf through the morning commuters, carriages and cars, until she reached Egorov's car parked at the end of the block. Anna got in on the passenger side.

"Where is she going?" he puzzled out loud. He stowed away a pair of small binoculars and put his hand on the wheel. Letting some distance build up between them, he pulled out into the street behind a slow-moving carriage.

Anna tracked the red swatch. On the opposite side of the street, a dark, broad-shouldered army coat was now following the girl – Sergei. She checked the scarf again. Then Sergei. Back and forth.

At the end of the block, the girl took a right onto the Old Arbat street. Here, the crowd got thicker. Egorov pulled to the curb at the corner and lit a cigarette, watching her cross the street towards a produce store. She stopped at the back of a canvas-topped delivery truck and talked to a man stacking wooden crates – apples or pears – Anna could not tell. The man, with a sailor's wide stance and a muscular frame under the worker's jacket, was definitely not Savinkov, but Anna scanned the surrounding area just in case.

Sergei crossed the street too, and stopped at a street vendor's stand, watching the girl and the man in the reflection of the store window. The man climbed into the back of the truck, disappearing behind the canvas top. Sergei edged closer to get a better view in the reflection. Anna saw him put his hand casually on his belt, close to the pistol hidden inside his coat. She checked the girl – she was still preoccupied at the back of the truck. Sergei adjusted closer again, pretending to be interested in some item and talking to the vendor, while glancing periodically into the reflection. "Move back, move back," Anna whispered under her breath. He could be so impatient sometimes, just like a little boy.

And then, the store window in front of him exploded into a myriad of sparkling shards, and a fraction of a second later she heard the pops of gunshots. Before she could even gasp and reach for her own gun, Sergei ducked into the store entrance, his gun in hand, as another window shattered behind him. And then everything around them set off in motion.

People ran in all directions, but the sounds of screams and gunfire were drowned out when Egorov revved up the car and launched it towards the truck. He spun the steering wheel and slammed on the brake lever, skidding the car sideways across the wet pavement, and before they had even come to a stop, he had already fired four or five rounds from his revolver at the truck's canvas top through his window. The man stumbled out and pulled what she instantly recognized as a Lewis machine gun from the back of the truck. The big black barrel raised towards them and a burst of bullets thumped across the side of the car and cracked through the windshield, spraying her with broken glass. The car had stalled, and the rattle of rapid firing was now the only sound, echoing sharply off the buildings all around them. She kicked open her door and took cover behind the front of the car. The spray of bullets pelted the hood and the engine block. When she peeked out from behind the front tire, Sergei was standing behind the man with his gun raised. The man's head jerked, and he took an unsteady step and toppled over. The Lewis went silent.

The street was suddenly quiet and empty. *Where was the girl?* Anna jumped to her feet and climbed up onto the rear wheel of the truck, just in time to catch a glimpse of the red scarf settling onto the pavement half a block away. The girl's dark overcoat was rounding the corner.

"There!" Anna yelled, pointing, and Sergei took off after her, shouting "Stop! Cheka!" with the pistol still in his hand.

Anna looked for Egorov and saw him emerging from the car with blood streaming from his head above his brow.

"Go, go! It's just a scratch," he shook his hand sharply down the street and then dove back into the driver's seat, trying to crank the engine. Anna threw off the trench coat and took after Sergei and the girl.

With the heavy pistol in her hand and her boots driving hard against the cobblestones, she charged past the ornate awnings, the large store windows and the arched stone entryways of the Old Arbat. People, starting to emerge again, hurriedly ducked out of the way, seeing another person running with a gun.

Turning the corner, she spotted the girl's figure up ahead, with Sergei not far behind. He shouted "Stop!" again and fired a shot into the air. She turned around for just an instant and fired three rapid shots that reverberated off the walls and the windows. Sergei stumbled and fell, and the girl vanished into an entrance of a building.

By the time Anna reached him, he was already getting up on his feet. "Go!" he yelled, waving her ahead. She flew into the entryway, thinking that it was a foolish thing to do. The landing was small and dim, and the stairwell above it was silent. But just ahead, the thinning wedge of sunlight betrayed a through door closing. She opened it more cautiously this time to find a narrow, short crevasse of an alley crisscrossed with clothing lines overhead. The girl was standing at the end, where the alley terminated in a blind courtyard with a patch of sky overhead.

Anna approached, with her pistol raised: "Natalia, put your gun down!" she mustered a shout with her burning lungs. The girl swung around, and her small pistol fixed on Anna. Anna took a step forward, her gaze locked on the girl's grey eyes over the sights of their guns. The girl's chest heaved in short, hurried breaths. She looked so young.

By now, Sergei had caught up, and the girl's eyes darted a quick glance at him, but she kept her sights on Anna.

"It's going to be OK, Natalia. We just need to talk." Anna tried her best calm voice although her heart was about to burst from her chest. "Don't do anything foolish. Put down the gun. Think about your son."

The grey eyes snapped back to Anna's, and she thought she saw a shadow of a thought pass through them, like a reflection in a window. Perhaps it was a resolution. *It's OK, we got you*, she thought, or maybe said, because the girl seemed to have understood. She shook her head slowly, her blonde hair clinging to her cheek in the light breeze. She never took her gaze off Anna as she moved the pistol up to her temple and, without hesitation, fired. Her body collapsed like a marionette whose strings had been cut.

The echo of the shot still rang in the courtyard. Stunned, Anna lowered her gun and approached. The girl was lying on the wet cobblestones spattered with blood, her blonde hair wisping in the draft. She was breathing – shallow, strained breaths in the damp air. Anna knelt down next to her, but the girl did not see her. Her eyes stared into the patch of the sky above, as if it were a distant horizon. The sky reflected back in her eyes. Her breathing stopped.

Sergei snapped closed his holster. A car squeaked to a stop in the street and soon Egorov stood next to them. He smudged thick blood away from his brow. "Fucking contra," he spit on the bloody ground. "The truck is full of guns. How does this counter-revolutionary scum just keep crawling out of every crack?"

*

Another letter was on her desk. Anna recognized the ivory-colored envelope the moment she crossed through the office door. The same postage stamps as before – one blue and one red. The same meticulous handwriting in blue ink. She sat down and felt the thin envelope in her fingers. She knew what was inside.

Sergei marched through the door at his usual energetic pace, but judging by the slight scuff of his boots, Anna could tell he was tired. He threw a stack of folders on his desk.

"You want the good news or the bad news first?" He turned to her and Egorov.

She let the envelope slip from her fingers into the trash bin.

"Bad!" Egorov said.

"We got nothing from the girl's apartment."

"What about the truck driver?" Anna shook off the thought of the girl, dead on the pavement, and her little son and elderly mother waiting for her in the apartment only to have a squad of Cheka agents show up and ransack the place.

"No ID, nothing. The truck belonged to a cannery before the revolution. Who knows where it's been for the last ten months?" He sat on the corner of his desk and lit a cigarette.

"What about the guns in the truck?"

"All British; new in crates – fifty Enfield rifles and six Lewis machine guns."

Egorov's giant fist slammed onto his desk, making Anna jump in her chair. "British guns?!" His bandaged head cocked to the ceiling and he raised his hands in a dramatized prayer. "God bless King George for sending us British guns! They will be in great company in Moscow. Look, I've already got a Belgian one here." He deposited his Nagant revolver on his desk with a heavy clang. "*Annochka* has a German one," his upturned prayer hand pointed at Anna's Mauser, "and Nikolaev there has an American Colt. It is as if the entire world has decided to lend a hand in this little civil war we are having here."

"And all those hands – they all want a slice," Sergei smirked. "Frankly, I am still surprised the British government has stooped to supplying guns to a known terrorist."

Anna shrugged. "I am not. They've been pissed since we've signed the treaty. Look –" she rifled through a stack of papers on her desk and pulled out a copy of *The Times*. She unfolded it and put her finger on a line circled in pencil: "*Bolshevism must be strangled in its cradle,*" she translated. "Do you know who said it? Their Minister of Munitions Winston Churchill, last week." She tossed the paper back on her desk. "Does that sound cryptic with regard to their intentions?"

"All this just because we pulled out of the war our tsar pulled us into?" Egorov picked the newspaper from Anna's desk.

"Well, I'd bet they also weren't too happy when we nationalized all the foreign businesses and investments in Russia," Sergei added. "I guess if they wanted to find someone to rattle us, Savinkov is certainly the right man for the job."

Anna tapped the pencil on her lips. "You said there was good news. So, what's the *good* news?"

Sergei laughed. "There is always good news! For starters, we are all still alive after this morning." He reached over and patted Egorov on the shoulder. "Great work today! But I really need you to not get hit in the head – *again* – next time. I don't want to have to answer to Katya for this." He tapped his temple with his finger. "Who knows how many lives you have left after the war?"

"When I find out, it will be too late!" Egorov barreled out a laugh. "And you are not one to talk; was this your first one? It's a nasty habit to pick up!"

"Not if you do it right! Managing to miss the head is a good place to start." Sergei put his foot on a chair and rolled up his pant leg, showing off the hole through the side of his boot and the bandage peeking out over the rim. "Clean through, just a small hole. I bet it will take less time to heal than to get the pants patched up."

Anna was feeling considerably less pleased with the day's outcome. "If you two are done comparing the holes in your hides, maybe we can talk about what we are going to do, now that our only lead on Savinkov is dead?"

"Oh, that's the other good news," Sergei straightened up. "Dzerzhinsky signed off on full surveillance on Lockhart. If Savinkov makes contact, we'll know."

"I hope we nail them both," Egorov muttered through his teeth, examining the pictures in the English paper.

Anna considered any other threads to pull on. "What about Lockhart's diplomatic cables? You said we may be able to intercept them?"

"Yes, and we've already got a few." He pulled one of the folders from the stack on his desk and tossed it onto Anna's.

She opened it and flipped through a few sheets of paper. There were no words on them – just a few neat columns of numbers. "What's this?" She gave him a blank look.

"Code of some sort. Our telegraph guys can't make heads or tails of it."

She closed the folder and kicked up her boots on her desk. "So, that's it?"

"For now," Sergei shrugged, seeming suspiciously content.

His lack of concern and a sense of urgency about this was irritating her like an itch she could not scratch. "Look, we know less today than we did yesterday. We have no active leads on Savinkov, we don't know what he is plotting with the British, we don't know what the guns were for, and we don't know what the British are reporting back to London from Moscow. Did I miss any other things we still don't know?" She gave him her most penetrating gaze and was suddenly convinced – *he was hiding something*. "Let's just grab Lockhart and have a little chat with him instead of dragging out this cat-and-mouse game. We know he had met with the SRs –"

Egorov perked up: "Now, that I can get behind! Let's squeeze the prick and see if he tells us where to find Savinkov. Let's shake him up a bit."

"Absolutely not! We can't touch him. Not now, at least. He is a diplomat, and Lenin wants to maintain civil relations with the West. And you know Dzerzhinsky wouldn't cross Lenin even if he wanted to. And he doesn't. Just have patience – we'll get Savinkov. Let the surveillance play out."

He walked to his desk, put out the cigarette and settled into his chair. "Hey, look on the bright side – two terrorists are dead, and a shipment of guns is out of the enemy's hands. Consider the case of Natalia Goncharova closed. Go home and rest. Tomorrow we chase a new one."

"Now, that sounds like the best idea I've heard the whole day." Egorov stood up, stretched, and scooped up his flat cap. "I will see you two tomorrow."

He was barely out the door when Anna dragged her chair around to Sergei's desk and straddled it offensively, blocking his route to escape.

She squinted intently into his face. "What are you not telling me?"

"What are you talking about?" He tried to restrain a grin, but she knew he would soon crack.

"I know you can't be OK with this lousy state of affairs. We can't just sit on our hands, watching Lockhart. There is something big here, I can feel it. Two people died today, to protect something. These guns were just one piece of the puzzle, and we have not the slightest idea what the rest of it looks like. And yet you don't seem to be concerned. That's not the Sergei I know. So, what are you not telling me?"

He leaned back in his chair, grinning and shaking his head. "Anna, trust me, I *am* concerned, very concerned, but I can't…"

"Damn it, Sergei, you've known me since childhood. You know there is nothing you can't trust me with. I've been working this case for weeks. If there is information that pertains to it, I should know about it."

"OK, OK!" He put up his hands in surrender. "But this absolutely cannot leave this room." He sighed, and the grin melted off his face. "You promise?"

She relented her assault and gave him a nod.

He lit another cigarette. "Do you remember my friend Uritsky?"

She nodded again. She remembered meeting him once – a congenial former teacher in his forties, smiling patiently in someone's Petrograd apartment amidst a throng of boisterous young revolutionaries who seemed to be content with drinking and orating radical rhetoric to each other on that particular night. He was not a partier. Nor an orator. He was a doer, a mentor, a *starík*. But he let them have their fun that night.

"He now heads the Petrograd Cheka, and I contacted him." His eyes fixed on hers. "Anna, you are right. Whatever this is, it is big. Bigger than just Moscow, and the British are right in the middle of it. Uritsky has been watching them too."

"Why? Whom?"

"The British Mission in Petrograd."

"They still have the Mission there? I thought they closed it after the treaty."

"Apparently, they left a skeleton crew. Just the spies, I imagine," he mumbled aside. "One of them – Cromie – the naval attaché – has been of particular interest."

"Why?"

"He's been poking around the Baltic fleet – trying to recruit contacts."

"For what?"

"Sabotage? Mutiny? Uritsky does not know yet, but he will soon. But that is not all. Lockhart has traveled to meet with Cromie in Petrograd two times this month alone."

Her pulse quickened. "This has to be connected to Savinkov. It can't be a coincidence!" She plucked the cigarette from his hand and inhaled, letting the long, hot stream flood her lungs. The nicotine rushed straight to her head, and she felt acutely that the whole picture was somewhere close within reach, just beneath the smoke. She just had to connect the right dots for it to reveal itself.

Sergei nodded. "I don't think it is a coincidence. But we don't know just how big this thing is, so I am staying in close contact with him. He is watching Cromie, and we'll watch Lockhart. And until we know exactly what this is, we need to keep this to the minimum number of people. We don't know the extent of their network or who else might be involved." He gently pried his cigarette from her thin fingers and took a drag. "Now you know everything I know. Satisfied?"

She shook her head. Nothing felt satisfying about this. "I feel like we are sitting on a ticking timebomb, and we don't know when it is going to go off, and yet all we are doing is watching and waiting for someone to do something. There has got to be more we could be doing!"

"I get your eagerness to do something. But if our leadership is going to accuse British diplomats of conspiracy, we will need to catch them red-handed. Surveillance will get us there. We just have to be patient. Trust me – soon Lockhart or Cromie will give us a thread to pull, and this whole thing will crack open."

But her mind was already racing back through the evidence and all the leads and dead ends, looking for another way in.

Sergei swept the papers on his desk into a messy pile and tossed them into the drawer. "I think we should call it a day." He leaned in. "Are you coming over tonight?"

*

Night had fallen outside, and Moscow's jagged skyline of roofs, cupolas and towers had dissolved into the darkness. Standing by the window in Sergei's apartment, Anna watched the gas lamps glowing ghostly along the boulevard on the other side of the Moscow River, illuminating behind them the fortress walls of the Kremlin. In the night, Moscow looked at peace – no soldiers, no beggars, and no food lines – only a constellation of beautiful lights.

Sergei's living quarters were carved out, along with a dozen of others, from the former mercantile office on the Balchug Island. This hook-shaped, two-mile-long strip in the middle of the Moscow River was once part marshland and part the city's market district. However, thanks to its fortuitous location at the very heart of Moscow, it was destined for improvements. A series of canal projects had drained the marshes and ushered in the era of gentrification and the mansions of aristocrats and industrialists to edge out the butcher shops and the livestock pens. Banks, factories, depots, and tenements followed. A marshy island no more, Balchug now presented to anyone viewing from the Kremlin side a respectable European façade all along the riverfront.

But on the inside of Sergei's apartment, the improvements ran in a different direction. The former refinement of what used to be a small parlor was still somewhat evident in the white wainscoting and parquet floors. But in every other way, the room had shed its bourgeois aspirations in favor of a more utilitarian disposition towards the future. This single space now served as a bedroom, a study and a kitchen all in one. The heavy, tall doors separated it from the hallway which led to the communal bathroom and a dozen of other similarly repurposed rooms.

Most of the wooden furniture in the city had been burned for heat last winter. Sergei managed to preserve a desk and a chair. A metal bed and a cast-iron wood stove in the corner completed the rustic decor.

Tonight, there was also a happenstance picnic taking place on an old blanket spread out on the floor – a cutting board with black slices of pumpernickel bread and a bottle of vodka. She thought of the abundant spreads at her family's table when she was younger. Her father would be appalled at this peasant meal, but she was perfectly content. And Sergei, too – but it seemed he always needed very few things in his life outside of work. He led a spartan existence, but she liked coming to his place. It seemed she was here more and more lately. He was her one unsevered connection to the past, and he was the closest she had to a home in this big city. Or anywhere, for that matter. And besides, his place had a much better view than her own small room in a blind alley of the old Kitai-Gorod neighborhood.

His leather boots creaked as he crouched in front of the wood stove and tossed a few planks of parquet into the flame. He blew into the small fire, trying to inspire it to heat up the tea kettle.

"You know," she said, "if you keep taking this building apart, one day it just may collapse on you."

He chuckled. "That possibility in the future seems an acceptable price to pay for hot tea today." He used his knife to liberate a few more planks from the floor in the corner and tossed them into the stove, watching the lacquer sizzle and hiss in the flames.

He turned the lights off, leaving just the flickering flames to light the room. She took another sip and set the glass on the windowsill. The vodka flushed her cheeks and lifted the weight of the day just off her shoulders only to leave it hanging above her like a leaden cloud. She gazed into the night, mesmerized by the lights dancing in the dark waters of the river.

"What are you thinking about so seriously?" He walked up behind her, his reflection materializing out of the darkness.

The water was as dark as blood. "Natalia." Her voice sounded detached from her.

"What about her?"

If we had not gone to work today, she would still be alive, and her son would still have a mother. "Her life ended so violently, and yet so easily. She did not hesitate. There was no fear, no shock, and no pain in her face. She seemed at peace when she pulled the trigger. She was prepared for this."

"Do you admire that? She was a terrorist."

"I know. But she did not die as a terrorist. She took only her own life today. She sacrificed herself for the cause. You can't help but admire that."

"I guess. But she and her machine-gun buddy could as well have killed us today – and they did try. It could have been me or you lying in the morgue right now. Dead for a cause – just like her. But a different cause."

"You are right." She turned the glass slowly on the windowsill, watching the lights reflect in its sides. "Her file said she was just a year younger than me, and also from Petrograd. We could have gone to the same school, mixed in the same social circles. But somehow, day by day, we ended up so different. Do you think when she tied her shoelaces this morning, she had even a thought that this could be her last day? I know I didn't."

Sergei watched her turn the glass. "Maybe she did. I think about that every now and then. When I pick up my gun in the morning, I think that I may have to use it that day, and that I may not live to see the night. It's the risk I take. At least I know that if I die, it is for something I believe in. Something that matters. I suppose that's how she felt."

"I suppose… and I suppose our time will come just as quickly. Unexpectedly. Maybe soon."

He took her hand into his and wrapped his arms around her. She moved her hands up to feel his muscled arms. Her head rested on his chest.

"No. Not soon." He rocked her gently side to side. "You and I will live a long life, you'll see. First, we will win this war. And then we will rebuild this city and this country, brick by brick, and rail by rail, better than the world has ever seen. And then, maybe we'll take on the rest of the world."

"You've always been a dreamer," she said softly, but without a smile.

"And you have always believed in my dreams."

"That I did. Despite my father's disapproval."

"The old man never did like me," he smirked. "I was tolerable as a playmate for his son, but too much of a peasant to go near his daughter. I am sure he still blames me for you breaking off the engagement to that noble prick – what was his name, again?"

"Victor Demidov. And yes, he does," she smiled. It was cute that he pretended not to remember her one-time-fiancé's name. "He believes you had forever ruined his chance of wedging the family name into the high society."

"And I am perfectly fine with him believing that. But you and I both know that's not what happened. With his complete disapproval, you were the one that snuck away again and again to spend all that time with Alexei and me. Why would you do such a thing?"

"Because you two were the most beautifully idealistic and passionately convincing boys I had ever known. No one else had ever measured up to that. You told me that if I made the choice not to accept the world the way it was, I could change it."

"I said that?"

"You did. And I believed you. After all, I was just an impressionable girl, smitten with my brother's best friend." She turned her head and gave him a teasing look.

He laughed. "Now wait, that's not at all how I remember it." His arms tightened around her, and he rocked her gently again.

She loved the warmth that radiated in his eyes when he looked at her. He never looked at anyone else like that. "I remember that summer before you left to study in Europe very clearly, and I don't recall the girl you are describing. But I do recall a young woman who couldn't be told what to do, not even by her father. She knew exactly what she wanted out of life. And what I wanted more than anything in the world was to ask you not to go. But I didn't. Do you remember what I told you?"

"You said I would accomplish great things."

"And look, here you are. Ruins of the old empire at your feet."

"And here I am," Anna repeated, mesmerized by the rocking and the glowing lights in the river.

His fingertips touched her cheek and brushed away her hair. "Does it feel awkward, at all? Us – working together?"

"You mean me working for you?" she smiled.

"Sure. I was surprised you wanted to transfer to my department."

"I transferred because this is the work I want to do. There is nothing else I'd rather be doing. Now, as far as it being awkward…" She held a long, teasing pause. "No. I am glad I did."

"I remember something else about that summer," he whispered in her ear and kissed the back of her neck. She lowered her eyes and bit her lip.

His hand moved slowly, tracing the contour of her body. She closed her eyes, her every cell and every little hair on her skin attuned to its familiar, gentle weight. Sometimes she hated that he could make her melt. His presence was always so safe and warm. A shelter she could never refuse.

She pressed into him. His hand cradled her cheek, and he turned her face to his, pulling her closer, until she could feel her own hot, intoxicating breath on his lips. He kissed her, and a fire spread. His fingers tightened in her hair, and her pulse pumped faster and faster, beating deep in her body and in every limb, like a maddening drum urging escape. But she knew she was not going to escape, unable and unwilling to resist the spine-tingling relish of feeling so safe and so vulnerable in one endless moment.

She turned toward him. He pulled her in tighter, but she thrust her hands into his chest, her fingers feeling their way to the buttons of his shirt, undoing the top button, and then the others, one by one, until her hands grazed his bare chest. She pulled his shirt back and put her hot, wet mouth on his chest – a yearning, warning bite. He laughed and picked her up, and she wrapped her legs around him, tightly, and pulled his hair back and gave him a bite on his muscled, musky neck and let him carry her, triumphant, to the edge of the bed.

She pulled him down with her, their hands hurriedly undressing each other, and their lips kissing whatever bare skin they could find. Free at last from her clothes, she climbed on top of him like summiting a conquered mountain, leaving him to struggle, laughing, tangled in the shirt she had left half-removed. Sitting on top of him, with her skin glowing in the flickering flames of the stove, she pushed him inside her, giving in to the fire, and letting it devour her completely, with only an ecstatic "Aah" escaping from her lips.

*

The fire in the stove had reduced into a crumble of glowing embers. Sergei was asleep, but Anna had drifted back into awakedness, and now her mind refused to settle. It seemed she had dreamt of Alexei but now could not recall the dream. She slipped out of bed and walked across the cold floor planks to the blanket in front of the still-warm stove. Her belt with the holster gleamed from the shadows. She pulled it closer and took out the heavy, angular slab of metal that was her Mauser C96. Sergei's gift. It felt cold against her bare thigh.

Alexei had always disliked guns. She did not realize until later how unusual that was for a young boy. All of their father's aristocratic aspirations for Sokolov family hunts at their country estate would have withered away were it not for Anna's ambitions for adventure as a child. She relished the times with her father in the woods. He seemed proud that she was a good shot, and to her it was like a game they played together.

She pulled back the bolt on the pistol and ejected one bullet onto the blanket. It lay there like a fish on the shore, cut off from its purpose. Alexei had never reproached her for bringing home the rabbits and pheasants she had killed.

But they were after different game now, weren't they? She had never killed a human. She hoped she would never have to. Alexei had always advocated against violence in their group. He said they should fight with words and with ideas. Even then, he was in the minority – a lone voice against the bombs and the bullets. Until he was killed by one. Real revolutions were not rational debates.

It had been eighteen months. Eighteen months since that last protest on the snow-swept square in front of the Winter Palace. Just thinking about it, she could feel the damp coldness of the air burning her lungs as the soldiers opened fire. And then there were screams, and more gunshots, and the clatter of hooves, and the stampede of the crowd running. Alexei was hasting her away, his hand on her shoulder. And then, that sudden unbearable lightness – his hand was gone. She turned around and saw him on the frozen ground. By the time she had fought her way back to him against the crowd, he was already gone.

A tear rolled down her cheek. She touched the leather strap of his watch on her hand, the one in which she had to punch an extra hole to make it fit her wrist. What would he think of her and Sergei now? Things had changed so much in eighteen months. The revolution had come and gone. Could he have known that right after the revolution, they would fall into a war? No longer with the Germans – with ourselves – the *other* Russians. Making peace with Germany was probably easier than it will be with ourselves.

Would he have joined the Cheka?

She pulled the bolt nine more times, ejecting bullet after bullet from the breech, until the gun was hollow and light in her hand. The embers still glowed in the stove – the hues of red, yellow and orange blazing hot, inextinguishable, in the heart of the night.

She took one gleaming bullet from the blanket and loaded it back inside the gun. The Mauser slipped back into its holster, and she put the other nine rounds into Sergei's desk drawer. With that, she climbed back into bed, into the crook of his arm, and closed her eyes.

*

She awoke to the sound of voices and the door closing. It was barely morning. Sergei was standing at the bed, barefoot and with his shirt unbuttoned.

"Are you awake?" He was looking for his other boot. "That was Nikolaev. We need to go to the office."

"Why?" she rolled over lazily, letting the sheet slip off her naked shoulder.

"The British have just landed 100,000 Allied troops on Russian soil."

NEW YORK

Crossing Central Park, William could tell that something was going on in the Upper East Side. Snippets of distant chanting, shouting and impatient car horns carried toward him in echoes through the blistering late-July heat. The noise got louder as he got closer, until he reached Fifth Avenue, where it exploded like a crashing wave in the raging sea of people – thousands of men in a flow that stretched for several city blocks, halting traffic and gathering crowds of onlookers on the sidewalks. The demonstrators – factory workers, judging by the signs they were carrying and by their clothes – were slowly making their way towards Carnegie Hill.

Escorting them, in the thick of all the yelling, the honking, the fist pumping, and the occasional trash being hurled, was a small army of policemen, some on horseback and some on foot, who had dispatched into the street in a valiant attempt to maintain civil order. Outfitted with billy clubs and whistles, they strained to hold the imminent chaos from erupting by keeping the gangs of counter-protestors, armed with their own signs and fists, from breaking through to the demonstrators. Were the peace officers to fail in their effort, the heated masses would, without a doubt, clash in an unrestrained bloody street brawl.

This unfolding live entrainment attracted a considerable and diverse crowd of spectators, from the paper boys and the shoe-shiners to the smartly dressed businessmen and socialites, some craning their necks, some climbing onto the light posts to get a look across the sea of hats and signs, and others observing with engagement from the windows and balconies above.

He pushed his way through the crowds to 60th Street, where a bottleneck of pedestrians and cars had accumulated, squeezed on both sides by the canyon of concrete and glass. He crossed between the bumpers of gridlocked cars and headed through the tall, gilded iron gates of the Metropolitan Club, past the doorman quarreling with a raggedy beggar who had set up a collection station just outside the gates.

From the foyer, he stepped inside the cavernous grand hall and felt as if he had just entered a cathedral. Here, in the cool, dusky air, the sounds of the demonstration had melted away into a barely perceptible distant hum. Around him, the marble slab walls soared several stories up, towards the stained-glass windows up high, the gold-trimmed colonnade and the massive pendant of the chandelier suspended from the coffered ceiling over his head. Coming here, he did not know what to expect, but now had to admit that the Metropolitan did not let down its reputation – it was a temple to wealth befitting the gods of American capital who had built it.

He gave his name to the concierge and took off his hat, baring a clean cut of light brown hair. The concierge took the hat off his hands and invited William to follow him up the grand staircase, which cascaded like a symmetrical, sprawling, monumental, kaleidoscopic convergence and the subsequent divergence of two identical reflected staircases.

Step after step, stiffness returned to his right leg, gradually growing into the familiar dull, gnawing ache. He gritted his teeth to drown it out.

Their destination turned out to be a small, plush lounge on the third floor with velvet-lined walls and high wingback leather chairs. The concierge took him to a table by the window, where two men were conversing.

Seeing him approach, one of them – a big, jolly fellow in his mid-forties with neatly parted dark hair and a goatee – bounced to his feet and spread open his arms like a portly bird taking to flight.

"Billy, my boy!" He beamed a wide toothy grin at William and gave him a tight, heartfelt hug. He then pulled back to an arm's length to get a good look. "My god, how you have grown! Last I saw you, you were barely ten or twelve, and now look at you – a decorated veteran and a worldly man. And look at that gallant mustache."

"You flatter me, Uncle Henry!" William smiled bashfully. "I suppose a year in Europe does change a man." He patted his uncle on the arm. "You look exactly how I remembered."

"Well, I know that's a lie, but thank you kindly," his uncle roared. "And listen to you – not a shred of that old Texas drawl!"

The second man rose from his chair, politely giving the two a chance to take each other in. He was older than William's uncle, and bald, and his tall, slim frame cut a polished, thin silhouette against the window.

Uncle Henry stepped back and extended his arm towards the thin man. "Billy, let me introduce you to Mr. Emmett Barr. Mr. Barr is a director at the National City Bank, and a former army man himself – a Colonel... if I am not mistaken?" His uncle tilted his head towards the man.

Mr. Barr nodded ceremonially and gave William a cool, polish-smooth handshake with a slight bend of the taut three-piece pinstriped navy suit. His already thin lips whittled into a paper-thin smile – an exercise that set off countless crackled runs of wrinkles in his long, cleanly shaven face disrupted only by his full, silver-white eyebrows.

"Sit, sit!" Uncle Henry ordered, gesturing to the chairs. The three settled in. "What can I get you to drink? Gin, whiskey?" He signaled to the steward waiting nearby.

William considered, glancing at the two glasses already on the table, and two cigars smoldering in the heavy, cut-crystal ashtray. "Whiskey would be fine. Neat."

"And bring the cigars! And I'll take another!" Uncle Henry leaned towards the steward, holding up his half-full glass.

"Did you get through the protesters unscathed?" Barr enquired.

"They are a spirited bunch," William nodded with a smile.

"Who is it today? The miners, the steelworkers, the Wobblies? Tuesday was the Women's Party... or was it the Women's Trade Union?" He turned to Uncle Henry. "I can't keep track... They were demanding a minimum wage..." He shook his head.

"And some of them were not all that bad looking." Uncle Henry nodded enthusiastically and winked at William with a conspiratorial smile.

William smiled a small, mollifying smile intended to both acknowledge and quell his uncle's crass jab. Had he always been like this? William suddenly understood why his father found his mother's brother insufferable.

"It was the factory workers, I believe," he offered.

Barr contorted the corner of his mouth around his cigar and shook his head. "I just don't understand it. It is as if striking and protesting have become a national pastime. Now that we are at war, the unemployment is virtually non-existent. And still, all they want is to work less and get paid more. We must find a way to get labor relations under control, or America will blow up like a powder keg."

William nodded politely and rubbed his knee.

"How is the leg?" Uncle Henry inquired, sticking his cigar in his mouth.

"It's practically healed now," he replied with a light slap on his knee.

"It'd probably be as good as new by now, if he weren't spending so much time dancing with the young ladies at society events," his uncle winked to Barr and rolled with a burst of laughter, his pomade-reinforced hair immovable like a trench helmet. "I'm sure they can't get enough of your war stories. Nothing like a good scar to get them excited, right?"

William reminded himself to smile as he mustered to shut down the reel replaying in his mind of the moment shells detonated above their trench line. *Before-during-after, before-during-after.* His uncle meant well, and William was getting better at this, but not to the point of laughing it off. At least not just yet. Relief came in the form of the steward returning with the drinks, followed by another steward with a tray of cigars. William picked out one, and the steward cut it with a swift metallic snip and then held the lighter for William until he puffed out a small thick cloud of blue smoke.

Barr raised his glass. "To the soldier's return home." They toasted with a clank.

"When did you get back?" Barr inquired.

"Three weeks ago."

"And he took that long to call his uncle!" Uncle Henry groaned, reaching over and shaking William by the shoulder.

"How do you find America after your time at the front? Your uncle tells me you have been quite a hit in the social circles."

He rubbed his cleanly shaven chin. *Smile.* "A passing novelty, I am afraid. In Europe, all everyone thinks about is the war. Here, I am sure the good people of society will soon tire of my war stories and find something new to entertain themselves." *War stories* – he'd had to work hard to scrape up a handful of bits tasteful enough for the glitzy midtown parties his veteran buddies from the boat had managed to coerce him to attend.

Barr nodded in understanding, as if he could read his thoughts. The half ringlet of short silver stubble around his bald crown glinted against the sunlight. "I had served in the Spanish War, and we had seen our share of hell, but from what I've heard, it fails in comparison to what our boys in Europe are going through now. Where were you deployed?"

"Northern France – in Cantigny, then at Belleau Wood. That's where the mortar shrapnel sent me to a first-class hospital in the South of France and then on the boat back home."

Uncle Henry shook his head enthusiastically, puffing out a cloud of smoke from his cigar: "My nephew is being modest. The French had awarded his division the War Cross. It was in the papers. *For exceptional gallantry in battle*, the article said. Must have been some battle. I am sure they don't give those to just anyone."

William puffed on his own cigar and kept his gaze on the swooshing amber liquid in his glass. *Might as well have been just anyone.* If there was any sense to this war – any logic to who got to live, who to die, and who got the medal – he was yet to uncover it.

"So, your uncle tells me you are interested in a career in banking?" Barr thankfully changed the topic.

William nodded and let out a plume of smoke to the side. "I am. I'd like to explore my options in New York; perhaps at Chase? I hear my uncle has made quite a name for himself there."

Uncle Henry chuckled. "Don't believe the rumors, my boy. But I do OK for myself. One thing is true – this city is filled with opportunities. Many more than you will have back home on the ranch in Texas. Each man here makes his own luck. All it takes is knocking on the right doors and knowing the right things to say when they open."

"And to a young, smart man like yourself, the right doors may already be open," Barr added cryptically and tapped the ash off the tip of his cigar on the edge of the ashtray.

His uncle nodded. "Mr. Barr and I have looked at a few options for you at both Chase and City. We can certainly put you in a junior desk position and have you work your way up through the ranks, but, frankly, I think that would be a waste of your time and talent. I think we have a better proposition for you. An opportunity more suited for someone with your qualifications and one that gives you high visibility to all the right people."

Barr puffed pensively on his cigar. "Your uncle tells me you speak Russian?"

"Some – I was stationed next to a Russian division in France."

"What do you know about Russia?"

"Not much. They fought hard and took heavy casualties. But after the revolution, things changed – most wanted to stop fighting and return home. And now that the Bolsheviks have signed a peace treaty with Germany, they made things much harder for our boys. That treaty freed up a million German troops to redirect back to the Western Front."

Barr nodded. "An unfortunate turn for the Allies, without a doubt. But we mustn't blame the Russian people for this decision. They've lost millions of their people to wars and revolutions in just a few years. Now their country is ravaged by poverty, hunger and disease, and their economy and industry are in shambles. And on top of all that, there is now a civil war brewing."

Uncle Henry leaned in: "Of all the nations, we Americans certainly can relate to revolutions and civil wars!"

William nodded. "So, what is our interest in Russia?"

Barr smiled. "As you probably know, both City Bank and Chase are financial institutions at the very heart of the American capital. The captains of industry like J. D. Rockefeller and J. P. Morgan are not only our clients but often also our venture partners and political advocates. These men drive American economy, but what you might not know is that they are also titans of philanthropy. Mr. Morgan in particular happens to be a generous benefactor to many charitable causes, and one project in particular is especially close to his heart: the American Red Cross. We truly believe this is your best opportunity to make a mark with all the right people."

"The American Red Cross?" William was puzzled.

"Yes. You see, he has already sponsored several American Red Cross Missions in Russia – to feed the hungry, heal the sick, etc., etc. Some of our top executives have contributed to this program in various capacities. And now there is a new Mission being set up in Petrograd. Now, I know you've just returned home from that side of the Atlantic, but if you were to help the Petrograd Mission succeed, all the right people would take notice."

"Petrograd?" William glanced at his uncle, with a shy smile of a man expecting to confirm he was being pranked. "Isn't it under the Bolshevik control?"

Barr nodded without a shadow of a smile. "It is, but the Bolsheviks respect the organization's neutrality. They let the Red Cross work in peace – after all, we are helping their people."

"It's God's work, Billy," his uncle nodded.

William let the reality of the offer set in. "This certainly sounds like an exciting proposition, but I must admit, I am not sure how I can help – I don't have any medical experience."

"Don't worry about that. They have plenty of people to do that part. The challenges at the Mission are more operational in nature. Russia is not an easy place to be right now. With all the civil unrest and disruptions of all sorts, the Mission could really use a man like yourself. You speak the language, and you know how to work under pressure. You would be indispensable."

"So, exactly what sort of things would I be doing?"

"The usual Mission work – managing the deliveries of supplies to the hospitals, distributing food shipments, helping the Mission director develop relationships with the local government and organizations. Whatever other odds and ends the Mission director may need help with."

William nodded and puffed out a pensive cloud of smoke.

His uncle leaned in. "It's an opportunity of a lifetime, Billy. We can get you in. You spend a few months there – half a year, tops – to help them get set up and make a real difference. Making the right impression on this assignment would mean virtually limitless opportunities when you return. With the experience you will gain and the connections you will build, you will be able to write your own ticket."

Mr. Barr nodded. "And, for the duration of the time you are in Russia, you will also get a stipend. $110 per week, and all your travel and expenses will be covered by the Red Cross. The money can go straight into your account, and it will be waiting for you when you get back."

"Heck, you could decide to pursue something completely different when you return, and still walk away with all that money," his uncle winked at him.

"That *is* a very generous offer," William politely agreed.

"It is commensurate with the value we feel you would bring to the project. Mr. Morgan has invested a great deal in this endeavor and would very much like to see it succeed."

Mr. Barr set down his glass. "I know it can't be an easy decision to pack up and head overseas again. Take the rest of the week to think it over. The job is yours if you want it. If you decide to proceed, just let your uncle know, and he will make the arrangements. Regardless of your decision, it was a pleasure to meet you."

He unfolded his thin frame from the chair, buttoned his suit. William stood up to shake his hand.

"I should get back to the office, too." His uncle gulped down the rest of his Scotch and hoisted himself out of the overstuffed cushions. He gave William another bear hug and two hardy slaps on the back. "It's really good to see you, Billy. Stay as long as you want. Have another drink. Or two. It's taken care of."

He turned to walk away but then turned back, the jolly lines now faded from his face: "Hey, I know this is not exactly the opportunity you were looking for. But sometimes, the right door opens without you knocking on it. Do give this offer a serious consideration, my boy. I can't tell you why right now, but just know that this Petrograd Mission is much more important than it might seem. I do hope you accept. But let me know either way."

Left to himself, William took a drag of his cigar, picked up his drink and walked to the large window. His head was full with questions and very few answers. From up here, the view was better than from the street. Bigger. On the other side of Central Park, behind the tops of the trees and the distant silhouettes of buildings, the sun was setting. The magical golden light made the surface of the pond shimmer and glow, sending dancing rays into the room. Three stories below, Fifth Avenue had recovered from its earlier disruption, and the steady flow of pedestrians and motorcars had been restored to its cobbled pavement. A man was sweeping on the corner. William gazed into the disappearing light. The blinding, blistering sun had been reduced to a thin fiery sliver hovering at the edge of the skyline, and he could look straight into it now. Under his feet, the earth was turning, and Manhattan would soon plunge into the night.

CODES

The basement of Lubyanka was a medieval dungeon with corridors of cinderblock and peeling plaster. Until today, Anna had no idea there were offices down here. And now that she had descended the stairs to the cool, quiet sublevel, she realized that there couldn't have been many, and quite possibly only one.

While the above-the-ground Lubyanka was bustling with growth, and each day, the previously empty offices were filling up with new people and new departments, below the ground there was no chatter, no shuffling of footsteps, and no clatter of typewriters. All the rooms she had walked past were occupied with surplus furniture, boxes and filing cabinets. Most of this stuff had probably been here since before the Cheka had moved in.

The room she needed was at the end of the hallway, beaconing her with light. The arched entryway was scraped and chipped – evidence of things being moved in or out. A few brick steps landed her in a palatial corner room topped with a shallow vaulted ceiling. It reminded her of a castle keep, like in one of the towers of the Kremlin. It was lit with several bare light bulbs wired roughly to the plastered ceiling and a row of small windows up high, flooding the room with fuzzy ambient daylight through the grimy glass.

The first thing she saw was books – two large tables piled with open volumes, and behind them several rows of bookcases obscuring the back wall. She flipped through the open pages on one of the tables – mathematics. She liked books. Her father had prided himself on assembling a considerable family library, and it was easily one of her favorite rooms as a child. She loved the feel of the old bindings in her hand, the scent of old paper, and the worlds that were just waiting to be opened.

"Hello?" she said into the empty space, and her voice echoed through the large space.

Papers rustled somewhere in the back of the room, and a small, thin man emerged from the stacks with a book in his hand.

"Yes?" he said, choosing not to approach any closer, as if an uninvited visitor was a cause for caution. He looked to be in his thirties and wore a brown vest over his white shirt and a pair of wireframe glasses on his thin, smooth face.

"Is this the Cipher department?" she asked, convinced that the man had no intent to initiate the conversation.

"Yes," he conceded with a slight inflection that betrayed disappointment at the realization that the uninvited visitor was not here in error.

"Are you Nekrasov?" she asked, finding the basement-dweller's lack of hospitability slightly amusing. She supposed a grumpy goblin was a fitting guard for this castle keep. She gave him a smile.

"I am. What can I do for you?" He put the book down on the table and adjusted his glasses, committing to the unwelcomed transaction. His eye ticked, likely from irritation.

"I am Agent Sokolova with the counter-terrorism department. I was told you might be able to help with these." She pulled out several sheets of paper from the folder in her hand.

"Counter-terrorism, huh?" He gave her a surprised glance, and she gave him another smile. "Well, let's see what you have." He took the pages and turned on the desk lamp.

One of his eyebrows floated up above the frame of the glasses. "British diplomatic correspondence?" This was a statement more so than a question, but she detected a spark of interest.

"Yes, how could you tell?" She was already impressed – there was nothing but rows of numbers on the pages.

He put one sheet on the table and swiveled the desk lamp towards it, motioning Anna to come closer.

"It's the format, see – a series of numbers of the same length? This means it's likely this message is encoded with what's called the *dictionary code*. It's a common cipher for sensitive British diplomatic communication."

"How does it work?" Her curiosity was piqued.

He darted a suspicious glance at her to confirm she was not leading him on and was genuinely interested in his craft. Satisfied, he relaxed his demeanor and seemed pleased to explain. "To encode or decode a message one needs a dictionary. You see here – each six-digit number represents a word. The first three digits are the page number in the dictionary, and the last three digits are the numbers on the code slip."

"What's a code slip?"

"A code slip is a strip of paper, like a bookmark, with a column of random numbers – one for each line of text on the dictionary page. Here, let's use this dictionary, for example." He pulled a small book from a pile and opened it to a random page. He placed a blank sheet of paper on it, overlaying half the width of the page.

"Now, let's put some numbers on here," he said, and wrote a column of three-digit numbers along the edge of the sheet. "It does not matter what the numbers are, as long as there is a different number aligned to each line of text on the page.

"Now, imagine we have a code like 063735. The first three digits denote the page number, so I would go to my dictionary and open it to page 63. Then I would overlay my code slip on that page and look for the word lined up next to the number corresponding to the last three digits of the code – 735." His finger traced to the word at the beginning of the line.

"Beware?" Anna read.

His eyebrow floated up again. "You speak English?"

She gave him a small smile. "That's pretty clever! But both the sender and the recipient have to have the exact same edition of the dictionary and the same code slip for this to work?"

Nekrasov seemed pleased with his new pupil's progress. "Precisely! And if the code is compromised, they just have to change the code slip and they can keep the same dictionary."

"So, does this mean there is no way to decode these without the right dictionary and code slip?"

For the first time, it was his turn to smile. "Actually, there is."

"How?"

"With something we call frequency cipher analysis. If we have a large enough sample and know the language of communication – in this case English – I can analyze how often each number and combination of numbers occurs and then compare this information against the most commonly occurring words and word combinations. For example, the words *the*, *of*, *and*, *to*, and *is* are some of the most frequent in the English language. I can also determine some of the words based on context, or from their relative position in the dictionary based on the page number."

"How long would this take?"

He flipped through the folder. "It can take a while, but the bigger the sample, the better. Do you have more?"

"Not at the moment, but maybe in the next few days."

"I can get started with this, but bring me more as you get them. I should have at least partial results for you by the end of the week."

AUGUST 3, 1918

The men's spirits are elevated. I am now in regular contact with General Alekseev's volunteer army in the Don region. They are fighting to retake Rostov. With God's help, we will regain this city and make it our stronghold in the south-east. In Moscow, funding is flowing steadily, enabling us to step up recruitment.

Recruitment status: 6,500 in Moscow and surrounding cities. We organize into companies of eighty-six, each with a commanding officer, adjutant, four platoon commanders, sixteen squad leaders and sixty-four soldiers. All officers are former military. The soldiers are workers, students, and former military. Secrecy is essential. Each officer knows only the identities of the men he commands and that of his own commander.

We are building an underground army. A first of its kind. Each man has only two imperatives: to maintain absolute secrecy and, when he receives the order, to arrive at the designated location with his weapon. Until that day, all of us exist only in the shadows.

– Boris Savinkov's Journal

THE DEVIL'S ARITHMETIC

The double-headed golden eagle had a rope thrown around it, like a noose across one head and one wing. Perched high atop a white marble obelisk, it still had the gaze of its two heads fixed to the east and to the west – the two distant ends of the empire, farsightedly oblivious to the impending doom. A crowd of passers-by had gathered in the Varvarka street below, gazing into the blue sky, where the familiar wings spanned supremely for a few more minutes yet, glimmering in the high-noon sun.

The soldiers gave the ropes a tug, and the eagle careened heavily to one side. One of its heads now peered into the sky, and the other down, at the faces staring at it from below. Several people in the crowd crossed themselves and murmured hushed prayers. Anna cast a sideways glance at Egorov – she knew he wore a cross under his peasant's shirt – but he seemed unaffected by the blasphemous affair. St. Basil's Cathedral bells struck noon a few blocks away at the south end of the Red Square. Like an echo, the bells of the

Znamensky Monastery joined in from down the street. The soldiers gave the rope another coordinated heave and the eagle snapped off and tumbled down to the crowd's collective involuntary gasp. It crashed to the stone sidewalk with a loud metal thud and broke into several pieces. The gilded imperial globe rolled down the street with the talons of the eagle's claw still clutched around it. A gang of kids chased after it, already arguing who was going to keep it.

Anna pondered the irony of this end to the three centuries of the Romanov dynasty.

Egorov spat on the ground and readjusted his flat cap. The crowd began to disperse, and he and Anna resumed their walk back to Lubyanka. "Speaking of the dead Tsar…" he stopped to light a cigarette, "… did you hear Yurovsky is now in Moscow?"

"He is?" Her heart skipped a beat. With the Savinkov ordeal preoccupying her mind, she had not thought of Ekaterinburg in a couple of days. But just hearing his name put her teetering at the top of that staircase again.

"Yes – he got an office on the third floor. He is with the new federal division now, the V-Cheka." He put out his match and glanced at her. "Are you OK? Do you know him?"

"Just briefly."

"A good man. Makes me mad the way some people talk behind his back." He shook his head and offered her his cigarette.

"Oh?" She accepted and took a quick drag.

"I guess some here in Moscow take an issue with him on the account of killing those Romanov children."

"And you don't?"

He shook his head with short resolution. "Not one bit. It was the tsars who spent hundreds of years convincing everybody that their blood was better than ours and that it gave them the birthright to rule over us. So, if that's the case, they really did not leave us any choice. They are the ones who made their children into more than just children. They are the ones that brainwashed people to believe this birthright nonsense. So, they are the ones who condemned their own kids. The way I see it, their birthright signed their death warrant. There is always a price to pay for privilege. You can't have a coin with just one side, and this is the other fucking side of the coin."

He took the cigarette from her, inhaled, and released a long angry plume of smoke from his giant lungs into the warm Moscow air. "I mean, can you think of anything more backwards than monarchy? And still, these so-called modern nations of Europe bow to their kings. And they are all related! Wasn't Nicholas related to the British King and the German Emperor?"

"First cousins," Anna nodded. "And to the kings of Norway, Denmark and Greece."

"One big, screwed-up family that can't get along. How many millions of lives do you think they've murdered between them all? Someone should do this world a favor and rip out that whole family tree. Maybe we'll start with the British, once we get their boots off our land."

"Monarchy *is* backwards," she agreed. "But I am more worried about something else." She grabbed him by the arm and turned him, pointing to a three-story white house set in the trees back from the street. "Do you know what that building is?"

He shook his head.

"That's the Old English Yard. Do you know why there is an English Yard in the middle of Moscow?"

He shook his head again.

"In the Middle Ages, the Germans ran a massive trade network called the Hanseatic League throughout Europe and much of the Middle East and Asia. They had monopoly over the trade routes, and the British wanted to bypass them and establish their own direct access to the resources they needed. They sent several expeditions east, and one reached Moscow. Ivan the Formidable was the tsar at the time, and he gifted that building to England as the first English trade mission in Russia. They traded English wool and wine for Russian fur and timber. Back then, they needed our timber to build their fleet. Now, they need our oil, coal and metals. And because of that, I am not as worried about their king as I am about the industrialists, merchants and financiers who really run England, and they are not likely to let Russia go without a fight. That's why they landed troops in Vladivostok and Arkhangelsk."

"But they have not declared war. Is Lockhart still saying the troops are there to protect the Allied munitions and supplies?"

She nodded. "He says the armaments and supplies were sent to the Tsar to fight the Germans. And now that we've signed a treaty with Germany, they don't want those supplies to end up in the hands of the Germans."

"But it just happens that those two cities give them control of our two main seaports! I say they are sticking their boot in the door to keep it open."

"Exactly. And besides, all they've been doing is bringing in more Allied troops and armaments through these two ports, instead of moving them out. It's nothing less than a build-up of force."

They turned down Nikolsky Alley, and Egorov stopped at the steps leading up to the wrought-iron gate. "Well, this is me. Are you sure you don't want to come up for a bit? Katya would be glad to see you."

"No, I should really get back to the office. Tell her I said hello. How is she liking the new place? It sure looks fancy."

"Oh, she could not be happier," he grinned. "Can you believe some petty aristocrat had this whole place just to himself?" He cocked his head and measured off three stories of windows towering above the entrance. "The housing committee carved out almost twenty apartments when they nationalized the place. Katya used to rent a bunk when she got to Moscow three years ago. Now we have a whole room to ourselves, with a door we can close."

"Sounds like there may be a baby on the way soon," Anna winked at his round beaming face.

His head rolled in laughter and he waved her away, turning to go in. "Tell Sergei I'll be back after lunch." She watched his broad farmer's frame disappear inside.

*

Mostly empty just a few weeks ago, the third floor of Lubyanka was now teeming with new faces. She made it almost to the end of the hallway before she found the right door; Anna stuck her head in and knocked.

Yurovsky raised his eyes from a book and glanced at the door over his glasses. He suddenly recognized her, and a barely discernable smile rendered on his lips. "The young commissar," he said in his raspy voice and put down the book.

"Come in, sit." He waved her in. "I heard you had moved up. How is the action in counter-terrorism?"

"I have to admit, we are somewhat in between actions right now." She shook her head with a sad smile and settled into the chair at his desk. "It's been a lot of watching and waiting lately."

He nodded. "I am sorry to hear that. I've never had much patience for waiting either. And yet it seems I have to do more and more of it these days. It seems the bigger we get, the slower we get it as well."

"I hear you are with the V-Cheka now?"

"Yes." He gestured to the hallway on the other side of his door: "This whole wing is now V-Cheka. We are growing fast." He paused in sudden consideration and his eyes narrowed to a squint. "Are you interested in moving up from the Moscow Cheka? We can use more smart people at the federal level."

His offer gave her a pause; it flattered her, considering he barely knew her. "Thank you. I really want to solve the case we are working now. Hopefully, it will crack open soon. After that, if your offer still stands, maybe we can talk again?"

He nodded.

She looked around at the bare office walls. "Are you going to stay in Moscow for a while? Is this a permanent posting?"

He shrugged. "As permanent as it ever gets. I moved the family here, but I am not getting too comfortable just yet."

She nodded. They sat in silence for a few moments. Outside

of his window, like a distant reflection, was the other wing of Lubyanka across the void of the courtyard.

"I am… glad our paths crossed again." She cleared her throat. "There is something I've been wanting to tell you."

The memory was like the edge of a dark pit opening at her feet. She swallowed. Her heartbeat seemed so tiny, as if crushed under the burden. "What happened last month in Ekaterinburg… I think about that night often." Tears welled up in her eyes. *Damn it.* She breathed in to restrain them and raised her eyes to him. "I wanted to say thank you. If you had not told me to stay behind… I don't know if I could have…"

He seemed to sink into his chair. "Those orders were for me. You did not need to be part of it." He shook his head. "That was a terrible night. Not many people can do that. I am not sure I could, if I had to do it again."

In an overwhelming impulse of compassion, she reached over and put her hand on his – the rough, callused hand resting on the open book. "How *are* you?" she uttered, suddenly certain that no one had asked him that since that night.

He lowered his eyes, lost in thoughts. A shadow of a smile moved across his lips. "You know, I didn't believe in fate until I got this order. I guess fate has a dark sense of humor. Tsar Nicholas and I had crossed paths before. When I was a boy growing up in Tomsk, I saw him once. He was just a young tsarevich then, passing through the city, on some grand tour to see the ends of the empire he would soon inherit. I was twelve or thirteen, and Nicholas was maybe ten years older than me. On that day, we heard all the church bells ringing in the city, and the streets filled up with people. I was apprenticing for a watchmaker then. I ran from the back of the shop just in time to see his mounted guards passing, followed by the imperial carriage. And there was he, behind the glass – this perfectly groomed young man in a white uniform. The whole city was in commotion around him – children were running alongside the carriage; beggars were prostrating themselves in the dirt, holding out their hats in their hands; old women were blessing him as he passed. It was as if the son of God himself had come down from the heavens. And Nicholas just stared through all of them, waving mechanically with his white-gloved hand, as his carriage rolled through. All I could think then was that if he would only stop, I could tell him how hard life was for his people, and he would order things to be better. But the carriage did not stop. He did not see them. He did not see me.

"Just as he did not see me years later, when his police threw me and my co-workers in prison for demonstrating at the factory, or on Bloody Sunday, when his guards fired on *his people* demonstrating outside of his palace. He did not see me when he sent me to die for him in his war with Germany. Where was he? Behind the glass somewhere, again, watching without seeing? All we wanted was change. I think the first time he really saw me was when my revolver was pointed at him right before he died."

He took off his glasses and rubbed his eyes. "And you know the irony of it all?" his raspy baritone quietly rolled on. "Even though he was a born despot – a real cruel, entitled, oblivious, and unapologetic bastard – I never really wanted to kill him. In my whole life, I never wanted to kill anyone. I had managed to avoid it through all those years in the underground. Even when I was sent to the war, I signed on as a medic. In the end, I think it is that experience that gave me the strength to do what I needed to do in Ekaterinburg." He nodded softly and put on his glasses.

"What do you mean?" She wanted to understand this. For the longest time, she had fought against ideas and institutions. But that seemed childish and naïve now, like dinnertime discussions about politics. All just empty rhetoric. In the end, what were institutions but people? And what was there left to do when these people refused to give up their ideas? Where was the line that made killing justified? He was an educated and introspective man. How did he make his peace with it? Was it a weakness that she couldn't? That every time she thought of it, she could still smell that nauseating metallic scent of gunpowder and blood?

"I was assigned to a field hospital. It was a visage of hell. Each day brought carnage. Mangled human bodies, hanging onto life by a thread, just alive enough to feel the pain and to writhe and scream in agony. Have you heard of that medical pledge, *first, do no harm*? Those are just four hollow words. I learned that quickly. In that place, harm was relative, and harm was often necessary. Every day, we had to cut off limbs to save the men. But sometimes, not saving the man was the right, most merciful thing to do. Harm is unavoidable. But it should be done out of reason, not anger. I had no anger towards Nicholas and his family. But I had the duty to cut off the festering limb so that our nation had a chance of survival. As long as they remained alive, they gave hope to those who wanted Russia to return to the old ways."

"So, you really had no choice. And you were following orders."

"I think we fool ourselves when we say we don't have a choice. There is always a choice. In the end, we alone are accountable for our actions. I take full responsibility for what I did. And I will for the rest of my days. Do you believe in God?"

She shook her head.

"I don't either. My parents did, but I never took to it. The idea of God just did not fit with the world I knew. Sometimes I wish I could. For those who believe, killing seems to be easier to live with – they have a mechanism for confession and absolution. They can pass the sin onto their god. The rest of us don't have this option. But I think we still seek absolution in some form. Killing is a terrible task. There is no way to make it not so. Every reason and every intention behind it may be right, but none of that will ever make it right in itself or make it any less terrible. It will eat at the soul. Even if we tell ourselves we had no choice. Even if it is for the greater good. All we can do is hope we are right. If God offers forgiveness, perhaps it is the Devil's arithmetic that makes all these terrible things we do add up to something good."

"Maybe they are one and the same."

He gave her a small, kind smile. "But this is the burden of *my* generation. We are the old guard. We had to do these things so that your generation and my children's generation would not have to. You can change it. You *are* the greater good. You should be builders, not executioners."

There was a solemn resignation in his words. A dark resolution in him, the same as she felt stirring in her own soul. It had been there since Alexei died. And lately, it had been growing wider, crumbling away at the edges of the pit. Its pull was growing stronger, seeming inescapable at times. She wanted to tell him that lately, when she tried to see beyond the stirring darkness, to *feel* beyond it, what she felt each time was nothing but more darkness. But she couldn't tell him that. It was just her, wasn't it? Overanalyzing again, picking off the chips of paint from the vision of the shimmering future at the end of all these terrible things. She used to see it so clearly with Alexei, but now it was only a worn-out postcard, growing grimier and more washed out with each day. *But what else could there be, in the middle of this insane war? What else but hope can keep people moving forward? And of course, hope is irrational. Hope is no more than a peasant's modest icon with a flickering candle. But without it, what is there left to believe in?*

"I hope you are right," she said. "Maybe by the time your children grow up, no one will need to do what we do."

She stood up and extended her hand over his desk. "Thank you."

He took her hand.

"I am glad you are here," she said. "It will be nice to see a familiar face among all these new ones."

"You take care of yourself out there, Commissar," he said, letting go of her hand. "And about your case… Consider this. When you wait, you have no control over what happens next. But if instead you make a move, at least you have a chance to force the events towards the outcome you actually want."

*

"How many?" Sergei said into the telephone. "OK. You, too." He hung up with a grim expression on his face.

"Who was that?" Anna sat on the edge of his desk, holding a folder in her hands.

"Uritsky in Petrograd."

Over the last week, she had become accustomed to his calls with Uritsky. She could tell when Uritsky was on the other end of the line because the confident Sergei she knew would suddenly sound like a student talking to his mentor, or maybe even a father figure. This heartened her because he never had a good one growing up.

"What's the matter?" she asked. "Anything to do with Cromie?"

"No," he shook his head. "It's worse. The Americans have decided to side with the British. They have just landed 3,000 marines in Vladivostok, and 5,000 more are on their way to Arkhangelsk."

"The Americans?" She was perplexed. "I thought Wilson was sympathetic."

"Apparently not sympathetic enough to cross his allies. We can expect more coming. The British are recruiting their war allies into this intervention." He nodded to the folder in her hands. "What have you got there?"

"Some timely information, I think." She pulled out a sheet of paper from the folder and placed it in front of him.

"What is this?" He looked up at her and then at the sheet.

"It's the decoded communication between Lockhart and London."

"How...?" He forgot to finish the sentence, absorbed in reading the memo.

"... How did I get it?" she smirked. "From a grumpy man in the basement who runs our brand-new cipher department."

"We have a cipher department?" he mumbled.

"We do now, courtesy of the V-Cheka. Now, that particular memo is pretty mundane. I think you will find this one a lot more interesting." She placed another page in front of him.

"Son of a bitch," he muttered and read out loud: "... *therefore request payment of one million rubles to Savinkov for the purposes of recruitment and arming of his Union.*" He looked at Anna. "Savinkov's building an army."

She nodded. "This is clear evidence of conspiracy, right? Is this enough to justify us going to get Lockhart?"

He chewed his lip, considering for a moment, and then shook his head. "I wish we could. We'll take this to Dzerzhinsky, of course, but I know what he will say – *he is still a diplomat, and evidence does not apply to diplomats.* London would raise hell about diplomatic immunity if we touched him. And now, with the Allied troops already on our doorstep, we can't afford to provoke them any more at the moment. Our army is already spread very thin fighting the Whites. We'll have to figure out how to eliminate the threat without poking the hornet's nest."

She smiled. "I figured you'd say that, so I have another idea for you."

He reclined in the chair and clasped his hands behind his head, giving her his full attention.

"Let's consider everything we know so far," she said and held out her open hand. "The British are building up a coalition force at the edges of our country." She folded her pinky finger into her hand. "Savinkov is building a secret army in Moscow." Her ring finger folded in next to the pinky. "And Lockhart is paying him to do so." She folded in her middle finger. "How is this all connected?"

"Well, the British want to displace our government, so they are backing Savinkov to lead the insurrection from within while they lead the Allied forces to invade from the outside. Classic imperialistic tactic."

"Precisely! Now, we know the plan is already in motion, and the clock is ticking towards the moment they decide it's time to strike. But Lockhart knows there is risk – Savinkov is their best bet but also the weakest link. Lockhart knows we are actively hunting down Savinkov and have recently eliminated two of his operatives and intercepted a shipment of weapons. Lockhart has to wait for Savinkov to build up the Union, but he also knows we could take down Savinkov tomorrow, and then his whole plan would collapse.

Without an insurrection in Moscow, with our central government still in place, the invasion would be immensely more difficult." She paused and peered at Sergei until he nodded in confirmation. "We can use that," she said.

"How?"

"We give Lockhart a better option."

"What's that?"

"We offer him an already formed and armed counter-revolutionary force. One beyond suspicion from our government."

"What force are you talking about?"

"The Latvian Rifle divisions. For one, they are not ethnic Russians, so the British would be more inclined to make a deal with them, like they did with the Czechs. Second, they have almost unrestricted access to our defense and security operations in Moscow and Petrograd. Lockhart would not be able to resist – it's over 40,000 skilled fighters. Whatever recruits Savinkov has scraped up for his Union can't be anywhere near that. If you were Lockhart and planning to topple a foreign government, would you not want to improve your chances of success with additional allies?"

Sergei rattled through his desk drawer for cigarettes, lit up and squinted into the corner of the ceiling, not saying a word. She knew he was hooked.

"So, you are proposing we run a sting operation on the British consul?" he finally said.

"Why not? We don't need to arrest him – we just need him to let us into his plan. Look, we can still keep trying to find Savinkov the way we have been, but you know he is really good at hiding, and we may very well not get to him before the British decide to make their move. But if we can get Lockhart to take the bait, we will find out the whole plan and get a lead on Savinkov in the process."

He sat up in his chair and squished the cigarette in the ashtray. A content grin spread on his face. "You know what, I love it. And the more I think about it, the more I love it. Since this involves

Moscow, Petrograd, and foreign diplomats, we will probably have to run it through the V-Cheka. Let me take it to Dzerzhinsky and see if I can get him to sign off."

AUGUST 12, 1918

The Bolsheviks talk about power. Denikin, Wrangel and Yudenich talk about power. They all purport to speak for the people of Russia. But neither the communists nor the monarchists promise the Russian people what they really need – ownership of their land and freedom to choose their leaders. This irreconcilable chasm between need and intention now pits us in a mortal fight for the future of true electoral democracy in Russia. We – the People's Union for the Defense of the Motherland and Freedom – are not only a fighting organization. We are the germinating seed of the new Russia. We are people's will, long repressed, now rising for reckoning. I know some in our leadership question if Terror is a justifiable means. As some had also questioned in 1905. I was there when our bomb ripped the Grand Duke of Moscow's carriage in two and tore him into pieces. One part of his torso and his head were in bloody shreds in the street. His bloody feet, still wearing his boots, were on the splintered floor in his wrecked carriage. Some of his fingers, it's been reported, still wearing his rings, were found on the roof of the nearby building. The rest of him had simply disappeared, obliterated by the blast. As did over 700 other government officials that year alone. Terror works because it is terrible. To those questioning the justification for Terror, I say Terror is the only instrument people have against tyranny. Only Terror can end tyranny. Tyranny must be cleared out, blasted apart, and obliterated to make way for democracy. Systematic Terror is what ended the centuries-long rule of the tsars, and it will end this brief rule of the Bolsheviks.

– Boris Savinkov's Journal

IRON FELIX

Anna had never been to Dzerzhinsky's office before. She had never even talked to him face to face and was pretty sure he had no idea who she was. Five days had passed since Sergei had pitched her plan to the director of the V-Cheka, and she could tell he was getting tired of having to tell her he'd had no updates from upstairs. But today she was summoned.

'Iron Felix' was the nickname Chekists gave their boss. A tall, thin man in army uniform, Felix Dzerzhinsky was easy to spot around the Lubyanka building. He was the top of the Cheka chain – above him only Lenin himself. To Anna, he was shrouded in the legends of his past – son of a Polish aristocrat who chose the life of a revolutionary that landed him years in political prisons and exile. But even if the legends were to be disregarded, no one could deny that he upheld his 'iron' reputation each day with his obsessive, almost super-human dedication to his work. He was married to it, it seemed, spending most of his life in his office on the fourth floor, keeping his lights on late into the night. One had to respect that – always at the helm, poring over the reports and the maps like a meticulous, tireless captain ensuring his ship stayed the course.

Walking up the steps to the fourth floor, she pondered any other possible reasons why she would have been called up, hoping this had something to do with her Lockhart plan, but also trying to be prepared if she were to be disappointed. When she entered Dzerzhinsky's office, Sergei was already there. Dzerzhinsky himself was behind two large desks pushed together to form an L-shaped surface that accommodated three telephones, several neat stacks of documents, and his tidy workspace. The windows of his office faced the square, and from up here, Anna could see the spires of the Kremlin in the distance.

Dzerzhinsky stood up and walked around the desks to shake her hand. Up close, she could tell that he was a man in his mid-forties with a thin, receding hairline. He looked at her, his lively eyes in a semi-squint, harboring a smile in the corner wrinkles. His lips were locked in an undiscernible wry squiggle. He had been handsome, at one time, but now his mustache and goatee did little to hide the grotesque asymmetry in his face, which she knew to be a vestige of an old injury at the hands of his Okhrana captors.

He motioned her to sit in the vacant chair in front of his desk next to Sergei.

"So, this is the famous Comrade Sokolova," he said, settling back at his desk. "I had actually heard of you a few days before Comrade Zaverin here had approached me with your audacious plan."

Heard from whom? she thought, slightly alarmed that her name had come up on the fourth floor. *Yurovsky?*

"All good things, don't worry." The corners of his eyes squinted. "I have good news I thought you would like to hear first-hand. I have approved your operation on Lockhart. I must commend you. I think it is an ingenious plan with tremendous potential."

"Thank you, Comrade Dzerzhinsky." Her heart wanted to beat out of her chest, but she tried to maintain composure. "When would you like us to begin?"

The corner of his mouth curved demurely. "We already have. Deputy Director Peters and I took the liberty to do a quick test to validate your proposal. Two days ago, we sent two undercover agents to approach Attaché Cromie at the British Mission in Petrograd. They introduced themselves as officers of the Latvian Riflemen division in Petrograd. They proposed to him that if there were to be an Allied invasion, the Latvians had no desire to fight the Allies and would surrender in exchange for a monetary compensation for their troops and the guarantee of safe passage back to Europe."

"And did Cromie buy it?" she asked.

"It would appear so. He told them to come back the next day, presumably to give him time to confer with London. When they returned yesterday, he gave them a letter of introduction to none other than Lockhart himself, and directed them to visit Lockhart in Moscow. They are on their way to Moscow as we speak."

She tried to breathe slow and deep to contain the excitement of seeing her plan unfolding and coming to life right in front of her. "So, does this mean the operation is a go?"

"It most definitely is a go," Dzerzhinsky nodded.

"So, what happens now?" Anna asked.

"Our two undercover agents will take the letter to Lockhart and we will find out if they can convince him. Since this was your idea, I thought your department should run the operation." He pushed two files towards Anna and Sergei. "I assume you won't object?"

She shook her head.

"Splendid. These are the files of your two operatives. Agent Buikis is using the undercover alias Shmidken, and Agent Sprogis is Bredis – both have been added to the rosters of the Latvian regiment in Petrograd to support their cover. Deputy Peters has also enlisted the help of Colonel Eduard Berzin in Moscow. He is the commander of the Latvian guards posted to the Kremlin, and under his real identity will provide credibility as a high-ranking officer, to help convince Lockhart. You will also have the full assistance of the Petrograd Cheka, as needed. I have informed Uritsky, and he is fully on board."

He shifted in his chair and smoothed his beard with his hand. He was no longer smiling.

"I need you both to be clear about one thing. This is going to be a complex operation, and we have to take the utmost care to get it right. I know you've been locked on Savinkov for a while now, but I need you now to mind the bigger picture. This is not about finding a lone terrorist. We are using undercover operatives to infiltrate a foreign network of unknown size. This means the chances of something going wrong are high. We also have foreign diplomats involved, so if our plan is exposed before we get results, Britain will find a way to use the scandal to their advantage. Failure is truly not an option here. Because of this, Deputy Director Peters will personally oversee the operation and ensure you have everything you need. You have two objectives. Your first priority is to determine the nature and the scope of the plot between the British and Savinkov so that we can take the appropriate measures to neutralize it. The second priority is to uncover the British network operating in Russia and obtain undeniable evidence of their efforts to subvert our government."

The corners of his eyes smiled again. "So, what are you waiting for? Go get these bastards."

ARKHANGELSK

Eight hundred miles north of Moscow, the boundless green expanse of the Siberian taiga forests reached the arctic waters of the White Sea. There, along the jagged coastline abounding with deltas, islands, bays and sounds on the map, William found the port city of Arkhangelsk nestled at the mouth of the Dvina river.

The journey to Arkhangelsk from the New York harbor was expected to take around two weeks, according to the Norwegian America Line ticket office, barring inclement weather and acts of war. After ten days of nothing but the cold, grey waves of the Atlantic, the sight of land brought the passengers out onto the decks to take in the mild northern August sun and watch the distant shores of Europe unfold along the horizon.

William scanned the glittering sea, squinting from the bright reflections. As a boy from rural Texas, he held no special fondness for boats and open water. Given his two prior transatlantic crossings, he had hoped that he would never again have to undertake a lengthy sea voyage, yet here he was again. It wasn't that he was afraid of water – he could swim as good as any other boy in his school – but he found it extremely tedious, trudging at barely twenty miles per hour for days on the open seas without land in sight. It made him impatient – he liked seeing progress.

"Worried about the U-boats?" English accent – a man in his forties in a grey business suit leaning on the railing next to him, taking in the moist sea air through his cigarette.

William returned a small, polite smile, doing his best to conceal his apprehension of the possibility of more small talk, which he had started to dread after all these days among strangers on the ship. Yet the man in grey did not seem overly talkative himself – his gaze was already on the water and his attention on his cigarette. He had the approachability of a salesman, and if he was one, he must have been a seasoned one, preserving his conversational prowess for a qualified prospect.

"Should I be?" William voluntarily stepped into the trap, his curiosity teased out by the possibility of seeing a submarine in real life.

"Oh, I can guarantee you, there is a couple of those buggers down there this very moment," the man pointed down into the sea. "We were stopped by one a few months back on this very route."

"What happened?"

"Well, it just surfaced like a bloody whale, that's what happened. And then a man popped out, turned this big gun towards us and ordered us to stop. Then a few of them came aboard to inspect the papers and the cargo. After a couple of hours, they let us pass. But a few days later, another Norwegian Line ship got stopped, only this time everyone got ordered off into the lifeboats, and then the Germans torpedoed it."

"Why?!"

"They said it was transporting munitions and supplies."

"But Norway is neutral."

The man nodded. "It is, but that does not mean the Allies don't ship with them. The Germans sink whatever they please.

The Norwegian flag just means they let the passengers get off first. That's why I don't sail on His Majesty's ships anymore. Not since *Lusitania*. Over a thousand civilians dead just because the Germans said it was carrying munitions."

"Do you think it really was?"

He shrugged. "We may never know. The Germans said it was, so that was all that mattered. I was supposed to be on it, but my business plans changed last minute. A fellow I knew went instead. Didn't make it off, poor bastard. Never found his body. Still probably down there, dead in his cabin at the bottom of the sea."

The thought of the grey-suited man's co-worker floating in the murk gave William the chills. The sinking of *Lusitania* made national news in the States – there were over a hundred Americans aboard.

"It's monstrous – the concept of collateral damage," he said, looking into the foamy dark-green waves lapping at the side of the ship.

The man gave him a sardonic grin. "Now, if you think that's monstrous, you'll love this twist." He puffed on his cigarette. "A friend of mine works for the British government and told me there was a rumor going around that the Admiralty itself had a hand in tipping off the Germans about *Lusitania*."

"The British? Why in the world would they endanger one of their own ships?"

"Because Britain was desperate for America to join the war, and because there were so many Americans on the ship. If one wanted to push America to enter the war, that would probably do the trick, right? A ghastly theory, but intriguing with its sheer magnitude of cold pragmatism."

Ghastly was one way to put it. William knew the Allies were desperate for the US to join the war, but could they have really sacrificed all those people to get what they wanted? He pondered the possibility. In the trenches, the reality of war seemed reassuringly black and white, but things quickly got murky away from the frontlines.

"For the sake of all humanity, I do hope it is just a theory," he said.

"I am sure it will never be proven. Nor disproven. But I do find the moral dilemma fascinating. I am not a callous man, but if getting America to join the war will help defeat the greater evil, will we say that the thousand souls of *Lusitania* were a terrible but necessary price for victory?"

"And what if we don't win?"

"Well, then I suppose the Germans will say the exact same thing."

The man stared into the sea for a bit longer, took the last drag of his cigarette and flicked the butt into the dark waters sloshing below. He tipped his hat to William and wished him a safe journey. The strip of Europe bobbing on the horizon was getting closer.

They reached Norway a few hours later without any U-boat incidents. They docked in Bergen, and most of the passengers disembarked into the dusk of the evening, the man in the grey suit among them. But for William, there were still three long days left to travel. It was dark when they cast off again to sail further north and east, towards the North Cape.

For the next two days, the land remained mostly in sight, which eased his disposition, although he had to content himself with the monotony of the rugged, rocky coastlines of Lapland and the Kola peninsula slowly drifting past. But on the morning of the third day, his tour of rocky desolation ended. Overnight, the ship had entered the inlet of the White Sea, and William awoke to the view of a forest scrolling on the other side of his porthole, as the ship was now making its way through the meandering delta of the Dvina bay.

On the deck, the crisp northern air greeted him with a breath of the arctic, even in the height of summer. His first glimpse of Russia was the low-lying coastline, unraveling like a green tapestry of grasses and trees, stretching as far as he could see. It looked uninhabited and completely wild, and even the ruins of an old fortress had been reclaimed by nature – the crumbled walls were overrun with moss and grass, and only the tree saplings kept silent watch over the water. He wondered if this was the route the Vikings took centuries ago to access Russia's rivers and inlands.

Several islands and bends scrolled past, and then the view widened, opening to the large harbor. Expecting Arkhangelsk to be a sleepy seaside outpost, he was surprised to see instead a large fleet of British and French navy ships anchored in the bay. He scanned the steel-sided armada and tallied up over two dozen ships – large destroyers, cruisers and aircraft carriers, and the smaller trawlers, subchasers, troop transports, river monitors. There was even a seaplane in the water.

Behind this unexpected display of naval might lay Arkhangelsk itself – a sprawling seaport crowding the shoreline with warehouses, quays, cranes, docks. Barges were being loaded and unloaded with timber and crates, and fishing boats bobbed in the waves, besieged by the gangs of seagulls fluttering about and quarreling over their pillaged catch. The thin, unmistakable pungency of fisheries reached him in the breeze.

And so, thirteen days after casting off from New York, they finally docked in Archangelsk, and William set foot on the Russian soil for the first time. A pair of British MPs checked his papers on the pier.

"Who is in charge here?" he nodded inland.

"Lieutenant-General Frederick Poole, sir," one of them replied, handing William back his papers and saluting him to pass.

He signed for the three wooden crates waiting for him on the wharf, looked around and checked his watch. No one appeared to be waiting for him. Archangelsk was a busy port, and around him everything was in movement – people, horses, crates. A shadow crossed the ground, and he looked up to see an airplane with its wings detached and strapped beside it, moving across the sky, swinging from the hook of the loading crane. Beyond the roofs of the warehouses, golden cupolas of a church glimmered against the grey clouds.

Among the stacks of cargo, a familiar patch of color caught his eye. He walked closer, past the pallets and the crates, to find a row of five long boxes draped with the Stars and Stripes. A pang of a memory: the unending flow of mangled bodies that poured from the frontlines into boxes just like these to be buried in the foreign land. They never left. Too many to bring home. Too far. He returned. They didn't.

Two American GIs smoking nearby took notice of him. They ditched their cigarettes and approached. Recognizing the silver bars gleaming on his shoulder loops, they saluted and snapped to attention.

"As you were, boys," William saluted back. They looked to be eighteen to twenty years old. One was thin, with shy eyes and a budding mustache. The other looked like a robust midwestern farm boy with rosy cheeks.

"What happened to these men, Corporal?" William asked, lighting a cigarette, and offering them the pack. They graciously accepted, and he held the match for them, watching their cracked, weathered hands shield the flame from the wind.

"These ones were killed Friday, sir," the farm boy responded. "Fighting the Reds up the river."

"What do you mean fighting the Reds? Under whose orders?"

"General Poole, sir," the one with the mustache said, squinting from the smoke.

"The British?"

"Yes, sir. He commands the Allied forces here."

"To what end?"

"To take control of the railroad to Vologda."

"Vologda? That's halfway to Moscow from here! And what happens when you get there?"

"We can't say, sir. But I am sure he will tell us, when the time comes," the skinny one nervously chuckled.

"And how long have you boys been here?"

"We landed in Murmansk in May and then got transferred here last month when the British took the city."

"Where were you deployed before?"

"This is our first posting, sir – straight from Detroit, same as most of the 339th Infantry. And you, sir? You look like you've seen action before. In Europe?"

"France," he nodded.

"France? Boy, that sounds awfully nice. Better than here, I'd bet." The farm boy rubbed his hands, the cigarette hanging from his grin.

"Better? I don't know about that," William said, looking at the flag-covered boxes.

A large, road-dusted automobile pulled up to the pier and honked the horn. On the mud-splashed fender, a tiny American flag proudly fluttered. A stout man in an army trench coat stepped out.

"Captain Arden, I presume?" he shouted to William.

"Well, you boys take care of yourselves." William put out the cigarette and saluted them goodbye.

He walked to the car, to the stout man who was leaning lightly on his cane. He looked to be in his late forties, with a cleanly-shaven face, a hawk nose, and a pair of dark, inquisitive eyes that sized up William as he approached.

William saluted. "Colonel Robins, sir?" he guessed, confirming the silver eagle on the man's sleeve.

"Just call me Raymond," the man said, dismissing formality and extending his hand to shake. "These Red Cross ranks are good only for getting through the bureaucrats' doors. Yours, at least, is not made up." He smiled, flashing a row of strong white teeth.

William shook his hand and then took a step back, studying the front of the car. He recognized it immediately but was sure that he couldn't possibly be right. Between the large, wire-spoked wheels, two burly leaf-springs lurched forward, carrying above them a pair of weighty round headlights. Behind the headlights rose the unmistakable gable-topped grille. Through the layers of road grime, patches of gold trim gleamed dully in the gray Arkhangelsk afternoon. "Is this... a Rolls-Royce Silver Ghost?" he finally said, grinning.

"Indeed," Robins grinned back. "At our disposal courtesy of the Petrograd Commissariat."

"I don't think I've ever been this close to one. Not even in New York!"

Robins shrugged lightheartedly. "Welcome to Russia, my boy. The wild, wild east. Here, the status symbols of the upper social crust are mere tools of the working class. I'm told this car belonged to the former prime minister Kerensky last year, gifted to him by the British government. Now it's ours to enjoy. But don't get too used to it," he said, patting William on the back. "The Reds give, and the Reds take it away. Are those my medical supplies?" He pointed his cane at the crates next to William's bag on the wharf.

"Yes."

"Excellent. Let's get them loaded." Robins pivoted on his cane towards the car and waived his chauffeur to come out.

"This is my assistant and interpreter, Mr. Gumberg," he introduced the man. "He has graciously agreed to accompany me on this little adventure to retrieve you."

Gumberg had a smooth, rounded face. He was of medium stature and was wearing a black leather coat and a black leather cap. "How do you do?" he said to William in near-perfect English and shook his hands.

"Are you hungry?" Robins turned to William. "I know a place."

*

Gumberg maneuvered the big car out of the wharf and through a crowded street market. Soon, the tires were rumbling on a cobblestone street, and the hustle and grime of the port began to fade away. The warehouses and log homes were replaced with white plastered façades and shop windows. The streets widened, and before long, they were driving down a broad, straight-as-an-arrow boulevard with trams, cars and horse-drawn carriages.

So far, Russia was not what he had expected. This sliver of European refinement was hundreds of miles away from any other cities and was surrounded with some of the wildest environment on the planet. And yet, there were smartly dressed pedestrians outside the car window, and stately mansions and government buildings with their Grecian columns, Palladian pediments and Venetian windows.

"This could be a boulevard in Paris," he said to Robins with amusement.

Robins chuckled. "Don't be fooled. In a couple of months, this place will be unrecognizable. Arkhangelsk is the northern-most large city in the world. Look how low the sun is over the horizon, and it's one o'clock in the afternoon! The sun here does not get much higher than that. Ever. In the winter, the daylight lasts barely two hours of the day. The port itself is frozen solid for more than half of the year, and you can imagine what the winters here are like for people, horses and machines. Believe it or not, Russian Tsar Peter the Great wanted to make this place the capital of Russia. Can you imagine? It's further north than Anchorage."

"I've never been to Alaska," William admitted. "Have you?"

"I have. And the Yukon. I spent some time in Klondike in my twenties, and take my word for it, it did not look anything like this."

"Did you go for the Gold Rush?"

"Precisely," Robins nodded.

"Did you find gold!?" Whatever the answer, he was already liking the Mission director. Robins had an adventurous spirit about him, like the covers of the dime novels William used to devour in his boyhood.

"Actually, I did," he nodded with lighthearted excitement.

"How did you know where to look? What's the trick?"

"It is really not a trick, and not luck. One simply has to be a student of the landscape and after a while, one learns how to read the signs. I had spent my youth mining coal in Colorado, and I've been learning geology ever since. I imagine I'll be learning until the day I die. Gold, coal, oil – they all have their own signs. It just always fascinated me to find all those riches lying just beneath the surface, out of everyone's sight."

Gumberg parked at the entrance to the restaurant sandwiched in a row of shop windows between a watchmaker and a furrier – *everything one needed to pass the long, dark winters*, William supposed. Across the street, the British flag flopped lazily in the wind atop a government building. The smell of food made William realize that he was indeed hungry.

Inside, the restaurant was, as expected, an upscale European lounge complete with white linens and a stocked bar clad in dark wood and gold accents. Most of the clientele were officers – English, French and Russian, with a few civilian suits mixed in. A pair of musicians in white peasant shirts and blue pants and equipped with a guitar and an accordion serenaded a tableful of Brits in Russian.

"I must warn you – the culinary scene in Petrograd is somewhat in a state of decline at the moment," Robins informed William as they settled at the table. "So, enjoy this meal – I am afraid your options will be less predictable from this point onward."

Robins took off his cap and brushed the raven's wing of black hair back from his forehead. The waiter appeared with a bottle of vodka and poured three small glasses. He returned and ceremonially placed in front of them a round loaf of bread with a small dish of salt in the middle.

"It is a Russian hospitality custom," Robins answered William's inquisitive look. "The bread is a staple in Russian cuisine, and salt was a precious commodity here for centuries." He broke off a piece of bread, dipped it in salt and ate it, gesturing William to do the same.

The bread was warm, with a chewy crust, like the sourdough his mother used to make.

Robins gestured to the vodka: "I don't drink, but I do wish to toast your successful arrival." He raised the glass, and William and Gumberg followed suit.

"Welcome to Russia, Captain! Here is to the success of our Mission, now that you are here." They clanked the glasses.

"*Za zdorovie!*" William said – *To your health* – the toast he had learned from the Russian soldiers in France. He took a gulp. The vodka was strong and better than what he'd had at the front. It spread like a wave of heat through his body.

Gumberg downed his and gave William an approving grin: "That's very good Russian!" he said. "You have excellent command of one of the most important phrases in the Russian language."

They laughed. "Being able to share a drink can certainly be a useful social skill, both at home and here," Robins nodded. "Perhaps, Captain, you can help hold up the American end where I fail."

William nodded. "I hope this will prove to be the most difficult challenge in my posting here." He took another pinch of bread. "But, speaking of cultural relations, I have just found out that there are now American GIs fighting the Bolsheviks under the British command. Has this resulted in any hostility towards the Mission in Petrograd?"

"No. Nothing to worry about," Robins reassured, chewing on a piece of bread. "They know we are doing good things in Petrograd. Trust me – it's in their interest to keep us there."

Trust? His trust was already being stretched to its limit. He had crossed the Atlantic on trust – in something his own uncle and Mr Barr could not quite tell him about this Red Cross Mission, and now the Mission director himself wanted him to believe that the Reds would welcome them in Petrograd.

"Do they need our supplies so badly?" He stopped himself, suddenly struck with a flash of realization that Gumberg, being Robins' assistant from Petrograd, was likely one of *them* – not just any Russian, but a Red.

"You'll see for yourself soon enough." Robins gave him a playful wink. "In the meanwhile, suffice it to say, the Bolsheviks have plenty of real enemies to deal with right now. Isn't that right, Comrade Gumberg?"

Gumberg nodded with a calm smile and poured William and himself another shot.

So, that was settled – Gumberg was a Bolshevik. Calmly drinking vodka in the middle of a city run by the Whites and the Allies. Why was he here? Why was he Robins' assistant? To spy for the Reds?

William's cautious wartime brain settled in, and he resolved to mind Gumberg's pours. Maybe that's why Robins did not drink? He had to acknowledge to himself – again – that everything would have been a lot easier if someone would have actually told him the real reason he was here. Were he and Robins in danger right now, just minutes from the American garrison? Yet Robins seemed completely relaxed and unhurried. William could not wait to talk with him alone. Until then, he could not afford to be a tourist. This was an active war zone.

"So, what *is* the current state of affairs?" He broke off another piece of bread and thanked Gumberg who nudged the glass of vodka towards him. "Things seemed to be escalating rapidly when I left New York. But I haven't been able to follow the news as much as I would have liked to during the two weeks at sea."

"Well, now it's a full-blown civil war and a full-blown intervention, a lot of pieces in motion. A real mess."

"What are the pieces?"

Robins looked around the table and then reached into his pocket and pulled out his wallet. "I am a visual person, so it might be easier to explain with this."

He straightened a banknote on the table. "Imagine this dollar bill is Russia." He put a wheat penny on top of the bill, just to the left of Washington's face, over the scene depicting Columbus sighting land from the deck of *Santa Maria*.

"The Bolsheviks control less than the area under this penny – maybe about 300 miles around Moscow and Petrograd. The rest of this vast country is peppered with forces hostile to them." He pointed at the top edge of the bill. "Here, to the north, in Arkhangelsk, you have the British-led coalition force which now includes French, Canadian, American, Australian, Serbian and Polish troops. The British want to overturn Lenin's government and replace it with one willing to rejoin the war against Germany and willing to reinstate British business interests in Russia which the Reds have nationalized."

He pointed at the right edge of the bill. "Now, to the east, 6,000 miles from Moscow, there is another Allied coalition force in

Vladivostok. This one is led by the Japanese, and includes British, French, Canadian, American, Chinese and Italian troops. The Japanese committed the largest army of the group and want to take control of Russia's far-eastern territories. Also in Siberia, there is the Czechoslovak Legion, which is a force of around 40,000 POWs who were captured by the Russian Empire in the war, and whom the British have now bribed to fight the Bolsheviks in exchange for a country of their own after the war. Right now, they are fighting to secure the Trans-Siberian railroad, which is a vital supply line across Russia." His finger traced a line from the penny to the right edge of the bill.

"And those are just the foreign intervention forces. Then the Reds also have domestic enemies." He semicircled the left side of the penny. "To the west and south of Moscow, there are several *White* armies. Most of these are led by former tsarist generals – Denikin, Wrangel, Alekseev, Yudenich and a few others. Some are monarchists, some anarchists, some socialists, but all want the Bolsheviks out of Moscow. And then all throughout Siberia," he swept right of the penny, "there are hundreds of bands of Cossacks. Many are just opportunistic marauders, but a few fight on the side of the Reds, or the Whites, or the Allies."

He pinched off another piece of bread and popped it in his mouth. "And that, in a nutshell, is the current state of affairs."

"You have very impressive knowledge of the political climate here."

"In Russia, one has to keep his ear to the ground."

"Be a student of the landscape?"

Robins smiled. "Precisely! Politics permeates every aspect of Russia right now. Every corner of the country, every town is polarized and pulled in different ideological directions."

The penny looked so small and lonely on top of the dollar bill. "Do you think the Bolsheviks can win?"

"I know it looks dire, but they do have a couple of things in their favor. First, even though their enemies are many, they are not unified, and not coordinated. Not yet at least. Second, unlike most

European nations, Russia is simply too vast and populous to be invaded from the outside. When Napoleon tried it in 1812 with a superior military, the Russian generals simply kept retreating east. They drew Napoleon's army deeper and deeper, burning down their own villages and slaughtering their own livestock along the way to strain his supplies. They even let him take Moscow, after they burned it down, too. And then winter came, and his soldiers dropped like flies from starvation and cold. The Russians are tough fighters, especially when defending their land. But in a civil war, of course, this applies to both sides of this conflict."

The food arrived, and Robins stuffed his teaching aide back into his wallet.

THE AMBASSADORS' PLOT

In the car, Anna picked impatiently at a piece of door trim with her nail. They had been parked with the engine off for close to a half hour now. The subject of their observation was building number 19 at the end of the block in Khlebny Alley. There, on the eighth floor, one Robert Hamilton Bruce Lockhart, the British Consul General, occupied a luxury suite less than a mile away from the Kremlin.

Sergei checked his watch: "Five minutes till the meeting. Looks like no one is showing up early."

"Unless they showed up *really* early." The anticipation was torturous. She wanted Lockhart to bite, and bite hard, but two meetings in, he was still testing the waters. Today, he was meeting Berzin for the second time, and there was nothing she could do now but wait. They had planned and coached the agents as well as they could. And now, the spring had been released, and the clock was ticking down on its own toward the end, whatever the end would be. If this meeting failed, the whole plan would need to be scrapped. The piece of trim was beginning to peel away.

Finally, someone. Her small binoculars darted up. "Berzin and Buikis." She watched their plain-clothed agents approach the building from the other side of the street.

"Don't you mean Berzin and *Shmidken*?" Sergei smirked.

She recorded the time in her notebook. "Do you think Buikis got to pick his own alias, or did Peters christen him?"

He laughed, peering through his binoculars. "Come on, boys, don't let us down," he muttered under his breath as the men entered the building.

"Maybe Savinkov will show?" She hoped he would, so she could catch a glimpse of the most wanted man for the first time, even though Peter's orders were not to take him – *only follow, until we know who is who, and what the plan is.*

"I doubt it – he is much too cautious. But he may send someone if it comes to it."

A car turned the corner and pulled up to the entrance. It pattered thinly in the distance while the driver walked around and opened the rear door.

"Who is that?" She held her breath and fixed the binoculars on the man emerging from the back of the car.

"Well, son of a bitch! That's the French Consul Grenard." He looked at Anna. "If Lockhart invited the French to the meeting… that means…"

"That means he is bringing us into the plan!" The warm tinge of vindication dissolved any traces of self-doubt. The cast of conspirators was now unmasking right before her eyes.

She made a record in the notebook and watched Grenard disappear into the building just as another car drifted into view and parked behind his. A man with a small mustache and glasses emerged from the back and adjusted his trilby hat.

"And that is the American Consul General DeWitt Poole," Sergei identified.

She recorded the time and almost missed a slender man in a

business suit and a bowler hat who briskly crossed the street and entered the building with a briefcase in hand.

"Who was that?"

"I don't know; maybe just a tenant?"

"Did you catch his face? Are you sure it wasn't Savinkov?"

"Too tall for Savinkov. Short dark beard and mustache."

It was eleven o'clock. The meeting had started.

Almost an hour later, the French and American consuls re-emerged, got into their respective automobiles and parted ways. Anna logged the time and returned to watching the door. Ten minutes passed. Then another ten. Sergei glanced at the piece of the door trim enduring the incessant plucking of her finger. Berzin and Buikis were still not out.

"Do you think something's wrong?" she asked.

He shook his head. "I don't think so. I think it's a good sign – it means they are still talking."

Five minutes later, Buikis finally emerged, crossed the street and disappeared around the corner. Berzin appeared shortly after and headed in a different direction, carrying a briefcase he did not have before.

She exhaled a sigh of relief and marked the final time in the notebook. They waited another ten minutes, but no one else emerged. Sergei started the car and pulled away.

*

Yakov Peters dropped two lumps of sugar into his teacup and clanked around in it with his spoon. Anna liked Peters. He was in his early thirties, with a smiling round face, a high forehead, wild dark hair, and a pair of lively intelligent eyes. He looked up from his tea and smiled at the three of them.

"So, did you know the French and the American consuls were going to be there today?"

Anna shook her head. "Lockhart must have felt confident enough in Colonel Berzin to have them attend."

"And who was the other person in attendance?"

Berzin cleared his throat. "Lockhart introduced him only as Mr. Constantine and said he was an agent of the British Intelligence Service. Constantine is likely an alias."

"Do we know anything else about him?"

Sergei shook his head. "We have found no record of him entering the country, but he may have assumed this identity afterwards. I have two of my men looking into this. We'll also put surveillance on him at the next meeting."

"Good," Peters nodded and took a sip of his tea. "So, what do the diplomats want?" He looked at Berzin.

"They want the Latvian divisions in the north to support the Allied troops when they march on Moscow from Archangelsk. They also want the Latvian divisions in Moscow to assist with an armed coup and the arrest of the Bolshevik leadership. In exchange, the Allies will provide monetary compensation of two million rubles to the troops and will support the creation of an independent Latvian state after the war." Berzin reached down and sat a thick briefcase on Peters' desk. He opened it and put a pack of hundred-ruble bills in front of Peters.

"What's this?" Peters asked.

"That's their first installment, 700,000 rubles: 200,000 each from the US and France, and 300,000 from Britain. Constantine promised more at the next meeting."

"Well, if that does not prove they've taken our bait, I don't know what else would." Peters leaned back in his chair and connected his fingers together. "This is phenomenal. Just like that, we have three global superpowers exposed in the act of plotting to overthrow our government. Can you imagine what will happen when the workers in their countries read this story and learn what their governments are doing? This is tremendous success! Now, do we know the timeframe of this planned coup?"

"August 28."

Peters furrowed his brow. "That's the day of the Executive Committee Summit."

Anna nodded.

"It puts the entire party and government leadership in one room at the Grand Theater," Sergei said. "That's Lenin, Trotsky, Sverdlov – everyone! And it's only two weeks away."

"Can we cancel the summit?" Anna looked at Peters.

He shook his head: "We are talking about a meeting between the Executive Committee, the Council of People's Commissars and the Moscow Soviet! Lenin would never allow a foreign threat to derail something so important and publicly visible. He would see it as a defeat to the image of our government. Besides, now that we know about the plot, we have a lot of control over the situation. We can take measures."

Anna shook her head. "We know only part of it – we still don't know how Savinkov fits into this plan and what it will take to stop him. Our Latvian play may be the sideshow, but what is the main act?"

Peters' gaze darted to Berzin. "Did anyone at the meeting mention Savinkov?"

"No. Constantine only mentioned that there will be a force of 9,000 Russian patriots leading the armed rebellion."

"Which must be Savinkov's Union," Anna said. "But we did not get any leads. We'll try to feel out more details at the next meeting, but we can't pry too hard, or it will raise suspicion. We've only got our foot in the door. We need more time to uncover the rest of the plot and identify their network."

Peters sighed. "OK, very well. I will see what I can do to get the Executive Committee to postpone the meeting by at least a week to buy us more time. I don't think they will agree to any longer than that. In three weeks, the summit is going to take place regardless of whether you find Savinkov or not. Let's hope you do." He looked at Berzin. "What is our next step with Lockhart?"

"The French and the Americans are evacuating their diplomatic staff due to the civil war and the intervention, so they will not be directly involved in the future. Lockhart said Constantine will be my main contact going forward – he will bring the money and provide further instructions regarding the coup. I think Lockhart wants to distance himself from the execution of the plot. The next meeting is this Friday at a different address. Constantine will bring another installment of money and the letters of safe passage for the Latvian divisions in the north to the Allied commander in Arkhangelsk."

"So, this Constantine must be their main field operative – the *agent provocateur*," Peters pondered. "And Lockhart is just the link to London and funding."

She nodded. "Constantine does seem to be at the center of all this. And this begs the question. Up until now we have assumed that the British have been helping Savinkov. What if it's the other way around? Lockhart brought in the French and the Americans – the same allies supporting the British in Archangelsk and Vladivostok. Maybe we should treat Savinkov as just one piece of the larger British plot? Maybe Cromie is another piece in Petrograd? Who knows how many others there are?"

Peters nodded, sipping his tea. "All right, let's focus on Constantine and see if he leads us to the rest of his network and to Savinkov. Given the deadline and the sensitive nature of this project, I will get a secured task room assigned to you on the fourth floor. Move all your files pertaining to this case there, hold all your meetings and calls there, and do not give anyone else access besides you two. And let's update Uritsky's office with the new intelligence and have him increase surveillance on Cromie. As you said, Petrograd may also be a part of this plot."

*

In the large unoccupied office on the fourth floor, the air was hot and musty. Flecks of dust, undisturbed for months or maybe longer, now took to flight around them, dancing in the rays of the afternoon sun that pierced through the broken shutters. Anna opened the windows to let in the light and fresh breeze. This was one of the inner offices, looking out into the angular well of windows and down into the bare Lubyanka courtyard below.

They cleared out a workspace for themselves by dragging most of the office furniture into the corner and keeping just two desks and chairs. They then scavenged a large and very heavy table in a nearby boardroom, dragged it down the hall and set it in the middle of their office. Anna took in the new arrangement and liked it – it was open, minimalist, and conducive to thinking.

Sergei split a stack of blank notecards in two and handed one half to Anna. "OK, let's get everyone we know or suspect to be involved out on the table."

He wrote on three cards and placed them along the far edge of the table. "We have the British, the Americans and the French."

"Then we have Savinkov and his Union." Anna scribbled on another card and placed it along the top.

"Right. For the British, we have Consul Lockhart and his assistant Captain William Hicks, who is likely with the Secret Intelligence Service." He placed those name cards under the *British* heading. "We also have Captain Francis Cromie in Petrograd, confirmed with the SIS; and Constantine in Moscow, also with the SIS."

"We also have two Russians under surveillance who are likely working for the British. Maria Fride is on the lease for the address Constantine gave Berzin, and her brother is Colonel Aleksander Fride, who works in the Office of Military Communications." Anna added two cards for them in the *British* column.

"Good! Now, for the French, we have the Consul-General Grenard, General Lavergne with the French army and Colonel Vertemont with the intelligence service."

"And for the Americans, there is Ambassador Francis in Vologda, Consul Poole in Moscow, and a Mr Kalamatiano who is registered as a businessman but actually gathers intelligence for the US State Department."

Sergei scanned the table. "And these are just the ones we know – there must be dozens more."

"Even with just these, Moscow is starting to look like a city of spies!"

"They gather like crows sensing a kill."

She looked at the empty column under the Savinkov card. "But what concerns me more is that we know nothing at all about the Russian piece. We've been chasing Savinkov for months now, and all the leads we've had on his organization have ended up dead ends. It's as if the ground opened up and swallowed him. And now we have just three weeks left to find him."

"We're bound to get something out of Constantine."

"You think so? As much faith as I have in Colonel Berzin, he may not have enough time to develop that level of trust with Constantine. If you were Constantine, wouldn't you keep the parts of the plan separate to reduce risk? Meanwhile, 9,000 Russians may be preparing to take to arms in this city in three weeks. Can you imagine the carnage?"

Sergei rubbed his jaw. "OK... so, if we can't get any leads at the top from Lockhart and Constantine, let's shake out the bottom. Let's brief with the vice departments. If Savinkov is outfitting a secret army, he must have used illegal supply channels. Who knows, Contraband or Gangs may find another way in for us."

THE GOLDEN ROOSTER

The boy's lip was split, and his face was smudged with dirt, dried tears and snot. His bare feet dangled and kicked under the table while Mironov, a stout old Chekist with a greying cavalryman's mustache, was pulling him up by the ear. On the table in front of the boy lay several gold coins.

"The little bastard won't tell me where he got these!" Mironov conveyed to Anna as she entered the room. He let go of the boy's ear and then raised his arm as if to strike him. The boy shrunk into the chair, jerking his handcuffed hands to protect his face. His little eyes flared with fiery hatred at Mironov.

"OK, OK!" Anna intervened. "Agent Mironov, why don't we step out for a minute so you can catch me up?"

Mironov shook his fist at the boy, scooped up the coins and followed Anna out into the hallway. He shut the door and postured in the corridor with comfortable authority – his barrel chest out, and one hand casually on the gun holster at his side. "I caught this little shit pickpocketing in the market in Kitay-Gorod this morning. He stole a watch, and when we caught him and shook him down, we found these." He opened his hand and passed the coins to Anna.

She took one of the small coins and turned it in her hand. A woman's head on one side and a rooster on the other. "French gold francs," she said.

"Right. Not exactly the usual tender in that neighborhood," Mironov pronounced, pointing his finger with the weight of a detective making a profound deduction. "Now, I remembered what Comrade Zaverin had said about foreign money, so I thought we had better haul him in. He confessed to picking the watch in the market, but he's mum about the coins. So, I know it's something else. Now we just need to beat the truth out of the little son of a bitch."

"Good work," she said, rolling the coins in her hand. "Tell you what – let me try. I'll come get you if I need you to take the next turn."

Mironov sighed with visible disappointment, shook his head and walked off.

Anna returned to the room a few minutes later. She uncuffed the boy and put a thick slice of white bread and a tin cup of milk on the table in front of him. His dirty fingers snatched the bread off the table, and he dug into it with his little teeth, keeping his sharp, cautious eyes on Anna. When there was not a smallest crumb left on the table, without a pause, he grabbed the tin mug with both hands and hurriedly gulped down the milk. He set down the empty cup, sniffled, and wiped his mouth and nose on his sleeve, all without taking his eyes off Anna. The whole process took less than a minute.

He was a scrawny little thing with light brown hair. He watched Anna with the willful fearlessness of an alley kid who learned to hustle and run before he learned to walk. One of his ears was glowing beet-red.

"How old are you?" she asked.

The boy swallowed. "Eight."

"What is your name?"

"Serafim."

"Do you have a mother?"

The boy nodded.

"A father?"

He shook his head.

"Do you have brothers and sisters?"

"Three brothers and two sisters," he enunciated clearly and with some pride. "I had another brother and sister, but they died when they were little."

"What does your mother do?"

"She works at a tannery," he declared and then hushed down, cautious not to give away too much.

Anna smiled. She put the coins on the table between them.

"Are these yours?"

He was silent, sensing a trap.

"Agent Mironov took these from you, right?"

The boy stoically stared at Anna.

"I don't want them. So, if they are really yours, I would give them back to you. You just have to tell me where you got them, so I can be sure they are not stolen."

The boy swallowed and stared at the coins. "My uncle," he finally said.

"Doesn't he need them?"

"He has more."

Anna pushed one of the coins to the boy.

"Does your uncle live with you?"

The boy shook his head. "No, he is visiting from Odessa."

Anna moved another coin to him.

"And if I asked him, he would *not* say you took these without his permission?" Anna shook her head slightly.

"No," the boy shook his head too, looking up at her sheepishly and clearly lying.

"OK, then!" Anna said with relief and pushed the rest of the coins to the boy. "I think this was clearly a misunderstanding. Here are all your coins back, and I will go tell Agent Mironov to let you go. Wait here just a minute."

Anna found Mironov at his desk. "It's his uncle," she said. "I need you to let the boy go and let him keep the coins. Borovsky will take a squad to follow him."

*

Michael Borovsky was a strapping, broad-shouldered former soldier and ironworker from Tula. He had a level disposition, a clean haircut and a jaw as square as a blacksmith's anvil. In all her time with the Cheka, Anna had never seen him unnerved, never seen him drink, and never heard him swear. In fact, he did not say much at all, and yet he had the reputation for getting the detainees to talk. After his squad had picked up the boy's uncle, Anna let him run the interview. Given the large sum of foreign currency and the counterfeit documents they had found in the apartment, she knew they had the right man. They could have tried sweating him out between herself and Sergei, but right now they did not have the luxury of time. Less than an hour later, Borovsky called her back down.

When she entered the interview room, the first thing she saw was the wide expanse of Borovsky's white linen shirt stretched over his muscular back and criss-crossed with suspender straps. He was hunched over the desk with his sleeves rolled up, filling out the report.

While he himself may have been a portrait of mundane office reality, the scene on the other side of the desk would have caused alarm under any other circumstances. A chair lay overturned amidst semi-dried pools of blood and what looked like several bluish-pale severed fingers on the floor.

"God, Michael, was this necessary?"

He turned his clean-shaven face and calm grey eyes towards her.

"You said you needed results and fast." He returned to the report. "I did try talking first, but that did not work. Pulling fingernails did not work. Fingers worked." He recounted the progression of horror with methodic dispassion and detached professionalism of an accountant explaining the tax code. "Don't worry, he can still sign the confession," he added without an ounce of humor.

She took a deep breath to get the image out of her mind. "So, what do we know?"

"He is a runner for Pashka Zalotin."

"The Odessa kingpin? Smugglers and thieves?"

"That's right. But this time they are not running furs and caviar. He says he was sent to arrange for the shipment of dynamite into Moscow from the Don region."

"So, the French currency we recovered from the apartment was…"

"A deposit."

"Did he name his contact in Moscow?"

He glanced at the severed digits on the floor, as if reconstructing the chain of events. "Oh yes. A former army officer, representing some unnamed organization."

"He didn't mention the Union?"

He shook his head.

"Did he tell you how we can find this officer?"

"Even better." He handed her the report. "He is supposed to come to a meeting at this address tomorrow night to finalize the delivery arrangements. He said someone from the leadership of the organization will be there."

She snatched the report from his hand and suddenly felt as if she'd been punched in the gut. "Number 2 Molochny Alley? That's… the doctor's office Natalia took her son to. The Union has been under our noses this whole time!"

He nodded without a word, and a shadow of a smile slipped across his lips.

*

The dusk came on like a dark tide, deepening fast, even as they drove. Egorov parked at the west end of Molochny Alley, under the old stone wall of the Conception Monastery. The second car pulled up behind them. They were about two blocks away from number 2. Three more cars were supposed to make their approach from the south. There were twenty-five agents mobilized for this. Hopefully enough for whatever they were about to walk into.

She got out of the car. The night air was still and damp. She had been in this part of the city once before. A sleepy old neighborhood near the river by day, it was now a dim, treed maze of narrow streets, hooked side alleys and walled dead ends. It was quiet. Even the dogs weren't barking.

Sergei checked his watch and gave her a nod. They proceeded on foot, with the other squad doing the same now – armed agents converging quickly and silently in the shadows towards the street corner where the house stood. The meager light cast by the sparse streetlights was to their advantage. In front of her, Sergei was pressing forward with a confident pace, and she tried to match his steps, placing hers carefully on the wet cobblestones, trying to avoid bottles and other trash underfoot that could betray their presence.

Would Savinkov be there? She gripped the pistol tighter in her hand and felt her pulse pumping forcefully in her thumb. The safety was off, and her index finger lightly checked the ridge of the trigger as she scanned the murky alleys and gaping dark voids of backyards and entryways.

Number 2 was a three-story building on a three-way corner at the end of the block. The windows were dark, and she wondered if perhaps Serafim's uncle had lied. Or maybe the Union had been alerted? Across the street, a pistol barrel glimmered in the shadows like the slash of a tiny razor in the dark – their second squad was in position.

She followed Sergei along the wall of the building, ducking under the windows towards the entrance, where they stopped under the brass placard engraved with *N. S. Aksanin, Doctor of Medicine.* They were now in position for the next part. Soon, footsteps approached in the street – Borovsky, dressed in civilian, emerged out of the dark and passed through the fuzzy light cone of the streetlamp. He knocked quietly on the dark window near the entrance, adjusted his flat cap and walked up the steps. A few moments of waiting followed, and then finally there was the sound of the latch.

The door opened, and she heard a man's muffled voice. She could see Borovsky up in the entryway but not the man who had opened the door. Suddenly, Borovsky exploded forward and disappeared into the dark void with a few muted thuds and moans. It all happened so quickly and quietly, and in the same instant, Sergei charged silently up the stairs, followed by Egorov and several others who rushed past her and through the door with their guns drawn. She followed.

The room smelled of an apothecary mixed with stale cigarette smoke and a tinge of something sweet. Their flashlights carved out snapshots of an empty reception room – desk, chairs, and a couch. On the floor, Egorov was helping Borovsky gag and tie a man. Anna turned on her flashlight and fixed its light on the coatrack near the entryway. Anna snapped her fingers quietly to Sergei and pointed to the seven or eight overcoats and military trench coats hanging on the coatrack. Where were the people belonging to these coats?

That's when they all heard the quick footsteps somewhere in the depths of the office, and the hairs on the back of her neck stood up. Somewhere, a door closed.

"Well, son of a bitch!" she heard Sergei curse under his breath.

So much for the element of surprise! His flashlight zigzagged across the wall to find the light switch. "Let's go! Let's go!" he urged them as the lights came on, and they followed him into the small hallway, kicking in the doors into a washroom and two exam rooms – all empty.

Only one door remained, at the very end of the hallway. Who was on the other side? She knelt on one knee next to Egorov, ready to fix her sights on the target inside. But when Sergei kicked the door open, all she saw was another empty room – an office with a desk and bookcases along the back wall. There were no doors left to kick in.

There was a scent of a damp cellar hanging in the room. "Look for a trap door," Sergei exclaimed.

They pulled back the Persian rug off the floor and found nothing and proceeded hurriedly tapping and pushing on the wall panels and on the wainscoting until one of the bookcases gave slightly under Anna's hand.

"Here," she said, putting her cheek to the edge of the trim and feeling a cool, damp breeze.

Egorov, using his hands like a pair of shovels and sledgehammers all at once, tore out the books and the shelves, until only an oak frame of the bookcase remained. They searched for a latching mechanism without success. The sturdy oak frame would not budge from the wall.

"Mus'be bolted from the inside," Egorov huffed, took a step back and bashed his boot into the middle of the bookcase with a thunderous crack. Without a pause, he stepped back again and repeated his technique vigorously until the frame splintered and snapped loose from the wall. He tore it away with his massive claws, revealing a small doorway and steps leading down.

The stone stairs terminated in a blind landing with light coming from around the corner. They reached the bottom silently, with their guns on the ready. Sergei peeked around the corner and was immediately met with three bangs of pistol fire. Bullets sparked off the cinder block wall and showered them with tiny stone shrapnel.

Sergei backed away from the corner and yelled: "Cheka! Put down your weapons. The building is surrounded!"

A bassy holler came back: "Fuck you, you Red pussies! Why don't you come over here and suck on some lead!" This suggestion was followed by three more blasts doling out the aforementioned lead to drive home the point. When the ringing of the gunshots subsided, they heard some hushed arguing coming from around the corner.

Sergei turned back to his team. "It's a large room with a barricade about ten yards out. Two shooters behind the barricade, possibly more in the room. Egorov – you provide cover. Nikolaev, Borovsky – follow me."

He gave a nod and Egorov leaned around the corner with his pistol and fired one round after another into the room. As soon as the first shot rang out, Sergei's assault team slipped around the corner.

Anna heard a scattering of gunshots around the corner and then shouts – Sergei and Nikolaev yelling something. Egorov ceased firing and advanced into the room. Anna followed him into the thin fog of gunpowder smoke.

The improvised barricade of upturned desks was piled at the front of the room, and behind it was a man writhing on the floor in a glossy, dark-red puddle. Blood was spattering and bubbling from his contorted mouth, and his hand was grasping at his blood-soaked chest. His eyes caught Anna's and he raised his hand towards her, perhaps mistaking her in his desperation for a sister of mercy. She turned away. In the room, Nikolaev and Borovsky had their guns pointed at nine men sprawled on their stomachs on the floor. Anna walked through and kicked away the pistols scattered near them.

"Everybody, keep your heads down!" Nikolaev barked at the group. "It's a good thing we brought the extra handcuffs," he smirked at Anna.

The basement room was a vast cavern finished in peeling plaster and propped up with stone support columns. Several bare lightbulbs hung from the ceiling, illuminating the space with weak light that barely reached the stacks of boxes and furniture at the very back. What must have been a storage cellar had been converted into a subterranean command center complete with maps on the walls, desks, chairs, filing cabinets, and stacks of papers. It was like a darker version of their office at Lubyanka. This was the place where their enemies came to work, just as she, Sergei and Egorov did above ground.

"Savinkov's not here," Sergei said quietly to her. "Do you smell that?"

She did – the sweet tinge she had smelled upstairs was overbearing here, an almost sickening aroma leeching through the smell of fired gunpowder.

"It's dynamite. And a lot of it." He pointed to the stacks of small wooden crates. "That's why they gave up so easily. One stray bullet and we could have leveled the whole block."

They both jumped when something metal fell with a loud clang at the far end of the room. Egorov pointed the flashlight at the murky corner but illuminated only stacks of upturned chairs and boxes.

"Who is back there!?" Nikolaev blared at the group on the floor, putting the gun to the head of one of the men.

Not waiting for a response, Sergei was already closing in on the dark far corner, with his flashlight and gun pointing the way towards the sound of something heavy being dragged across the floor. Anna was right behind him when he rounded a stack of boxes.

"Stop right there!" he shouted.

Her eyes followed the line of his flashlight and she saw a dark, rough-edged opening in the stone of the foundation wall. On the other side of the void was a silhouette of a man. As if in a dream, she saw him turn around and she instantly recognized the thin, hard features and steely eyes looking back at them. It was Savinkov! In the split second it took her to draw a breath, Savinkov had vanished into the pitch black of the void. Sergei managed to fire two shots into the dark, and then there was a bright flash of light that filled everything around them.

When she came to, she was on her back on the floor, and her ears were ringing, and her eyes still burned with the flash of the explosion. Egorov was saying something to her, and she felt his hands helping her sit up. The room was slowly re-emerging from the blinding blur, and there was dust and a strong smell of chemicals filling the air and stinging her nose. Sergei was sitting up against the wall, holding up his bloody left hand.

"That was fucking Savinkov!" he grunted.

"It's the Moscow sewers on the other side," Nikolaev said, examining the rubble with the dust-filled wedge of his flashlight. "There are hundreds of miles of it underground. He's gone – no telling where he will pop up."

"The fucker took off two of my fingers!" Sergei growled through clenched teeth, wrapping his hand in a rag.

"We are lucky he did not set off the dynamite," Egorov said.

Through the daze and the ringing in her ears, an odd sound was cutting in. Anna looked around the room and realized that she was hearing the strained, irregular rattling gurgle of the man dying behind the barricade. Several Chekists stood nearby watching, mesmerized by the gradual, inescapable tightening of the death's grip. Borovsky walked over and shot him in the head.

*

Sitting on a hospital bed, Sergei waited for the nurse to return and finish changing his dressing.

"Look at this!" he said, holding up his left hand with two raw stitched nubs in place of his pinky and ring finger.

Anna reached over and put her hand over his right hand.

"You are lucky to be alive. It could have been a lot worse."

"Yes, it could have been my shooting hand." He examined his shortened digits and shook his head: "I still can't believe that bastard slipped away. Again."

"You've got to let it go. What matters is that we got *to* him. Finally. Let him run – he is finished. We took down the entire leadership of the Union. We took his dynamite and his weapons.

He's got nothing left. I'll bet you the British won't go near him now. The Union is done. He is done."

"I'll believe it when I see him dead."

She nodded. "Look, the hard part is over. Peters and Dzerzhinsky are ecstatic, but we still have work to do and only six days until the summit. With the Union liquidated, the British will have to rely even more on our Latvians. Which means we have a chance to get closer to Constantine and his network."

Egorov's bandaged head popped in the door. "Oh, man," he grinned. "I heard you won't be able to count to ten anymore!"

Sergei scrunched his face into a wry smirk: "Hey, why don't you come over here and help me check if I can still use my foot!" he invited.

"You should really try getting hit in the head for a change," Egorov chuckled in the hallway, walking away.

THE MECHANISM

The sun had set, but the crowd was not dispersing – it seemed it had grown larger. The factory lights glowed bright overhead, against the darkening inky sky, making Dora's eyes hurt. The rally had overflown from the shop floor, and the large loading yard was now filling with workers and soldiers, men and women pushing her from behind and from the sides, moving her about like a sea.

"There he is! Look!" a man next to her said to his little son, hoisting him onto his shoulders. He pointed inside the factory, through the tall open loading doors.

Yes, there he is. A sudden outburst of cheering and applause spread from the crowd inside the factory out into the yard. A sailor in front of her blocked her view and yelled something, pumping his fist in the air. The spontaneous, disorganized shouting rolled into a public chant that spread through the crowd like a tidal wave, reverberating in the air, and in her own body.

They are triumphant. They think they've won. But in the war of ideas, ideas don't die. They just smolder at the end of a wick. They re-ignite.

The crowd quieted down, and the fragments of his speech reached the courtyard again in waves, like broken echoes. Next to her, the boy on the worker's shoulders was studying her. She looked up, meeting the unblinking stare of his big brown eyes. It was like looking into the horizon. He raised his little hand and gave her an uncertain wave.

Breathe, she thought to herself. It had been so many years since she had felt this.

The steel spine of the pistol grip had warmed in her fingers. She squeezed it. The small Browning fit perfectly in her hand in the pocket of her coat. Her thumb gently circled the checkered ridge of the safety switch. This tiny metal lever was the only thing restraining the trigger under her index finger.

The speech was culminating. She could not make out all the words, but she heard the crescendos in his sentences which were becoming shorter and more forceful: "*... our enemies! ... only one way out! ... victory or death!*"

She scanned the crowd – they were seized in rapture. But she was not in their reality. She moved in a different plane. The present – *their* present – did not matter – it was just a false façade behind which the mechanism was already in motion. What mattered was what led to this and what would come out of this. Cause and effect. She was a lever in the mechanism. The trigger was a string tied to a life. A decision executed. A future corrected.

The crowd broke out in applause and shouts. The band began playing. He was done. People were moving – some leaving, and some closer toward the front.

He descended the podium and was now walking towards the exit. She pushed forward, her hand in her pocket. His car was waiting. No armed guards. She squeezed in between people to the front of the crowd. They let her through without really looking at her – she was just a small woman, maybe a child. He was almost to the car. A throng of people surrounded him. He stopped, talking to someone. Now he was shaking hands with someone. Her heartbeat was pounding in her ears. His driver walked around and opened the rear door – a gun holstered on his belt.

Her thumb flipped the safety lever down. When she took her hand out of her pocket, it was holding the gun. She stepped out of the crowd towards him.

Breathe.

Click.

The clap of the small pistol was barely perceptible over the spatter of the engine and noise of the band. A spark and a puff of gunpowder smoke erupted at the end of the barrel. She felt the hot breath of the opened breech as the discarded shell ejected from the firing chamber, burning a black sooty smudge onto the knuckle of her index finger.

He turned towards her, his eyes not yet bearing recognition of what had just happened. People started running. Some away and some towards her. She pulled the trigger again. And again.

Someone grabbed her arm from behind and pushed it up. She tried to pull away, but her lace-up ankle boots slipped on the cobblestones. Someone's fingers pried the pistol from her hand. The weight of many hands latched on to her coat, her arms, and her neck, pushing on her and pulling her down to the ground.

Someone's heavy body was now on top of her, and someone's hands were holding her wrists behind her back, and a sharp pain was piercing into her shoulder and her neck. But, with her cheek pressed hard into the warm pavement stone, her eyes were still on him. He was on the ground, too. His head was propped against the wheel of his car. He was holding his neck with his fingers slick with blood that was spurting through them and flowing onto his red-soaked shirt.

EXIGENCIES

Anna tossed a stack of files back into the box and shoved it aside with her foot. Outside the window, the afternoon shadow had moved up higher in the well of the Lubyanka courtyard. She wished the windows of their task room faced the street, but maybe it was better this way – less distraction. She stood up, stretched, and pushed the finished box to her 'done' pile. She made a detour and opened the windows, but the meager breeze did not make the room any less stifling – the scent of the cellar and dynamite had now permeated into everything, including her own fingers. She caught herself sighing as she grabbed another box from the stack. Eighteen to go. She was tired of sitting, and she was tired of looking through these papers.

"How can there be so much bureaucracy in an underground terrorist organization?" she asked Sergei, settling back into her chair and picking a file from the box. "Purchase orders, meeting minutes, payment slips."

"The better for us," he shrugged. "I wish all criminals kept good records." He seemed content with digging for the truth in the stacks of paper.

"It will take months to *really* go through all of these." She sized up the boxes of papers they had removed from the Union office.

"Just keep skimming! There's gotta be something."

So far, in all these papers, there was no mention of any foreign agents or the Allied military plans. It was as if that reality existed only in her's and Sergei's minds.

"Maybe Savinkov was not privy to the larger plan," she said. "He was never at any of the meetings with Berzin. Maybe he was just a pawn in Constantine's game? The rest of the Union leadership don't seem to know much about it."

"It's possible. But we won't know for sure until we check." He stood up, stretched his back, and walked over to the door to turn on the lights. She was still getting used to the snow-white flash of the bandage on his hand.

She pulled a notebook from the box and paged through it – more tedious meeting minutes.

"Whoa!" Sergei said. "I think… this is the roster of the Union army." He flipped through page after page of a black notebook. "*Commanding Officers, Platoon Commanders, Squad Leaders, Recruits* – names and addresses." He turned it around to show her the rows and columns on the page.

"Are you serious? All 9,000 of them?"

"Could be."

He turned more pages but was interrupted by an urgent knock at the door. They exchanged an inquisitive look – they did not get visitors here. He walked to the door to unlock it and returned followed by a grave-faced Peters.

"What?" Anna stood up from her desk.

"Have you been here all day?"

"Since the morning, why?"

"Then you have not heard. Uritsky has been killed."

"What!?" Visibly shell-shocked, Sergei crumpled onto the edge of his desk.

"When? How?" Anna asked.

"This morning. Outside of his office in Petrograd. A man walked up and shot him point-blank. Uritsky died on the spot."

"Did they get the shooter?" Anna asked.

"He ran but was eventually apprehended."

"Who is he?"

"A nobody, as far as we can tell. Last name Kannegisser. A kid in his twenties; a former military cadet. The Petrograd Cheka is still processing him, so maybe they will figure out something that makes sense."

Peters walked up to the table and studied the notecards. "Have you seen anything – anything at all – in the course of this operation that would indicate a threat against Uritsky?"

"No." Sergei looked at Anna and shook his head. "Lockhart and Constantine have discussed arrests of the Soviet leadership, but never direct action like this."

Peters chewed his bottom lip. "OK. So, here is what I need you to do. I need you to evaluate the impact of this on our operation. Talk to Petrograd and determine if this could have anything to do with Uritsky's surveillance on Cromie's network there. Maybe this is unrelated, but I don't believe in coincidences. Berzin goes back in to meet with Constantine tomorrow, so I need your assessment and recommendation on my desk first thing in the morning: are we compromised? If so, to what extent, and what countermeasures are needed? OK?"

Peters marched out and they sat in silence, stunned, their minds trying to process this new turn.

"I just talked to him on the phone yesterday," Sergei muttered distraughtly and settled into his chair, his gaze fixed aimlessly on the surface of his desk.

Looking at him, she knew there was grief churning in him, even though he might never surface it. He had been dealt a blow and lost someone important to him, like when they lost Alexei. She came to him, put her hands on his shoulders and kissed the back of his head. Under her fingertips, his heart was beating fast, like a cornered animal's.

She wiped a tear away from her cheek.

"Who do you think is behind this? Cromie? Savinkov? Maybe there was a Union cell in Petrograd?"

He shook his head. "I don't know. I should call Petrograd. We'll see what we can piece together. Can you check with the ops teams and see if there's been anything out of the ordinary on our end?"

She left him alone to talk to Petrograd and went downstairs and tracked down everyone and anyone involved in the operation. When she returned a half hour later, he was standing over their card table, examining the names.

"What do you have?" He looked up.

"Not much." She shook her head. "Berzin and Buikis are both certain that their covers are still intact. The surveillance squad confirmed that the French and the American diplomats had left the country last week, as planned. Lockhart is up to his usual activities, and Constantine has not left his apartment for two days."

"So, we really don't know where Constantine is. He could have slipped out. He could even be in Petrograd."

She nodded. "But if we raid his apartment now, it will end the operation. Berzin is supposed to meet him tomorrow, so I guess we will know soon enough. What did you find out from Petrograd?"

"It's a strange deal." He shook his head. "This kid – Leo Kannegisser – guess where he was arrested?"

She shook her head.

"Leaving the British Mission!"

"So, this was the British?"

"Could be, but he did not admit to it. He said he was trying to get political asylum but was turned away."

"Do you believe it? The British certainly would have benefitted from getting Uritsky off Cromie's back. But it seems too clumsy for the SIS to have an operative return to the Mission right after the assassination. So, if he did not do it for the British, why did he do it?"

"He said Uritsky had ordered the execution of several White officers who were plotting an uprising in Petrograd. One of those officers was his lover."

"Kannegisser is a homosexual?"

He nodded.

She sunk into her chair, feeling suddenly exhausted from the last few days of long hours and little sleep. "So, do we just file this away as a crime of passion? The chief of the Petrograd Cheka gets murdered in the midst of an international spy sting operation by a grieving lover of one of the men he had executed?"

"I agree – it sounds implausible, but maybe too implausible to be made up?"

"So, if that is true, then this is completely coincidental to our operation, and does not change our tactics, right?"

"Does it feel a little too convenient?"

"Maybe." She tapped the pencil on her lips. "I think we should review all of Uritsky's reports from the last two weeks just in case, before we tell Peters the operation is in the clear."

"I agree." He pushed the papers aside, propped up his elbows on his desk and let his head sink into his hands.

She looked at her watch. "But first, why don't I get us some food from the cafeteria? It's almost seven, and we have not even had lunch today."

She got up but did not make it far. Heavy footsteps rumbled hurriedly in the hallway, and Egorov burst through their unlocked door: "There you are!" he huffed, out of breath. "I was looking all over for you. He's been shot!"

"We know – Uritsky?" Anna said.

"What? No – it's Lenin! Lenin has been shot!"

Sergei jumped to his feet. "What the devil is going on?" he growled under his breath.

They hurried after Egorov downstairs to the main foyer, where a hundred or so Chekists still remaining in the building at this hour had gathered. Dzerzhinsky's tall, lanky figure loomed from the top of the staircase.

"Comrades." His normally quiet voice carried in the open space. People hushed. "As you may have heard, about a half hour ago, Comrade Lenin was shot while speaking to the workers at the Michelson factory. He sustained three gunshot wounds and was taken to the Kremlin in a serious condition. The shooter was apprehended on site and is in our custody.

"But that is not all." He raised his voice over the erupted agitation. "Earlier today, the chief of the Petrograd Cheka Moisei Uritsky was shot and killed outside the Cheka headquarters in Petrograd. The assassin was apprehended and is now in custody of the Petrograd Cheka."

Anna's mind raced, checking off possibilities. This was not a coincidence – it couldn't have been. *Lenin?! They got to Lenin?!* And then, a terrifying, sickening thought: *Did we do this? Did I miss something? Savinkov? Lockhart? Constantine?* The name cards on the table scrambled into a tangled mess. Who was this other shooter? Was it a name on a card on their table, or another nameless nobody? She looked at Sergei. His steely gaze was transfixed on Dzerzhinsky. He was still hiding his emotions, but she knew him enough to see the welled-up tear glazing the corner of his eye. She knew it was not sadness – it was rage. Like when he was bullied by older boys in the street, long ago, and his hands were clenched into white-knuckled fists, just before he started punching. If Uritsky was the father he never had, Lenin was his prophet. No other two men had shaped him more in his life. She wanted to take his hand.

"I consider these events a clear declaration of terror on our government and the Cheka organization. The nation looks to us to ensure that there are no more attacks on our leadership and that all those responsible for these cowardly acts are brought to justice. I have assigned additional security at the Kremlin as well as to Comrade Trotsky and other members of our government in Petrograd. There is a lot of work to be done over the following hours and days, and I know I can count on each and every one of you. I know you are eager to get started, but first, let us take a moment of silence for our fallen comrade." Dzerzhinsky bowed his head.

Anna looked down and closed her eyes. There was a darkness rising – she felt it. How far they had fallen in just a day! This morning, the world made sense, and she felt in control. And now they were two moves behind, and the sense of control had been supplanted with uncertainty and fear. What was next? Who was next? The darkness was rising like a thousand anonymous hands trying to pull her down. There was no control. There was never any control.

"I know it is late, but I want everyone called back in." Dzerzhinsky's sullen face gleamed down on them like a grim moon. "And I want to see all the department heads in my office now." He turned and walked up the stairs.

Sergei looked at her, and she, maybe only she, could clearly see the shadow of that helpless anger in his eyes.

She was going to say something, but he shook his head. "I don't know. Make sure everyone's called back in." He turned and began his ascent after Dzerzhinsky.

*

Sergei returned to the task room a half hour later. "Come on," he said. "This may be connected to our case."

"Connected how?" she asked, following him down the corridor.

"The shooter is an SR."

"So, this was Savinkov?" She wished they had not let him slip away into the rat tunnels under the city. "Is Kannegisser an SR?"

He did not answer, striding next to her, lost in his own head.

The shooter was a small woman in her mid-twenties. Her cheekbone was scraped, and her dark hair was pinned up and disheveled. Anna squeezed through a group of department heads crowding the hallway to observe through the glass-lined partition.

Her hands were shackled to the table, and her gaze was fixed somewhere in the distance past the empty patch of the wall on the other side. Peters sat down across from her, put his gun on the table and opened his notebook.

"What is your name?"

She did not look at him. "Dora Kaplan." Her voice was small, gruff and detached.

"How old are you?"

"Twenty-eight"

"What is your political affiliation?"

"I am a member of the Socialist Revolutionary Party."

"Do you know why you are here?"

"I shot Lenin."

"Who told you to kill Lenin?"

"Is he dead?" The last word glinted with a thin facet of inflection.

Peters looked up from his notebook and examined her face, as if trying to detect a crack in her impenetrable façade of detachment. Perhaps it wasn't a façade, Anna thought. Perhaps it went to the core of this woman. Peters turned back to his notebook.

"I will be asking the questions. Who told you to kill Lenin?"

"No one. It was my decision alone."

"Why did you decide to kill Lenin?"

"Because he betrayed the Russian people."

"What do you mean by that?"

Her gaze shifted and fixed on him. Distant and dispassionate. "You'd have to be blind to not see he has betrayed the revolution. He disbanded the Constituent Assembly. He suppressed all other parties. He deprived the Russian people of choice. Do you need more reasons?"

Her gaze released Peters and drifted across the front of the room and all the eyes watching her from behind the glass. She passed calmly through Anna's gaze and diverted back to the empty wall.

"Who else was involved in planning and executing the assassination?"

"No one. I acted alone."

"Where did you get the Browning pistol?"

"I have nothing else to say."

Peters looked at her pale, stone-like face. His pen hovered above the page.

"You do realize that you are facing the firing squad? I can promise you that you will not live much longer if you don't give me information on your co-conspirators."

She met his gaze with indifference and said not a word more. The show was over.

After Peters had her taken away, Anna pulled Sergei aside in the corridor. "We need to get some time with her. Let her sleep on it and have Borovsky take a crack at her tomorrow, find out if Savinkov is behind this."

He shook his head. "She'll be dead before then."

"Sergei, we need her!" she whispered. "You have to try. We still don't know how she is connected to Kannegisser!"

"Look, Anna, it does not matter," his voice cracked. "We are at war. They are shooting our leaders in our streets. Right now, five doctors are trying to keep Lenin alive. Uritsky is already dead. We are done talking to these people. Kaplan and Kannegisser *need* to be shot! Our sting operation has been terminated. We've been ordered to sweep everyone up."

"Like whom?"

"Everyone – British, French, American, Russian – every name on the table, starting with Lockhart!"

"Lockhart? But what about diplomatic immunity?"

"It's just run out. Dzerzhinsky's order. An attempted assassination of our head of state changes things."

LOCKHART

No one spoke as the motorcade sped through the night. Up ahead, the Kremlin was aglow with lights, and as the cars flew past, Anna saw soldiers, trucks, and machine guns at every entrance, gate and intersection. But Sergei didn't look – his gloomy gaze was lost somewhere ahead, in the darkness beyond the headlights.

Egorov drove fast, and it took them less than ten minutes to pull into Khlebny Alley and stop in front of the building. After the car doors thumped shut, the only other sound in the night was the cocking of their pistols. One team covered the fire escapes in the back and another the elevators, while the rest of them ascended the stairs. It was just past one in the morning when they reached the penthouse apartment number 24 and kicked in the door.

It flew open with a crack, sending metal hardware clanking and scattering on the floor as they proceeded inside, turning on lights and checking the rooms.

Lockhart was in the bedroom, looking even paler than usual,

but then again, Anna had never before seen him this close. Standing next to the bed in his pajamas, he was squinting at the lights and the people stomping through the rooms. Without his suit, and with his dark hair tousled, he looked even younger than his thirty-one years. *How on earth did he get this posting?* Anna wondered. Examining him now, she thought that his messy hairdo actually better suited his protruding ears than the shiny, heavily pomaded part he typically sported.

"What is the meaning of this? Who are you?" he squeaked in Russian with a Scottish accent. She could tell he was inebriated and not trying to veil his annoyance with what in his mind certainly must have been the ultimate display of incompetence on behalf of the dimwitted peasants running this backward land. She'd read his memos. Seeing the uniforms, he postured arrogantly, assured that this mounting blunder would inevitably precipitate in a diplomatic fallout of unprecedented proportions. But behind his eyes, Anna saw a thread of fear.

"Cheka. You are under arrest," Sergei replied.

A woman turned in Lockhart's bed, trying to cover herself with a blanket, clearly not sober enough to be alarmed by the presence of armed men in the bedroom.

Egorov pushed in Lockhart's assistant Hicks from another room. Hicks was in his pajamas and had papers in his hand: "What is your authority? You cannot do this! He has diplomatic guarantees."

Sergei took the papers from Hicks and folded them into his coat pocket without looking. "You, too – get dressed. You are coming with us."

He then turned to Anna: "Please have this young lady get dressed and bring her down."

*

Robert Hamilton Bruce Lockhart had sobered up sitting in the small processing room in Lubyanka. He took a sip of his tea and his tired, bloodshot eyes scanned the pale green walls again but could not find anything to hold his attention. He studied Anna standing by the window – she watched him in the dark reflection. The black void of the courtyard glared into the room.

"How long will this continue?" His nasal broken Russian cut the silence. "I demand to speak to someone in charge."

He probably thought she was a secretary. She could tell he despised her, and it made her smile.

"I wonder if you can hear it – that obstinate conviction of your own entitlement?" She responded to him in English and could tell that it startled him. "I am curious if you can recall a time before it had been hammered into your head and ruined you. You probably can't. When I was in England, I had met many naïve young men just like you, who were taught to believe in the superiority of the British man. They measured their egos by the size of the British Navy and the conquests of the British Empire. Your country has done all of you a grave disservice. You've been taught that you are the master race and the master gender, and that you have the right to take and destroy anything you please anywhere in the world. But take heed, Mr. Lockhart, here you have no entitlements."

Sergei entered with a file in his hand, glanced at Anna and settled in the chair across from Lockhart. He studied the British Consul's face.

"What was your involvement in the assassination attempt on Lenin and the murder of Uritsky yesterday?"

Lockhart sighed, crossed his arms and glared. He replied with the patiently patronizing tone of one speaking to someone else's child: "As I have already told your Deputy Peters who came in before you, I am a diplomatic representative of the British government, and I demand to be released immediately."

"How do you know Dora Kaplan?"

Lockhart tightened his lip and gazed into the corner of the ceiling.

"What was Cromie's involvement in the assassination of Uritsky?"

The mention of Cromie's name seemed to give him a startle. He straightened up in his chair and crossed his legs. "As I have already said, I am a diplomatic representative of the British—"

He did not get to finish because Sergei exploded out of his chair, making it fly back and slam into the wall behind him. He grabbed Lockhart's teacup and drove it with full force into the table in front of Lockhart, showering him with ceramic shrapnel and leftover tea.

"You do not want to test me! *NOT-TO-DAY!*" he blared, measuring out each word at the visibly rattled Lockhart.

This outburst rattled Anna, too. In all the years she had known him, this was the first time she had seen Sergei give in so completely to anger.

"There was an attempt on the life of the Russian head of state, and your name is at the very center of it all. Do you think your title will protect you? What is it? *Special Envoy?* What does it even mean? It sounds made-up to me. Your government does not recognize the legitimacy of the Soviet government, but you demand that I recognize the legitimacy of yours?"

"You can try to defy it, if you dare." Lockhart wiped his face with his handkerchief and tried to recompose himself to the best of his circumstance.

Sergei was still livid. "Oh, I do dare. What are you doing here, really? Britain closed the official embassy in Russia and sent *you* instead? That's quite a vote of confidence, wouldn't you say? You must be a diplomat extraordinaire, at your tender age, for them to entrust you to single-handedly mend the relations between our people."

Lockhart puffed up in the chair, avoiding eye contact. Anna took a turn.

"You do have a remarkably poor track record abroad, don't you?" she said. "You had to flee the family rubber plantation in Malaya in 1911 after an affair with a married girl. Seems it was quite a scandal, was it? Did her family really try to poison you?" She checked his defiant gaze and knew that it masked his unease

123

at the fact that they knew this. That was exactly what she wanted to see. "But you managed to land a job in the Foreign Office, and even got posted to the embassy in Moscow, only to disgrace it with another affair and be sent home by your own ambassador in 1917. Tell me, how did your young wife take the news of your indiscretion? You did tell her *why* you were recalled from Russia, no? She must have heard by now, even if you didn't tell her. How do you suppose she will react when she sees your name in the papers? When she learns that you've been up to your old habits since you had managed another posting to Moscow? All the drinking, the late-night cabarets on Ohotny Ryad, and then, of course, Ms. Maria Budberg – your live-in mistress. I am sure the newspapers in London would love to get a thoroughly documented account of your lifestyle in the service of your country. The British do so love a good public scandal, don't they?"

Sergei picked up his chair and settled in it again across from Lockhart. "Let's add to that the charges of espionage and the assassinations. Just how eagerly do you expect the Foreign Office would rush to your defense? After all, you had already disgraced them in Russia once before. Unless… it's not the Foreign Office you are really working for. Maybe you came back here with new orders from a new master?"

Lockhart crossed his arms and grimaced in indignation. His eyebrows lifted.

"This is all conjecture," he muttered through his teeth. "You can threaten to humiliate me personally, but that is the extent of it – hardly the grounds for the diplomatic hysteria you are suggesting."

"That's where you are wrong. We are way past conjectures. We know that over the last several months you've been engaged in the acts of inciting and funding anti-government activities including sabotage and terrorism. In fact, we have enough evidence on your involvement to justify having you shot. And believe me, there are many people in this building who would very much like to see that. But, lucky for you, I am interested in more than just a washed-up junior diplomat. I know you weren't the brains of this operation. You were just the messenger boy. So, from this point on, your fate is in your hands – it all depends on whether or not you choose to cooperate."

He opened the file and pulled out a stack of papers.

"On August 14, you met at your apartment with Lieutenant Colonel Berzin of the Latvian Rifle detachment. How do you know him?"

Lockhart's face turned pale. He looked down at the table, at the thick file in front of Sergei. He looked away. "He was introduced to me by two Latvian officers from Petrograd."

"Who directed them to you from Petrograd? Was it Cromie?"

"Yes."

"What did you and Berzin discuss?"

"He said his men were dissatisfied fighting for the Reds and wanted to return home. He said he could broker a surrender of the Latvian divisions in the north to the Allies at Arkhangelsk."

"And you agreed to it?"

"Yes"

"What else?"

"That was it."

Sergei placed several pages in front of Lockhart, one by one.

"Here is your coded communication to Cromie informing him of the arrangement with Colonel Berzin and his officers. Here are the passes you provided to Berzin for General Poole in Arkhangelsk. And here is a receipt for 700,000 rubles you had disbursed to Berzin. Here is one more for 700,000 and another for 600,000. This is your signature, isn't it?"

Lockhart looked away.

"That's two million rubles, and it wasn't for surrendering. So, what are you not telling me?"

Lockhart was silent.

"What about the Latvian troops in Moscow?"

He glared at Sergei. "Well, I suspect you already know the answer to that question."

"Given the seriousness of this matter, I am giving you the opportunity to tell me."

"Fine. Berzin agreed that his division of the Kremlin guards would support a coup in Moscow to overthrow the Bolshevik government."

"Now we are getting somewhere. When was the coup to take place?"

"At the meeting of the Executive Committee, at the Grand Theater. We had learned that it was rescheduled to next week, so we had adjusted our plans accordingly."

"Why did you authorize the assassinations ahead of the coup?"

"I absolutely did not!" Lockhart turned red. "I had nothing to do with that!"

"How do you know Dora Kaplan?"

"I do not!" He was clearly flustered.

"Then who does?"

"I do not know."

"What about Cromie?"

"I don't know – ask Cromie!"

"Cromie is dead."

"What?!" He glared in confused incomprehension. "That's impossible! I just spoke with him yesterday."

"He decided not to cooperate with the Petrograd Cheka. They came to question him about Uritsky's murder. He fired on them, and they shot and killed him. Hardly the actions of someone innocent if you ask me."

Lockhart covered his face with his hand and shook his head. "Stupid son of a bitch," he muttered under his breath.

"He might as well have painted a bullseye on you," Sergei continued. "You two have had a lot of meetings and a lot of communication over the last few months. If you did not know about the assassination plans, then who did? Who else was involved in this plot?"

Lockhart stared silently into the table.

Sergei sighed. "Here is the thing. Right now, you are the highest-ranking British official left, and there is plenty of very incriminating evidence against you. If there is no one else connected to this plot, then you are the only one left to be held accountable. Cromie has chosen his way out. Do I need to paint you a picture of what will happen to you?"

Lockhart set his jaw.

"OK, there are several ways this could go," Sergei elaborated. "We could do a show trial publicized to the entire world. This could take some time. In that time, Lenin could die from his wounds, and that would be the worst possible turn of events for you. On the other hand – as satisfying as the public trial would be – we could save everyone some time and just make you disappear. Maybe let you rot in one of Russia's many prisons. Or release you only to fish your body out of the river the next day – a street robbery gone wrong. Very plausible, given that Russia is so dangerous these days, as you yourself have written to your wife."

Sergei tapped his pen on the table.

"You *are* guilty. Maybe not of the assassinations, but you *are* absolutely, undeniably guilty. The only way you could possibly get out of this alive is if you help us find those actually responsible. So, let's try this again."

He pulled a sketch from the file and placed it on the table. "Who is Constantine? Berzin met with him three times – once in your apartment. You referred to him as ST1 in your messages to Cromie. What is his real name?"

Lockhart studied the artist's rendition.

"Come on, Consul! This is how you work your way up from the firing squad."

Lockhart cleared his throat. "Reilly," he sighed. "His name is Sidney Reilly."

"What other identities does he use?"

"Constantine Reiss is the only one I know of."

"Who does he work for? Does he report to you?"

"No. Directly to Cumming – head of Secret Intelligence – MI section 1c."

"How do you know Reilly?"

"He contacted me shortly after I arrived in Moscow in May."

"What did he want?"

"To make an arrangement. I was to secure the funding and he would organize the network and handle clandestine operations."

"Why this arrangement?"

"It would protect my position, knowing that I would be under scrutiny, and it would allow him to operate mostly underground, away from the high-profile individuals connected to the money."

"Who else is in his network?"

"He did not bring me in on the details."

"Fine – when you requested the funds, where did this money end up?"

Lockhart pursed his lips.

"Several places. General Alekseev's and General Kornilov's volunteer armies in the Don; the Latvians – as you well know; several Socialist Revolutionary organizations."

"Like Boris Savinkov's Union?"

"Yes."

"Why didn't Savinkov just come directly to you? You did meet with him personally earlier this summer."

Anna knew Sergei had just bluffed – this was merely a guess, but Lockhart did not deny it.

"Because, as I told you, I was no longer to handle the operatives directly," he said, visibly exhausted and annoyed with the interrogation.

"Where is Reilly now?"

"Petrograd, I suppose. That's where he went."

"When did he leave for Petrograd?"

"Two days ago."

"Why did he go to Petrograd?"

"I don't know."

Sergei scribbled in the file. "So, Reilly was in Petrograd at the time the head of the Petrograd Cheka, Uritsky, was murdered? And on the same day, an SR operative shot Lenin in Moscow? And you expect me to believe you knew nothing about any of this? With a trail of money leading from your office to the SRs?"

Lockhart turned pale. He shook his head. "I did not know she was an SR. You must believe me – I had nothing to do with this. Reilly never mentioned the assassinations to me – only arrests. That was always the plan he discussed with me. I suppose he could have plotted something else with Savinkov and kept me in the dark… it would not be much of a surprise."

"And why is that?" Sergei peered.

"Reilly is a wild card, a provocateur. I'd heard he had spied for the Japanese, the Germans, the Americans, and the British since the war had started. He has so many schemes in play, half of the time I can't even be sure he himself knows for which side he's working. I can't be held accountable for his actions."

Sergei closed the file. "As you say, *we are the company we keep*. And you too have played a major part in this. You best hope we find him."

AUGUST 31, 1918

As the arrests in Moscow continue, we mourn the many patriots being put to death by the illegitimate Soviet regime. And even though we have lost the fight in Moscow, we have taught the enemy to fear. The tide is turning all over Russia, and all the pieces are being moved into their positions. The enemy has no idea that the final chapter of this war has already commenced. Kolchak is on his way as I write this.

– Boris Savinkov's Journal

THE PIECES

Sergei did not come back to the apartment. He had sent her home at 4:30 in the morning to get some sleep and said he would follow soon. Anna could have gone to her own flat in Kitai-Gorod, which was closer, but she took a car back to his place instead. It seemed natural now, after all these days and nights together. Over the past few weeks, her existence had moved, a few possessions at a time, into Sergei's place. At first, she wondered if she would be tired of him, after working together all day, but she found that she liked being with him. She liked being in this space and having his presence near her. He always seemed to have this life figured out, and she appreciated that. It's what had always made him so comforting, warm, and familiar. Being here with him in Moscow was like resuming an interrupted story or going back to a place with fond memories. She liked that feeling. And so, she chose to return, time and again, staking her claim, one little thing at a time, to his space – the space he willingly shared with her.

She had managed only a few hours of sleep before the morning light and street noise pulled her awake. He was not there. She freshened up and drove back to Lubyanka. Moscow was on high alert, with more checkpoints around Red Square and a whole battalion of soldiers outside the Spassky Tower gate.

But inside Lubyanka, things were surprisingly quieter. After yesterday's events, she had expected to walk into a maelstrom of activity, but instead, the hallways were silent. She passed one empty office after another. Somewhere in the depths of the building, a lonely typewriter was clanking out rapid staccatos in spurts punctuated with the end-of-the-line rings and carriage returns.

In the department was only Egorov, packing a few things from his desk into a bag.

"Where is everyone?" she asked.

"Number 11," he grumbled, referring to the previous Cheka office a block down the street. "Looks like I'll be stuck there the rest of the day."

"What's going on there?"

"The arrests. There wasn't enough space here. Over 500 just this morning. Now everyone's busy processing—"

"What arrests? Who?"

"Everyone. Everyone we had on file plus the Union rosters you and Sergei found. We'll be going at it for days. The paperwork will never end—"

"What are we doing with all those people?"

"Questioning and detaining for the time being. Peters said not to leave a single stone unturned until we find everyone responsible... Want to come help?"

"I don't know... maybe. I'll catch up with you later. Is Sergei there?"

"He was earlier, but then came back here. He could be upstairs or in the courtyard..."

He was in the courtyard. She descended into the cool, shadowless pit saturated with damp cigarette smoke. Sergei was perched on an upturned wooden crate.

"Did you get any sleep at all?" she asked, approaching. He looked up at her. The unshaved dark stubble made his cheeks look sunken in and gave his tired face a completely depleted appearance. A long-ashed cigarette was clamped absentmindedly in his partially bandaged hand.

He shook his head. "Didn't have time," he said hoarsely and cleared his throat.

She knew that hoarseness – it meant he had been smoking for hours, keeping himself going with nicotine. The ground behind him was a carnage of cast-off cigarette butts.

He gazed at her through the fog of exhaustion. His usually lively eyes now glowed faintly like embers slowly fading deep inside a dormant furnace.

"Did you find Reilly?" she asked.

He shook his head. "But we found his apartment. The real one."

"Not the one Maria Fride leased for him?"

"No. Fride knew him only as Constantine Reiss. This apartment he took out under the Reilly name. We went there."

He discarded his cigarette and mechanically lit a new one.

"What did you find?"

"A woman."

"Who?"

"Elisaveta Otten. She is either extremely naïve or she is in on it. She said she moved in with him in June. He told her he was a British government employee with the Moscow Mission. He traveled a lot. Paid her to deliver packets throughout the city on many occasions, saying they were short-handed at the Mission. Promised he would marry her and take her back to England with him. He told a similar story to Maria Fride, except he told her he was a merchant and promised to take her to Greece. The two women evidently had no idea of each other's existence."

"So, he lied to them both to use them? Does either of them know where he is?"

"Otten said he left for Petrograd on the 28th."

"Which is what Lockhart said too. Do you think he was involved in Uritsky's murder?"

"If he was, then he is definitely working with Savinkov."

"Why?"

"The Petrograd Cheka has uncovered that Kannegisser is a cousin of Max Filonenko..."

Filonenko was a known associate of Savinkov. Anna pulled up a crate and sat down. This revelation made her feel both relieved and tired at the same time. "So, this is it, then... Savinkov was behind both assassinations."

Sergei smoked mechanically in silence.

"So, this is good, right?" She tried to catch his gaze. "Now we know who we need to look for."

He nodded silently, dropped the half-finished cigarette, and ground it into the pavestones with his boot. "Do you think we are making a difference?" he asked, fixated on the charred, wrecked hulk of the cigarette at his feet. "Are we making any progress, doing what we do?"

His question unsettled her. Sergei was never uncertain. He was always the one to see the path forward.

"Of course, we are. How could we not?" she responded.

He shook his head. "I don't know that it's working. No matter what we say, no matter how many agents we put in the streets, *they* just keep coming. It's like trying to untangle a knot of snakes. Each one more vicious and lethal than the one before. We thought we had made a difference eliminating the Union, and in return they killed Uritsky and almost killed Lenin. And now we can go get Savinkov and Reilly, like we got Lockhart, and Kaplan and Kannegisser. But before we are even done putting them away, more will emerge. Another Savinkov, another Kaplan, another Reilly and Lockhart." He fumbled for his pack and matches and lit another cigarette.

"What else can we do, Sergei? Our job is to defend the revolution, and every day, we do it the best we can. New threats will continue to emerge—"

"Yes, but why? Look at the big picture, Anna. They will continue to emerge because the West will continue supplying money and guns to anyone willing to walk up to one of us in the street and pull the trigger." The temper in his voice elevated. "When will be the next time? Who will be next? We may have beheaded the Union, but that does not change the fact that 9,000 people in this city pledged to take up arms against our government. Are we just supposed to forget it and wait until they kill our politicians one by one and undo everything we've done?"

The embers in his eyes had flared up and now burned like two furies feeding on nicotine and rage. She had never seen him so distraught and ready to take on the entire world with just his fists.

"Of course not," she said. "We can't forget this. But until they commit a real crime, they are just Russians. Just like us. You've said it yourself – we are working to change Russia. If we just lock up everyone who disagrees with us, we are no better than the tsars before us."

She put her hand on his. "Look, Sergei, I know you. Right now, you are tearing yourself apart, wondering what you've missed and how you could have prevented this. But you couldn't have. *We* couldn't have. We acted based on the best information at our disposal. Uritsky died not because of what we did, but because of what these bastards did. And now the one thing we can do is go get them before they do it again. Let's get them."

He exhaled a forced sigh and gave her a tired nod. He flicked his cigarette in a sparking arc and then reached into his shirt pocket and pulled out a small notebook. He handed it to her.

"What's this?"

"Reilly's notebook from his apartment. He hid it in the mattress. It's all in English, so I need you to take a look. Maybe there is something we can use here to help us find him."

She snagged it from his hand – a small, fabric-bound pad with a brown cover. A stub of a train ticket stuck out from the pages. *Samara–Moscow*, she read.

"This was last Monday," she said. "What do you think is in Samara?" she asked.

He shrugged. "The Whites."

She scanned the first few pages. "It *is* his journal, but it seems to cover only Moscow – I am not seeing anything about Petrograd or Samara," she noted, paging through. "These are his logs of meetings and money transactions."

She flipped through a few more pages, going from the most recent to the older entries. And then she froze on one page, reading and re-reading the same line over and over. An impossible and yet indisputable realization seized her and pulled her down into the spiral of doubt.

"What?" he said. "What?"

She read out: "Met Buikis and Berzin. Transferred 600,000 rubles."

"Right – that was the meeting last week. What's wrong with that?"

"Nothing. Except for one very small detail – he used Buikis' real name."

*

Dzerzhinsky looked glum. Peters was still staring blankly at Reilly's notebook, his lips twisted into a wry squiggle.

"So, this Reilly, or Constantine, or whatever his real name is… he knew that the Latvian regiment plot was a ruse? How do you suppose he found out?" Dzerzhinsky asked.

"I don't know." Peters shook his head and raked his fingers through his hair with an exasperated sigh. "We must have a mole. Not many people knew about this operation. I will personally question everyone involved. I will conduct a thorough internal investigation to find the source of the leak."

Dzerzhinsky nodded. "This does beg another question. If Reilly knew about our operation, why did he continue to play along? Why did he keep paying out the money if he knew the Latvians were not going to back the coup?"

"Because it was to his advantage to know and ensure that we did not know that he knew," Sergei grumbled. Despite a shave and a shower, he still looked like a pale, sleep-deprived phantom of his former self.

"What do you mean?"

"He wanted us to continue thinking that he was planning a coup on the day of the Executive Committee Summit. He knew that this would keep us in a false sense of security and control. And that gave him time to put together and set in motion a contingency plan. A plan that did not rely on the Latvians. A plan about which we knew absolutely nothing."

"And what is this contingency plan?"

"One he hatched with Savinkov. When we liquidated the Union, we found plans for a bombing campaign. Reilly funded Savinkov to buy and smuggle explosives from the Don region. They were going to blow up the railroad bridges leading to Vologda and Petrograd, leaving Moscow cut off from military reinforcements. But the timeline in these plans was off: four days before the summit, and that did not make sense until now. Now we know they knew that the Latvian coup was not going to happen. So, while we were expecting them to make a move on the day of the summit, they were planning to take us by surprise."

"Were the assassinations part of the plan?"

Sergei nodded. "I believe so. I think that was Savinkov's contribution, since this is where his talents lie. I think he provided Kaplan and Kannegisser for the assassinations, which, if the attempt on Lenin had been successful, would have weakened our government just in time for the Union coup. But Agent Sokolova and I believe there was also another part of the plan."

"What's the other part?" Peters asked.

"The military invasion. From the beginning, the British plot relied on a combination of the coup and military intervention. They had always intended to march on Moscow once the government was toppled."

Anna cleared her throat. "And even though we took down the Union and averted the Kremlin coup, there is still a considerable Allied force building up in Arkhangelsk and Vladivostok. I – *we* – believe they will still attempt to take Moscow by force, and Reilly and Savinkov are going to support them with more terror and sabotage from behind our frontlines."

Peters looked at Dzerzhinsky, who gave him a nod. "Your theory certainly seems accurate in light of some new intelligence we received today. The British have landed several additional battalions in Vladivostok and are now advancing west with the intent to establish an alternate government in Siberia."

"What alternate government?"

"A centralized, anti-Soviet government. Instead of rushing to storm Moscow, they will just set up a new capital. With sufficient military and financial support, a capital can be anywhere they want."

"… And it will give all the opposing factions a single flag to rally around. That's very clever." Sergei rubbed his chin pensively.

Dzerzhinsky nodded. "This is exactly our concern. All those disconnected White armies and breakaway territories can now be unified and centrally commanded. This would make them a significant threat. If the Whites unify under a strong leadership, they could overwhelm our army."

"Who is going to lead this new government?"

"We don't know yet. The British effort is headed by General Knox. He is their liaison to the Allies and the White armies in the east of Russia. He'll probably pick one of the White generals to head the new government. Maybe Denikin or Wrangel. Someone they can control, same as they did in Arkhangelsk."

"In that case, we definitely need to find Reilly," Sergei said. "With Lockhart in our custody and Cromie dead, Reilly must be their key remaining link behind our frontlines."

"You really think this Reilly is still a threat?" Dzerzhinsky raised his eyebrows. He turned to Anna: "What about you, Comrade Sokolova? You dreamt up this whole operation. Do you think chasing this mystery man is a wise use of our resources given that Savinkov is still on the loose?"

"I think Reilly should not be underestimated," she responded. "He was in Moscow for only a few months and was able to build a clandestine network including foreign diplomats, Russian civilians, a possible mole in the Cheka, *and* the most wanted terrorist in our country. And that's just in Moscow – we don't know anything about the extent of his activities in Petrograd or anywhere else. I think if the British have a plan for Russia, Reilly is likely playing a part, with or without Savinkov."

Dzerzhinsky looked at Peters. "Very well, then why don't we make this Mr. Reilly feel unwelcome. Let's launch a nationwide manhunt. His picture will be in all the papers first thing tomorrow morning."

Sergei leaned in. "I think we should hold off on publicity for a few days, if possible."

"Why would we do that?" Dzerzhinsky scrutinized him.

"Because if he is still in Petrograd, Reilly most likely still does not know that we now know his real identity. Going public with a manhunt will spook him and make him that much harder to find. Can you give my team a few days to try to locate him and Savinkov?"

Dzerzhinsky tapped his finger on the table. "OK, you've got it. But in two days, if you have no leads, I want to proceed with a public release."

*

"So, how are we going to do it? How are we going to find Reilly and Savinkov in just two days?" Anna studied the network of notecards on the table in the task room.

"Well, first of all, we need to stop trying to solve the assassinations. There may be more people involved, but we can't afford to be distracted by the minor players right now."

He swept all but two cards into a box and centered the

remaining cards on the empty table – *Reilly* and *Savinkov*. "We will have to divide our efforts."

He pushed the Reilly card towards Anna and looked at her. "We know Reilly went to Petrograd, so I need you to go there and work with the Petrograd Cheka to find him. Take Egorov with you. Uritsky had a special source in Petrograd who had been useful in the past. I will give you his information – he may be able to help."

"What about you?"

He massaged his bandaged hand. "I'll stay in Moscow and continue to squeeze Lockhart and the Union leadership for more information. Between the two of us, we are bound to get a lead."

She walked up to him and took his hands in hers. His eyes were like a wolf's – tired but hungry and restless.

She touched the frayed, stained bandage on his hand. "OK, but I am worried about you. You are not sleeping or taking care of yourself."

He looked at her, and a spark of familiar warmth glimmered in his eyes. "I know... I am sorry – everything that's happened over the last few days... it has completely taken over everything." He brushed a strand of hair away from her face. "We just need to push through this. We need to see this through to the end, or else we may lose everything."

She touched his cheek and kissed him. His lips felt rough.

CITIZEN DORA

Dora awoke when the orderly slid a tray with bread and water into her holding cell. She lay in bed for a while, watching a cloud move slowly in the small window.

Today she was going to die. She was informed so yesterday by the awkward young guard who escorted her to the washroom. He seemed apologetic and somewhat ashamed in telling her this, as if he was bringing news of an inconvenience to someone important. He looked barely older than she was when she had disappeared into the vast prison system of the Russian Empire. She was sixteen. He had a revolver in the holster on his belt. She doubted he had ever had to fire it at someone.

She did not ponder her fate. Death seemed an appropriate sentence for her crime.

She made her bed – a habit of eleven years she had spent in the prison labor camp. Her shoulder started to ache again – echoes of an old injury. It was one of several such souvenirs courtesy of the prison system's affinity for corporal punishment – the disciplinary method proven most effective at maintaining order.

She was given a death sentence then as well. A death sentence reduced to life in labor camps. A perverse mercy judgment on account of her young age.

There'd be no trial this time – the Reds were furious. She did not want one, anyways.

She sat on the bed. Waiting.

The thought of her youth burrowed in. She had not thought of her childhood often – that part of her life was severed long ago and seemed to be someone else's story now. The event of her birth to a family of poor Jewish peasants in Ukraine signified only that they now had one more mouth to feed along with her six brothers and sisters. It was an arbitrary, insignificant happening in the vast universe. To her, the particulars of her birth and childhood seemed like a random fact that could have been attached to a million random people. Her life did not acquire significance until she was taken in by a group of young radicals. They wanted a revolution. Their bomb killed a tsarist official in Kiev. She got caught and was convicted for life. The act and the consequence.

She was sent to the hard labor camp, one of hundreds in the Katorga system, used by the tsars as the source of free labor in the sparsely populated expanses in the north and the far east. A second, shadow empire entwined into Russia – hundreds of shadow cities with millions of shadow citizens. And so she became a shadow. One of a thousand souls bound to the Nerchinsk lead mines gouged deep into the Siberian steppe. Four thousand miles from Moscow and only a hundred miles from China.

Perhaps the endless stream of lead ore that passed through her hands had given lead to the three bullets she had fired at Lenin.

By the time the revolution had freed all political prisoners, she had already spent eleven years in the camp. Eleven years a shadow. Eleven years a convict. A convict lives trapped each day in a single consequence. For eleven years, each day and each minute of her existence reduced perfectly and undeniably to the consequence of a single act. It was the invariable answer to every daily aspect of her life for all those years. Consequences define our lives. Without consequences, how do you know what your life was worth? Nothing worse than being inconsequential.

Outside the prison walls, one has to make her own consequences again.

She looked at the window once more. The cloud was gone. This was her last day. Minutes and seconds were dissolving away, unstoppably, like grains of sand falling away inside a sand clock. One could scream, claw at the walls – does not matter.

That old rage that used to snap at the chain like a captive wolf had recoiled over the years, beat down by the Katorga guards. Time after time she swallowed it down, into the pit of her soul, and from there it growled at the world. Raw like a nerve.

She came of age at a time when words had lost their power, lost their significance, and all that was left was action. The hand holding a bomb imparted direct, offensive terror against tyranny. The hand holding a pistol corrected the future.

Sometimes the future needed to be corrected again.

Eleven years a shadow. Just a few months to realize that nothing had changed. And neither had she.

Maybe she was spared death eleven years ago so that she could once more emerge out of the faceless masses to punish a betrayal. Once again, the public servants had become the wardens and executioners of the people they were supposed to serve. Two days ago, they did not know she existed. Today, they were afraid of her and anyone else who may come after her.

She took a deep breath.

Steps approached. A burly soldier and the boy guard. They led her to a courtyard filled with warmth.

She squinted, looking up at the sun.

The soldier's hand on her shoulder stopped her in the middle of the courtyard. He said something, but she did not acknowledge. He did not matter anymore. She was miles away, gazing into the distance over the courtyard wall, not hearing the city beyond it, not seeing the soldier raise the revolver to the back of her head.

She thought she felt a wisp of air on the back of her neck, like the pull of the undertow gathering strength and pulling her off her feet right before the crushing wave. Once, she was a child at the sea, feeling the warm water, the sun and the sand. Before the prison. Before the bomb. She did not feel the lead tear into the back of her skull.

She lay in the courtyard until the burly soldier checked to make sure she was dead.

The boy guard stood to the side, unable to take his eyes off her figure on the ground. "What do we do with her now?" he asked.

"The order is not to bury her," the soldier said. "No bones, no ashes. They just want her to disappear, completely."

After a while, the soldier dragged her body like a rag doll to a metal barrel at the edge of the yard. He lifted her off the ground and lowered her into the barrel. Her slight body took up surprisingly little space in the void. He poured a jug of kerosene over her and set her on fire. The kerosene combusted into a hot blaze and smoldered upwards, carrying flakes of her ash drifting into the sky above Moscow, across the Moscow river, and higher.

PETROGRAD

It was still dark when Robins woke him up to go 'on a mission'. Rubbing his eyes, William made it downstairs and into the street outside the hotel to find a convoy of six canvas-topped trucks with red crosses painted on the sides waiting at the curb.

"You drive, my boy," Robins said, getting into the front truck. Robins sounded entirely too awake and chipper for this hour. William drove off, trying to shake off the sleep. He had not slept well the last two nights at the hotel, after two weeks on a ship at sea. Occasionally, he still felt the ground move and sway under his step like the deck rolling over the waves.

Their destination was the Finland station on the northern bank of the Neva river, near the city arsenal, Robins told him, guiding him down the murky streets. They cut through the Palace district, empty at this hour, and crossed over the Liteiny bridge – a long, wide span of trellised iron flying just above the dense blanket of fog on the Neva. The fog was flowing west, towards the Gulf of Finland and the distant cathedral spires of the Petropavlovsky fortress that shimmered in the first rays of the morning.

At the station, Robins directed him past the passenger terminal and across the tracks to the loading docks at the far end. They stopped at a security gate, where two Red Army soldiers checked their papers. Having found their documents satisfactory, one of the guards hopped onto the sidestep outside of William's door and navigated him past the long row of wagons and depot buildings to find the train. Once the right train was found, they rattled and bounced through the potholes down the length of the train to the right dusty, weathered boxcar. The guard dismounted the sidestep of the truck and went to the wagon, double-checking his papers on his way.

William and Robins climbed out of the truck. The sun was rising, and its rays were slowly beginning to warm through the chilled air, accentuating the scents of the sea, burnt coal and motor oil. A dozen men emerged from the other trucks. A handful of them William recognized as the other Americans he met at the Mission the other day. The rest looked like Russians off the streets of Petrograd – workers, soldiers and sailors in shabby clothes and uniforms.

"Time to get to work," Robins said, handing William a pair of leather work gloves.

"What are we doing?"

"God's work, my boy," he grinned. His lighthearted mischievous nature beamed through even at this hour. He clearly relished keeping William in the dark.

The barn door on the side of the railcar was rolled open with a weighty rumble, revealing rows of wooden crates inside.

"Condensed milk?" William read the stenciled markings on the crates.

"All 100,000 cans of it!" Robins proclaimed with a clear sense of joy and pride. "It took some politicking to get this shipment here from Murmansk."

"From Murmansk? But Murmansk is under British control. Why would they let you take it to the Bolsheviks?"

"That is the power of the regional Soviets, my boy!"

"The Soviets? What do you mean? I thought *soviets* was just another word for the Bolsheviks."

"Not at all! The Bolsheviks are a political party, and the Soviets are local councils all throughout Russia. The Soviets had existed for years before the Bolsheviks ever came to power. What the Bolsheviks did do, however, is unify and centralize the Soviets. So, all I had to do was let the Central Soviet in Moscow know that this shipment was held up in Murmansk, and they directed the Murmansk Soviet to release it. And the British could not do a thing about it."

"So, you spoke to the Central Soviet?" In William's mind this seemed equivalent to asking for a favor before the entire US Congress.

Robins smiled. "I know the right people. Now, come, help me translate." He turned around and walked to his work team to relay how he wanted the crates unloaded into the trucks.

They backed the first truck to the railcar, and the crates began flowing along the human daisy chain. The Russians chattered as they worked, occasionally bursting out in laughter.

William smiled, listening to their banter.

"What are they saying?" Robins inquired.

"One man said he had never seen canned milk before, and the other said it comes from canned cows, which are in the next wagon."

Robins laughed. "I'll see if I can get a shipment of canned stew or corned beef next time."

"Who are they?" William asked. "Where did you find them?"

"Russians, mostly. Maybe a Pole or a Latvian in the mix. The streets of this city are full of people willing to work, especially for provisions."

It took them almost five hours to transfer the contents of the boxcar into the trucks. They loaded one truck after another, listening to the suspension springs creaking as the rows of crates stacked higher and higher.

When they were done, Robins checked and counted each load and instructed the Mission staff to take the shipment to the city food bank and to give each worker ten cans after they'd helped unload. The trucks drove off one by one.

"Do you want me to follow them?" William asked hopping into the driver's seat.

"No," he said with a sly smile. "With this load we will have some fun. This is the best part, my boy," he added.

They drove out of the loading depot back onto the city streets and across the bridge to the Central district. The city was now awake, and the cobbled streets were bustling with people and vehicles.

After several days, Petrograd was beginning to grow on William. Beneath the grimy crust of wars and revolutions, the city's elegance and grandeur shined through. It was a city-palace, planned and born into the beauty of the European Baroque without having to grow into it awkwardly through the putrid, cramped darkness of the Middle Ages. It had been furnished for the royalty with broad boulevards, imperial façades, wrought-iron trim and a myriad of fountains and statues. Yet there was no highbred society left here to roll about in their carriages – these streets now belonged to the throngs of the homeless, gangs of alley kids and packs of feral dogs digging in the rubbish.

"Turn here." Robins interrupted his musings pointing left to an upcoming cross-street.

William complied, and suddenly he knew exactly where they were. They had driven straight onto the Palace Square – the vast granite-lined plaza flanked on one side by the grandiose span of the Winter Palace and on the other by the sweeping arc of the General Staff Building.

It was almost noon, and the square was stirring with activity. Robins directed him past several battalions of soldiers engaged in exercises near the General Staff Building and past the makeshift market set up by a handful of enterprising merchants under the Alexander Column at the center of the square. They turned just past the man orating from the back of a truck to a gathered crowd and circled to an open area in front of the Winter Palace.

"Right here?" William asked, looking up with uncertainty at the tall gates of black iron and gold, and long façade of hundreds of columns and windows. Up above, the statues of saints, emperors or maybe gods towered from the roof-top parapet.

"Yes – it's fine. We will not be here very long," Robins reassured.

William turned off the truck, and they got out. Two Red guards armed with rifles took notice of their arrival but continued conversing at their post at the entrance to the palace. Robins walked around to the back of the truck, pulled down one of the crates and set it on the ground. He pried the lid off with a crowbar, took two cans of milk and offered them to an old woman walking by with her head wrapped in a scarf. She looked at him with apprehension at first, but he nodded enthusiastically and said "Moloko" – *milk*, extending the cans towards her. She took them cautiously, one at a time, with a shaking hand and stuffed them inside her robes. She bowed to Robins humbly, mumbling some sort of a prayer and making the sign of the cross in the air with her weathered fingers.

She had hardly moved on when a gaggle of kids descended on Robins, tugging on his coat and noisily demanding their share, like a flock of birds who had spotted spilled grain. He turned to William with a grin and gestured for more cans. William grabbed a handful from the crate and passed them on, and then repeated, until Robins had put one into each pair of little, dirty hands. The kids ran off with triumphant shouts, but several curious people were already waiting their turn. Robins retreated closer to the truck and now reached back without looking, waiting for William to reload his hands with more and more cans.

Before long, a large crowd had gathered around them, with more converging from across the square, sensing that there was something being given out. Robins was now surrounded by what looked like a hundred open hands reaching out to him. He flipped over an empty crate and stood on it to get above the crowd. William had to climb into the cargo hold and keep pace, frantically prying open the crates and handing can after can to Robins. He barely had time to toss the empty crates out to the side of the truck.

In the midst of the frenzy, Robins turned to William, his face beaming in a broad grin. "You try it," he said, climbing into the back of the truck and handing William a few cans. William took his place on the crate and, looking around, felt adrift on a moving sea of faces and hands. Hand after hand touched his as he passed them the cans. Rough hands and soft hands, large, small, old and young. At first, he tried to favor the children, the women and the elderly, and tried his best to ensure no one got the handout more than once. But eventually he lost track and just tried to keep up with the never-ending demand of open hands. The canned milk was flowing out of their truck and into the hands of the people of Petrograd, and with them, throughout the city.

He was thoroughly enjoying this carefree giving when, at some point, he reached back for more cans, and did not feel one being placed into his hand. He turned around and saw Robins toss the last empty crate outside the truck. The disappointed crowd dispersed.

The cargo hold was completely empty, except for a few splinters and planks. Even the empty crates they tossed to the side of the truck had disappeared, probably pillaged for firewood.

"Wasn't that fun?" Robins slapped him on the shoulder and sat down next to him on the tailgate. He wiped his forehead with the sleeve of his shirt. He was still beaming.

William had to admit to himself that he too felt a bit of euphoria from this rush of spontaneous giving.

"It was," he smiled back. "It took us almost an hour to load this truck, and just a few minutes to empty it."

*

The American Red Cross Mission to Petrograd was headquartered in several adjacent suites at the Hotel d'Europe. According to the very amiable concierge, the hotel was refurbished just before the war in the airy and elegant style of art nouveau and was now the most luxurious accommodation in the city – a four-story edifice occupying the entire block at the corner of Nevsky Avenue and Mihailovskaya Street.

After the day of loading and unloading crates, William hoped he would never see another can of milk, or even a truck or a freight wagon, for that matter, as long as he lived. His back was sore, and his leg wound was gnawing with a dull ache again. Having cleaned himself up in his room, he decided to head back downstairs and have a drink to dull the pain. Robins did not drink, but it was all for the better – after spending the last few days in the company of the old man, William welcomed a few waking hours on his own.

He crossed the palatial lobby awash with marble and gold and descended down a few steps through an arched entryway into the bar. After the bright glitz of the lobby, the cool, murky cavern felt welcoming. A row of narrow stained-glass windows dispensed warm glowing twilight from the deep cut-outs in the thick stone walls.

He settled at the mostly empty bar and lit a cigarette. The bartender approached – a thin, middle-aged man trimmed impeccably in a crisp white jacket with a black bow tie.

"Do you have American whiskey?" William asked in Russian.

"Of course, *m'sieur*," the bartender responded in English with a French accent and went to get the bottle. *Of course they do*, William thought to himself. This was by far the nicest hotel he had ever stayed at. Anywhere.

He rolled up the sleeves of his shirt and inhaled the hot jet of cigarette smoke. A man a couple of seats away turned toward him and saluted him with his glass. He was older, wore glasses and looked familiar.

William pivoted toward him. "Excuse me. Are you with the American Red Cross Mission? I think I saw you when I first arrived but did not get the opportunity to introduce myself."

The man gave him a weak smile and extended his big hand to William across the empty seat. "Yes," he said dryly and cleared his throat. "Dr. George Saunders."

"William Arden"

"Pleasure. So, you are the one that arrived a few days ago? What will they have you do?"

The bartender returned with a bottle and poured him a double. William clanked glasses with Saunders, noting that he said *they* instead of *we*.

"I am not entirely sure yet. So far, it's been some driving, some translation, and moving about a thousand crates."

The man nodded without a smile. "That's right. Robins did say he wanted to bring on an American instead of relying on Gumberg so much."

"What's wrong with Gumberg?"

"Oh, nothing. But I guess there are things Robins needs done without a Bolshevik always at his side."

"So, his driver was really a Bolshevik? I wondered as much."

Saunders shrugged. "This is Petrograd. It's full of them." He lit a cigarette. "And where are you from?"

"Texas. And you?"

"Chicago. I came with the first team last August. But I am going home tomorrow." He finished his drink and set the empty glass on the bar.

"Well, in that case, let me buy you another round," William offered. "Going home is a reason to celebrate."

"Much obliged," Saunders gave him a nod.

"One more for my friend here, please," William asked the bartender.

"This is quite a swank place!" he turned back to Saunders. "I had no idea charitable work could be so comfortable."

Saunders smirked. "Yes, this place puts most of the Chicago hotels to shame. But you should have seen the first place we landed at – Hotel de France – nothing but roaches and fleas in every room! Thompson, our first director, could not stand it. He paid his own money to move the entire mission here. And I think he is still paying, even though he went back to New York months ago."

They clanked glasses.

"Wow, that's very nice of him!"

"Nice? I doubt it." Saunders turned glum. "There is nothing *nice* about this." He levied a disdainful emphasis on the word *nice* as he swished his drink in the air.

William peered at him, perplexed by his sudden pessimism. *He's pretty drunk*, he decided. "I know. In here you can almost forget there is a war going on—"

"No!" Saunders interrupted with exasperation and took an anxious puff of his cigarette. "I am talking about the Mission. The whole thing is bullshit. A sham."

"Why do you say that? What about all the medical aid?"

"We don't do medical aid here," Saunders sneered. "Not in Petrograd. Have you seen this city? The hospitals are half-empty, and they have plenty of their own doctors and nurses. When we arrived, there were five other doctors that came with me. All of them have left – either returned home or reassigned to the other Missions – there is nothing for them to do here."

"So what about the supplies we distribute? The provisions?"

"What? The milk? The flour? Just for show. You'll be lucky if there is a shipment every couple of months. Just to keep up the appearances – not enough to make any difference. But that was never the purpose."

"What do you mean?"

Saunders leaned in, almost spilling his drink. "This is not a real Red Cross Mission, is what I mean! Want to know who came with this Mission? Six doctors and sixteen bankers, lawyers and business executives. Five of the doctors have already left, and I am leaving tomorrow. But the Mission is doing swell. You do the math."

"So, if we are not here for charity, why are we here?"

Saunders chuckled into his drink. "Ask Robins. Maybe he'll tell you. But I'll tell you this much. They funnel more cash here than they do milk or antiseptics. Thompson himself had paid a million dollars of his own money to the Bolsheviks before he left. And it wasn't for the hospitals and orphanages, I guarantee you that!"

"What was it for?"

"Ask Robins! Ask him about the American International Corporation." Saunders put out his cigarette and gulped down his drink. "I should have left a long time ago," he grumbled. "The Spanish flu is killing more Americans than the war, and I am sitting here twiddling my thumbs. I can't do it anymore. Won't play their crooked game anymore…"

He stood up shakily, put on his hat and tossed a few bills on the bar. "Thank you for the drink. Best of luck to you, Mr. Arden." He shook William's hand. "I hope they let you get out with your soul intact."

He shuffled unsteadily out of the bar. William took a drag of his cigarette and swirled the whiskey in his glass, pondering what just happened.

KOLCHAK

The black ribbon of the train cut through the yellow expanse of the Siberian steppe, puffing out a steady sooty wake of coal smoke into the blue sky.

Rear Admiral Alexander Kolchak was at his favorite position on the train – the forward flatcar. Here, on the open deck, he had not only the fresh air, but also the wide, unobstructed field of view, unlike in one of the stuffy, sealed-off armored wagons, where one had to squint through the narrow slits of rifle embrasures or climb into the hot metal observation turret to get a look at his surroundings.

Around him, the flatcar's low walls were lined with sandbags through which the snub barrels of six Vickers machine guns bristled at the plains, hills and groves steadily rolling past. The sight of the black gun barrels lined up and ready for action gave him a sense of satisfaction, as he used to get on a ship at sea, where everything and every man was in its place and everything and everyone had a specific purpose.

He had lost that sense of purpose when sailors had mutinied, and the entire Russian fleet fell into the hands of the Bolsheviks. He had thought about that day a lot. Losing the fleet was like losing his home. He drifted through the world for months – America, Singapore, Japan, Manchuria – a passenger rather than the captain, a man without a clear purpose. But now everything had changed. He was back in Russia, and he had purpose. And that purpose was now taking him across Russia in an armored train, with the Vickers guns in front of him and the 127mm naval cannon mounted in the railcar behind him, pointing the way forward with its smooth iron barrel. It was now day six since he had crossed the East Sea from Hiroshima to Vladivostok and set off on the Trans-Siberian railroad westward, to where thousands of miles away lay Moscow and Petrograd.

His adjutant of the last two weeks Staff-Captain Victor Demidov was studying the horizon through his pair of binoculars. *Praying for a horde of bandits or a stray Red Army division; anything to break up the monotony* – Kolchak thought. He knew his prayers would be answered soon.

He liked Demidov – young, but already christened in battle under Kornilov's command. He reminded Kolchak of himself twenty-some years ago: driven, focused, given in fully to the service. *Without service, discipline and hierarchy, what else is there? Chaos and anarchy.* Kolchak brushed off his crisp black uniform. Two rows of gold buttons gleamed from the front of his coat with their embossed two-headed eagles. These eagles had flown over the waves of several oceans to protect the Russian Empire, and now they flew over its lands.

Six days of this railway stupor! The floor of the railcar swayed, rolling over the rails, like the deck of a ship at sea. In the midday heat, if he closed his eyes, he could almost forget he was on land – the warm scents of timber, steel and gunpowder, just like at sea. Only the scent of the sea itself was missing.

He tried not to dwell on being out of his element. He supposed that the armored train was in a way like a battleship that had been dissected into compartments and strung together into a single chain. And yet, there was no grace left in it. It had been transmogrified into an armored iron beast chugging and clanging about with its various mechanical limbs and organs. Its heart – the locomotive – was unrecognizable inside the thick angular shell of steel panels, tucked behind the forward artillery car. Behind the locomotive were the officers' quarters – two armored passenger cars: a 'Russian' one for his staff and the 'British' one for General Knox and his entourage. Behind them were three long boxcars carrying 200 troops, followed by a wagon with horses, two tarp-covered cargo cars, and finally the tail flatcar with more sandbags, soldiers and machine guns. It was a long, inelegant, grotesque daisy-chain of appendages.

Demidov handed him the binoculars: "Camp up ahead, Admiral. Must be Semenov's."

Kolchak took the binoculars and studied the distant encampment at the edge of the woods – tents, wagons, people and horses. These must have been the 2,000 Cossacks Semenov brought from Irkutsk.

"Prepare to stop," he said.

Demidov shouted out the order and it echoed in several voices down the train towards the locomotive. A few moments later, the train gave a double whistle and the tone of its chugging engine shifted lower as it began to slow down.

Kolchak had met Semenov in Japan. Semenov was an Ataman – a Cossack general. He was also in the employ of the British and the Japanese, who paid him to inflict damage on the Bolshevik strongholds across eastern Siberia. He proved apt to the task, gaining a reputation for unrestrained violence. This earned him Kolchak's secret contempt, for Kolchak scorned lack of restraint in general, and particularly took issue with it when it manifested in violence against fellow countrymen.

He had already heard of Semenov by the time they first met. And then, when they did meet, he thought there was a hint of madness in Semenov's eyes. But maybe it was just the only explanation he could construe for a man who relished the indiscriminate plundering, terrorizing and murdering of the local populations, and even took pride in the disdain from some of his Western Allies who found his methods unpalatable.

From everything Kolchak had heard, the essence of Semenov distilled to him being a brutal warlord. But as much as he detested Semenov, he had to rely on him now. And this, Kolchak detested even more.

Two Cossacks on horses rode out to meet them on the dusty embankment by the rails. Semenov was not one of them. Kolchak had their own horses brought out, and he, Demidov and Knox climbed into the saddles and followed the Cossacks to Semenov. This was a campsite of nomadic horsemen, disorganized and crowded with tents, campfires, horses and wagons. Kolchak suspected this sight (*and the smells*) had not changed much since the first barbarian ancestors of these men roamed these plains.

Semenov's was the large tent at the back of the camp, and at the front of his tent was a scene Kolchak did not expect to see in the middle of the steppe – a small table set up in the grass, topped with crisp white linen and a formal dining place-setting of china, crystal and silver. Was this a mockery or a megalomaniacal whim? With Semenov, it was probably both. Semenov himself was perched at the table, gnawing the meat off a large bone in one hand and clutching a glass of red wine with his thick fingers in the other.

Seeing him again instantly reminded Kolchak just how much he detested being around this man. There was something animal-like about his stout build, his pointy mustache and quick, beady eyes set deep in his full face. And there was something else now. When he first met him among the Japanese, he did not realize just how dark Semenov looked. Now, even among his own men, his complexion betrayed the lineage of Mongols or Tatars – definitely not a pure Slav. This sudden realization gave Kolchak some unexpected comfort.

Semenov raised his head towards the visitors and straightened in his chair without putting down the bone or the glass. The black

Georgian burka coat draped on his shoulders revealed a cross of St. George pinned to his breast pocket (Kolchak had one as well but did not feel compelled to wear it around every day). Next to Semenov stood a chubby, rosy-cheeked, snot-nosed youngster of ten or twelve in a black, furry papakha hat, outfitted with a bandolier of bullets across his coat and a saber and a dagger hanging off his belt. The boy must have been a future Semenov in tutelage. Kolchak shuddered at the thought.

Semenov put down the bone and wiped his hands on the tablecloth.

"Admiral, General! Come, come!" He did not bother getting up. He grinned broadly at them and his beady eyes glistened. "Are you hungry? Some wine perhaps?"

"Thank you, Ataman," Kolchak answered with a civil but cool nod. "I'd rather get to the matter at hand, if you don't mind."

"Ah, very well then," Semenov said jovially. He gulped down his wine and wiped his mouth with his sleeve. "If you please, Your Excellencies, join me in my humble command center." He stood up and extended himself in an intentionally exaggerated courtly gesture, inviting them into the tent.

Inside, he leaned over the map rolled out on the table and pointed to the dashed line of the railroad. "We are here." He moved his finger down the line to the intersection of the railroad and the river. "And this is Novo-Nikolaevsk, about two miles out. The Reds have control of the city and the bridge, so we can't get through to Omsk. They have barricaded the railway and set up defense positions at the edge of the city – here, here and here, on the east side of the river." He drew three red exes on the map.

"How many men?" Kolchak asked, fixated on the greasy print left on the map by Semenov's finger.

"The man I sent estimated around a thousand. Well armed."

"What kind of armaments?"

"Two entrenchments with heavy machine guns here and here," he pointed at the exes. "Field cannons here – two or three. He could not get close enough to verify. There is another entrenchment near the rail station and another by the river on the western side of town. Without artillery support, my men would be mowed down. But I guess that's where your big cannon is going to help."

Kolchak focused on the map, trying not to make eye contact with Semenov, aware that the latter was squinting at him, beaming with that idiotic wide grin again.

"We have brought something else that might help," Knox smiled coyly. He seemed quite at ease with the barbarian.

Kolchak nodded, still avoiding eye contact. "Can your men be ready to move out in an hour?"

"They'll do it in half that time!" Semenov stretched his mouth into another grin.

Kolchak responded with a curt nod and walked out of the tent. As they rode back to the train, a loud whistle launched the camp into a frenzy of preparation.

At the train, Kolchak watched as the British soldiers went to work on the two canvas-covered flatcars behind the locomotive. Under Knox's command, the ropes were undone, and the tarps were pulled down to reveal the tall green riveted iron sides of two British Mark V tanks. Kolchak had known they were carrying tanks, but this was the first time he saw them in person. The tanks looked so new, that he could practically smell the paint. Without the tarps, the metal behemoths looked even more massive – their nine-foot-tall sides towered over him from the cargo platform like fortress walls with fat cannon barrels protruding from the angular side turrets.

The soldiers hammered open the shackles and loosened the pulleys that bound the tanks to the platform. The heavy chains rumbled loose. Two of Knox's men scaled the first tank from the back, swung open the heavy hatch on top and squeezed themselves into the machine. The face-sized hatch next to the forward machine gun popped open. The engine spattered and coughed and then rattled to life, filling the air with mechanical squeal, black smoke and the smell of burning oil. The clutch engaged with a loud metal clank, and the tank jerked to life and began uneasily turning in place.

Another crewman directed the driver from the ground, aligning the tank with the ramp. Rocking back and forth and clanking with its tracks, the tank drove down the ramp and onto the ground with a deep thump that made the earth tremor under Kolchak's boots.

"What an infernal machine," he said over the noise to Demidov standing next to him.

Demidov leaned into his ear: "I've seen these used in the Don region. Very effective against the enemy, but also hell on the crew. Several of the crewmen passed out from the heat and the fumes and had to be carried out after the battle."

"Marvelous!" Semenov roared from the saddle, grinning at the tanks over the ruckus they were making.

Kolchak did not hear him ride up. Knox, who stood in front of them with his officers, turned around and grinned back at them through the pipe clenched in his smooth, square jaw.

"This is the new model," he shouted over the noise, "straight from the factory in Birmingham! The old one required four men to drive it. This one needs just one. The new Ricardo engine puts out 150 horsepower. Each of these units has two six-pounder Hotchkiss naval guns and four machine guns. The armor is 16mm thick in the front. They can cross trenches ten feet wide!" He recited the specs by heart, clearly proud.

"British engineering at its best!" Kolchak tipped his cap in acknowledgment.

The second tank was now down on the ground along with the first one, lined up next to the train. The gun barrels moved about as the crews climbed in and settled into their positions.

The Cossacks gathered by the tracks, curious about the noise and the commotion of unfamiliar machinery. A few rode up closer to inspect the tanks and knock on their iron sides. Some of the horses, spooked by the mechanical ruckus, reared and turned their heads, neighing. The Cossacks laughed.

"Shall we, gentlemen?" Kolchak turned to Knox and Semenov. He was ready for the circus to end and for them to concentrate on the business of war.

The locomotive puffed, hissed, and a cloud of steam poured from behind the steel armor plating protecting the driving wheels and the piston cylinders. Kolchak climbed into the artillery wagon and ordered the crew to ready the cannon. The tanks idled noisily by the tracks like a pair of bulldogs growling at the end of a chain. The train billowed a breath of black smoke from its iron lungs, and the land armada set off, creeping ahead inch by inch. Apparently, Knox had failed to mention that despite their marvelous specifications, these behemoths were unable to go faster than five miles per hour. And so, the tanks set the pace, squealing, rattling and clanking, but steadily ratcheting forward. The train followed, chugging and clanging heavily on the rails with slow, restrained force. The Cossack horde paced along, the hooves of their horses beating a leisurely gait.

After about a mile, the railroad began to curve like a long, polished metal bow around the edge of the woods. And that's when the town came into view. Spread on the hilly banks of the River Ob, Novo-Nikolaevsk emerged in a spattering of simple log homes and shacks that further in the distance melded into a sea of roofs punctuated with golden spires and crosses of churches. It was a town like hundreds of other towns in these parts of Siberia – hammered together from the plentiful Taiga timber by the miners or the railroad builders who had, decades ago, pressed deeper and deeper into the eastern frontier to assert the influence of the Russian Empire.

Kolchak ordered full stop, and the land armada of men, horses and machines rolled to a standstill. Using the binoculars, he could see the brick building of the railroad station on the northern edge of the city. The breeze was light, he noted, watching the red flag turn lazily above the station. The tracks were blocked with trucks and wagons. Near the station, a jagged trench line was cut into the steppe, with two crescent-shaped machine gun nests fortified with sandbags and logs. He searched the hills for the other red 'ex' Semenov had marked on the map. He found it nestled in a low ridge on the outskirts: a battery of three field cannons next to a few log buildings.

"Let's take care of those cannons before they spot us," he said to Demidov.

Demidov confirmed and gave the order. The artillery crew of seven men snapped into action at the twenty-foot-long barrel.

"Range to 1,600 yards," Demidov commanded.

Each man in his place, and each with his purpose. All seven were former sailors and knew how to work as a team. The sight-setter shouted back the order and cranked the dial to adjust the range. Before he was even done repeating the command, the line-layer and the elevation-layer both got to work on their adjustment dials to get the cannon to line up on the first target. The barrel turned slowly, rising towards the city. The familiar clanks told Kolchak that the shell was loaded into the breech, followed by the cartridge. With another clank, the breech door locked, and the firing pin clicked into place.

"Ready!" Kolchak heard the acknowledgment, his gaze still locked in the binoculars. The target was almost a mile away. He breathed in, as if before firing a rifle. Everything seemed still and quiet, except for the thin rattle of the tanks idling slightly ahead. A bird called somewhere in the tall grass.

"Fire," he said.

"Fire," Demidov repeated without tearing his gaze from the binoculars and plugged his ear closest to the cannon with his finger.

The deafening boom jolted the wagon and knocked a layer of dust off the railing. The fifty-pound shell hurled upward and away, disappearing into the blue sky. Through the ringing in his ears, he heard the breech snap open and closed, and then another "Ready!" from the crew – the next shell was loaded.

He watched. One of the log homes behind the cannons exploded into a ball of fire and flying timber like a box of matchsticks. *Overshot.*

"Right twenty, drop one hundred." Demidov shouted the adjustment without looking away from the binoculars.

The second round must have hit a cache of shells stored near the cannons. A fireball flashed in the distance, and a thin mushroom of smoke rose above the city. The Cossacks hollered in excitement. The rumble of the far-off explosion reached them a few seconds later.

"That takes care of the artillery," Kolchak said to Knox, putting down his binoculars. "The machine gun entrenchments are too close to the railway tracks. I don't want to risk damaging the railroad. Shall we see what your tanks can do?"

Knox smiled through his clenched pipe and signaled his men to let the tanks loose.

The iron bulldogs revved up, belched out several sooty puffs and rolled noisily into the steppe, bobbing over the uneven ground towards the city. Their clanking, squeaking and rattling soon thinned out, and the landscape was quiet for a short while. And then, the ra-tat-tat of a distant machine gun cut the silence, and soon was joined by another in a discordant polyphony of echoes.

Through the binoculars, Kolchak watched the trench line come to life. Like ants defending the anthill, a battalion of the Reds spilled from the station and into the trenches. He saw the flashes of their gunfire and puffs of smoke, while the heavy machine guns continued hammering out their lethal bursts from their nests. But the tanks continued rolling forward, without returning fire, undeterred by the hail of bullets unleashed at them.

And then the trench line disappeared in plumes of exploding earth and he heard the delayed pops of the tanks' cannons, one after another. One of the machine guns fell silent.

A Red cavalry squadron emerged from behind the station and charged towards the tanks, their pistols and rifles popping in the distance. They made it halfway between the trenches and the tanks, and then the sound of the tanks' machine guns interrupted their advance. Kolchak felt unnatural watching the battle unfold from afar, not being in it. Through his binoculars, he saw several dozen men and horses cut down in just a few seconds. The rest of the cavalry dispersed and began retreating.

A burst of Semenov's deep guttural laugh tore him away from the battle. Semenov was on his horse next to the flatcar, watching the battle through his own binoculars with the excited smile of an entertained child.

"They are retreating!" he exclaimed delightedly, looking up at the wagon.

"Without artillery, there is not much else they can do against a tank," Knox replied. "I would bet you most of them have never seen one before. Welcome to the future of warfare, my dear Ataman – superior technology means not a single casualty to your men," he grinned through his pipe. "It should be safe to send them in now, to clean up."

Kolchak ordered the train to advance, and his gunners in the flatcar tucked in behind the sandbags, ready to fire and be fired upon. But no one did. Up ahead, the tanks were at the trenches now, and the bursts of their gunfire were amplified to an exterminating crescendo. And they just crept on forward, across the trenches, unstoppable, towards the city. The Cossack horde poured into the valley behind them, cutting across the steppe like a spreading fire, hollering and whistling on their way.

By the time the train reached the entrenchments, the town's defense line had already been overrun. The landscape had fallen quiet once again. A steady breeze surged in waves through the tall grass, carrying the cloud of smoke and dust away from the city. Rolling up to the station, Kolchak examined the entrenchments torn and cratered by shells and strewn with bodies. The massive tanks had rolled through it all, implacable, grinding the carcasses of men and horses into the dirt under their tracks. He had seen his share of blood on the seas, but the gore seemed much more intense and primal on land, seeping into the earth right before his eyes. Amongst the dead and the dying, a disfigured white horse brayed, trying to get up off the ground. He tried again, his hooves digging in and his mane whipping back and forth, but he grew weaker.

The tanks stopped in front of the railway station, and their hatches propped open. A white-sheet flag was now flapping from the station window. The Cossacks began rounding up the surrendered Reds. Several Cossacks rode up to the tanks and kissed their hot, dusty, bullet-pocked iron sides.

The battle was over.

*

They had spent the night in Novo-Nikolaevsk to give the train crew time to refuel and resupply. In the morning, Kolchak was awakened by the sounds of gunshots. He jumped out of bed and stuck his head into the corridor. Demidov was already outside of his cabin, dressed and groomed, peering through the thick armored shutters of the window.

"What's going on?" Kolchak asked.

"I am not quite sure. Sounds like the Cossacks are celebrating again," he said, referring to the late-night pandemonium of drinking, yelling, singing, and periodic shooting that had kept Kolchak sleepless into the early hours of the morning.

The Cossacks did not know the meaning of the word *discipline*. He cursed them in his head, got dressed and walked out onto the platform. Demidov followed. The shooting was continuing in intervals. Not disorderly. Purposeful. He feared he knew exactly what was going on. He walked briskly along the brick façade of the station and then down the side alley to cut to the plaza behind it, to the wooden church of St. Daniel where he had taken mass last night.

The plaza was filled with a rowdy mob of several hundred Cossacks. He pushed through the sweaty, vulgar mass, inebriation thick on their breath, until he reached a clearing at the back of the station, where he saw exactly what he suspected – an execution squad. Four Cossacks were reloading their rifles and four more were at the brick back wall of the station, using their bayonets to methodically stab the nude bodies lying on the ground.

But what drew his eye next was even more horrific. It was the large, fleshy pile almost chest-high against the station's back wall. It took him an instant to comprehend that he was looking at human bodies hashed together into one pale, amorphous mass protruding with limbs and heads and staring out with dead eyes. The sight disturbed him. There must have been close to a hundred. He felt nauseated. The stones on the ground were wet and dark with blood.

The Cossacks dragged more limp bodies to the pile and heaved them on top.

"Son of a bitch," he gritted through his teeth, looking around for Semenov. He spotted him at the center of the square, surrounded with a crowd of his own. What sideshow was he presiding over in this rendition of hell?

Semenov's stout frame loomed over a man slumped in a chair that must have been dragged from a nearby building. The man was covered in blood, and his shirt was hanging in red tatters off his shoulders and his wrists. Kolchak approached, and with the next step, he realized that it was not the man's shirt. What hung off his wrists like torn sleeves dripping with blood was his own skin, flayed off in crude, jagged strips, leaving his exposed muscle and sinew glistening in the mid-morning sun.

Kolchak froze in a sick mix of horror and revulsion. He knew of Semenov's reputation, but this eclipsed all reasonable expectations. Semenov's men were cheering him on, their contorted, scowling mouths spitting out obscenities, and Semenov's boy soldier was watching wide-eyed, mesmerized as Semenov, his boots sprayed with blood, hunched over the man and slowly peeled a five-point star out of the man's chest with a small, curved knife.

"Stop! What the devil are you doing!?" Kolchak yelled over the noise of the crowd.

Semenov turned around. The front of his clothes and his face were spattered in blood, and the jagged star-shaped patch of bloody flesh was still in his bloody fingers.

"Ah, Admiral!" he roared, seemingly delighted to see Kolchak, as if eager to share his accomplishments. "How kind of you to come. Would Your Excellency like to join us in exorcising the Red Menace? *This* Red Menace, specifically." His knife pointed at the carved-up body as he raised his voice to draw cheers from his audience.

Kolchak was aghast. "What the devil are you talking about!? Whose body is this?"

"This?" He smirked deviously and lifted the lifeless head by the hair. "This here is Comrade Petrov – the chairman of the regional Soviet. A Bolshevik, and also a Chekist!" he added dramatically and let the head fall back.

"Have you gone completely mad? These men are local townspeople. They are Russian subjects. They are our prisoners! Was it necessary to execute them?"

Semenov straightened up, still holding the bloodied knife in one hand and the flapping sliver of flesh in another. He looked perplexed for a moment, and then exploded with rolling laughter. "Was this NECESSARY?!" he roared, turning to his Cossacks.

He wiped a tear from the corner of his eye, smudging blood. "...the hell do you mean was it *necessary*?" he annunciated, stepping closer and peering into Kolchak's eyes, as if trying to comprehend how his men's performance could be misconstrued as something offensive and deciding whether to get offended in return.

"What is it you think we do with the Bolsheviks here?" His eyes glinted maniacally. "Siberia is not one of your gentlemen's wars where you just wave your white glove when you don't want to play anymore. My men don't run prisons. We are fighting a war, and there are millions more of these animals out there. If we catch and release, this war will never end. We *must* exterminate to make an example. They need to know what they are signing up for, before any more decide to join in. So, yes – it is, as you put it, *necessary*."

He walked back to the body and picked up a small sack from the ground. He scooped what looked like a handful of salt from it and poured it over the skinned flesh.

What happened next shocked Kolchak to his core. The body came back to life, convulsing with a harsh, muted moan and shuddering uncontrollably, with its limbs jerking powerlessly at the ends of the straps that bound it to the chair.

Kolchak glared at Semenov with repulsion, pulled out his revolver and shot the trembling, bloody mass that remained of the man in the head. The figure slumped forward, held by his bounds like a limp, bloody rag doll.

A shadow crossed over Semenov's face.

"I do believe you are forgetting where you are, Mr. Admiral. You are a long way from Moscow. My people have roamed this land for centuries before Your Purebred Russian Excellency took your first shit. And while you and your high society pals were suckling on your mothers' white aristocratic teats and wearing out the seats of the best academies in St. Petersburg, I was raised by these people among these steppes and these horses. And yet, when the war came, your tsar needed me and my men the same as he needed you. And I fought for the Tsar and country same as you did. And now that the Reds are here, where are all your aristocratic chums? Scuttled like roaches from under the Bolshevik boot! And who is left to defend this land from the Reds? Me and my men."

Kolchak had just realized that the commotion in the square had ceased, and everyone was watching him. Semenov moved in closer, his blood-spattered face contorted and his eyes burning with venom. "So, let me give you some advice, Admiral. If you are finding my method too unsavory for your pedigreed taste, you had better learn to swallow it or we are going to have a real fucking problem going forward."

Kolchak holstered his pistol without looking at Semenov. He turned and was about to walk away but the Ataman seized his arm with his bloody hand. Demidov stepped in with his hand on his holster but Kolchak held him off.

Semenov was livid. His beady eyes bulged like they were about to pop out of his beet-red face. "And one more thing," he whispered loudly into Kolchak's face. "Perhaps you are under some misguided impression that my men and I are fighting to restore your Slavic master race back to power, so let me clarify things for you. Just because my people have been vassals to the tsars for the past 300 years does not mean we will kiss the ring of the next government in

Moscow or in Omsk. We may have helped Russia defeat the khans and spread the empire across this land, but you are standing on the very tail end of that arrangement. Today, you and I have a common enemy and common allies. I promised to protect your passage to Omsk, and I will stand by my word. But once the Bolsheviks fall, God help you and your new government if you stand in my way."

Kolchak pried his arm free and straightened his coat. Anger pulsed in his temples, but he did not let it show. He turned and walked back towards the train through the parting sea of Cossacks. Semenov's voice rose behind him:

"Now, if you would not terribly mind, kindly inform your British master that we will do our best to expedite these proceedings and should be ready to depart for Omsk within two hours."

*

He went straight to Knox. *This will not stand!* He burst into Knox's cabin, not waiting for the general's assistant to finish announcing him. Knox was drinking tea by the window.

"Did you know about this?!"

"The executions?"

"And the torture! Have you seen it? It's gratuitous sadism!"

Knox gave a vague upward nod and sat down his tea. Despite the many days on the road, his mustache was perfectly trimmed, and the thinning hairline was neatly combed back from his forehead.

He gestured Kolchak to the other chair, but Kolchak was too agitated to sit. Another round of gunshots rang out outside.

"Come, see for yourself! The man is a raving lunatic taking genuine pleasure in flaying people alive and executing prisoners by the hundreds. This violates the rules of the Hague Convention! We can't ally with him."

"I admire your principles, Admiral, but the Hague rules don't apply here."

"What possibly do you mean by that?!"

"The Soviets are not an internationally recognized government. They have never signed the Hague treaties. At this point, they are the illegitimate usurpers of power, entangled in a civil war. The Hague Convention treaties apply only to conflicts between sovereign states."

Kolchak was aghast. "That's a bureaucratic loophole – you can't seriously be using it to turn a blind eye on what Semenov is doing! The point of the Hague treaty is in the principle. Don't tell me you actually approve of his methods!"

"Of course not! But my approval is not important here. You have to admit that he has proven effective."

"At what? Killing Russians? Cut him loose! There are other Cossack armies out there. What about Ataman Krasilnikov?"

Knox shook his head. "Admiral, I do understand your apprehension. But I am afraid he is our best man right now. Siberia is rife with feuding warlords, and new governments pop up like daisies after the rain. Semenov has the largest Cossack force and also the support of our allies in Vladivostok. The Japanese back him with their army of 80,000 men. With the war in Europe, Britain can't come close to matching that. Incidentally, the Japanese find his methods admirable. Even the French and the Americans have found him to be useful in the course of the intervention."

"I can't justify having atrocities committed in my name! I can't be in alliance with a man like that for the sake of statecraft. He relishes in his own barbarianism!"

"At times, diplomacy calls for making odd bedfellows. You need him."

"He is not even Russian! He is a half-breed Mongol who hates Russians!"

Knox shrugged. "And that is one of the reasons the Japanese back him. Admiral, you'll have to learn to manage the lesser races. It's unavoidable. Like the British Empire, Russia is a veritable powder keg of racial conflicts. The burden of the master race is to not only keep this mix from blowing up but also to find ways to channel their nationalism and self-interests to further the greater ideals to the benefit of the whole empire. In the end, this is in their own best interests. We learned our hard lessons in the Indies and in Africa. And you have hundreds of ethnic groups in this country. If you can't find a way to manage the Tatars, the Uzbeks, the Ukrainians, the Belarusians, the Poles, the Czechs, and the others, the Bolsheviks will."

Kolchak was silent, his gaze fixated on the façade of the station beyond the steel shutters of the window. He reluctantly pulled out the chair and settled himself into it.

"I am a soldier, not a politician," he said, and immediately knew that it sounded false.

"I believe you will find, Admiral, that in Russia today you have to be both. A civil war is a war of ideas first, and weapons second. The Reds won the revolution with an idea. And a man with an idea is a hundred times more dangerous than a man with a gun. A man with a gun fights to not die. A man with an idea is willing to die for it. The Reds know what they want. What about you? Have you changed your mind about what you want?"

"No," Kolchak shook his head. The slaps of gunshots resounded from behind the station.

"When you came to me, you said you wanted to see the Russian Empire restored to its greatness. To be ruled by Russians, not mongrels like Lenin and Trotsky. To fight the German aggressors, instead of slicing away Russia's territories to appease them. Is this still what you want?"

"It is."

"Then the question you have to ask yourself is if you believe in it enough to stomach the cost. We are in this together. The Reds must be defeated in order for the Eastern front to re-open, and for *your* Russia to have a fighting chance. Right now, you have the full support of my government. You have powerful champions in the War Cabinet and the House of Commons. You have Allied reinforcements at your disposal, and more to come. You have me, and I believe you are the right man for the job. I know that you care about this country. But the choice is yours. Should you find this task to be beyond your ambition, I will, with regret, have to explore other options."

Outside the window, the Cossacks began to load the train.

*

Demidov was waiting in the corridor. As they walked back to the 'Russian' wagon, Kolchak felt hollowed out. It was as if Semenov himself, with his small, curved knife had carved out all the bits deemed no longer pertinent – principles, decency, self-restraint. Was there to be no honor in this war? Was this how Russia was to be rebuilt – by boorish, bloodthirsty brutes and thugs?

"Is everything in order, Admiral?" Demidov's springy, youthful step was in infallible measure with his own.

"Tell me, Victor, do you think making a deal with monsters in order to survive makes us monsters too?"

"I believe it makes us survivors, sir," he responded without hesitation. "Russia needs us to survive."

"Russia…" Kolchak mulled the word. "Did you know that *Russia* was the name of the first minelayer I was assigned to command when the war started?"

"No, sir, I did not." He shook his head.

"Do you know the first key to successful minelaying? *Know your enemy* – his routes, schedules, and defenses. With just a small vessel and a few well-placed mines, you can cripple the enemy's fleet and shift the entire balance of war."

Demidov nodded.

"But there is the second key to minelaying: *Always know where you laid your own mines*. You never know when you will need to sail through these waters again. Mines have no allegiance. Russia today is a minefield, and I am afraid we are about to lay a lot more."

THE WINTER PALACE

It was only the second day of September but, standing at the open window of the General Staff Building, Anna could already smell autumn in the air. The northern autumn – smelling of the sea, a damp chill and the forest. It was the smell of her childhood in Petrograd. When she drove through the streets this morning, the pavement was wet and remnants of the morning fog were drifting through the city, lingering in the alleys and in the canals. And now, outside the window, the vast, granite-lined field of the Palace Square extended into the grey haze, towards the ghostly silhouette of the Winter Palace looming over the river embankment.

The last time she was here, she was on the other side of this window – in the square, where Alexei died. She could see the spot now through the patchy fog, out there, by the palace gates. There, she sat beside him on the frozen stones and held him in her arms. All of her life, he had always felt so strong and full of light to her. Until that day. When she pulled him close that day, she could no longer feel him.

His blood must still be there, seeped into the stones and into the ground beneath them, forever part of this place, of this city. She wished she believed in heaven. She wished he could see that they had won. The palace, the city – it all belonged to them now.

Maybe he did.

"Are you OK?" Egorov tossed a stack of documents on the table and stretched in his chair.

"Yeah."

Captain Lavrov of the Petrograd Cheka backed in through the door with a file box in his hands.

"Well, this should be the last of it," he said and set the box on the table next to the two others.

He adjusted his glasses. For a man in his fifties, Lavrov looked lean and carried himself with a sense of taut sturdiness. With his uniform, his full, neatly trimmed mustache, and his full head of wheat-colored hair, he looked more like a cavalry commander than a department administrator. When he walked, the heels of his boots drove confidently into the floor, hinting at the former swagger of his youth.

"Thank you," she said. "So, let's start with the assassin. What do we know about him?"

Lavrov rifled inside one of the boxes and pulled out a file. He flipped through a few pages. "OK. Leo Kannegisser; aged twenty-two. Wealthy middle-class family. Before the revolution, he was a military cadet at the Mikhailov Artillery School of the Imperial Army. His detachment was assigned to the Winter Palace on the night of the Bolshevik revolution. He could have been one of the cadets shooting at our people during the storming of the Winter Palace, but he claims he was among the group that had disbanded voluntarily. After the revolution, he was moderately active in the Popular Socialists Party, but mostly had aspirations to become a poet. He is marginally known in the local literary circles."

"So, no prior counter-revolutionary activity?"

"Nothing we know of. Certainly nothing like his cousin Max Filonenko, who, as you know, has very close ties to Savinkov."

She nodded. "So, what happened the day Uritsky was killed?"

Lavrov opened another file. "It was around nine in the morning. Uritsky had just arrived in his car at the People's Commissariat entrance, over there." He pointed through the window to the other curved wing of the General Staff Building.

"According to the eyewitness reports, Kannegisser approached Uritsky's car on a bicycle. He stopped and fired three times. One of the bullets hit Uritsky in the head. When the medics got to him, he was already dead."

"And Kannegisser?"

"By the time the guards ran to the car from the entrance, he was already riding away on his bicycle, heading towards Admiralty Boulevard. They gave chase but he managed to lose them down a side alley."

"How was he apprehended?"

"We launched a manhunt and his description was given to every agent in the streets. Let me see here…" He flipped the page and scanned its contents, following with his finger. "There. It was a little after ten later that morning. One of the patrols identified him as he was exiting the British Consulate. He ran from them but was apprehended."

"Why did he go to the British Consulate? Did he know Cromie or Reilly?"

"No. He said he had never met Cromie and never heard of Reilly. But he did admit to meeting Savinkov. He said Savinkov directed him to meet at the Consulate after the assassination, to get British papers and leave the country. But Savinkov was not there, and no one would help him."

Finding Reilly was proving to be as difficult as catching a ghost. It did not make sense that he was not part of this picture. They knew he went to Petrograd, and there was clearly a British connection here, but where was Reilly himself? She would have been inclined to dismiss his participation and perhaps his existence altogether, had she not seen him once in Moscow, from a distance, entering Lockhart's building, before she knew who he was and the intricate conspiracy he had orchestrated before disappearing. And now, she could practically feel his invisible hand all over the Petrograd plot, and yet there seemed to be no trace of him.

She turned to Lavrov: "And Kannegisser still maintains the assassination was motivated by revenge? That his lover was an imperial officer executed on Uritsky's orders? Have we confirmed this?"

"Yes. The name he gave us was on the list of men executed last month for conspiracy to commit sabotage."

"And he says Filonenko and Savinkov helped him plan the assassination?"

"Not exactly. Filonenko introduced him to Savinkov and a Turkish merchant Konstantine Massino. Massino gave him money to purchase the bicycle, and Savinkov supplied the pistol and Uritsky's schedule on the day of the assassination."

"Have you located this Massino?"

Lavrov shook his head. "We have found no record of anyone by that name."

"How many times did they meet?"

"Just twice. On the 27th and the 29th, the day before the assassination."

"Where?"

"Balkov Café – just a few blocks from here."

Anna tapped a pencil on her lips.

"And what about the shoot-out at the Consulate?" Egorov asked.

"That was the following afternoon, on the 31st. I took a squad of agents there to question the staff about Kannegisser and the assassination. When we entered the premises, we were fired upon from the top of the stairs by Captain Cromie. He wounded two of our men. My agents returned fire and killed him. In his office, there was evidence that he was destroying records – we found burnt papers in the fireplace."

"Was there anyone else? Reilly?"

"No. Just a few junior staff members."

"How can you be sure? Do you know what Reilly looks like?" She opened one of her files and pulled out the sketch.

Lavrov smiled and opened another file. He took out a photo and placed it on the table, next to Anna's sketch. "It's from 1911, but I think the resemblance is definitely there," he said.

"Where did you get this?!" Anna bolted forward in her chair to examine the photo. It was definitely him – the clean-shaven, middle-aged man in a dark suit with a bow tie. The same elongated face, full pursed lips, bulging dark eyes, and dark hair slicked and parted on the right.

Lavrov tapped the file. "This is Reilly's Okhrana record. Straight from their Petrograd archives."

"Okhrana? Why would they have a file on an Englishman?"

"Because he is not really an Englishman, and Reilly is not his real name."

"What do you mean he is not an Englishman?" This Reilly plot was thickening.

Lavrov handed her the file. "According to this, he is Russian. He was born in Odessa under the name Georgi Rosenblum. He left home at the age of seventeen under rather suspicious circumstances surrounding an unsolved murder. He surfaced in England several years later and managed to obtain a British passport in the name of Sidney Reilly, but the file indicates that he also has several others, including German and American ones. He returned to Russia in 1906, working for the Okhrana to infiltrate Russian revolutionary groups. According to the file, his handlers did not trust him and suspected that he was also spying for the British at the same time. He left Russia at the outbreak of the war, and this is where this file ends."

Anna paged through the papers. "It feels like now we are hunting a completely different man. He has spent a lot of time in Russia, knows Petrograd well, and probably has many old contacts here. He may have even met Savinkov in those years."

"Russian, British, Greek, German, American…" Egorov murmured and scratched the back of his head. "How can one man keep so many identities straight? Most days I can hardly be myself."

Anna stared at him.

"What?" he said.

She turned to Lavrov. "Have you shown this photo to Kannegisser?"

"No; we've just located this file last night. Should I?"

"Yes, and right away. I have a feeling."

Lavrov left and then returned fifteen minutes later, put the photo back on the table and settled back into his chair.

"That Turkish merchant Massino is Reilly," he said. "How did you know?"

"Reilly went by the name Constantine Reiss in Moscow, so I figured he could be Konstantine Massino in Petrograd." She closed Reilly's Okhrana file and put it back in the box. There was satisfaction in pieces finally beginning to fit. "Now we have a lead to follow."

Lavrov got comfortable in his chair. "So, if I may ask, Agent Sokolova, why expand so much effort on capturing this single operative? We have already apprehended the two shooters, and now both Reilly and Savinkov are on the run."

She considered how much to tell him. Sergei had warned her that there could be a mole in the Petrograd Cheka who leaked Uritsky's schedule. Could it be Lavrov? She doubted it. She considered herself a good judge of character, and if Lavrov were a mole, why would he bring them Reilly's file? Unless somehow this was a diversion. Distrusting people took a lot of energy. Right now, she had a job to do, and she needed support from Lavrov and his men. Being paranoid wasn't going to help.

"We have reasons to believe Reilly is not on the run but is working on a bigger plot to support the establishment of a White government in Siberia." She watched Lavrov's reaction.

He sat silently for a few moments, processing the information.

"So, the assassinations were not the end of it?" he said.

"I am afraid not."

He smoothed his mustache. "If the British are supporting a new government in Siberia, that means they are not going to give up on the intervention. That means more troops, more weapons, and a bloodier war."

She nodded. "That is what we are trying to prevent. In Moscow, we have managed to dismantle the Union and the Ambassadors' plot, but in every other way, Reilly and Savinkov have been a few steps ahead of us. We know virtually nothing of their operations in Petrograd. This is what Uritsky was working on, but now he is gone. We have to assume they have a plan in motion, and the clock is ticking towards the next big thing, but we don't know what it will be."

Lavrov gazed darkly at the window. "Uritsky was my friend, my brother in arms. He was by my side when we stormed the Winter Palace. Somehow it was easier to think that he was cut down by some random cadet out for revenge. It was easier to make peace with something unpredictable, like fate, like being struck by lightning. But to find out that his death was a calculated move planned by a foreign operative, precisely because of who he was and what he stood for... that makes me angry. Savinkov and this Reilly have no conscience at all. They manipulated this young man, gave him a gun and pointed him at my friend. And then they hung him out to dry – the kid will get the firing squad. What kind of men do something like that?"

He looked back at Anna. "What else can I do to help you catch him? I believe we've gotten everything we can out of Kannegisser."

"Anton and I are going to check out this Balkov Café you mentioned. Can we have one of your men take us?"

"No need," he said, closing the file and getting up. "I will go with you."

*

Balkov Café was not really a café at all. At least not one that specialized in serving coffee or even food, for that matter. It was a smoky, side-alley bar in the Jewish quarter in Petrograd's west side. In the early afternoon, the clientele was sparse. Unlike the ritzy establishments off Nevsky and Admiralty Avenues, which were still occasioned by the sharply dressed remnants of the city's aristocracy and the pre-war nouveau-riche, Balkov clearly catered to the working class. Contributing culture to the place was a man with rolled-up shirt sleeves and suspenders at the piano in the corner, tenaciously trying to clank out the right melody from some once popular vaudeville tune, like a blind man trying to feel his way out of a labyrinth.

The bar-keeper shot a quick glance at the newcomers from beneath his heavy brow. Lavrov positioned himself at a table near the door, and Anna and Egorov went to the bar.

"Are you Balkov?" Anna asked.

"Who wants to know?"

"Cheka." She showed her ID.

The man glanced at the unfolded card and proceeded to wipe the counter with a towel. "What can I do for you?"

His tone was not unaccommodating but also not friendly. She guessed he had honed this tone over his previous brushes with the authorities, probably even before the revolution. He did not seem trustworthy to her, but in these hard times, everyone had something to hide.

She pulled out Reilly's photograph. "This man has been here. Do you recognize him?"

Balkov studied the photo while she studied his eyes. He did not flinch. "Yes. He has a beard though."

"When was he here last?"

He looked at his watch. "About two hours ago. He looked like he was waiting for someone, but then he left."

Anna and Egorov exchanged a glance.

"Do you know where we can find him?"

"No. But he's been here a few times. She might know." He pointed to a girl reading a book at the table by the window. "He talked to her for a bit. He likes the theater girls."

The thin, pretty girl by the window was absorbed in a book, oblivious to the questioning at the bar. Anna walked up and sat across from her, and Egorov pulled up a chair and straddled it next to the girl, like a broad, smiling wall blocking her escape.

The girl's thin eyebrows crumpled into two startled coils. Anna guessed she was in her early twenties. Short, dark hair framed her fine white face.

"Hi," Anna said.

"Hello," the girl responded. "Do I know you?"

"No. We are with the Cheka. I am Agent Sokolova, and this is Agent Egorov." Egorov touched the tip of his flat cap with a gallant wink. "What is your name?"

"Vera. Vera Rosenberg." The girl picked up her cigarette from the ashtray.

"Vera, we need your help finding this man." Anna placed the photograph on the table. "He probably has a beard now. Do you know him?"

Her eyes darted to the photo and then back to Anna. "Yes." She took a short drag of her cigarette and let out a nervous burst of smoke towards the window. "What do you want with him?"

"I can't tell you the details, but it's important that we speak with him as soon as possible. People will die if we don't."

The girl glanced back at Reilly's face on the table. "I don't know him very well. I only met him a couple of times. My girlfriend knows him better. We went to a party at his apartment once."

"Do you remember where he lives?"

"Yes. It's not far."

"Vera, I need you to take us there now."

"OK," the girl said simply and gathered up her things.

Outside, she took them down the back alley to Torgovaya Street and pointed to the pale-yellow five-story building at the end of the block: "Second entrance, top floor, apartment on the right."

"Are you sure?" Anna asked, examining the windows on the top floor.

"Yes."

Lavrov pulled the car around. Anna leaned into his window: "Can you drive her back to HQ and have someone take her statement? We can't risk Reilly seeing her here. Also, have someone locate her girlfriend and take her statement, too. And send a squad for backup."

Lavrov drove off with Vera, leaving Anna and Egorov in the alley. A streetcar rolled by, chiming its bells. They crossed Torgovaya and made their way towards the building, blending into the scattered flow of people.

The door squeaked open and closed on the rusted iron hinges, and they found themselves deposited in the cool, murky staircase. There was no elevator. On the way up the five flights of tiled stairs, Anna tried to breathe slow and deep, like before firing a gun, as her mind played through the scenarios of what would happen if Reilly were there. Egorov huffed next to her, his revolver clutched in his massive fist.

The fifth-floor apartment on the right was number 20. She nodded to Egorov and let him go ahead. He took a few steps back and rammed his shoulder into the door. It burst out from the splintered frame like a nut from a cracked shell. There were no sounds inside. They hurriedly checked the rooms; the apartment was empty.

Someone definitely lived here. There were dishes in the kitchen sink, and a lukewarm kettle on the stove. In the living room – a couch and a simple desk with a telephone and a few newspapers. Anna opened the desk drawer to find only a lonely pencil rolling around.

"These are today's," she said, showing the newspapers to Egorov.

They checked the bathroom – no soap, razor, comb or toothbrush. In the bedroom, the wardrobe held a shirt and a suit, but no travel bag.

"He is leaving the city – his bag and toiletries are gone," she said to Egorov. "But it looks like he is planning to return. Can you call Lavrov and tell him to send several squads to the station to check for him on any outbound trains?"

Egorov nodded and stomped off to the phone in the living room.

She tried to picture Reilly in here. There were no books, no mail, no family portraits. The apartment wasn't a home. Like a hotel room, it was devoid of anything that would betray its occupant.

She went into the bedroom as Egorov began rattling through the drawers in the kitchen. Sergei said Reilly's notebook was hidden in his mattress in Moscow. She pulled the blankets and the sheets off the bed and ran her fingers along the edges of the mattress. Near the headboard, she felt it – a small tear in the side seam. She dug her fingers in and fished out a small, folded piece of paper.

"Got something here!" Egorov yelled from the kitchen. He came into the living room, holding a rolled-up paper in one hand and a metal tube in another.

"It was inside the hollow leg of the kitchen table," he said, proudly showing her the tube.

There were footsteps in the stairwell, and Lavrov and several of his men appeared in the doorway.

"I sent two squads to the Finland station with photos of Reilly," he said. "Let's hope he has not left yet."

Egorov sat on the couch and unrolled the paper on the coffee table. It was a detailed map of Russia with multicolored spiderwebs extending out of Moscow and Petrograd in fine lines across the country.

"It's a railway map," Lavrov said, examining the contours. "Looks like military-issue – it shows the non-commercial lines."

"I've got something, too," Anna said and opened her hand. She unwrapped the folded piece of paper and laid it on top of the map. It contained a handwritten sequence of numbers.

"This looks like the same code I saw in Moscow," she said. "I am going to go back to HQ and call Moscow to get them started on decoding this. You finish taking this place apart. Every joint and every seam."

THE INSTITUTE FOR NOBLE MAIDENS

William's first week in Petrograd had been spent in the driver's seat of the Rolls-Royce, with Robins sitting next to him and either going over his notes while giving occasional directions or telling him stories of his adventures while his gloved hand polished the silver eagle's head on the handle of his cane.

The business of the Mission took them to the doors of the countless administrative offices, banks, factories and depots. William suspected that, in the course of just the first few days, they had covered the whole wide Neva river delta, set foot on Petrograd's every large and small island, and crossed every canal and bridge at least once.

From the very first day, William realized that the task of driving was not at all about driving. It was actually Robins' way of tutoring him on the ins and outs of this country's government and infrastructure. He could tell Robins was impressed with his sharp memory and learning aptitude. Saunders' parting words still rang vivid in the back of his mind, but he wanted to observe and learn more before he confronted Robins with any troubling questions.

He was surprised to find that they were effortlessly admitted anywhere they went, as if they were not wearing the uniforms of the same country that had just landed two occupation forces in Russia. He had half-expected to be shot at with some regularity, but instead found himself being warmly welcomed, as if they were the trade delegation of a friendly nation. Simply saying that they were with the American Red Cross seemed to put people at ease.

He was also impressed with Robins. His new boss had an almost encyclopedic knowledge of the city, government officials and current affairs. He was charismatic and a master at building relationships and getting people to talk. The working people appreciated his down-to-earth disposition of a man who had toiled in the mines of Colorado and roughed through the wilderness of Klondike. On the other hand, the managers and the administrators appreciated his ability to see the big picture and his astute business pragmatism.

The sphere of Robins' acquaintances spanned the city and included everyone from the top municipal officials to the lowly depot guards. In the back of the Rolls-Royce was a crate filled with everything from cans of Carnation milk to Hershey chocolate bars and packs of Lucky Strike cigarettes, and Robins never missed the opportunity to gift these out to his connections, who were always happy to see him and returned the favor with the only thing he ever seemed to want – information.

William expected this particular Monday to be no different, but Robins assured him it was going to be a short day. There was a shooting in Petrograd on Friday, and the city had been on lockdown through much of the weekend. Some high-ranking security official got killed in the Palace Square, and in Moscow, Lenin himself had been shot and wounded.

Robins took this forced downtime as the opportunity to have the Rolls-Royce washed and polished at the hotel the night before. William had never seen this car so clean.

"Where to?" he asked Robins, squinting from the blinding sun reflecting in the car's long, angular hood.

"Let's hit the bank first," Robins remarked, not lifting his gaze from the notebook.

The bank was the Petrograd branch of the National City Bank of New York, and they had made several stops there during their rounds last week. William knew the way and cranked the steering wheel to make a turn onto Nevsky Avenue.

But when he looked up to the street sign at the intersection, he was reminded that since two days ago, Nevsky was no longer Nevsky. The Reds had been renaming streets all over the city, which, according to Robins, wreaked havoc with the post office. Anything named after a saint or a tsar was guaranteed to be renamed to something more proletarian, but even the more innocuously named streets were not exempt from the 'out-with-the-old' revolutionary enthusiasm. And so, Nevsky, the major thoroughfare of Petrograd named after the river it was built on, had just been re-christened as ProletKult Avenue – named after the artists' collective for proletarian culture which took residence somewhere down the street. (This bit of trivia was volunteered to him by Robins, who was naturally in the know.)

Personally, William thought that all this was way too much trouble for the sake of a name change, but the Russians did not seem bothered. The previous tsar himself had renamed the whole city from St. Petersburg to Petrograd when the war with Germany broke out because *Petersburg* sounded too Germanic. If they had renamed the whole city overnight, William supposed a few dozen streets did not seem like a big deal.

Robins normally did not take long at the bank. Indeed, he had soon re-emerged – with his briefcase in one hand and his cane in another – and re-deposited himself in the front seat of the Rolls-Royce. He directed William back to the Central district and then down Suvorovsky Boulevard.

"Turn in there," he said, pointing at the driveway entrance in the middle of a long stretch of iron fencing surrounding a large, treed estate.

William did, and drove down the long driveway towards the sprawling palatial edifice that was unfolding up ahead.

"What is this place?"

"The Smolny Institute for Noble Maidens. But don't get too excited. There aren't any left inside." Robins chuckled, seeming pleased with his own humor.

"This is Smolny? The government building?"

Robins nodded. "Before the revolution, it was a boarding academy for the daughters of Russian aristocracy. Now it is occupied by the Petrograd Soviet and the whole lot of regional commissariats."

They drove up to the inner iron fence and stopped at the guard shelter. The soldier guards with rifles seemed to recognize the car. A serious-looking sailor diligently peered inside and in the back seat. He gave Robins barely a glance but studied William's papers thoroughly before returning them. With his nod, the heavy wrought-iron gate was swung open, and they were allowed to pass.

William parked alongside the wide, temple-like stone steps leading up to the towering columns of this Parthenon-like grand structure topped with a red flag waving in the warm breeze. Robins got out, and, without waiting, began to climb the stairs with his cane and his briefcase in hand. William followed. At the top of the stairs, a Red Army guard standing next to a Maxim machine gun pulled open the tall, heavy door to let them in.

They took the grand marble staircase to the third floor. There, at the very end of a long wing of offices, they found themselves in a quiet and spacious hall with a reception desk next to a set of large double doors. The receptionist, a young man in uniform, recognized Robins with a nod. Robins signed the book, and the young man stood up and disappeared behind the double doors.

Of all the reception rooms William had waited in since his arrival in Petrograd, this one was by far the grandest. A row of large, discolored rectangles in the wallpaper adorned the walls. William had seen similar rectangles on the walls all around the city – the burnt-in shadows of removed portraits, probably of the former emperors, empresses, and other patrons of this once fine institution.

"I'll need you to translate for me," Robins said.

"Are you sure?" William grinned. "I've noticed you understand Russian more than you like to let on."

Robins chuckled. "My Russian is passable. I could probably get by, but there are many advantages to not having people know that you can understand them."

"So, essentially I was shipped across the Atlantic to be your driver?" William feigned being lightly insulted.

"More of an apprentice," he winked. "And a driver," he added with a smirk.

The young man returned and invited them to proceed through the doors. With its bookshelf-lined walls and floor-to-ceiling windows, the large room resembled a library more than it did an office. Behind an expansive desk was a man of medium build, dressed in military uniform. His face was rounded, with round wireframe glasses, a dark mustache, a goatee, and a mess of dark curly hair atop his head.

William could have recognized that face anywhere, even though he had seen it only in the newspapers. They were standing before none other than Leon Trotsky – the chief commander of the Red Army and the second most-powerful man in all of Bolshevik Russia.

Trotsky stood up and shook hands with them. William translated, as Robins introduced him as his associate from New York.

"How is Comrade Lenin?" Robins enquired with sincere concern, as they settled into the chairs.

"Thank you for asking," Trotsky replied. "He is in a stable condition, although I am afraid still a long way from full recovery."

"I know he has the best doctors caring for him, but please do not hesitate to let me know if the American Red Cross can provide any assistance."

Trotsky gave Robins an obliged nod. "So, what is it that I can do for you today, Comrade Robins?"

"I have received a report that there is a train in Vyborg with fifty-four cars loaded with metals and other raw materials. I am told it is destined for Helsingfors in Finland, from where it is to proceed to Sweden and from there to Germany."

Trotsky's lips curled into a thin smile. "That is *very* specific information. I am impressed that the American Red Cross is better informed on this matter than I am. I must admit, I have no knowledge of the train in question."

"I suspected as much. Perhaps, it is one of the regional Soviets or some other local government that made a deal with German agents. Still, as you are aware, if this train were to make it into German hands, it would constitute a definitive violation of the embargo on trading with the Central powers. Despite the fact that your country has signed a peace treaty with Germany, any evidence of trading in violation of the embargo would put your government's neutrality in question by the Allied powers, which is something I am sure you would want to avoid."

Trotsky nodded calmly. "Do not worry, Comrade Robins. We have no intention of sending supplies to the Germans. Russia is being bled dry by the occupiers and the profiteers. If the train is, as you said, at Vyborg, it will be detained on my orders. Consider it done; and thank you for bringing it to my attention. Will there be anything else?"

"No; that is everything," said Robins and stood up.

Trotsky shook hands with Robins and then turned to William: "Comrade Arden, I was told you had fought in the war in Europe and were wounded in France."

William was quietly startled that Lenin's second in-command knew about him.

Trotsky continued: "As a man who has survived the war in Europe, you must have strong feelings about our peace with Germany. For whatever it's worth, believe me this is an uneasy peace, and I wish our country was in a position to not enter into it."

William nodded in respectful acknowledgment and shook Trotsky's extended hand. It was smooth but strong.

When they left Trotsky's office and were walking down the wide, carpeted hallway again, Robins turned to him: "One thing I appreciate about Trotsky is that there is never small talk – he is all business, and I can get more done with him in five minutes than with a room full of Wall Street lawyers and bankers in a week."

"You seem to have a great rapport with him! But tell me, why isn't our Ambassador Francis handling issues like this?"

Robins laughed: "Ha! Francis? My dear boy, Francis is a nearsighted imbecile. He still stubbornly refuses to deal with the Bolsheviks. He does not understand the power they hold through the Soviets throughout Russia. Instead, he has chosen to retreat to the White territories and be wined and dined by the Whites, who hope he will convince the president and the State Department to go to war with the Bolsheviks."

"So, you are saying the task of diplomacy is left to the Red Cross Mission?"

"Why not? Someone has to do it. Right now, the US has no official relations with the Soviet Russia, so diplomacy falls to whoever has boots on the ground. Speaking of which, we have one more errand here."

They descended to the second level of Smolny and went down a busy wing of offices ringing with typewriters and phone conversations.

Robins stopped at the frosted glass door marked *People's Commission for Railways – A. V. Grigoriev.* He knocked, and a man's gruff voice shouted "*Da, vhodíte!*"

"I'll need you to translate again." Robins winked at William and opened the door.

Inside was a small office with no receptionist. An older man in a suit sat behind a desk, his head propped up on his hands over a stack of papers. The grey caterpillars of his eyebrows scrunched upward as he peered at the visitors without raising his head from the papers. Having recognized Robins, he straightened up in his chair.

"Ah, Comrade Robins!" he greeted, rising from behind the table. He was of a shorter stature, and his grey thinning hair matched his mustache and goatee.

"Artem Vasilievich," Robins exclaimed. "It is great to see you again!"

They shook hands.

Robins gestured to his companion: "Please meet my interpreter and associate from New York, Mr. William Arden."

William introduced himself and shook Grigoriev's hand. It was strong, wide and calloused, hardened by decades of manual work.

"I've not seen you for a while. What brings you my way?" Grigoriev inquired, inviting them to sit.

"It is the matter of the Railway Mission from America."

"Are you referring to the group that landed in Vladivostok several months ago?"

"Yes – it's called the Russian Railways Service Corps, and it is a team of 300 expert American railroad engineers. They have been assembled with the singular goal of helping repair, improve and organize the Russian rail operations."

"But if I am not mistaken, they were invited under an agreement between your government and the former Prime Minister Kerensky's provisional government?"

Robins lowered his head in an exaggerated nod.

"I am sure you are aware, Mr. Robins, that my government does not honor the agreements made by the former provisional government."

"It is true that the original arrangements were not made with the Bolshevik government, and I fully appreciate that you have inherited this arrangement with no obligation of honoring it. I also suspect that you have inherited the many issues that have plagued the Russian railway system for decades, and I know that your young government has many, many other priorities at the moment. However, I do sincerely believe that the Russian people can benefit greatly from the expertise and the services provided by these men.

After all, the railway infrastructure is of such critical importance to this vast country, and I am certain your department is spread very thin."

Grigoriev leaned in over the table, looking alternately at Robins and William, as the latter translated.

"Believe me, we are not in a position to turn away expert assistance," Grigoriev responded. "However, you can imagine that the disposition towards this mission is suspicious at best, given the recent landing of the American troops in Vladivostok and Archangelsk. Why would the American government sanction this peaceful mission and at the same time send troops to support the hostile British and French invasion? Our military leaders worry that these *experts* as you call them, are actually here to assist the Allies in sabotaging or overtaking the very railroads they promise to repair."

Robins nodded politely and responded casually, in short snippets that allowed William time to translate. "I understand that, given the current circumstances, America's approach towards Bolshevik Russia may seem contradictory at best. The American political system is a complex apparatus in the best of times. In the times of war, it can become downright incomprehensible. Right now, the president, the State Department, and the War Department don't quite see eye to eye on the question of Russia, which is why we find ourselves in this situation."

"Mr. Robins, are you saying that your president did not order troops into Russia?"

Robins smiled abashedly. "He did, and although I can't purport to speak for the president, I know he was pressured to appease the Allies and the War Department. Certainly, this small number of American troops sent to Russia cannot be mistaken for an invasion. On the other hand, the Railway Service Corps is a purely civilian effort with no ties to the American military or the Allies. It was organized by American businessmen, several of whom I personally know. Their only goal is to build trust and trade between our two countries."

Grigoriev leaned back in his chair and clasped his hands behind his head, studying Robins. "Suppose I believe you. What is it exactly that you are asking?"

"The members of the Railway Service Corps have been stranded out east, unable to reach Petrograd. These men have travelled a long way from their families and are anxious to start their work so that they can eventually return home. However, the civil war has complicated things. I ask that you permit their passage through the Bolshevik-controlled cities and railway segments, and that you grant your approval for them to commence work with your Railway Commission, which was the original purpose of their journey."

Grigoriev nodded. "Even if I wanted to, this type of a mandate would require a lot of convincing in Moscow."

"Of course. But consider the situation. If they are unable to commence their work, soon they will be forced to turn around and return home, without benefitting your people. In the meanwhile, they are being forced to spend a lot of time in the areas controlled by the British, the French, and the Whites. The men of the Railroad Corps are not soldiers or spies – they are simple, working men. But I am afraid that the longer they are stranded in the company of your enemies, the more your enemies may be able to benefit from them and their expertise."

Grigoriev's face was polite but impenetrable.

"Artem Vasilievich," Robins continued. "I understand that this work was not planned and that there may be concerns that this could create disruptions to other projects. I am sure you have limited resources, even without this additional undertaking. However, my sponsors strongly believe that collaboration on the reconstruction and modernization of the Russian railway infrastructure could be of great benefit to both of our countries and could act as the foundation of a long-lasting trade partnership after the war. That's why I've been asked to deliver a seed budget of one million rubles to help this project get started on the right foot."

William stumbled in his translation as Robins opened his

briefcase and unloaded five thick stacks of Russian rubles onto the desk in front of Grigoriev.

Grigoriev looked at William, who hastily finished translating. Grigoriev stroked his goatee and looked at the money and then back at Robins.

"Rest assured, these funds are provided by a private foundation interested in seeing an improvement in the business relations between our countries. This seed capital is a gesture of good will to ensure the success of the men who had left their families and regular jobs to help Russia rebuild. There are no additional conditions or obligations."

Grigoriev sat silent for a few moments, stroking his beard. He finally reached over his desk and extended his hand to Robins: "Very well. I will recommend to Moscow that this project be approved and that we are permitted to utilize the expertise of your men to the fullest."

Robins closed his briefcase and shook Grigoriev's hand, beaming contently.

*

In the car, Robins clearly had no intention to discuss what had just happened. He seemed pleased with the day, and, as he often did on the way back, was scribbling in his journal. But William had decided this was a good opportunity to have a talk.

"So, did we just bribe the People's Commissar for Railways?" he asked, pulling out of the Smolny driveway.

Robins smiled, still focused on his journal. "Oh, don't be silly. I know you've learned better than that this week." He looked up at William. "What was your assessment of Grigoriev?"

William considered the question for a moment. "Well, judging by his calloused hands, he came from the working class – maybe a foreman. This means he is likely ideologically driven, as opposed to the officials who have retained their posts from the imperial days and would be more likely motivated by personal gain."

"Very good!" Robins was pleased with his pupil. "So, you see – it wasn't a bribe. It was an investment. I guarantee you – he won't keep a ruble of that money. The whole amount will make it to Moscow. Now, here is a bonus question for you: why do we care about the Railroad Commission?"

"Because Russia has over 60,000 miles of railroad, and it is the only reliable transportation infrastructure for moving supplies and resources."

"Very good!" Robins refocused on his journal.

They drove in silence for a few blocks.

"But whose money was it?" William was determined.

"Just a group of enterprising American investors aiming to develop American interests abroad."

"The American International Corporation?"

Robins looked up, surprised, and a grin spread on his face. "Well, very good, my boy! I see you have done your research."

"Who are they?"

"The very captains of industry: J. D. Rockefeller, J. P. Morgan, and many other visionaries from the greatest American banks and manufacturers."

"And what does the American International Corporation do?"

"It develops new opportunities for America. These men have industrialized America, and now they look beyond her borders to apply their expertise and investment on the world stage."

"So, you mean to tell me that none other than J. D. Rockefeller and J. P. Morgan, the icons of American capitalism, are willingly signing over millions to the Bolsheviks?!" This sounded even more ludicrous out loud than it did in his head.

Robins smiled coyly.

"But why—"

"Why Russia?"

"No, I get that – the resources, right? Timber, oil, coal, metals? That's why *you* are here."

Robins nodded.

"But why are we betting against our allies? By giving the

Bolsheviks money, aren't we basically funding them? That money we left back there will go towards the weapons and provisions to be used in their civil war. By giving them money, we are essentially taking their side, just as the British and the French are taking the side of the Whites!"

Robins turned to him, his dark eyes lively and engaged: "You are right! And I know this must be hard for you – betting against our allies on this one, after you had fought alongside them in Europe. But here is the thing. You must realize that the war in Europe no longer matters. Forget whatever you've heard. Forget all the propaganda. It is not about freedom or even political power. It is all about the economic power of a handful of empires. To us, the war in Europe is just a sideshow now. Russia is the new world. You and I are here because America needs us to secure its access to Russia. We are here to make the necessary investment to make it happen. In Russia, our European allies are our economic competitors. We are actually playing catch-up here. The British, the French, and even the Germans have spent centuries developing their Russian investments. And they want to protect and expand their interests. Once the war in Europe is over, they will turn their attention to carving up this country."

William tried to digest the new information. It made practical sense, but it just wasn't sitting right. "But... by taking sides in the civil war... it feels like we are meddling in their affairs. Our interests may be all-business, but aren't we crossing the line from business to politics?"

Robins laughed heartily. "My dear boy. I do admire your idealism! It's healthy. I was just like you when I was young. Everything was either black or white. But let me tell you something that will save you some grief in the future. Politics is just another name for business. There is only the economics of supply and demand. That is what has started and ended every war and revolution since the dawn of humanity. It's all business. Politics only happens when there is more demand than supply."

His gloved hand polished the eagle's head on his cane. "The best opportunities don't just materialize by themselves – they must be developed. Gold nuggets did not just appear under my feet one day – I had to go to the Klondike and fight for them – fight the elements, the animals and other men just for the opportunity to mine that land. It's the American way. If we had capitalized only on those opportunities that occurred of their own nature, America would still be overrun with savages."

William stopped at an intersection, waiting for a tram to move. "But aren't you worried about supporting a government that's diametrically opposite to our own? The Reds don't believe in free market economy, they don't believe in wealth, they want our workers to revolt. Aren't we being short-sighted by enabling them?"

"That's exactly how the Allies think, my boy. They lack the vision. They don't see the opportunity. All they know is the old colonial mentality – find a slice of land rich in resources, and then slowly drain it while turning it into a caricature version of the motherland. They fail to see the potential of what's going on in Russia politically. The Bolsheviks don't want to turn Russia into a version of England or France, or even America. And we don't want that either."

William gave Robins a perplexed look. "Why is that? Don't we want them to be like us?"

"Heavens, no! If Russia became a capitalist country like the US, that would make it into our direct competitor on the global stage, with considerably more land, resources and trade influence. We *absolutely* don't want that."

"So, what *do* we want?"

"We want them to succeed. We want them to build their government-controlled economy with absolute government monopoly over production and the markets. Why? Because it won't be self-sustaining. Not for a very long time. Russia is too vast, hungry and underdeveloped. After the Bolsheviks win, it will be decades before they can ramp up their own manufacturing and agriculture on the scale they need to provide for their people. So, they will have to rely on the outside supply of goods and services.

The Red Russia will be the largest captive market the world has ever seen, and we will have the connections needed to become its supplier."

William had to admit that this was a very audacious and elegantly simple plan. "So, we basically want to turn Russia into one massive company town? Like Pullman?"

"Precisely! Except Pullman's company town failed because all the risk and all the burden of labor relations was on the Pullman company. But with Russia, all the burden and all the risk will be assumed by their government – not our corporations."

"And you think the Bolsheviks will allow capitalist companies into its markets? You've seen their propaganda – they are violently opposed to capitalism."

"They will, just as they took our money today." He returned to the page in his notebook. "And have been taking it since day one."

"You mean to tell me we've been financing the Bolshevik government for almost a year now?"

Robins smiled mischievously. "Consider that branch of City Bank you and I visited today. Why do you suppose this American bank remains open when the Bolsheviks have nationalized and closed all other foreign banks in Russia? Because that bank is their sole conduit for foreign investment. They are short on allies right now, and that's why the relationships we build now are so important. Of course, they will never admit to taking our help openly, but we don't need them to. They will keep taking it. Right now, they need our money so they can feed their people and fight the war. After the war, they will need our machinery, engineers and consumer goods. And we'll be here to provide all that, while our allies are still scrambling to rebuild after the war."

William turned the car onto Nevsky-Proletkult. "But what about our government? Do you think Washington will go for it? So far, Wilson seems ambivalent on the topic of Russia."

Robins waved him aside dismissively. "Don't worry about Washington! Sometimes those bureaucrats lack the imagination to see the possibilities and need to be shown the way. There is one thing you can always count on. American policy will follow the interests of American business."

William turned down Mihailovskaya Street and parked the car in front of the hotel.

Robins turned to him: "Look, my boy, I know you didn't know the whole picture when you signed up, so you have a lot to think about. But just know that this *will* work. We can help America prosper and help the Russians build the country they want."

"How can you be certain?"

"Because it's worked before! It's all a game, and we wrote the damn playbook. The Persian Revolution in 1906, the Mexican Revolution in 1910, the 1911 revolution in China – all of them have resulted in lucrative investments, industrial contracts and trade deals for America. Not by chance, but because our top men from oil, steel and banking were right there, on the ground level. Just as we are here today in Russia. Who knows, next time around, wherever in the world that may be, you could be one of those top men."

HOME

The Sokolov household was in a state of disarray. Just off the entryway, the sitting parlor – normally pristine and ready to receive callers – was now littered with boxes, trunks, suitcases, and piles of clothing from dresses to coats, strewn over the furniture.

Anna quietly closed the front door behind her and stealthily made her way past the parlor and through the dining room towards the kitchen, trying, from memory, to avoid the creaky floor planks. The sounds of someone rummaging through the pots and pans in the kitchen helped cover up her advance.

Fedosha, the family cook, backed out of the pantry and turned around. Suddenly noticing Anna standing in the kitchen doorway, she shrieked and dropped an empty pot from the stack in her hands onto the floor. Anna put her finger to her lips, trying to contain laughter.

"Ms. Anna!" Fedosha flung open her arms and hugged Anna, tears welling in her eyes. "When did you come back?"

"I am not back, Fedosha. I am in Petrograd for just a little while," she said, closing her eyes and smelling the collar of Fedosha's apron, which still smelled just as it did when she was a child – of pot roasts and freshly baked bread.

"What's going on here? Are you going on a trip?" Anna asked, nodding back towards the parlor.

"Oh," Fedosha wiped the tears with her apron. "You had better talk to your Mamá – she is upstairs, packing with Masha."

Anna kissed Fedosha's familiar cheek and left the kitchen to go find the rest of the Sokolov clan. It was strange, being back in this house. It had been just over a year since she was here last, but it seemed like a lifetime ago now. She had barely turned the corner at the base of the stairs when she heard a scream up above followed by the stomping of feet running down the stairs towards her.

"Annochka!" Masha flew into her arms. "I knew I heard your voice!" She squeezed the breath out of Anna and held her for a long minute.

"When did you get in?" She finally let Anna go, and stepped back to examine her older sister. "What are you wearing?" she rattled off without waiting for a response to her first question. "Are you dressed as a soldier boy?"

"This? Most certainly not!" Anna feigned indignation and turned around, showing off her polished black boots and military breeches. "I'll have you know, this just happens to be the latest in women's frontline fashion. Straight from the trenches of Europe! Thanks to the women's battalions, we don't have to wear men's uniforms anymore."

"Oh my god – you have a gun!?" Masha's eyes turned into saucers in combination of terror and awe. She hugged Anna again "I missed you so terribly. Where have you been? It's been over a year! Did you hear we are leaving for Switzerland? Mamá has an old aunt there." Masha's eyes lit up with a glimmer of hope: "Are you coming with us?"

Anna shook her head.

"Mamá! Come, see who is here!" Masha yelled up the stairs.

"I can't believe how much you've grown!" Anna said, stepping back to take in her little sister. Masha spun around in her light-blue day dress with a lace collar. She was breathtaking – her golden hair piled into a messy bun at the base of her slender neck and her iridescent blue eyes sparkling like a pair of clear aquamarines. "You are just beautiful! Are you sure you are only seventeen? If one did not know better, they could mistake you for a proper young lady."

"I know! And this corset makes my boobs look huge!" Masha gave her pushed-up bosom a vigorous squeeze, making Anna laugh.

"Mamá!" Masha yelled again up the stairs. She grabbed Anna's arm. "Did you see Fedosha? We had to let Petrovich go last year after the workers' strikes. Papa's factory was nationalized. And the head housekeeper at the manor, and the stablemaster and his boy – do you remember little Nikolai? He grew into a dashing young man overnight, it seems. I do miss seeing him around. I pray there will be eligible young gentlemen in Switzerland. I do hope not all of them have been sent to war. So dreadful."

Anna just smiled, taking in her sister as she chattered on. Masha had never shown interest in politics – she was too young to remember the time before the wars and revolutions became regular topics of dinnertime conversations. And Anna and Alexei had never exposed her to their revolutionary activities, as if by an unspoken agreement. Maybe it was for the better, and that's why Anna never felt bad about indulging her sister's childish and superficial infatuations with fashion and boys. Masha had managed to carve out her own sheltered childhood in the middle of a violent time. Maybe someone had to stay innocent. She brushed a lock of hair from Masha's temple.

Out of the corner of her eye, Anna saw the slender figure of her mother appear at the top of the stairs. Seeing Anna with Masha clinging to her arm, Mrs Sokolova sat down on the top step, and tears rolled down her cheeks.

Anna walked up and sat next to her mother. She hugged her and felt her sob. Her mother's body felt so much smaller in Anna's arms than she had remembered.

Her mother wiped the tears with a handkerchief. Her face had aged, but it was still so very pretty; Anna studied the familiar delicate features she used to love tracing with her fingers when she was little. Her mother clasped her hands onto Anna's.

"I sent you letters in Moscow, but never heard back."

"I'm sorry, Mom – I moved around a lot," she lied. She did not want to start the argument.

"It's been over a year; I thought I might never see you again." Her pale eyes searched Anna's. "How are you?"

"I am fine. I am good," Anna said, holding her mother's hands in hers. "So, I hear you are leaving?"

"Yes. In two days. Your father is out, finalizing the travel papers. We are going to stay with your Great-Aunt Clara in Switzerland until we find a permanent place."

Anna nodded in silence, considering the odd prospect of being the only one from her family left in Russia.

"I tried to let you know in the letters," her mother said, dabbing her eyes with the handkerchief. "How long are you staying in Petrograd?"

"I don't know yet. Maybe a few days, maybe longer. I have some urgent work, but I wanted to at least stop by and see all of you. I really can't stay long."

The front door opened. Anna's father stopped in the doorway. His gaze traveled from Masha and up the stairs, finally fixing on Anna's face, as if it were a barely recognizable specter from the distant past.

"Hello, Papa," Anna said, rising up from the step.

Seeing him made her want to cry. He looked thinner and had a lot more gray in his hair now; it struck her how much he had aged since she last saw him. More so than her mother. She came down the steps towards him. He stood in the doorway for a few moments, as if unable to move. Finally, he set his briefcase down and walked to his daughter. He took her head into his hands, kissed her forehead and pressed her face into his shoulder, wrapping her in his arms. Anna swallowed a lump in her throat, trying not to cry.

"You are staying for dinner, aren't you? You must stay for dinner!" Masha hugged them both.

*

The dinner table was set as for a special occasion – fine china, crystal and silver. Anna smiled to herself at the formality of the traditional family seating arrangement she had forgotten since last year – Father at the head of the table, with Mother to his right. Today, Anna was given the seat of the honored guest to his left instead of next to her mother, where she had sat all of her life. It was strange to view the table from this side, but Masha settled down next to her, ignoring her mother's subtle directions.

The smallest daily details of the past seemed so foreign now. Like waiting to be served. The silent waiting seemed awkward now. She wished she hadn't agreed to stay for dinner now. The idea sounded nostalgic, but the reality of it was strained. She studied the china plate in front of her. The scroll of violet flowers and green vines seemed so colorful and vivid when she was a child. Now, she really noticed the spiderweb of cracks in the glazing.

Fedosha put the wine and bread on the table. Anna wondered if she had baked the bread this morning like she did when Anna was little, waking her up with the aroma spreading through the house. For an instant, she longed for those mornings.

Her father looked around the table and put his hands in front of him, facing upward. *Prayer!* – another tradition Anna had not thought of for some time. She used to dread these times before and after each meal when she was a child. The long-forgotten dreariness crept on. What could be more moot?

Her father closed his eyes and bowed his head. Fedosha stood at the kitchen door, her hands clasped in front of her, and head bowed.

"Through the prayers of our holy fathers, O Lord Jesus Christ, Son of God, have mercy on us. Amen."

Her father, mother, sister and Fedosha all crossed themselves. Anna looked down at the violets behind the cracked glaze.

"The poor shall eat and be satisfied, and those who seek the Lord shall praise Him; their hearts shall live forever!"

A thousand years of Russian prayers for the poor to eat – maybe this one will finally do the job, she thought to herself.

"Glory to the Father, and to the Son, and to the Holy Spirit, now and ever and unto ages of ages. Amen."

They crossed themselves for the second time. Masha was looking at her out of the corner of her eye, pretending to pray. Anna smiled at her.

"Lord, have mercy! Lord, have mercy! Lord, have mercy!"

Anna must have grimaced, because Masha snorted, trying not to giggle. Anna nudged her with her elbow, noting her mother's disapproving glance.

"O Christ God, bless the food and drink of Thy servants, for Thou art holy, always, now and ever and unto ages of ages. Amen!"

The family crossed themselves the third and final time. Mr. Sokolov gave Masha a reproachful look and she blushed. Fedosha disappeared into the kitchen and started bringing out bowls of Uha – fish soup with perch, carrots and potatoes. Anna's father broke off a piece of bread.

"Fedosha could not get butter yesterday," Mrs. Sokolova said. "The rations had run out and the line was still out the door and around the corner. Luckily, the butcher always remembers your father and had saved us some roast."

Fedosha poured the wine.

"Drink it up," Mrs. Sokolova motioned to Anna. "Not you – half a glass is enough for you," she pointed a finger at Masha. "We can't take it with us. You probably can't buy French wine in stores in Moscow. How are the provisions there?"

"The same. There are shortages everywhere."

"And we thought things were bad during the war with Germany! They have gotten so much worse after the Bolsheviks came to power!"

Sensing her mother's thinly vailed jab at her chosen political conviction, Anna took a breath and tried to enjoy Fedosha's soup.

But her mother went on.

"At least, under the provisional government, we could still get milk, eggs and flour with some regularity. There was even chocolate in the stores once a week!"

Anna sighed and put down her spoon. "That's odd, Mother – I remember people starving by the thousands in this city under the Tsar and then under the provisional government. They must have missed the news about the chocolate in the stores! The Bolsheviks did not cause food shortages. We are in the middle of a civil war. The whole country's economy and infrastructure are disrupted."

Her father, who was eating in silence until now, looked up at Anna. "I hear they are now taking grain harvests from the farmers by force," he said.

"We have to – to feed the people. Otherwise, the farmers will horde it or sell it to the highest bidders, and the cities would starve."

"But it's their grain! Shouldn't they be able to do with it whatever they choose?"

"Not right now, they can't. We can't afford to think of *mine* vs *yours* when it comes to food. We must think of the common good. We just can't afford to permit profiteering when millions are starving."

Her mother looked at her sternly. "How can you defend them, Anna? All they do is take everything away! We have nothing left here. The factory, the stores – all gone. Everything your father has worked so hard to build – all of it gone!" She teared up again and dabbed her eyes with her napkin. "We are being forced to uproot, to leave our home, while we still have some money left."

Anna tried not to lose her temper. Her mother had not changed. This is why Anna could not stand to even read her letters which somehow managed to follow Anna wherever she moved. Her letters were nothing more than rambling pages of self-pity and grievances against whatever people or forces she had perceived to have conspired against the Sokolov household. Throughout her childhood, her mother had always been so overprotective of everything – the china, the floors, the children themselves. It was as though there was meaning and happiness in the simple fact of possession and preservation of the domestic cocoon she had built around them. Change devastated her. It threw her whole world off the equilibrium. First there was the war, then the first revolution of 1917 and Alexei dying – as a revolutionary, of all things. When Anna left this house last year, her mother had not gotten out of bed for almost a week. She was a victim, of course. It pained Anna to see her mother suffer. But she also could not stand the underlying sense of entitlement with which her mother wore her victim badge.

"No one is forcing you to leave," Anna said as calmly as she could. "That is the choice you are making, based on what's important to you."

"To us? How about what's important for your little sister? All we've ever done is care for our children. What kind of a future will she have here? She did not even get to finish her last year at Smolny because the Bolsheviks disbanded the institution and took over the building for their headquarters."

Anna looked at Masha: "Ooh, are you sad that you did not get to graduate from the Institute for Noble Maidens? I'd bet Prince Gorchakov was devasted at the news that one of his protégées now goes around utterly uncultured! Do you miss wearing his blue ribbon around your neck, like a trained poodle?"

"Woof," Masha barked at Anna and laughed. "Mamá, you know I couldn't care less about that place! Eight hours a day of French lessons, botany and sewing. How was this education supposed to prepare me for the modern world? Not to mention, our Class Lady was a mean hag, and all the male teachers were old."

· Her sister's list of grievances made Anna smile.

"Masha!" her mother cried out in indignation. "You have no idea the strings your father had to pull to get you a sponsor to the institute! A lot of respectable ladies came from such institutions!"

"Your mother is right," Anna wagged her finger sternly at Masha. "You do know that Vera Figner graduated from the Institute for Noble Maidens in Kazan? And by the age of twenty-seven she was the leader of her own terrorist group and took part in the assassination of Tsar Alexander II."

Masha's eyes widened, and her mother gasped and crossed herself.

"Don't you put those ideas in her head!" her mother exclaimed. "That's what got your brother killed."

Color rushed to Anna's face. "No, it's *your* world that got him killed. The world you seem so eager to defend and lament. Alexei rejected it and wanted to change it, and for that it killed him."

She stood up, infuriated. She wanted to leave. "You don't get to judge the value of his life and his choices. He died fighting for something bigger than him, bigger than this family. I know you may never comprehend why he chose to give his life to something bigger than the family business."

Anna's father put one hand on the hand of his wife and the other on his daughter's. "Stop it, both of you." He squeezed their hands. "Alexei was an adult, and he made his own choices. As much as I wanted him to take over the factory business, he had his own ideas."

Anna glanced at Masha who was sitting quietly, staring into space.

Her mother teared up into her napkin again and looked up at Anna. "You know, you left right after Alexei's funeral. It's like we lost two children at once."

Anna bit her lower lip. "I know. And I am sorry for that. I love all of you, but I had to do something. I could not carry on like nothing had happened. I could not go back to the debutante balls and the Sunday promenades while this country was drowning in the blood of our people."

"Things were not so bad," her mother said, looking down into her plate, her trembling voice a plea of affirmation for a memory of the past that was now forever lost.

"Not so bad?" Anna leaned towards her. "What prospects did I have in your world, Mother? To wait for you and Father to find me a match that would elevate the family name? To be married off, to have children and to spend the rest of my life sitting at home? That may have worked for you, but I want more out of my life. It's 1918; the world outside these walls has changed, and I have actually helped change it. Outside these walls, women can now vote and have the same jobs men can. Emancipated women, even though I know it means nothing to you!"

"And we understand that, Annochka," her father spoke up, patting his daughter's hand. "I understand why you want to work and have a different life than your mother and I had. But why must you work for the Cheka?!" His lips contorted into a grimace of disdain. "They are butchers!"

Anna withdrew her hand away from her father and straightened up. Her pulse pumped furiously. "I don't *work* for the Cheka, Father – I *am* the Cheka! Because someone has to be. Someone has to protect the people and their future because your generation did not care to. And we are not the butchers. If you want to see the real butchers, take a hard look at your precious Denikin, Wrangel and the rest of the White generals. Take a look at what atrocities these fine, well-bred Russian aristocrats are inflicting on the Russian people, all in the name of bringing back your precious lost world."

She leaned in towards her father's face and uttered with calm intensity: "I will *die* before I let them undo everything we've accomplished. Just as Alexei died."

She stepped back from the table and pushed her chair back in. The ends of the chair legs slipped naturally back into the divots pressed into the thick carpet over the years. "I understand why you want to leave. I can see you will never believe in what it is we are trying to build in Russia. All you can see is what you've lost, and not what there is for everyone to be gained. You are blind to the fact that your old ways are what got this country to the boiling point. We have made a clean break with the old ways. If you are looking for the old ways, there is nothing left for you here."

Her father stared vacantly at the empty chair at the far end of the table. He looked even older to her now. He looked worn out.

She put her hand on his shoulder. "I want you to know that

I appreciate everything you did for me when I was a child. Both of you," she glanced at her mother. "I know you thought you were doing this for us, your children. But this lifestyle we were able to afford – the country estate, the stables, the servants, the vacations in Europe – it was all just a mirage. It was a fantasy at someone else's expense – a brightly painted bubble of pretending in the middle of a stark kingdom where millions were being starved and worked to death so that a few could live in luxury. Alexei helped me see it. This is not the Russia we want. I understand why you want to leave. But please know that I do love all of you and wish you only the best of luck. I hope you find the life you seek."

"Come with us!" Her mother rushed to her and grasped her arm. "You can get a job in Switzerland. Women can work in the West, too."

Anna shook her head. "I have no interest in being a secretary." She embraced her mother and then gently pushed her away. Masha jumped up from her chair and threw herself at Anna, squeezing her tightly in her slender arms. Anna wrapped her arms around her sister, too, and they held each other, neither wanting to let go. Would she ever hold her sister again?

"Do we need to call you a coach? It's getting dark," Masha said quietly.

"I brought a car."

"You drive yourself around in a car!? How un-lady like!" Masha looked at her with feigned horror as a tear ran down her cheek.

Anna slapped her playfully on the cheek and pulled her in close.

"You still have much to learn about what it takes to be a real lady." She gently curled her sister's lock of hair around her finger, whispering to her in half-voice. "Ladies can drive cars just fine, thank you very much. And they can fly airplanes if you must know. And so can you. You can be whatever you want, my sweet child. Don't you forget that when you get to Switzerland!"

She kissed her sister's soft cheek and walked out into the night.

ON REILLY'S TRAIL

Number 2 on Gorokhovaya Street was a light-grey, four-story building of no particular distinction. From the street, its modest stone façade appeared unremarkable in a city abounding with ornate architecture, and William had driven past it on several occasions without giving it a second glance. Even when standing at its unassuming entrance on the corner of Admiralty and Gorokhovaya, one was not likely to give it any consideration at all, distracted instead by the neighboring landmarks: the lush green lawns of the Alexander Gardens wet with the morning dew, the golden spire of the Admiralty shining in the rising sun, or the Palace Square beckoning with its majestic span just two blocks away.

And yet, William now knew that despite its innocuous appearance and location, everyone in Petrograd (and St. Petersburg before it) knew this building, just as they knew the Tsar's palace.

This is because, for half a century, this building had served as the headquarters of the Okhrana – the all-powerful national security agency established by the Russian tsars to protect them from the revolutionaries and the terrorists. And when, despite the decades of spying, infiltrations, arrests and executions, the Okhrana had failed to prevent the downfall of the crown, this building passed on to the victors and became the Petrograd headquarters of the Cheka.

It was in this very building that William now found himself, along with Robins, wondering what they were doing here. It was Monday, and in his typical fashion, Robins said nothing about whom they were waiting to see or why. It was one of his typical *missions* – urgent and secretive, as always.

William leaned in and whispered to Robins: "Should I be worried? This is not exactly a place one would expect to find two Americans."

"Relax, my boy. They asked for our help."

"The Cheka does not exactly have a spotless reputation."

"What intelligence agency does? They are doing what they must to protect the revolution. Did you know that we had a similar agency in America during our revolutionary war? Ben Franklin was in it. Their job was sniffing out British spies... Funny how things have not changed 150 years later," he smirked, amused by the realization.

Observing the bustle of office activity around them, William noted that the Cheka did not seem to have a standard uniform – a few of the men wore what looked like Red Army fatigues and shirts devoid of any insignia, while others were in sailors' black-and-white striped shirts, and others still were in plain civilian clothes. He supposed this helped them blend in with the crowds in the streets of Petrograd. Some favored black leather jackets similar to ones he had seen pilots wear on the western front. Some also wore leather caps ensigned with a red star.

When Robins and William were finally admitted, they were taken to a large room where half a dozen men were discussing something around a large table covered with files and rolled-out maps. One of the men, with wheat-colored hair, a mustache and round glasses, held up his index finger to Robins, requesting another minute of their patience.

Robins nodded and pulled William towards the couch and some chairs in front of the large fireplace. They settled in, waiting once more. William poured himself some water from a pitcher on the coffee table and examined the room. The bare wallpapered walls had the same discolored rectangles on them as the walls in Smolny. He wondered about the fate of all these portraits of Nicholas and his predecessors – at one time there must have been thousands of them in the offices, palaces and schools across Russia. What happened to them? Were they burned? Or perhaps just dragged into the basements, condemned to stare into the darkness.

The discussion at the table ended and three of the men left the room. William examined the three remaining at the table. The one that had signaled to them looked to be in his fifties. He was sitting down now, busily writing in a file. The other one was a barrel-chested young giant with closely cropped sandy hair. He was leaning over a map on the table, and his olive-green peasant's shirt did nothing to hide his big arms and broad shoulders, made even more prominent by the taut straps of his suspenders.

The third one had his back turned to William and was a fellow of smaller stature. He had his elbows on the table and his head down, reading something. His uniform was unfamiliar – darker and slimmer than the traditional army attire William had seen in Russia so far. Perhaps a pilot, he wondered. His black boots were highly polished, like an officer's, and rose up to just below the knee. The breeches were a trimmer cut than cavalry or infantry, and they were black rather than one of the many shades of olive, grey or blue commonly seen around Petrograd. There was something odd about the uniform or perhaps the man himself.

William's examination was interrupted by an impatient "*Ahem,*" and when he looked up, he was met by the penetrating glare of two blue, most definitely woman's eyes looking right back at him.

"Do you like what you see?" Anna asked in English.

He choked on his water and the room busted out in laughter.

Anna straightened up and turned around, fixing her humorless gaze on the American.

He held up his hand in surrender and shook his head. "No! I mean yes... I mean..." He cleared his throat, mentally prodding his suddenly dumbfounded brain to sort through the jumble of Russian and English words. "I am sorry. It's just, in my country, I've never seen a woman in uniform."

"Naturally; unless of course she was a nun, a nurse or a maid?" The pretty female warrior seemed to be enjoying her merciless interrogation despite his panicked embarrassment.

"No, ma'am... Miss," – he stumbled over and silently cursed his Texas drawl which betrayed him now, as it sometimes did in the moments of politeness or abashment, which made him even more self-conscious. Next to him, Robins was not much help, having covered his eyes with his hand and shaking with silent laughter. Wiping away the tears, he looked at William, clearly amused with observing the utter devastation a pretty, confident girl could inflict on a young man.

The man with the mustache walked around the table and shook Robins' hand, smiling.

"Thank you for coming, Comrade Robins," he said in Russian.

He extended his hand in greeting to William. "I am Captain Lavrov with the Petrograd Cheka, and these are agents Anna Sokolova and Anton Egorov from the counter-terrorism department."

"Counter-terrorism?" William shook Anna's and Egorov's hands.

"And sabotage, and espionage, and any other active counter-revolutionary measures." Anna shook his hand and granted him a small smile of clemency. Her hand was soft and delicate, and he feared he had turned even more red at her touch. What was the matter with him?

"Thank you for coming," the pretty Chekist said to Robins. "Sergei spoke very highly about the assistance you have provided him and Uritsky in the past."

She looked at William and he cleared his throat and translated.

"I have enjoyed working with them both on a few occasions," Robins responded. "And I am happy to provide any assistance I can with this Reilly affair. Have you made any progress in your manhunt?"

"Not much, except we've discovered that he was actually born in Russia and that Reilly is not his real name."

"Really? Well, that certainly casts a strange new light on this man," Robins uttered.

"Why do you say that? What do you know about him?"

"A few curious things." Robins pulled out his notebook from the briefcase. "I personally had never heard the name Reilly before, but, after I received your inquiry, I spoke with Mr. Thompson, the former Mission director. He is well connected in Washington and was able to do some additional enquiring on the matter."

He flipped through a few pages in his notebook. "I was surprised to find that Reilly was well known to our State Department. Evidently, he had resided in the United States from 1915 to 1917. He had set up an arms trading company and managed to make a small fortune at the beginning of the war, brokering armament sales to the Allies, including to Imperial Russia. But in 1916, he was extensively investigated by the State Department."

"Why is that?"

"That year we had several major incidents at the munitions manufacturing plants across the United States. Fires and explosions. The State Department suspected sabotage. The biggest one was at the depot on Black Tom Island in New Jersey, just a stone's throw away from Manhattan. Over one million pounds of munitions had exploded there while awaiting to be transported to the Allies in Europe. Ten people were killed, and there was destruction all the way to Manhattan."

"What did this have to do with Reilly?"

"Well, all the sabotaged locations had ties with Reilly's company, and it was one of few with access to the Black Tom depot. There was even a witness who claimed Reilly was involved.

The State Department investigated but could not find credible evidence to incriminate him. Officially, the sabotage was blamed on German agents. However, in the course of the investigation, the State Department discovered that Reilly had provided falsified information when he entered the US. They contacted the British government who confirmed his identity and that he had been in the services of the British SIS."

"Do you think he did it?" Lavrov asked.

"Blow up the munitions? I think it's likely that he was involved."

"I don't understand," Anna said. "If he is a British agent, why would he blow up munitions headed for the Allies?"

"Perhaps to pin it on the Germans and compel America to enter the war," William offered.

Robins nodded. "Thompson said that was the popular opinion on Wall Street."

"If that was the opinion on Wall Street, why was he allowed to leave?" Anna raised her eyebrows.

"I suppose not many on Wall Street objected to America entering the war," Robins smiled. "But there is one more curious bit of information, and I'm afraid it's rather bad news," Robins said, turning the page of his notebook.

"You see, the global banking system is a rather small club, and a single financial deal of a large size doesn't go unnoticed. And what Reilly has in the works is a very, *very* large deal."

"What sort of a deal?" Anna asked.

"According to my contact at City Bank, Reilly is attempting to secure financing for a very large arms order with Vickers and several other manufacturers, to be shipped to Russia to support the White armies."

"How large?"

"My source said he is trying to secure a one-hundred-million-dollar credit line. The order is to include over one hundred heavy tanks, several hundred pieces of artillery, and hundreds of thousands of machine guns and other firearms."

Egorov let out an astounded whistle.

"That is…" Lavrov uttered and stopped, lost for words.

"… enough to completely turn the course of the war," Anna finished for him. "They must intend for this order to support the new White government in Omsk. Against these kinds of armaments, our army won't stand a chance. The Whites will be able to roll over Moscow and Petrograd in a matter of weeks."

"Do you know anything else about this deal?" Egorov asked. "Can we stop it?"

"The order has not been placed yet," Robins said. "Before the manufacturers begin fulfilling, Reilly will need to secure a line of credit to cover the payments. That's what he is trying to establish now. There is no guarantee that he will succeed in securing such a large amount. But I'm told he has promised to deliver twenty million dollars' worth of gold as collateral." He looked at the group. "Now, do you have any ideas where a British agent might be able to get his hands on so much gold?"

"Samara," Anna looked back at Lavrov and Egorov. "That's why he went to Samara."

"What is Samara?" William asked, looking at Robins and the Russians.

"Samara is the city where the Imperial Russian gold reserve is currently located," Lavrov answered. "Over one billion rubles worth of gold."

Anna nodded. "At the start of the war, the Tsar moved the gold reserve out of Petrograd to Kazan, 1,000 miles back from the frontlines, to prevent it from being captured by the Germans. After the revolution, Kazan fell under the White control. We've tried to take it several times without success. About a month ago, we received intelligence that the British were using the Czech legion to move the gold reserve deeper into the White territory. Currently, the gold is in Samara. We assume it is going to be moved further east to Omsk, to support the new White government. It sounds like part of it is going to be used as collateral for this arms deal."

Robins leaned forward in his chair, tapping excitedly on the eagle's head of his cane. "If that is the case, Reilly will have to get this gold to an international bank, which is not so easy in Russia today. The only one he can access that is still recognized by the West is the Russo-Asiatic Bank in Vladivostok. From there, it can be transferred to any bank in England to finance his order."

"So, if we stop the gold, we can stop the deal?" Egorov studied the spiderwebs of roads on the map. "It's a very long way from Samara to Vladivostok."

"Is there anything that can be done to stop him along the way?" William asked.

"Well, Samara is controlled by the Whites," Anna said. "Assuming Reilly makes it to Samara, from there, he will be under the protection of the Whites all the way to Omsk, and then under the wing of the British to Vladivostok. Still, it's a long way to go and there is some ongoing fighting along the way, so it will take him weeks to get the gold from Samara to Vladivostok. I'll alert Moscow and see if there is a way to engage the army or the Red Cossacks to make an intercept in Siberia."

"Let's not forget that Reilly was still in Petrograd yesterday," Lavrov said. "So, he is either on his way to Samara now, or maybe he is still trying to get out of Petrograd. Either way, if we make the manhunt public, it could slow him down."

Anna nodded and pulled Reilly's photo from a file. "You are right. I'll ask Dzerzhinsky's office to proceed with the manhunt story. Being identified as the British spy implicated in the plots to assassinate Lenin and Uritsky will put a target on his back. And I'll also see if we have any assets in Samara," she added.

OMSK

The grand ballroom on the second floor of the Governor-General's mansion in Omsk could rival some of the ballrooms in the palaces of the capital. Standing here, Kolchak was awash with the white and gold glow from the bright chandeliers above, the crisp linens on the tables and the polished mirrors of the marble floors. The preparations were in progress, and servants dashed hastily about the tables, folding the napkins and clanking and chiming with knives, forks and glasses.

He had positioned himself away from the commotion on the perimeter of the room, at one of the tall windows. In the thickening dusk, he could still make out the river and the bridges, churches and the boulevards of the city outside. They had made it to Omsk – the largest city in Western Siberia, which wasn't saying much. Two thirds of the way from Vladivostok to Moscow, it was probably the furthest one could go inland on the whole continent. If everything went according to plan, this city was to be his home until the end of the war. He hoped it would not be long but knew it could be years – they had a frontline longer than the war in Europe, and that war had been raging for four years now.

Seeing himself in the reflection, he thought he himself looked like the ballroom, trimmed for the formal occasion in his white parade uniform, glistening with the gold eagle buttons, the gold cords, the gold bars, and the black epaulettes on his shoulders. He had forgotten how much heavier the parade uniform felt than his black field one. It felt premature to wear it now.

Demidov approached. "We will begin in five minutes, Admiral."

Kolchak nodded. They've come to hear him. He was supposed to give them confidence and hope. What could he say that hadn't already been said? Didn't everyone want to hear the same thing – *Freedom, Justice, Destiny*? Didn't *every* side fight for these? What more could he promise them?

The crowd began to fill the room. In the reflection of the window, he watched the flow of men in officer uniforms and business suits, and women in formal evening gowns and hairdos adorned with jewels and feathers. The high society of Omsk – provincial aristocracy, government officials, merchants. He felt as if he were standing at the edge of a sea of waxed mustaches, surgically precise hair parts, powdered faces, plunging necklines and glimmering fabrics. The old social uneasiness returned, carrying him off to the crowded events he had attended in his youth in St. Petersburg. He tried to shake it off. The orchestra began softly playing a waltz. The scent of the perfumes was suffocating.

"Don't be nervous." Knox appeared at his side. Kolchak eyed his field uniform with envy – a soldier's general through and through.

"Everything has been settled with the council," he reassured, patting Kolchak on the shoulder.

Kolchak shook his head. "I am not worried about that. It's this politicking thing I am not good at. Put me at the frontline and give me soldiers, and I can lead them into battle, but these people…" he gestured at the assembly with his hand. "What can I say to them?"

"These people are soldiers in their own right. They've found themselves in a battle for their way of life, and they need a strong, experienced leader just the same. This city is hungry for a renewal. The whole of Siberia and the entire Russia are. What they want is an end to the barbarianism, and a return to the sensibilities and values that once made Russia part of Europe."

A fork chimed on the side of a glass, calling the social sea to calm. The band stopped, and the room hushed as the guests settled at their tables.

A man ascended the orchestra stage. It was Peter Vologodsky – the chairman of the Council of Ministers, whom Kolchak met upon his arrival yesterday. Vologodsky had introduced himself as a former lawyer by trade, and Kolchak could now see that he carried himself with ease in front of the crowd – his appearance as polished as his demeanor. Nothing on him was out of place – from the balding half-crown of closely cropped dark hair to the groomed mustache and the short, pointed goatee presiding confidently above the starched white wingtip collar, a narrow black bow tie and a black suit. From the first moment of meeting him, Kolchak distrusted him. Vologodsky had a disarmingly casual yet eloquent parlance in which every sentence seemed to harbor a hidden point and end with a slight mustached smile and a squint at the corners of his eyes. There was indirectness in his approach. This was not how Kolchak talked to his men.

From the stage, Vologodsky's voice rang out in clear, trained enunciations. "My dear distinguished guests. Dear members of the Council of Ministers of the Provisional Siberian Government. Today we have the good fortune of celebrating not one but two momentous developments in our fight for Mother Russia.

"It is not for the lack of effort, but rather due to the fragmented nature of resistance across our vast country that we have been unsuccessful to date in defeating Bolshevism. But today, we are taking a significant step towards coordinating and focusing our efforts. Ladies and gentlemen, it is my great pleasure to announce the unification of two of the largest anti-Bolshevik governments of Russia. From this day, and until Moscow and Petrograd are liberated, the Constituent Assembly Government of Samara and the Provisional Siberian Government of Omsk are unified into a single Provisional All-Russian Government."

The crowd broke out in cheers and applause, and Vologodsky smiled benevolently and nodded, waiting for the excitement to subside before proceeding.

"We are thrilled to welcome our talented and dedicated compatriots from Samara to join forces with us in giving the Russian people a capable and democratic government in these hard times. But that is not our only good news today. I am also delighted to announce that Admiral Alexander Kolchak, Russia's fearless explorer and a distinguished hero of the Japanese and German wars, has accepted, at our request, the post of the Minister of War in our newly unified government."

Vologodsky extended his hand towards Kolchak, and the crowd exploded in applause again, turning around to get a glimpse of him standing at the back.

"We are honored to have Admiral Kolchak join our cabinet, and I am confident that under his experienced, battle-hardened leadership, our armies will deliver the decisive and fatal blows against the Reds. Ladies and gentlemen, please welcome our Minister of War, Admiral Alexander Kolchak!"

Kolchak walked up the steps onto the stage to a thunderous applause that turned, like a wave rushing towards him, into a standing ovation. He wasn't prepared for that. Humility and gratitude flooded him. He had traveled to and addressed audiences in many countries. But these were Russian people. *His* people. He bowed his head. The crowd settled back down into their chairs.

Kolchak surveyed the room. "Ladies and gentlemen. Members of the council."

He paused, absorbed in momentary contemplation.

"I get asked often about my political alignment. Am I a Socialist Revolutionary? A Constitutional Democrat? A Menshevik, a Monarchist, a Republican? To which I have to say I am none of those things but one: a Russian patriot. I have resolved not to align myself with any party until the greater threat at hand has been defeated. Until the Russian Empire breaks free of her oppressors, both internal and external, and can rule with sovereignty over its dominion once more."

A scattering of spontaneous applause made him pause.

"This is why I accept with gratitude and honor the power and trust the council has invested in me with this post. I take this appointment with a sense of responsibility and patriotism. Our country has been through much hardship over the last several years. The wars and the revolutions have led her off course. We've been attacked and fragmented, and our lands have been decimated and squandered. And despite our most valiant efforts and the lives of countless patriots, we've been largely ineffective against the centralized and strategic actions of the Reds. But all this is about to change."

He glanced at the darkening windows, beyond which, in the descending dusk, the waters of the Irtysh river cut through the city in their languid, ever-moving flow.

"That river out there, wide and powerful, it starts as just a tiny trickle high in the Altay mountains of China. But mile after mile, other streams join in, and it grows stronger and flows 4,000 miles across Russia so that it itself can join the ocean. That is how our power will spread. From Omsk to Moscow, until the entire Russia joins in. But it is here, in this city, in this room that this movement begins. It begins in your hearts. With this position entrusted to me, I promise to be your sword. I will organize and lead a unified fighting force that will reverse the spread of Bolshevism and defeat it, paving the way for the government our great nation deserves."

Vologodsky handed him a glass of champagne, and he raised it to the crowd.

"Ladies and gentlemen, to the rebirth of the great Russian Empire!"

*

In his office, Vologodsky poured vodka from a fine cut-crystal decanter into three heavy crystal glasses. He handed one to Knox and one to Kolchak and settled into the chair behind his desk.

"Tonight was a great success," he said. "With the new Directorate and the Council of the Ministers, we now finally have a government with the power to challenge Moscow. I must thank you both for helping bring this about."

"Chairman, I am glad that our arrival has helped you reach an agreement with Samara, but I am afraid we'll need more than a new government to defeat the Bolsheviks," said Kolchak. "It does not matter how many ministers we put in Omsk, they won't change a thing unless we begin pushing back the Red Army."

He wondered if he had been too direct, and when Vologodsky's usual half-smile came out contorted into a half-frown, he knew that he had hit a nerve.

"Admiral, I appreciate your eagerness to fight the Reds." Vologodsky had regained his demure composure. "We all do. But we must also think about giving people something tangible to fight for. The Reds have changed the laws of this country and made promises to the masses who were voiceless under the old regime. If we wish to defeat them, we must think of what laws and promises our new government can offer. But let me and the council worry about that, while you worry about the Red Army. I do hope you truly are up to this task. To be completely frank, your nomination was not a foregone conclusion, and there were several highly and – some would say – more qualified men considered for this job. But it was ultimately the military and financial support promised by your British sponsors that swayed the council in your favor."

Kolchak considered whether he should be offended, but Knox intervened. His head shook slightly as he spoke, which, after spending several weeks on the road with him, Kolchak knew meant he was irked:

"Chairman, let's not delude ourselves. Your list of viable candidates for this job was much shorter than you presume. Kornilov is dead, and Wrangel and Alekseev have their hands full in the south. The next most experienced candidate would be Denikin, but his reputation leaves much to be desired. The pogroms and the mass murders of the Jews make for very poor press in the West. And, frankly, this is representative of the public image problem of the entire White movement. The White generals and Atamans have been accused of crimes against the Russian common folk, of indiscriminate marauding and executions, of ignoring the needs of peasants and workers, and of being more interested in setting up their own petty fiefdoms than in unifying and liberating Russia. Someone like Denikin can't be the face of new Russia. What Russia needs is someone fresh, someone with his reputation unmarred by genocide and personal ambition. And who better than someone who is already a national icon? The Russians already know Kolchak. He is an explorer and a war admiral. He is already a respected Russian hero, and people love and follow heroes."

Kolchak fixated on the cut sides of the crystal glass of vodka in front of him, feeling somewhat awkward to find himself the third-person subject of this verbal tug of war. The diamond-like facets on the outside of the glass all faced in different directions and all refracted the same light in their own different ways. And yet all had to come together to create a single vessel. Much like the current situation. So many sides and inclinations. He was finding political machinations increasingly frustrating and unnecessary. This conversation was mind-numbing.

"And that is why the British government supports him," Knox continued. "Because we believe he is in fact the most capable candidate to lead the military effort and inspire the Russian people to overturn Bolshevism. We have already committed significant military resources, and this is only the beginning. Several very large shipments of armaments and supplies will be heading for Omsk in the next few months. We have also secured the cooperation of Colonel Gaida of the Czechoslovak Legion to fight the Reds on your side. And we have facilitated the relocation of the Imperial Gold Reserve from Kazan to fund your new government. Very soon you will have the purse and the guns to engage the Bolsheviks on an unprecedented scale."

"And we do deeply appreciate your government's support." Vologodsky bowed his head.

"The crown does its best to protect its investments. We are confident the admiral will do his part, and we are also relying on you to do yours."

"And what is it that you envision as my part in this?" Vologodsky's eyes glinted with unease.

"To truly bring this new government together. This unified government looks good on paper, but you and I both know the parties don't see eye to eye. There are too many competing political agendas, with everyone squabbling for their own gains. You must get them to come together and create a government that has the backing of the Russian people. Without it, any gains the admiral makes at the front will not last. That is the condition of our aid."

Vologodsky lingered, his gaze fixed in the distance. "You are right, of course," he finally said in his casual provincial parlance. "It is a tall order, but it must be done if we are to succeed."

He squinted demurely at Kolchak, and Kolchak could tell he was ready to be done with this conversation as well. Yet he was sure he and Vologodsky weren't settled with this matter.

"Gentlemen, I believe we are all committed to the common goals here. To defeat the Reds, to re-instate the Russian Empire, and to rejoin the war in Europe." Vologodsky looked at them both, and they nodded in agreement.

Vologodsky smiled and raised his glass. "To victory, then!"

"To victory!" three glasses clanked.

SERGEI

Petrograd had changed overnight. Driving down Moyka embankment in the early hours of the morning, Anna saw shopkeepers boarding up their windows as if a storm were coming. The clumps of the homeless, typically still sleeping at this hour in entryways and on the canal footbridges, were nowhere to be seen. Turning into the Palace Square, she encountered a new checkpoint – a group of soldiers armed with rifles, huddled around the crude campfire they had built in the middle of the street. Their bayonets rose like hackles at the sight of the approaching car. One of them stepped forward, shaking off the morning chill. Anna slowed down. He inspected her face and her black leather cap and coat. She was about to reach for her badge, but he waved her through.

In the square, a crowd was gathering, too early for the usual rallies. Some were waiting in the backs of trucks and others were warming around the fires that smoldered with blue acrid smoke that ate its way into her car. In this square infamous for revolts and bloodshed, this gathering at dawn seemed ominous. She drove slowly as they parted before her. Their eyes glared gloomily from under the bills of their workers' caps; their mood was dark. She read the banners they were hoisting on the trucks – large white letters on red canvas sheets: *Long Live Red Terror!*; *Death to the Bourgeois!*; *For Comrade Lenin!*

She felt them. They had been pushed too far. She too had been here, in this square, in front of the palace. More than once. She could almost taste that perceptible mixture of their anger and anticipation hanging in the air like the sickening thickness of kerosene fumes. She knew this energy all too well. It tingled in her fingertips again – that combustible charge hanging about a crowd on the precipice of turning into a mob.

In the General Staff Building, she headed straight to Lavrov's office: "What's going on out there? The city looks like it's ready to go to war."

He looked glum, with dark circles behind his wireframe glasses. "You could say that." His voice cracked uncharacteristically.

"You haven't seen it?" He pulled a newspaper from under a stack of files on his desk and plopped it in front of Anna. "The Reilly story is in the papers. The people are furious."

From the front page, Reilly's photo and sketch stared at her. Four bulging eyes – two with a beard, and two without. "I get that, but it's just a manhunt. What's this whole *Red Terror* thing? *Death to the Bourgeois?* The mob in the square looks ready to begin stringing up shopkeepers."

He reached over and unfolded the front page. Below the fold, the words *The Red Terror!* were splashed in bold heading, right under the Reilly article.

He moved the paper closer and grimly read out: "*In the state of war, the use of violence is demanded by the task of eliminating the enemy. We do not make war against individual persons. In the class war, we must exterminate Bourgeoisie as a class of exploiters, landowners and capitalists. Do not look for evidence that a suspect acted or spoke against the Soviet authorities. The first question you should ask him is what class he belongs to, what is his origin, education, profession. These questions should determine his fate. This is the essence of the Red Terror."*

He turned the paper around and placed it in front of Anna.

"This can't be," she muttered, re-reading the words. Her mind raced, feverishly trying to grasp onto any sliver of reason. This wasn't part of the plan. *Her* plan. "This reads like a declaration of war. Martin Latsis wrote this? I don't understand this... All we need to do is catch Reilly and Savinkov... I have to call Moscow."

"No need," Lavrov said. "Your boss is already here. Check the courtyard," he nodded over his shoulder.

"Sergei is here?"

She rushed down the stairs and then past the dark row of empty offices to the end of the hallway. The courtyard door was cracked open, and through the crack, sunlight cut in from the outside like a burning wedge of a knife's blade. She pushed the door open.

The sunlight smelled of morning dew and gunpowder.

She squinted in the bright light. Sergei's familiar frame loomed in the group of soldiers, but he looked different. His old army trench coat had been replaced with a black leather one. He turned around, hearing the squeak of the door, but Anna's gaze was no longer on him – it froze on the bodies on the ground – eight or nine – she could tell one of them was a woman. The door squeaked shut behind her.

Reading the expression of horror in her eyes, he holstered his revolver and walked to her. In the still air, the creaking of his leather coat and boots sounded deafeningly loud.

He took her by the elbow and walked her back inside, where he flung open the door of a vacant office and pulled her into the dusky space.

"Anna."

She wriggled her arm from his firm grip and backed away, putting the corner of the desk between them.

He took off his leather cap. His face was cleanly shaven, and the bandages were off his hand.

"What is this? Did you…?" Her eyes darted between his face and the soldiers dragging the bodies outside the window.

"Those were the orders."

"Why? Orders from whom?"

He sighed and put his cap on the desk. "Peters… Latsis… Dzerzhinsky… Trotsky… why does it matter? Orders are orders." He met her gaze impatiently.

"Who were they?"

"The people who got Uritsky killed. Traitors. Right here, inside the Petrograd Cheka. They leaked the information to Filonenko. That's how Reilly found out about our operation."

"All of them?"

He nodded gravely. "We had evidence."

"Evidence? Where did it come from? We had no evidence just two days ago."

He rubbed his forehead. "I don't know, Anna. It came from Peters."

"Did it go through the Commissariat of Justice? Was there a tribunal?"

"Peters and Dzerzhinsky had reviewed the evidence."

"There was no trial?" She was dumbfounded. "You executed people without a trial?"

"We had to. Peters asked me personally."

"Why you? I thought you were working on finding Savinkov."

"Savinkov has escaped to Paris. We have confirmation. He is not a threat; not for the time being."

"So, Peters put you on *this*?" A chilling realization formed. "Are you… Tell me you have nothing to do with this Red Terror thing in the papers today?"

"It is our new mandate."

"What do you mean?"

"Exactly what it sounds like, Anna." He locked his steely gaze on her. "What we've been doing up to this point isn't working! To curtail terror, we must instill terror. From now on, we are to exercise zero tolerance. For every communist who falls to the White terror, we are authorized to shoot ten."

"Ten of whom?"

"Any suspected counter-revolutionaries. Former imperial officers, opposing political parties, profiteers, bourgeois. We have the authority to arrest and execute without a trial."

"Can you hear yourself, Sergei? Why would we want that kind of authority?"

He sat on the edge of the desk. "Because it's the only way we can turn the tide. Open your eyes, Anna! We don't have the luxury to follow due process right now. Our enemies have brought the war right to our city streets. Our frontlines now run through Petrograd and through Moscow. We are fighting for survival. We have to eliminate, or we will be eliminated."

She did not know what to say. Was this the same Sergei she had known most of her life? His gaze was morose, and his jaw set with resolve.

"Do you know how insane that sounds?" She searched his eyes. "We are the Red *counter*-terrorism department. How can there be a *Red Terror*? How can we build a better tomorrow if we are standing knee-deep in blood?"

He smirked bitterly. "Don't be naïve, Anna! We signed on to defend the revolution. That means doing whatever it takes. Anyone can dream about a better tomorrow. Not everyone is willing to do what's necessary to make it happen. We must be prepared to spill blood for what we believe in. We can't keep playing by the same rules while our enemies play dirty! There must be consequences. The White Terror is spreading across our land like a plague. They butcher entire villages just for electing their own Soviets. They murder our leaders in our streets."

Anna shook her head. "But this isn't the way! This can't happen—"

"It *is* happening, Anna. It is already underway. Last night, we swept up 300 suspects in Petrograd. And another 500 in Moscow. Many of them will be executed today, and more will follow. We've been much too tolerant. We've taken one hit after another. But if you beat a dog long enough, even a good dog will turn vicious. From now on, that's what they get: we counter terror with terror."

He shook his head at her, exhausted. "Don't look at me that way. This is the way it has to be for now. We did not invent it. The French had to have the Reign of Terror after their revolution, too. They executed tens of thousands – that was the price they were willing to pay for liberty."

"That was over a hundred years ago! They cut off the heads of the aristocrats and carried them through the streets on pikes. Is that our real goal here? To incite a class war? Are we after the terrorists or the middle class here?"

"This has always been a class war! Since the revolution! The bourgeoisie is the breeding ground for counter-revolutionaries. They've been rotting our country from the inside for decades. They've been leeching off the working people like parasites. They are a festering wound that has to be cut out."

"And how deep should we cut?" She felt her pulse pumping at her temples and tried hard to contain her outrage from boiling over. "How about Lenin? Trotsky? Dzerzhinsky? They all came from wealthy families. Am I next, because my father owned a factory? How about my mother? Or Masha? Think about what you are saying! Just because I don't agree with how they live does not mean I want to see them put up against the wall! We are supposed to be changing people's minds, not killing them."

He let out a deep sigh and hung his head low and remained silent for a moment. Then he looked up at her, walked around the desk and took her hand.

"Of course. You are right. Those who are not guilty of counter-revolutionary activities have nothing to worry about. The Red Terror is just an instrument we *can* use – when we need to."

Outside the window, the soldiers dragged away the last body.

"Look, I know this is hard… for you. I know what happened before you transferred to my department," he said. "In Ekaterinburg."

Her pulse tightened and the heavy pit turned in her stomach again.

He squeezed her hand. "You never told me this, but... I know what happened. I can't even imagine what you had seen there. And now this... this must not feel any different."

A powerless tear welled up in her eye. "I had no say in that, Sergei. And... it was different. It was a strategic move, a single act that turned the course of the war. But this – this is different."

"But it is not, Anna. It is that same circumstance. The same single act, that we have to do over, and over, until we've won. We can't stop now."

He picked up his leather cap and held the metal star between his fingers. It glistened with red enamel.

"Do you ever look at this star? I look at it often. It is red for a reason. For me, it's red with the blood of my fallen comrades. With Alexei's blood. With Uritsky's, and with dozens of others. And now I am continuing down the path they had forged. They have sacrificed their all to get us here. I can't abandon this path now, just because I may have to do things I don't like. I must do them because someone has to do them. Because without them, the world we've been fighting for, the world Alexei died for, will not happen."

"The devil's arithmetic," she muttered to herself.

"What?"

"Nothing," she said and took a deep breath to clear out the tears.

He put the cap back on the desk and took both of her hands in his. He looked deep into her eyes – still Sergei, but so distant now, too far gone. He raised her hands to his chest and rocked them gently, as if in a desperate prayer to transport them both to a time long before or maybe long after this moment.

"Anna, I can protect you. I won't let Red Terror affect you. Nothing at all has to change for you. You just keep working the Reilly case for now, and then we'll figure out what's next. But I do need you now. I don't want to lose you. Are you still with me?"

His hands felt rough and, for the first time in her life, strange. She gently pulled one of her hands free and placed it over his.

"Yes. But you have to make me one promise."

"Anything."

"My parents and Masha are trying to leave the country. Please see that they do. Promise me they will get out safely."

He nodded. "You have my word."

She nodded and gently squeezed his hands before letting them go.

ACTIVE MEASURES

Two of the executed men turned out to be from Lavrov's department. Anna watched him work now, back in their task room, his gaze occasionally drifting off into the distance. Egorov seemed mostly his usual self, maybe a bit less cheery. She too tried to focus on the matter at hand. Whatever the events of the morning, whatever the new agenda from Moscow, Reilly still needed to be stopped.

She had received a message from Nekrasov – he had decoded the note she found in Reilly's apartment. She read it several times, considering her options. If she was right about what it meant, she did not see any. She called in Robins again to review the situation – perhaps he'd have some useful new intelligence. Everything seemed to have changed since yesterday.

Robins arrived with his young assistant again. The two of them studiously read the note and then re-read it.

"And that is all it said?" Robins asked.

She nodded.

"Baku. Consul MacDonell will assist transfer," Captain Arden read out loud. "Do you think this has something to do with the gold for the arms deal?"

She nodded again, tapping the end of a pencil on her lips.

"Why do you think that?"

"Our source in Samara has notified us that there are currently two armored trains there. Both are heavily guarded by the Czech Legion. One of them is being prepped to depart south for Baku in two days, while the other is going to go east to Omsk."

"So, you think this means Reilly is going to take the gold out of Russia via Baku instead of Vladivostok?"

She nodded.

"Why Baku?" William asked. "That seems too close to the Ottoman Empire. Too close for comfort for the British."

"Moscow says the British took Baku late last week to capture the oilfields." Anna cleared off the map on the table and circled the dot on the peninsula protruding like a falcon's bill into the Caspian Sea. "If Reilly wants to move the gold out of Russia, going through Baku is a faster route than through Vladivostok. She traced the line of the railroad across eastern Russia. "To get from Samara to Vladivostok, he would have to cross 5,000 miles of Siberia and fend off dozens of hostile warlords and Cossack armies. But to get to Baku," she traced the route south from Samara, "is just a quarter of that distance, and it is mostly through the territories controlled by the Whites."

Robins leaned over the map. "And from Baku, he can easily move the gold to Teheran. The Imperial Bank of Persia is a British colonial bank. Once the gold is there, the arms order can proceed with just a phone call."

Lavrov took off his glasses and rubbed his face. "Do we have any actual intelligence that either Reilly or the gold will be on this train to Baku?"

She shook her head. "No, but right now this is the only lead we have."

*

William had managed to cast a couple of curious long glances at Agent Sokolova – *Anna* – since he and Robins had arrived back to the Cheka task room on Gorokhovaya. She intrigued him. She was young, beautiful and intelligent, and she had a large Mauser pistol strapped to her belt and intense blue eyes he tried very hard not to gaze into inappropriately for too long. Her eyes seemed sadder today, and he felt it had to do with something more than just this British spy's gold train.

"OK, so if we assume that Reilly is going south to Baku instead of east to Vladivostok, that means it will now take him days instead of weeks to get the gold out of the country," Lavrov said.

They stood in silence for a moment, examining the map and considering the implications of that statement.

"So, that's it?" Egorov cut in gloomily. "We didn't get him in Moscow, we did not get him in Petrograd, and now he will ride that gold train all the way to Baku, and we can't touch him."

"Are there any Red Army divisions close enough to intercept the train between Samara and Baku?" Robins asked.

Lavrov shook his head "Not on such short notice. Our closest garrison is in Voronezh, and they would not be able to move fast enough and that far into the enemy territory to intercept. Not to mention, the Whites would see a large force coming from a hundred miles away."

"What if we could mobilize a much smaller, faster strike force?" Anna said.

Lavrov shook his head again. "You can't take on an armored train with a small force. You need at least a few hundred men and artillery. Even if we tried, our forces from Voronezh still won't get there in time to intercept." Lavrov was exasperated.

"Are you proposing to rob the gold train?" William asked Anna, unable to restrain a smile. "I thought that was something only we Americans did in the Wild West!"

"*Rob* is probably not the right word here," Robins smiled. "I've seen a few of these trains, and I am afraid the word *rob* does not even come close to what it would take. *Storming a fortress* may be a better way to describe it. A Russian armored train is a far cry from a Wells Fargo stagecoach. It's like a navy destroyer on rails."

Lavrov dug through the drawer of the desk and pulled out some files. "Here," he said, flipping through their contents. "We build armored trains for the Red Army at the Putilov factory right here in Petrograd."

He placed several photos and design drawings in front of them. William studied a photo of a blocky railroad car without windows crowned with two massive gun turrets at either end.

"These may be comparable to what they would use," Lavrov pointed to the photos. "These trains can be quite formidable, and each one is unique. The Whites don't have access to the production plants like we do in Petrograd and Moscow, so their trains are outfitted with whatever they have collected along the way. It could be anywhere from a few to a dozen wagons, armed with anything from machine guns to field artillery and even heavy naval guns."

He flipped through the blueprints of various train configurations. "Besides the armaments, they will usually also carry a raiding party consisting of cavalry and infantry onboard. All told, you may be up against 200 or more well-protected and armed men onboard."

"What about the armor?" William asked, fascinated with the concept.

"It depends on the part of the train, but usually anywhere between half an inch and one-inch-thick steel. Some areas like the sides of the locomotive may have more than one layer and may even have concrete between the layers. You'd definitely need artillery if you want to do any damage to it."

"But it's on rails, so can't you just blow up the tracks and put this thing out of commission?"

Lavrov nodded. "The railroad is its greatest weakness, so they protect it well. There will be scouts riding ahead of the train to spot for any sabotage or ambush. The trains also carry their own parts to repair any railroad damage."

"So, we need an army to stop it, but we can't get an army there in time," Egorov summed up, examining the map.

"What if…" Anna said. "What if this army did not have to travel so far?"

"Then where would it come from?" Lavrov stared at the map.

"What if we could get help from someone who already has a large army in the area, and who hates the Whites and the Allies as much as we do?"

"Oh, no!" Egorov shook his head. "No, no. Are you talking about Makhno? Have you gone mad?"

"Who is Makhno?" William inquired.

"He is the leader of the Anarchist Army!" Egorov said, visibly heating up.

"And you think he would help you stop this train?"

Egorov shook his head vigorously and Lavrov shrugged.

"Well," Robins replied, "as Comrade Sokolova noted, Makhno does hate the Whites and the Allies as much as the Reds do. He would definitely not want them to receive the arms shipment. Trouble is, he hates the Reds just as much."

Egorov nodded affirmatively, but Anna did not seem to register his agitated protests. William watched as she became completely consumed with the idea and began marking the map with her pencil and a ruler.

"Look here." She drew an X just above the Azov Sea. "Makhno's army is here, near Lugansk, and he controls the area all the way east past Yuzovka. Reilly's train will have to come through Rostov-on-Don here, and that is less than fifty miles from Makhno's territory!" She was getting visibly excited at the plan. "This could work! We would just need to intercept around Rostov before the train retreats deeper again into the White-controlled territory in the Caucasus."

Lavrov sat down in his chair, shaking his head and looking completely flabbergasted: "What are you suggesting? That we just call Makhno and ask him to stop the train for us?"

"Of course not." The corner of her mouth curved up into a tiny smug smirk. "We can't just *call* Makhno. We don't have his phone number…"

Egorov and William laughed out loud, but Lavrov was not amused.

"... we will have to go to him," she added nonchalantly.

Egorov stopped laughing.

"Anna, he is an anarchist!" he exclaimed. "He'll probably shoot us before we can even say hello!"

"That *is* a possibility," she nodded.

"We probably can't even get there in time..." Egorov made no attempt to veil the glimmer of hope in his voice. "If the train is leaving in two days..." He looked up at the ceiling and began folding his fingers, his lips silently counting the days.

Lavrov kicked his boots up on his desk and pensively smoothed his mustache. "Well, the armored trains *are* very heavy and can't travel fast," he admitted grudgingly. "And they have to stop for water and fuel regularly. This means it will take them two or three days to get from Samara to Rostov. So, if they are departing the day after tomorrow, that would give you around three and a half days to get to Makhno, convince him to help, and then travel with his army to Rostov if that's where you want to intercept the train."

Anna leaned over the map. "So, let's say it is a day's ride from Lugansk to Rostov with Makhno's army. That means we have two and a half days to get to Lugansk and persuade Makhno."

Lavrov looked at his watch and shook his head. "It's almost noon now, and Lugansk is about a thousand miles away. That's a lot of miles to cover in two and a half days, even by car. You don't know the condition of the roads south of Moscow, and you also don't know all the enemy locations."

"We will just have to take our chances. If we drive through the night, we should be able to make it in a day and a half." She looked to Robins: "Can we take your car? It is much faster and better equipped for something like this than our pool cars. Comrade Lavrov will gladly requisition a replacement for you."

Robins nodded: "Of course! You are kind to ask. That car belongs not to me but to the people's commissariat."

"Very well," she nodded. "Egorov and I will equip the car and will depart this afternoon."

Lavrov waved his hands. "Hold on – you are really going to do all this on just a hunch? Do you think Moscow will approve this?"

"They will," she reassured him. "Don't worry – I'll take care of Moscow. They won't want to miss a chance like this. The Cheka is all about active measures."

"OK, well, at least take some of my men, I can spare five or six." Lavrov reached for the phone. "Who knows what kind of reception you will get with the anarchists."

"Thank you, but no. If we show up with a squad of armed men, I doubt we will get a welcome reception. We don't need a show of force. Besides, we'll get there faster with just me and Egorov in one car."

William watched Egorov begin folding the map, having accepted his fate. At this moment, without the benefit of forethought, and forfeiting any possibility of better judgment, William heard these words come out of his own mouth: "I'd like to volunteer to go with you."

The room fell silent, and everybody's eyes fastened on him.

"What are you doing?" Robins whispered.

"It makes sense," he whispered back. "If Reilly's deal goes through, everything we've worked on will be jeopardized. If the Whites win, we will get nothing. If I can help, it's worth the risk."

"This is dangerous, my boy. It is not what you signed up for." He stared an unblinking stare into William's eye.

"I know," he nodded. "But we must do it to protect our investment."

Robins squinted at him and a small smile formed at the corner of his lips.

"You know, that is an excellent idea," he declared, turning to the group. "Having a Red Cross officer with you might help smooth things out. I am sure even the anarchists hold no ill will toward our organization."

Anna measured William with her penetrating gaze, as if trying to figure out what to make of him. He tried his best to look disarmingly sincere.

"I can't possibly ask you to do that," she said. "Getting to Makhno is going to be dangerous enough, and no one knows what will happen once we find him. There is a very strong possibility that you could be killed."

Egorov sighed and raised his eyes at the ceiling.

"Oh, I don't think that will deter this one." Robins gave William a whack on the shoulder. "This young man is a war hero – fought the Germans in France for two years. Adventure is in his blood."

William gave Anna a goofy smile meant to reassure her.

She raised an eyebrow: "Very well, Captain Arden. I accept your offer."

"Just William, please," he said and stood up, already feeling the rush of the upcoming adventure pumping through his veins. "I will prepare the car and come back to pick you both up. What time shall we say?"

"No need," she said tersely. "We'll meet you at the hotel in an hour."

"Thank you," she added, still looking puzzled by the arrangement.

ROADS

When William stepped out into the sunny street from the cool lobby of Hotel d'Europe, Anna was already waiting outside, smoking a cigarette and leaning on the side of the big Rolls-Royce. The car's mirror-like polish gleamed in the midday sun. She passed the cigarette to Egorov who was sitting on the curb next to the car's big wheel.

"So, this is the humble abode of the American Red Cross missionaries?" she said to William, glancing up at the stacked façade towering above the sidewalk.

She was wearing a short black leather peacoat. The top two buttons of her shirt were undone, and he could not help but momentarily fixate on the slender line of her neck and the alabaster-white curve of her collarbone.

"Yes," he smiled abashedly. "Not exactly understated, I know, but it is quite nice. Would you like to see inside?"

"No, thank you."

He felt like an idiot. "I suppose it's foolish of me to offer a tour of a Russian hotel to a Russian in Russia."

She glanced at him with restrained humor. She seemed to find him amusing. "I've seen it already," she said. "And Russians don't stay here. Not anymore. Not the honest ones, anyways. It might as well be in another country."

William nodded. "In either case, we probably should get going." He opened the back door of the car and tossed his travel bag onto the floor of the spacious rear passenger compartment.

"I've got some water and spare fuel." He tapped the two large canisters strapped down to the wide sidestep behind the spare tire.

"Good! We brought food." She picked up one of two rucksacks sitting at the curb and tossed it in after William's bag. Egorov lumbered up from the sidewalk, picked up the second rucksack and climbed into the back seat.

"I'll drive," Anna said.

*

On the map, the pencil-traced route from Petrograd to Lugansk fell steeply south from the Gulf of Finland almost all the way down to the Azov Sea, cascading along the jagged hair-thin veins of roads that connected the black dots labeled *Petrograd, Moscow, Voronezh* and *Lugansk*.

They had passed through Moscow in the night, stopping only to refuel. By the morning of the next day, they were already halfway from Moscow to Voronezh, and in the glowing light of the dawn, William could see that the dense northern woods of birch and cedar had thinned out overnight into sparse groves and grassy steppes.

The long, heavy car heaved up and down and side to side on its hefty leaf springs as Anna flew along the unpaved road, steering strategically to avoid potholes and deep wheel ruts. With the exception of the front windshield and the canvas top, the cabin of the Rolls-Royce was open, letting in warm air and the smells of late-summer countryside and dusty roads mixed with the occasional breath of hot motor oil and gasoline. Every now and then, William tuned his ear to the engine's roar, listening for any signs of trouble, only to be reassured by the even choir of a hundred mechanical tics, clicks and tiny detonations melding into a single deep vibration emanating from under the long, pitched line of the hood.

Having driven through the night, Egorov was now struggling to stay awake in the plush, sofa-like back seat. Anna drove fast. Too fast, perhaps, William thought. But as the golden fields flew by, he had to admit that sailing over the rough country roads of Russia in the long, smooth Rolls-Royce was a far cry from bouncing about in his father's Model-T over the dusty roads of rural Texas.

He cast a side glance at Anna. Having thrown himself into this journey with little thought, he had now had plenty of time to consider his reasons for doing so. Having itemized all the possibilities, he had to be honest with himself and admit that he couldn't care less about protecting the interests of the American International Corporation and that he was here now because he was utterly fascinated with his beautiful companion and he did not wish to see any harm come to her on this journey.

Anna swerved to avoid a rut, causing William to slide towards her on the smooth, button-tufted leather seat. In the back, Egorov plopped up and down with an "Oh!" as the car sailed over the uneven washboard surface.

William chuckled and she smiled, clearly taking delight in going fast.

"Have you traveled this far by car before?" he asked.

"No, but I can see why people like it," she replied.

"What's not to like? It is faster than the train and more comfortable than the horse. And of course, a Rolls-Royce is not just any car! What do you think of it?" He brushed the road dust off the gold clock on the wood-trimmed instrument panel.

She took stock of the cabin. "It's a bit overdressed for the Russian roads, but fast enough for our needs, I suppose."

"*A bit overdressed?*" he laughed. "The Rolls-Royce Silver Ghost is the most expensive, luxurious and technically advanced car in the world today. There really is nothing else like it! Eighty horsepower and the top speed of eighty-five miles an hour."

He had always been mechanically inclined and could not help but feel veneration at the genius of engineering that had conjured this machine out of a pile of raw materials. This car would have turned heads in any town in America. And yet this Russian Cheka girl did not seem impressed.

"And it's extremely reliable," he added in one last attempt to get her excited, already knowing it was going to be in vain. "Before the war, it underwent cross-country and alpine trials, and set numerous records. It was all over the papers!"

"And did you get to drive one of these in your country?" Anna asked disarmingly.

He shook his head with a grin. "Not in my wildest dreams! This car costs over $7,000 in America! That's more than most people make in ten years. It's the car of royalty and millionaires. As the press called it, *a car for the classes and not the masses.*"

"Well, I suppose the previous owner of this car would be aghast to find the likes of us using it as mere transportation," she smiled. "We might not be the classes your papers had in mind."

He looked at her and glanced back at Egorov, who was now passed out, sitting in the back seat. "We do sound like the opening line of a joke," he admitted.

"You mean the one about the two Chekists and an American going to see an anarchist about robbing an Englishman's train?" She laughed for the first time, and he saw the sadness in her eyes retreat.

"That's the one," he nodded with a smile.

A deep snore cut over the drone of the engine. Egorov's head rolled heavily from side to side as Anna navigated the car.

"So, what is your friend's story?" William asked, pointing back at the big fellow. "He does not talk much."

"Who, Anton?" she glanced back. "You want to know his story?

I suppose it is the same as of most of Russia. He is a peasant's son. His parents were serfs bound to a land estate near Kostroma."

"Serfs?" William was surprised. "As in *medieval* serfs? Weren't they basically slaves?"

"Yes. The Romanov dynasty had built their empire on slave labor. The serfs were bound peasants belonging to the landowners. Their lives, their families, and all of their possessions were the property of the landowners. The serfs could not even get married without the consent of their owners. Buying and selling serfs was still legal in Russia just fifty years ago when Tsar Alexander II abolished the practice. At that time, over ten million Russians were privately owned. Unfortunately, the reform was too limited and focused on minimizing the impact on the landowners. The serfs were obligated to keep working for their masters for two more years following the abolition. After that, few had money to buy their own land, and most had no choice but to keep working for the same landowners."

She slowed down to negotiate a washed-out part of the road.

"That is what happened to Anton's father. He died working another man's land and left his wife with four young boys. She was illiterate and unskilled, like most peasant women. She took any work she could find to support them. The boys too had to start working when they were young. When the war started, all of the brothers were drafted into the army and sent to the front. All but Anton were killed in the first year. At the front, he became involved with the soldiers' soviet and learned to read and write. After the revolution, he came home and found out that his mother had died while he was at the front. He ended up in Moscow and was one of the first to join the Moscow Cheka."

She glanced at William. "And that's the story of Anton Egorov, as he told it to me. He is a good friend and has saved my skin more times than I can count."

"His family had paid a terrible price for Russia."

She shook her head. "Not for Russia – for the old regime. Anton is the first in his family to fight for Russia."

"And what about you?"

"What about me?" She gave him a sideways glance, keeping an eye on the road.

"Well, for starters, where did you learn to speak English so well?"

"The perks of a privileged childhood. I had English and French tutors, and my father sent me to study in London one year."

"So, you came from an aristocratic family?"

"Not exactly. Bourgeoisie. New money – *nouveau riche,* as they say. My father opened several furniture factories and did quite well for our family. We were not born into high society, but the money did buy quite a few privileges and a few rungs on the social ladder."

"So, how does one go from the schooled-abroad socialite to a card-carrying Cheka agent?"

She smiled at his question. "I suppose I have my brother to thank. He opened my eyes. I watched him become consumed with political activism as I was growing up. He used to tell me: *We live in the largest country in the world, rich with every resource imaginable. There is no reason why every Russian should not be clothed, fed, and educated.* I guess he planted the seed of the revolution in my heart. He made me want to build a better world."

"What does he do now?"

"He was killed last year during the protests."

"I am sorry. I…"

"No need," she shook her head. "He died doing something he was passionate about. He knew the risks." She gave him a reassuring glance. "But enough about me. Tell me about you – how did a Texas boy end up in France fighting the Germans?"

He covered his eyes with his hand and shook his head.

"What?" she asked, laughing.

"I wish I could claim being compelled by my innate high ideals, but it would be more honest to attribute it to the naïvete of youth. All it took was just one recruitment poster at the South Plains Fair in Lubbock," he laughed, "and the next thing I knew I was on the boat to Europe with a rifle in hand and some silly romantic notion of saving the world in my head."

"There is nothing silly about saving the world," she flashed a smile, "but this truly must have been a very inspiring poster!"

"Indeed, it was exceptionally compelling. I can still see it clearly in my head. It depicted a monstrous ape wearing a Kaiser helmet, and in one hand he was dragging a bloody club, and in another he was grasping the swooned, half-nude body of Europa as a beautiful maiden. The ape had the ruins of Europe behind him, and he was stepping out of the ocean onto the American soil. After seeing that, all I wanted to know was where to sign."

"And so, you rushed to aid the damsel in distress?"

"I am afraid so. I was a hopeless romantic at eighteen."

"Did you succeed in your heroic quest?"

"I am afraid not. The situation was mis-advertised, to say the least. There were no brute apes at the front, and the only damsels I saw were the nuns who took care of me at the hospital at the very end."

"That would explain your fondness for women in uniform," she jabbed.

He laughed and they drove in silence for a few moments.

"Can you tell me about the war?" she gave him a glance. "What was it like from your experience? Anton does not like to talk about it."

William nodded and considered what to tell, staring at road unfolding ahead of them. The few stories that befitted social events in New York seemed insincere to share now.

"It was nothing like what I expected. Nothing at all like the stories about battles I read as a boy. In books, death was heroic and sterile. I was not prepared to see so much death. And most of it was not heroic. One should never have to get used to death. But we did, over the many months in the trenches. We had to, or we would have gone mad. Death was just always there with us. At any moment, the man next to you could be cut down by a sniper bullet or torn apart by an artillery shell. Our daily existence was in a very violent place. I've seen men die from bullets, disease, trench clubs, bayonets, mines, bombs, shells, planes, tanks and machine guns. So many died senselessly, without heroism or even dignity. I remember one cold October morning last year. We had been dug into the same trench for over two months. I was talking to my sergeant when I smelled almonds in the frosty air. Before I realized what was happening, my men down the line collapsed to their knees, wheezing and vomiting."

He had not thought of that memory for so long. And now, the images, the smells and sounds were pulling him in again.

"A German gas attack?" she asked.

He shook his head. "No. French. They had fired canisters of hydrogen cyanide gas at the German side. But they did not realize that this gas was lighter than chlorine or mustard gases. It did not sink down into the German trenches. Instead, the breeze carried it across No Man's Land toward us. By the time we got our masks on, five of my men were dead. Just like that, they were gone."

She did not react with the horror or indignation he had expected. But he could tell it wasn't from indifference but quite the opposite. It was from the kindred experience of someone who had first-hand lived through a senseless loss and still felt it deeply.

"I had to write letters to their families. I told them that their sons and husbands died heroically for the great cause. It was a lie, but I couldn't tell them that their deaths were senseless and unfair. None of it was fair. No matter how I rationalized it, this was a mistake that was both no one's fault and everyone's fault. Everyone was just following orders. I realized that the war had become a self-sustaining machine that took lives whenever it wanted, and any control we thought we had over it was just an illusion."

He gazed into the steppe racing past his window and pulled away from the reel replaying in his head.

He smiled and turned to Anna: "So, tell me about this new world you want to build."

She smiled back. "What do you want to know?"

"What do you want it to be like?"

"Fair," she said.

A town appeared on the horizon.

SOMEWHERE ELSE

The Red Army garrison in Voronezh was the final outpost of Red Russia along their way and the last opportunity to top off fuel and water until Lugansk. Unlike in Petrograd, where fall was in the air, here it was still the high heat of summer, and every breath Anna inhaled was humid, hot and dusty.

While William refueled the car and the spare canister, Egorov walked back up the hot dusty road to the nearby market to purchase provisions. Two cavalry officers rode up to the car to strike up a conversation and investigate the fancy car, the girl driving it, and the man in the foreign uniform. They were both young and Anna could tell both wanted to impress her.

She redirected their enthusiasm towards something useful by producing her map and asking them for the best routes to Lugansk. They studied the map with resoluteness, pointing to the various roads, discussing the merits of going through this town or that one, and authoritatively disagreeing with each other. By the time Egorov returned with a couple of wrapped packages and a newspaper under his arm, Anna had her map marked with half a dozen penciled Xs designating reported enemy positions.

She settled back into the driver's seat and started the car.

"They said there is a build-up of Denikin's forces around Belgorod, but we should be able to avoid them if we keep east. We are making good time – I think we will reach Lugansk by nightfall."

Having thus lifted the spirits of her team, she got back onto the main road and headed out of the town, towards the lush grassy expanse and green groves extending all the way to the horizon.

"So, have we officially left Red Russia?" William asked as they crossed a bridge over a narrow river.

She nodded.

He gave her and Egorov a concerned look. "Did you two bring any other clothes? Won't the Red uniforms invite people to shoot at us?"

She smiled and shrugged. "It won't matter. In this car, we are going to draw attention no matter what. We just need to not run into any of the Whites. We are hooking far enough east, so that shouldn't be a problem."

"Hey, look at that – our man made it onto the front page of the local paper!" Egorov passed the newspaper to the front.

Anna glanced down at the front-page article that looked to be re-printed from the Petrograd papers. Reilly's bulging eyes and full bottom lip seemed even more pronounced in the poor-quality print.

"So, what will happen to this Reilly, if we manage to catch him alive?" William asked.

"A bullet to the head would be a good place to start," Egorov said morosely.

Anna shook her head. "I am sure Moscow will want to talk to him first. He will be interrogated and tried. Then, given his role in the attempt on Lenin, he will likely be executed, unless our government decides to trade him back to the British for something or someone of value."

"You must admire him on some level."

"Admire!?" His comment incensed her. "What are you talking about?"

"Professionally, I mean. He has managed to maintain three identities, infiltrate the Cheka, set off several major plots against your government and has evaded capture so far. The man's got talent."

"I suppose if we consider being good at lying and manipulating people a talent, then yes, I guess he has a talent. But that hardly makes him someone I would admire. From what I've seen, he seems to be a man with no decency and no loyalties except to his own ends. Did you know that he lived with two women in Moscow? And he lied to both of them about who he was. He worked his way into their lives, got them to betray their country and got what he needed from them. And now they will be executed for treason, and he has hightailed out of town."

William nodded, "I see your point. He does exhibit extreme moral flexibility. I am not saying this in his defense, but I am sure in his mind the end goal justified the means."

Before Anna could respond, Egorov's big hand appeared between them, pointing into the sky up ahead. "Look!" he said.

Anna looked, and after a while made out a dark speck in the blindingly bright blue sky. The speck was growing larger. In a few seconds, she heard the insect-like droning over the sound of their own engine. The dot gleamed in the sun and turned into a biplane that roared over them and disappeared behind the trees. Egorov stuck his head out of the back window, eyes squinting under his hand pressed into the forehead. After a few intense, silent moments, the plane emerged again from behind the woods and caught up with them on the left side, probably expecting to see the driver. The plane dipped its wings towards them, and Anna saw the pilot's goggles glint with reflected light as he examined William's side of the Rolls-Royce. She saw the banded circles of red, blue and white on the wings – White Army. William gave the pilot a short salute with his left hand. The plane pulled up, made a long arc above them, and headed back west.

"The Whites?" William asked.

"The Whites," Egorov responded.

"Probably heading to the frontline for reconnaissance," William said.

"Well, at least he saw your uniform and not ours. If he could make it out, hopefully he will assume we are with the Allies."

She glanced at the map on the seat next to her. "Let's hope that's as close as we are going to get to them. We should be crossing the river soon, and then it's maybe five hours to Lugansk," she said, accelerating through the straight stretch of the road.

Indeed, after a few miles they turned right at a crossroads, where the map promised to lead them to a bridge. Anna shifted down, smoothly accelerating out of the turn, but then immediately yanked on the handbrake, causing the large car to skid to an abrupt stop and Egorov to fly off his seat forward, and his surprised face to suddenly appear, punched in between her and William. The engine stalled, and in the ensuing silence, all of their eyes were fixed on the road ahead. There, past a grove and barely fifty yards away was the bridge they needed, and at the bridge was a cordon of half a dozen soldiers on horseback and a flat wagon with a machine gun mounted on it. The soldiers were looking at them.

The dust was still settling around the car, as her fingers were already frantically fiddling with the fuel mixture, the gears and the throttle to get the engine going again. She watched with concern as the grey-uniformed gunner turned the end of the heavy barrel towards them and the riders began to approach the car with their rifles on the ready.

"The Whites?" William asked, as Egorov got out his revolver and counted the bullets in the drum.

"The Whites!" Anna gritted through her teeth.

The engine revved to life, and she launched the car forward. She spun a hard left, and the massive Rolls carved a broad arc right in front of the enemy, bucking across the road, spooking the horses and raising a cloud of dust. When they emerged from the dust on the other side, they were speeding away from the bridge.

She kept her foot firmly on the accelerator, no longer worried about avoiding the minor ruts and potholes. The car was jolting violently over the rough road, but her sole focus was on getting them out of there alive. In this moment, she found herself being grateful to this overpriced marvel of British engineering which was getting them out of here with such confident, easy haste.

Even without looking back, she knew the Whites were giving chase. Gunshots popped over the roar of the engine, the noise of the road, and the merciless thrashing of the car's chassis against the ruts and the bumps. A few bullets thumped into the back of the car and tore through the canvas top.

In the passenger seat, William was weathering this wild ride with composure, having latched himself firmly onto one of the roof supports and monitoring their pursuit through the oval cut-out of the rear window. In the back, Egorov managed to stop rolling around and had wedged himself, facing backwards, against the back seat. Having secured himself in this position, he stuck his gun out of the window and began retuning fire. But the chase did not last long. As the car quickly built up speed, the sounds of gunshots faded. When Anna glanced back, she saw only the trail of dust behind them.

The road was taking them east again, and they needed to get back on course heading south, towards Lugansk. She tasked William with finding a detour on the map.

"That was close," he remarked, studying the paper terrain.

"Too close," she agreed. "The Whites aren't supposed to be this close to Voronezh."

"Could you tell whose army they belonged to?"

"It's hard to tell in these parts. Could be Denikin, or Alekseev, or Wrangel, or Yudenich. In this area, the frontlines can shift daily."

The detour turned out to be a single-track country road cutting through fields of wild golden wheat. As she sped through, making up for the lost time, she considered the prudence of continuing deeper into the enemy territory. *How did Reilly do it, month after month?* She knew the risk; she knew exactly what would happen if they were caught. The Whites made an example of any captured Bolsheviks, and for captured Chekists, it was the worst. A few days ago, she would have probably felt differently, but today she was not inclined to turn around. Here, in this vehicle hurling her deeper into danger with each passing minute, she felt more at peace with herself than she would in Petrograd or Moscow right now. Here, there was clarity.

She knew that even Egorov, despite his grumblings, would not be anywhere else right now but here, protecting her – the big brother role he had taken on with such comforting ease since the first day they met. She did not ask him to be here. But she never had to.

She glanced at William. The American probably had the highest chance of surviving this. The Whites would not knowingly harm an ally, even one caught with two Chekists. She was not sure what to make of him. He seemed utterly, disarmingly earnest, despite whatever role he had to play in the self-serving Red Cross Mission charade. What was he doing with them? This boy, around her age, who had already lived through a year of hell in Europe – why was he really here?

She wondered what was going on in Petrograd. By now, Lavrov must have found out that she had not cleared her little operation with Moscow. She smiled to herself. She wondered who was furious. Did Sergei take it all the way up to Dzerzhinsky? What would they do with her when she returned? *If* she returned. Memories of Sergei had turned into a deep sorrow, but she swallowed down the rising tears. Was he right? Was she just being naïve? She felt like a child sometimes, playing pretend among the adults.

Next to her, William was vigilantly watching the road ahead for any signs of danger. She watched too, but they seemed to be in the clear now. It had been almost two hours since their encounter at the bridge, and they had not seen any more signs of the enemy. Or anyone else, for that matter. Just mile after mile of the steppe. No matter how fast she sped through it, it seemed it would never end.

The steady hum of the engine stuttered, disrupting her thoughts. The car lurched forward a few times and she felt it lose power. The exhaust sputtered, popped, and then the engine went completely silent. She coasted it quietly to a stop.

"We need to refuel," she said and got out of the car.

William followed to stretch out. Egorov climbed out of the back and went around to the other side to fetch the spare gas canister. A few seconds later, she heard a barrage of choice Russian expletives, some unfamiliar even to her. She turned to see Egorov shake the spare gas can in the air and launch it into the field, sending a few more insults after it.

"Bullet hole," she succinctly interpreted to a puzzled William and reached for the map inside the cabin.

She followed the line of the road with her pencil and marked the spot where she thought they were now. She assessed the remaining length of the thin line stretching towards Lugansk. It would have taken them maybe another hour to reach the city by car, but now it seemed an impossible distance to cover. William and Egorov leaned in to see the map. There were only two towns – or most likely small villages – along the way. She pointed to the first one – a small grey dot labeled Zachinka that looked to be about twelve miles away on the map.

"Let's hope we can find some transportation there," she said and checked her watch. It was almost one in the afternoon.

"Do you think we can still make it to Lugansk in time?" William asked.

"As long as we reach Makhno by nightfall tomorrow. Otherwise, we risk missing the window to intercept the train."

There was nothing else left to do but to top off their canteens with water, grab their bags and set off on foot down the dusty road. Walking away, Anna looked back one last time at the grand-ducal Rolls-Royce glimmering on the side of the road like a misplaced relic from another civilization. The vast Ukrainian steppe was about to swallow it out of sight.

"You are right – the Rolls-Royce is a good car," she admitted to William. "But do you suppose they had anyone shooting guns at it during all those tests and trials you mentioned?"

"No, I do not believe they did," he conceded.

"Doesn't it seem like an oversight?"

*

Zachinka was not a village. Not anymore, at least. The patch of white that had beckoned William in the sea of green for the last half hour turned out to be the crumbling side of a whitewashed wall of a hut. The village looked like the war had rolled through it years ago, and the dozen or so remaining houses now stood reduced to carcasses of walls and chimneys protruding from the ground and besieged by the advancing tide of grass and saplings.

"I don't think they have transportation," Egorov said, taking off his army cap and wiping sweat from his forehead.

The sun was hanging low over the horizon. Anna knocked the dust off her boots and pulled out her map. "Well, we are still about twenty-five miles away from Lugansk," she said. "And the next village is about ten miles away."

William put down his rucksack. His feet were burning from the long march and he had a stinging blister on his heel. Egorov grunted and stretched out in the grass next to the road, closing his eyes and covering his face with his cap.

"It's going to get dark soon," he said, glancing at the glowing horizon in the west. "We should spend the night here and head out at first light."

She nodded. "Let's hope the next town has a car and a telephone – we need to get an update on the train."

Zachinka was situated at the edge of a birch grove next to a creek. They chose the ruin of a house by the water and cleared off a patch of the dirt floor to build a fire. While Egorov and Anna gathered straw and firewood, William went down to the creek to fill the flasks. The sun dipped below the plain, and shadowless twilight fell all around him in the cool dampness of the ravine.

Breeze rustled through the trees overhead, and one by one, cicadas began probing the approaching night with their resounding buzz. It was peaceful here. The water was clear and cold. He walked back to the house looking at the first few stars shimmering brightly in the deepening indigo sky.

The fire was just big enough to make the inside of the four ruined walls feel homey. Settling next to it on a heap of hay, Egorov produced a knife and a few bundles from his rucksack. He unwrapped one to reveal a round loaf of bread. The other one contained a small white slab. He cut a few slices from the slab and offered it to William along with the bread.

"Salo?" he said with a nod.

"Thank you. What is it?" William asked, tearing off a piece of bread and taking a white, buttery slice. He passed the bundle to Anna.

"It's salt-cured pork belly. Kind of like bacon but cured like a ham instead of fried," Anna explained.

William took a bite. The salo had a scent of garlic and black pepper. Its light, creamy saltiness melted into the sweet, chewy crust of the sourdough. It tasted like bliss.

"This is a welcome improvement over the road dust I've been chewing on for the past three hours," he said and nodded to Egorov.

Egorov laughed and outstretched his hand to William again, this time holding a flask – "Vodka?"

William raised the flask to Egorov, took a swig and wiped his mouth. The vodka coursed downward and spread through his body like a wave of fire, instantly dulling the soreness from two days on the road. He passed the flask to Anna.

Egorov grinned and gave him a hearty slap on the back. "I think a few more days of salo and vodka, and we will turn you into a proper Russian, yet," he said, making Anna laugh.

"I don't think Mr. Robins would appreciate it." She took a drink and passed the flask back to Egorov. "We should try our best to return Mr. Arden to Petrograd in his original condition."

Night had fallen around them as they finished eating. The light of the fire bounced softly off the walls, playing with the shadows and mesmerizing William's gaze. Egorov piled up the straw higher and stretched out on this makeshift bed with his eyes closed. Anna leaned back and gazed into the sky through the non-existent roof over their heads.

"I forgot how many stars you can see out in the country," she said.

William had to tear his gaze away from the line of her neck and the profile of her face glowing in the light of the fire. Her eyes sparkled with reflected flames. He piled up his own heap of straw and lay back, taking in the black vastness of the sky alight with a myriad of stars.

"This reminds me of my childhood," he said. "I used to lie in the field on our ranch, staring at the stars. The longer I stared, the more stars I could see."

"Did you ever think you would be a traveler when you grew up, and one day would be looking at the stars from another side of the world?"

"No, I don't think I ever did."

"So, what did you think you would be when you grew up?" Anna asked, turning her flushed face towards him.

He laughed. "An outlaw, like Billy the Kid. For a while, I even insisted that everyone call me Billy instead of Will."

She smiled. "So, what happened, *Will*? Why aren't you an outlaw?"

"You know, I don't know..." He puzzled the mystery for a moment, having never in all those years asked himself that question. He liked the way Anna's mind worked – with the cleverness and intelligence of someone who had lived through and seen many things, and yet with the childlike directness and fearlessness most people lost when they grew up.

"I suppose my mother is to blame," he finally said. "She succeeded in teaching me manners and not to take what is not mine. And then, when I got older, I learned that Billy the Kid was never the free-spirited American Robin Hood I had idolized as a child."

"What was he, then?"

"A murdering, self-serving lowlife with no conscience."

She took a swig from the flask and passed it to him. The vodka went down much too smoothly, and he thought to himself that this was probably enough for him.

"Well, perhaps he was both," she said.

"What do you mean? Both what?"

"Both the lowlife and the idol. His spirit – it resonated with you as a growing boy, as it did with millions of other people in your country. The spirit of rebellion and freedom – don't we all have it to some degree? We all want to rise above everyone and everything that wants to control us."

William shook his head. "Freedom is one thing. But the things he did… we must all be responsible for our actions."

She turned her face back towards the stars. "Precisely! We *are* responsible for our own actions. And so, you are not responsible for his. You should not feel guilty to admire some of his traits and not the others. I don't think a person can be summed up just from everything they've done. Think of the things you had to do in war. How much of you do they define now? And if my father only knew some of the things his daughter and her revolutionary friends were doing, he probably would have called the Okhrana himself! But that does not mean my father did not love me. You don't have to reject what Billy the Kid meant to you just because you reject some of his actions. His spirit was just as true as the fact that he was only a human, and a murderer and a thief."

She took another swig from the flask. "And besides, stick with us long enough, and you'll get to rob your first train yet." She gave him a coy smile.

He laughed. "And what about you? What did you want to be?"

"An explorer," she said without a pause.

His smile widened.

"Are you laughing at me?" Her sparkling eyes fixed on him.

"No, not at all. I just pictured you outfitted in a big fur coat, fur boots, and one of those massive fur hats."

"You don't think that look would become me?"

"I think you would pull it off better than anyone I know. But why an explorer?"

"I had always felt the draw of the new, the undiscovered, for as long as I can remember. My parents said that once I learned to walk, I had to be watched constantly at our country estate – I would just wander off. Evidently, I went missing a few times, causing quite a stir. Growing up, I read the stories of Kipling and Jack London and could not wait to experience the world."

Her face glowed, flushed with the fire, the vodka and the daydream.

"Was that hard... for a girl? Weren't most explorers in those books men?"

"Honestly, it never bothered me. As a child, I did not see a difference between what a man could do and what a woman could. My father had created his fortune from nothing and had always told me that I could accomplish anything I wanted to."

"So, your turn now." William propped himself up with his elbow and gave her a devious smile. "What happened? Why are you not slashing your way through the jungles of Bolivia or riding a camel across the Sahara right now?"

She gazed into the fire, and the daydream faded from her face. "I became a revolutionary instead."

"What was *that* like?"

She considered for a moment. "Like a hard lesson. One you can't unlearn. You realize that the world is like those street posters in the city – the ones that get covered by another, and another, until no one knows what is under them all. But you pick at the corners and begin to peel it all off, piece by piece, because you want to know. That's what I did. And what I found was a fundamental injustice – the ugly, unforgivable truth covered up with all the other versions of the world I thought I knew. And with each piece I peeled off, I saw that it went deeper than I had ever expected, to the very core of this country, and maybe the whole world. It permeated all, yet we were taught to not see it. Somehow, I grew up not seeing that the great majority of Russians lacked not only equality and opportunity, but also the basic necessities like food, clothes and education. And the world around me was rigged to keep it that way. To keep certain classes, races, and genders powerless. To keep giving more to some, and to keep denying others."

"So, what did you do?"

"Same as you did after you saw that recruitment poster. I had to act. I found others like me, wanting change. And together we pushed against the system. And the system pushed back, and with so much force. And when it killed my brother, I decided I no longer wanted to change it – I wanted to eradicate it."

Her voice was getting softer. She turned onto her side towards him and closed her eyes. A log cracked in the fire, and a flare of sparks rushed swirling upward. He watched as they disappeared among the stars.

"I am sorry you did not grow up to be an explorer. But I think if the girl you once were met you today, she would be rather impressed and inspired by you."

"You too," she said dreamily, after some delay, without opening her eyes.

"I'll take the first watch; you get some sleep," he said, sitting up and stoking the fire with a stick.

*

He must have drifted asleep. He realized that in a split second when nearby rustling suddenly pricked him awake. He opened his eyes to a silhouette of a large figure blocking the night sky above him.

"Who are you?" William tried to sit up, feeling around for something to use as a weapon and fuzzily attempting to sort through the Russian words jumbled in his mouth. "Red Army? White Army?"

"Black Army, bitch," a man's deep voice replied and knocked him out with the butt of a rifle.

FREE TERRITORY

William came to with the measured squeak of a wheel circling ceaselessly in his ear. He squinted his eyes open to the painfully bright light and the white fuzzy blotches of clouds floating in the blue sky. He was lying on his back in an open wagon. He lifted his hands to find them tied with a rough burlap rope. He could tell his feet were likewise secured. He nudged himself across the thin layer of straw and propped up as best as he could against the low side of the wagon. Anna and Egorov were sitting up against the opposite side. They were also tied up, and Egorov had a large bruise on his forehead.

William took stock of the situation. Beyond the side rail of the wagon, the same grassy steppe as yesterday was rolling by. At the front of the wagon, the view was obstructed by the broad back of what must have been an enormous man in a white peasant shirt. Next to him, dwarfed by comparison, sat a man in a black papakha hat, holding a rifle across his lap.

Behind the wagon, a dozen riders were following them. They rode at a leisurely gait and in a relaxed, noncommitted grouping no one would ever mistake for a military formation. Their attire, equally flexible in its commitment to a single style, was a mismatched assortment of military uniform articles sourced from disparate armies and branches of service. He recognized the coats from Austrian, German, and Russian militaries, and several others he did not know. This motley band was armed to the teeth, with rifles slung over their shoulders, bandoleers of bullets draped across their chests, and a mobile arsenal of pistols, sabers, daggers, and even grenades tucked into their belts. Their faces were youthful and cleanly shaven, and their long hair sprouted in bunches from under their military hats and caps – all *sans* the insignia, naturally. Given their wild appearance and affinity for weaponry, William decided they were bandits.

He turned his attention back to his companions. Egorov looked grumpy, throwing occasional hateful gazes at the back of the giant driving the wagon. Looking at the welt on his forehead, William recognized in it the likely explanation for his own splitting headache. He touched his forehead to confirm this suspicion and recalled the rude awakening and the fleeting encounter with the rifle butt in the night. Anna's face looked untouched.

He cleared his throat. "I thought you were all about gender equality in this country. Where is yours?" he said, pointing to the throbbing bump on his head.

The corner of her mouth curled in a small smile. "Are you proposing I must allow myself to get hit in the head for the sake of equality with men?

"And besides, I thought you were going to keep the first watch?" she added.

He hung his head in an exaggerated show of shame. "I was just now hoping you did not hear that last night," he said. Egorov gave him a reproachful glare from under the low brow.

"Who are they?" William asked, nodding in the direction of their escort.

"Makhno's army. They are taking us to him."

"Oh, well, see – this has worked out splendidly," he said, trying to make himself comfortable against the hard boards of the wagon. His head was splitting, and he wanted to close his eyes again. "I hope he won't shoot us quite right away."

*

The distant sounds of children shouting pulled William out of the state of semi-conscious stupor induced by the heat and the hypnotic consonance of the endlessly echoing squeak of the turning wheel and the lazy monotone beat of the hooves. He looked at his watch, edging the ropes down on his wrist. It was almost noon. Grey storm clouds were gathering on the horizon behind them.

Anna gave him an inquisitive look, and he stretched his neck over the side railing to see past the front of the wagon. Up ahead, in the low grassy valley at the edge of a forest was a scattering of white huts. "It's a village," he said.

The village was small and simple but not shabby, he observed. Not like some of the war-torn, broken-up settlements he had seen in Europe. Neat, whitewashed walls and thatched straw roofs rolled past – one-story huts with plots framed in stretches of low, woven-branch fencing. A few white goats were grazing in one yard. In another, an old woman picking apples from branches hanging low under the weight. A band of barefoot children ambushed the wagon, shouting and brandishing sticks and chasing after it, scattering spooked chickens from the road. William smelled the rain approaching.

Their cavalcade rolled into the yard of a large house with brightly painted orange shutters and a garden of tall, colorful flowers rocking in the breeze. At the front of the house sat a man with a trench coat draped on his shoulders. He was running a sharpening stone along the edge of a saber in smooth, unhurried strokes that carried through the yard in languid, metallic swooshes.

The man looked up, hearing the wagon and the horses. He put down the sharpening stone and picked up a cigarette off the bench, watching them.

The giant hopped down from the driver's seat and walked around to the back of the wagon. One by one, he untied Anna, William and Egorov, and helped them get down to the ground. From the front, he was a barrel-chested, round-faced and rosy-cheeked farm boy in his mid-twenties with short, sun-bleached hair. Evaluating his mountain-like frame against the sky, William concluded that he was the most probable match to the dark figure responsible for knocking him out in the middle of last night. With amusement, he noted that Egorov, himself of an imposing stature under any other circumstance, was unaccustomed to having to look up at anyone, and now seemed visibly uneasy around the big peasant who stood almost a head taller than him. William nudged Anna with a smirk and nodded at the odd pair.

The man on the porch stood up and slid the saber into the scabbard on his belt.

"That's Makhno," Anna whispered to William, watching the man walking towards them.

The rest of the motley riders had dismounted and now stood nearby, watching the meeting unfold and awaiting the outcome, likely hoping it would precipitate that their services be required for the purpose of shooting the new guests.

William examined the approaching figure with curiosity. The leader of the anarchists had a boyish frame. Despite his shorter stature and a slim build, he carried himself with calm confidence. Like most of his merry men, he looked youthful and was cleanly-shaven, with long, dark hair parted in the middle, cascading down in waves past his smooth cheekbones. Only when he got closer did William discern the fine wrinkles on his forehead and at the corners of his eyes, placing his likely real age in the thirties. As with the others, his cavalryman's uniform was stripped of any signs of rank or regiment.

The rosy-cheeked farm giant reached into the front of the wagon, gathered Anna's and Egorov's pistols in his shovel-sized hand and tossed them on the ground at Makhno's feet. Makhno brushed the raven's wing of hair from his high forehead, cocked his head to the side and inspected the visitors from head to toe with a mischievous gaze.

"Reds!" he finally declared, and a wide smile beamed across his face, making his cheeks dimple. "And what is this? An American?" He studied William's uniform.

"What an uncommon commission." He took a step back and rubbed his chin. His grin subsided into a slender smile of dreamy contentment. "I must say, many people come, wanting to join our army, but they normally don't demand to see me. So, who are you, and what do you want?"

"I must disappoint you," Anna said. "We are not here to join your army. I am Agent Sokolova, and this is Agent Egorov. We are with the Cheka. And this is Captain Arden of the American Red Cross," she nodded towards William. "We have a proposition for you."

"American Red Cross?" Makhno's lips rearranged into a puzzled twist as he examined William with amusement. "You don't look like a doctor to me," he noted. "This is indeed one very peculiar delegation. But regardless, I welcome you to the Free Territory." He spread out his hands, sweeping the horizon in a hospitable gesture. "Now, what is it that I can do for you, Commissars Sokolova, Egorov, and Arden?"

"We need your help stopping an armored train."

He smiled again. "And why would I do that for the Bolsheviks?"

"Because if this train makes it to Baku, the Whites will have hundreds of British tanks rolling over these fields before the end of the year."

Makhno was silent for a moment, stroking his chin and studying the visitors. Finally, he slapped his hands together: "All right, in that case, let's hear it." He turned towards the house and waved them to follow.

Inside, they settled at a long table in a large room with a map hanging on one wall and a black battle flag riddled with bullet holes on another. The flag carried a white skull with crossbones and the words *Death To Those Who Stand In The Way Of Freedom Of The Working People!* Makhno's giant followed them in and wedged himself on the bench at the other side of the table.

Makhno poured them tea from a dented brass samovar while listening to Anna's recap of Reilly's plot.

"So, this train is leaving Samara tomorrow?" he asked, keeping the third cup for himself after Egorov politely declined.

"That was our initial intelligence. I will need to call Moscow to get an update from our source."

"Sugar?" he offered, pushing a small bowl of cubes towards them. "We don't have a telephone here, but I can have someone take you to Lugansk – it's not far." He sipped his tea. "And this man – Reilly – he will be on the train with the gold?"

"That is correct. We would need him alive, if at all possible. But the train is the priority. It must be stopped by whatever means necessary." Anna took a sip from her cup.

Makhno walked over to a map on the wall, stirring the spoon in his cup.

"I think we should intercept the train before it gets to Rostov," Anna said. "There are too many White reinforcements there."

He nodded. "I agree. I think the terrain here, north of Aleksandrovsk, would be most advantageous for an ambush." He circled his finger on the map. "It's away from any major White outposts, and it's less than a day's ride from here. But moving my men that far into the enemy territory is still very risky."

He studied the map, stirring his tea. At last, he turned around and set the tea on the table.

"All right, Commissar Sokolova. I'll do it, but on two conditions."

William watched Anna in her negotiation with the leader of the anarchists. If she were nervous, she was not showing it. Across from her, Makhno was casually businesslike. Egorov seemed more relaxed now as well, probably assuming that the negotiations meant they were not going to be shot, although William suspected it was too early to rule anything out just yet.

"First, my people will keep the gold," Makhno said.

She shook her head. "I can't do that," she said quietly but firmly.

"*Can't?*" Makhno burst in laughter. "How do you intend to stop me, Commissar?"

"I won't have to stop you – you will stop yourself. You have the reputation of being a man of honor who serves the interests of the common people. I know you will not keep the gold that the Russian people have earned with their blood, and that now has been stolen from them. This gold will help feed and clothe our people through the winter. I can't give you all the gold. But I will split it with the people of the Free Territory."

Egorov darted a worried look at her, but she kept her gaze on Makhno.

Makhno crossed his arms and gave her a long, penetrating stare. He grinned. "Very well, Commissar. I admire your verve and your devotion to your people. Half it is! You have my word."

Anna nodded. "And what is your other condition?" she asked.

"My army will keep the train, which means it must not be destroyed or disabled."

"You must be joking!" she said and glanced at William and Egorov for confirmation.

"I assure you, I am not," Makhno said. "The road there is risky enough and taking the train will require considerable effort. I might as well keep it – my Cossacks could really use it to defend our land."

"Are you mad?" Anna was bewildered. "Surely you are aware that a train like that has enough firepower to kill a thousand men. And if we must not derail or disable it, taking it will be practically impossible! It will cost you so many more lives of your men."

Makhno watched her calmly. "My men will be willing to take that risk. I guess you have to decide if you are willing to take that bet, too. This train is no use to me if it is disabled deep in the White territory. If I can't drive it out of there, you have no deal." His grey eyes squinted at her. "So, what are you willing to risk in order to stop this train?"

She looked at Egorov and William; they both gave her silent nods.

"OK, you have a deal," she said.

Makhno smiled and put out his hand to shake.

The giant murmured something in Ukrainian and Makhno laughed: "Petro has just reminded me of the old Russian proverb – *it's bad luck to measure the bear's skin before you kill the bear.*

"So, here is to killing the bear!" he said, raising his teacup.

Outside, thunder rumbled, and drops began softly pelting the thatched roof.

*

Makhno directed Petro to return to Anna and Egorov their guns. Anna checked her Mauser before sliding it back into the holster. With a grin, the giant also presented William with a Colt revolver that had somehow ended up in the anarchist's arsenal.

Anna watched William fit the heavy chunk of classic American iron to his hand with a smile.

"Do you like it?" she asked.

"It has a nostalgic feel," he said. "The service pistol I had in France was the 1911 semi-automatic. It's a good pistol, but it's modern and angular, without much personality." His thumb traced the elegant curve of the handle of this descendant of the infamous American peacemaker. The gun molded into his hand with ease, directing his index finger to rest naturally on the thin curve of the trigger. He turned the cylinder a few times and they heard the confident mechanical clunks of the firing chambers.

Petro returned with a small, bouncy car to drive them to Lugansk, to a rural post office with a telephone. The rain had moved on, leaving only the mirrors of puddles in the road and the fresh grassy smell over the steppe.

Anna listened to the clicks as the call was connected and transferred several times. Sergei was back in Moscow and picked up in his office. There was familiar gravel in his voice – he had been smoking too much. She felt a pang of sorrow hearing him again.

"Anna! Are you OK? Where are you?" He sounded worried.

"Yes. We are in Lugansk now." She forced herself to detach.

She heard him sigh. "Are you completely insane?! To pull off something like this, without even telling me!? Peters had just about lost it when he found out." He came across sullen.

She gazed into the bright light of the window. In the sunlight, she could see the car with William engagingly narrating something to Egorov and Petro.

"There was no time. You had asked me to take care of Reilly, and I had a very small window of opportunity to act."

He sighed again darkly. He was displeased. "That's what Lavrov said too. Still, you should have taken more men than just Egorov and this American? I would have never approved it. And what about this Arden? Can we trust him?"

She watched William through the window. "As much as anyone."

They were both silent for a moment. She felt lost in the strangeness of this exchange between them. It felt unnatural and strained. There was no trust left, probably on both sides. And yet there was still familiarity and comfort, and safety, just within reach. Just a word or two could probably put everything back in place. And yet she found herself unable to step onto that crumbling bridge. Not yet, at least. But she knew it would crumble even more if she didn't.

He finally broke the silence. "So? Where do we stand with Makhno?"

"He has agreed to help us stop the train and apprehend Reilly."

"That is excellent!" He sounded encouraging. He probably made a point to. Sergei could just flip a switch like that. "That's an amazing thing to pull off. Great work. What does he want in return?"

"He will get to keep the train and half of the gold."

"OK, that's fine. This was a long shot, but you did very well!"

Again, there was a reconciliatory note in his voice. He was stepping onto the bridge. She twisted a coil of the telephone cord around her finger.

"What is the latest intelligence on the train?"

"Our source in Samara said it departed around two this afternoon. Where are you planning to intercept?"

"Before it gets to Rostov-on-Don."

There was the sound of papers rustling on the other end of the line. "OK, that should give you about a day and a half before it gets there." He was silent for a moment. "Anna, listen, this train is serious business. It's heavily armed. Artillery, machine guns, over a hundred men onboard. It's a fortress on rails. I want you to let Makhno's men do the fighting. You are not a soldier."

"Sure, Sergei." She studied the coils of the cord wrapped around her finger.

"There is one more thing," his voice got quieter.

"OK."

"Can anyone else hear us?"

"No."

"Good. Listen to me carefully, Anna. Trotsky wants us to use this opportunity to take out Makhno."

She closed her eyes. "What are you talking about, Sergei? Why would we do that? He has just agreed to be our ally."

"Yes, all thanks to you. And we might not get another chance. We can't lose sight of the big picture. He is our ally only because now we have a common enemy. But he is not fighting for us. As soon as he is done fighting the Whites, he will turn on us."

"We don't know that." The thought sickened her and she did not want to be discussing this.

"We can't risk it. He is building up his army. Our own soldiers are deserting to join him. Trotsky said 10,000 men just last month. We can't allow this. You've managed to get close to him and get him out in the open, and we don't know when the next opportunity like this will present itself."

She couldn't speak. In the window, Egorov and William were laughing at something Petro was saying.

"Don't worry, you won't have to do anything." His tender inflection felt abrasive like gravel. "Here is the plan. If he succeeds in taking the train, have him take you up to Voronezh. I will have men waiting there. All you have to do is get them onboard, and they will take care of it."

The very thought of it was like a caustic pill slowly dissolving its poison.

"Did you hear me, Anna? We need to take advantage of this. You don't have to do anything. Just make sure that our men get on the train in Voronezh. Tell me you understand."

She swallowed. "I understand."

*

Makhno declared they would leave at first light. He ordered more of his men and equipment from Lugansk, and they arrived late that afternoon by horses and wagons. William watched them set up camp in the fields around the village. In the dissolving daylight, the smoke of their campfires drifted into the steppe in a bluish-grey blanket of fog.

Makhno invited his guests to dinner at his house that night. The dinner turned out to be a party, with more and more Cossacks packing into the yard and the house in various states of drunkenness. They had built a fire in front of the house, and now the night air was filled with music, singing, and the occasional quarrel.

Makhno chased off a few partying Cossacks into the yard to make room for his guests at the long table where they had discussed the plan earlier the same day. But instead of tea, he was now pouring vodka.

"*Za svobodu*," he said, raising the glass.

"*Za svobodu*." They raised their glasses and drank.

"Freedom from what?" William asked Makhno. He had raised many glasses to many things in Russia – *to health, luck, those no longer with us* – but this was the first time he had drunk to freedom.

"From whatever is holding you back, brother man!" Makhno grinned at William, flashing his strong, white teeth. "Most of us are so used to living without freedom that we don't even remember how to live with it. Let me tell you a story – it's a short one. Ten years ago, I was arrested in Lugansk and sentenced to life in prison. Three times I picked the locks on my ankle irons and attempted to escape. After the fourth time, my jailors spared me from future attempts by riveting my shackles closed. And for eight years, those shackles did not come off. Do you know what happened when I was freed after the revolution? The ankle irons were cut open, and I could not walk on my own without them! That's how used I had become to their weight pulling me down – *Halina!*" Makhno spotted a young woman who had just entered the room. "Come, meet our guests!"

Anna watched as the pretty girl with snow-white skin, black hair, and big, dark eyes sailed with elegance through the room full of drunken soldiers. She was dressed with elegance, too – a long skirt and a jacket more befitting a big city than this rustic country home. When she neared, Makhno took her hand and suddenly pulled her into his lap, leaned her back and planted a full kiss on her lips before she had a chance to resist. She playfully slapped him on the cheek, stood up and straightened her clothes.

"Halina, my love," Makhno said, grinning and rubbing his jaw, "I'd like you to meet our distinguished visitors: this is Agent Sokolova and Agent Egorov from the Moscow Cheka, and this is Captain Arden of the American Red Cross, all the way from New York. Comrades, please meet Ms. Halina Kuzmenko, a schoolteacher and, despite her protests, my future wife."

"Welcome," Halina beamed a smile at them. "And please excuse this man's abhorrent manners. I am afraid he gets only more ornery the more he drinks."

"Sit with us." Makhno moved over to free up a spot on the bench. He poured her a drink.

"What do you teach?" Anna asked.

"Ukrainian language and literature," she responded. "Now that the tsars no longer rule Ukraine, we can teach our language to our children again. I am also coordinating a new school system for the Free Territory, independent of church or state."

"Halina is my muse for Ukrainian independence," Makhno attested. "Among other things." He grinned and put his arm around her.

"When is the wedding?" William asked.

"Whenever she finally says yes!" Makhno darted a feigned reproachful glance at the girl. "I'll have you know, this woman relishes torturing the most eligible bachelor in the entire Free Territory. And I have even heroically recovered her flower wreath from the river on Kupala Night last year! Can you conceive anything more unfair?"

"It is just a silly tradition." Halina rolled her big eyes and shook her head.

"If you don't believe in it, then why did you put the wreath in the river?" He turned to his visitors: "The river at Hulaipole is wide and fast, and I came very close to meeting my demise trying to retrieve her flowers."

Halina laughed. "The river at Hulaipole is a creek. You can walk across it."

She turned to William: "So, tell me, how did you come to join the Red Cross? Are you a doctor?"

Makhno shook his head categorically, putting his drink down: "I'll wager you, this man's job is not saving lives."

William smiled with a nod. "No, I am not a doctor. I was a soldier, but after being wounded, I was forced to abandon the front and find an alternate occupation."

"I knew I recognized a fellow soldier!" Makhno's eyes lit up. "Where did you fight? In Europe?"

"Yes, in France."

"And how did you end up in the present company of my two new best friends from Moscow?"

"He thought you would be less likely to shoot us, seeing an American in our midst," Anna replied for him.

Makhno slapped his hand on the table and erupted in laughter. "You probably figured right," he said. "And now look – who knew the communists, the capitalists, and the anarchists could come together with a common goal. What times we live in! It gives me hope for this world." He poured more vodka into their glasses.

*

Anna watched Makhno with attention to every detail. His face was handsome and animated. His hands were rough – hands of a working man, hands of a peasant. He did not have a large physical presence, but his charisma filled this room. He joked with his soldiers, related to his guests and showered boundless affection onto his future bride. He came across as a simple man, just one of the Cossacks, yet she knew he was an apt military commander whose guerilla fighting tactics were already inflicting significant damage on the occupying White forces. She could see why men followed him into battle. She wondered why men so easily followed charismatic leaders. It took discipline to follow the right ideas instead.

Her thoughts were interrupted by a rising commotion at the other end of the table. Two Cossacks engaged in a drunken argument which rapidly escalated into shoving and then punching, which resulted in a violent jolt to the table and knocked over glasses and bottles that sent a flood wave of vodka pouring into Anna's lap. She jumped up, but it was too late.

"Hey!" Makhno jumped up, his eyes burning into the offenders. They immediately broke apart and began to apologize profusely.

She brushed off the front of her uniform, but it was soaked through. Never the one to miss an opportunity for a punchline, Egorov stretched out his neck towards her and sniffed the air: "My, this new perfume you are wearing is simply intoxicating," he grinned. "You will need a stick to beat the men off you now."

She was about to tell him she was going to start with him when Halina rushed to her aide with a towel. "Here, come with me, dear." She grabbed Anna's hand and lead her into the other room, as if Anna was one of her schoolchildren who needed fixing up during playtime.

She allowed herself to be led through the narrow doorway with a curtain, into a room that was smaller than the one where the party was noisily going on behind them. The room was cozy. There was a bed, a few chests, and a large clay stove painted white like the outside of the house. A bed of embers glowed inside the stove. Anna felt its radiating warmth.

"Luckily, we are about the same size," Halina said, unbuttoning Anna's shirt and helping her take it off, her hands moving quickly and purposefully.

There was a colorful rug on the wall, a few icons on a shelf in the corner, and an arsenal of rifles and sabers hanging from the nails hammered into the logs.

"What are these?" Anna pointed to the white cloths with red embroidery, draped around the frames of the icons and the windows.

"*Rushniki?*" Halina followed Anna's gaze. "It's a Ukrainian tradition. Pure white cloth embroidered with the symbols of old Slavic gods are supposed to protect the home from evil entering through the portals."

"Portals?"

Halina smiled. "Doors, windows, pictures, icons – they are all portals to somewhere else. Evil comes from the outside, and the home needs to be protected from it. I know you probably think it's superstitious."

"No," Anna shook her head. "I think there is truth in that."

Halina put her hand on Anna's elbow to help her balance while she took off her boots and the army breeches. The touch of another woman's hand – soft and warm – felt strange but also comforting. It reminded Anna of being at home, with Masha. She always had such a gentle touch. Anna realized just how much she had missed it, having lived and worked surrounded mostly with men.

Halina opened a trunk and rummaged through folded clothes. "Sorry, it's a bit… traditional," she said, laying out a long black Ukrainian skirt with colorful flowers along the bottom and a white long-sleeved blouse with red flowers embroidered on its sleeves.

"It's fine; thank you," Anna said, her fingers tracing the daisy chain of flowers on the fabric.

She put on the clothes, realizing that it had been close to a year since she had worn a dress or a skirt. This place – the hearth, the bed, the weapons – so similar but so different from Sergei's apartment. Softer, homier.

"It looks good with your boots," Halina said.

Anna smiled. The thought of coordinating her clothes and shoes had not even crossed her mind.

"So, do you two live together?" Anna asked.

"Yes, but he is old-fashioned – he wants to actually get married, have a farm, a house, kids, the whole bit. And you? You have a man back in Moscow?"

Sergei's place was not a home. It was just *a* place away from Lubyanka. To crash, and to occasionally get drunk and screw. They never talked about marriage, kids. There was always something else more urgent and more important than that. She didn't even think she had ever wanted that with him, but she never missed the thought of it till now.

She shook her head: "No."

"Well, don't you worry," Halina beamed at her. "A pretty girl like you won't have any trouble finding a man when you want one."

She laid out Anna's clothes on the stove to dry while Anna fixed her hair in a small mirror hanging on the wall.

"Are you ready?" Halina asked.

"Almost." Anna strapped on her heavy leather belt and holster around her waist. She met Halina's amused look and smiled back.

The noise in the room died down when they stepped through the curtain. Egorov, who was in the process of saying something to William and Makhno, froze in mid-sentence with his mouth open. He put his hand to his chest and closed and opened his mouth several times, stumped for words, for the first time since she'd known him.

"Mother Russia," was all his drunken mind was able to assemble into a slurred mutter.

William, sitting next to him, stared at her, completely transfixed. Makhno turned around to look, and several excited whistles and hollers signaled approval from the drunken Cossacks in the room.

"Not a word," Anna said sternly to Egorov and William, settling back in her spot on the bench.

Egorov leaned in towards William and Makhno with wide eyes and whispered in full voice: "I've never seen her in a skirt... I don't think anyone has!" He grinned back at Anna.

"Well, if you ask me, this is a considerable improvement over the standard issue Cheka uniform," Makhno declared. "I admit that I've never seen this outfit with a gun before, but somehow, it just works." He winked at Halina and she gave him an eyeroll.

"Don't mind them," William whispered to her. "You look beautiful."

She turned to him, his face the closest it had ever been to hers. His brown eyes glowed warmly, and the contour of his lips was handsome and kind. "Thank you," she said. And added: "You are drunk."

He nodded with seriousness. "The tip of my nose is beginning to tingle."

Makhno poured another round.

"To the beauty of women in our lives," he toasted, putting his hand around Halina's waist.

"To the beauty!" they drank.

"Do you have a woman back in America?" Makhno turned to William.

"No," he shook his head. "I've been away from home for too long."

"That is unfortunate." Makhno shook his head with earnest inebriated exaggeration. "We soldiers need love, and we need to be in love. Without it, we turn hard and mean." He wagged his finger at William: "Captain, you must find yourself a woman when you get back home."

Egorov finished his drink and stood up. He mumbled something about fresh air and, swaying unsteadily, like a sailor on the rolling deck of a ship at sea, went outside, into the sounds of soulful drunken singing in the yard. A few Cossacks followed suit, leaving one of their comrades sleeping at the end of the table. The room quieted down.

Anna gazed into the black night outside the window. Somewhere out there, in the darkness, an iron leviathan was making its way towards them, bringing death.

She turned to Makhno: "So, how are we going to stop this train?"

He looked into the bottom of his empty glass. "I have a few ideas," he said and lit a cigarette. "But we can talk through it tomorrow on the road. We'll have plenty of time." He yawned and stretched out, his arm coming to rest around Halina. His fingers played with a lock of her hair.

William scanned the quiet congregation and tapped his hand on the table. "Well, I think I had better turn in and get some sleep. Sounds like tomorrow will be a long day."

Makhno nodded. "We'll leave before dawn. Come, let me show you where you two can sleep." He got up and motioned them to follow.

In the yard, several Cossacks were passed out, snoring into the starry sky. Egorov and Petro were sitting by the fading fire like two long-separated brothers, sharing a bottle and singing some sad peasant song.

"They sound horrible," William remarked.

Anna nodded. "Well, at least they have made up."

"Don't worry about them – they can sleep it off on the way tomorrow," Makhno said and led William and Anna to the house across the road.

WITH THE ANARCHISTS

By the time the first sunrays pierced through the horizon, they had already been riding for almost an hour. Anna looked back to see the long dark line of Makhno's Cossacks behind her, moving like a chain of ants across the steppe.

They moved quietly – as quietly as 150 riders and four wagons could move on an old country road. There was no singing and no loud conversations – Makhno explained to his city guests that in the steppe, voices could carry in the wind for miles. So, it was only the sounds of wheels and hooves, the occasional clank of sabers or other weapons, and a few hushed conversations.

Two of the horse-drawn wagons were what Makhno called *tachankas* – open carriages with a heavy machine gun mounted in the back, pulled by a troika of horses. "They go very fast," he said with pride.

Anna, now back in her uniform and leather jacket, was riding at the head of the line, next to Makhno. William rode on Makhno's other side. Egorov, not a fan of the saddle on a good day, chose to ride in the supply wagon driven by Petro, nursing a hangover in a nest of crates and sacks.

The road looked disused, with grass reclaiming the worn wheel tracks that would probably completely disappear in another year. It was a ghostly road with no towns or villages left along the way – '*from here to the Volga river*,' as Makhno put it – perfect for someone trying to avoid crossing paths with a larger enemy force. Here, there was nothing but the steppe around them. Quiet. Peaceful. She watched as the wind chased waves of feathergrass upon the endless green sea that extended to the horizon and vanished in the light blue haze of the sky.

"Are you sure we should not have brought some artillery?" Anna asked Makhno.

Makhno shook his head. "Hauling cannons and shells would slow us down. It would take us three days instead of one. But don't worry, we won't need them – I am wearing my lucky hat." He pointed to his light-grey papakha and grinned.

By ten in the morning, they reached the ruins of a village. A few walls still stood, but most of the huts had been burned down into piles of black and grey rubble in the tall grass. The landscape was pockmarked with artillery-shell craters. There had been a battle here. Anna wondered who had fought whom, and for what? Now it was just a ghost village on a ghost road. But the well turned out to have clean water, and so they stopped to let the horses rest.

Makhno checked the map. "We are making good time," he said. "We should reach the railroad in a couple of hours."

Anna left William and Makhno at the head of the line and went to check on Egorov.

*

William had discovered that he liked the steppe. It was peaceful here. Bountiful. A field of golden wheat, heavy with its own weight, swayed and rustled in the breeze right next to the road. Makhno picked a stalk and rolled it in his hand.

"Spring wheat has not been harvested," he said, letting the seeds and the chaff fall through his fingers onto the ground. "I don't know how this earth still manages to produce a harvest after all the dead we've buried in it through this war."

"Look at that." William pointed past some trees, where an abandoned tank was rusting in the field.

They walked over to take a look. It was a medium-sized tank. The small turret at the top pointed to the village with the snub barrel of its cannon. The split doors of the crew hatch were left open, flung apart like wings of a metal insect, revealing inside the cramped compartment where humans used to fit. William walked around, examining the damage. The left-side track lay broken, unraveled on the ground, with grass now growing though it. The front driving wheel was smashed and missing big pieces, probably the aftermath of an artillery round.

"Looks like it's been here a while," William said, touching the rough, riveted side.

"Two years? Maybe three," Makhno said. "There's been a lot of fighting in these parts."

What few patches of paint still remained on the tank were blistered and peeling and revealed no national designations. But William knew this model. "It's a Renault," he said. "How did a French tank end up in Ukraine?"

"Either the French or the Belgians brought it," Makhno shrugged. "Before the war, this part of Ukraine was carved up into four sectors: French, Belgian, British, and German."

"Why? I thought this was part of the Russian Empire."

"It was, but it was also rich in coal and iron, and the Tsar was eager to make money. He sold mining and manufacturing rights to foreign investors. Whole new towns sprung up. When the war broke out, each side fought to protect their investments and ensure the resources kept flowing. Then, the German and the Austrian armies rolled in and took control."

It was the story as old as the world – the fight for resources. William wondered if Robins and the American International Corporation already had plans for Ukraine, too.

"You know, this may actually be a good spot to test something," Makhno said and headed back to the supply wagons. "Come! You said you are pretty good with a long rifle?"

"I did?" William was baffled, regretting having drunk so much last night. "I suppose I am." What else did he blabber about last night?

"Good; I have something for you." Makhno shifted a few crates to expose a box almost long enough to be a skinny coffin. He pried open the lid to expose the long, black, oily barrel of a rifle.

"What is *this*?" William examined the unfamiliar weapon. It looked like a common bolt-action rifle, but considerably bigger. The core of the weapon was the massive, machined steel cylinder – the firing chamber with a wide breech and a thick-walled cut-out. Inside the cut-out, the long firing bolt darkly gleamed, ominously hinting at the sizable round of ammunition it must accommodate. The breech and the chamber tapered into a long, black, polished barrel with iron sights at the end. This whole hunk of cylindrical iron was mounted to a thick wooden stock with a pistol-grip trigger and a pair of spiked bipod feet.

"It's a present from the Kaiser," Makhno introduced. "This is the Mauser anti-tank rifle. The Germans just started making it this year."

"How in the world did you get this?"

"Let me just say that the Germans were not always scrupulous in guarding their supplies during their withdrawal, and the Ukrainians are naturally a very enterprising people. I won't bore you with the details." He gestured towards the rifle. "Pick it up."

William reached into the crate and had to use both hands to pull out the big gun.

"Weighs over forty pounds, and it's almost six feet long," Makhno said with the satisfaction of a proud owner.

William set the rifle's bipod legs on the side of the wagon and looked down the long, dark stretch of the barrel.

"What kind of round does it take?"

"Here." Makhno opened a box and pulled out a cartridge around six inches long. William weighed the heavy round in his hand.

"13.2-millimeter with a hardened steel core," Makhno said. "I was told it would penetrate armor three-quarters of an inch thick from 500 yards away."

He looked back at the tank in the field and then at the ruins of the village on the other side of the road. "It's at least a hundred yards to the tank from that hut, wouldn't you say?"

William nodded.

"Let's give it a try. Let's see what it can do before we point it at the train."

William heaved the massive rifle onto his shoulder and carried it to the ruins of the hut. A few Cossacks followed them to observe. In the semi-collapsed, open-sky room, he set the rifle down in the frame of the window. The spiked bipod feet confidently dug into the weathered wood of the windowsill. The tank sat helplessly up ahead.

"Now, do brace yourself," Makhno warned him. "This thing kicks hard. The man who sold it to me said he's seen it crack a man's collarbone and dislocate his shoulder."

"It can't possibly be any worse than waking up to get hit with a rifle butt in the head." He gave Makhno a wry smile.

He examined the rear sights and slid the adjustment bar back to the 100-meter mark. The well-greased bolt handle turned and pulled back with ease. He inserted the weighty round into the firing chamber and slipped the bolt closed and locked with two reassuring clicks.

He set up in front of the window on one knee and fit the blocky stock firmly into his shoulder. The rifle smelled of clean machine oil. Moving it around, he felt its heft. The sights aligned on the turret of the tank. He exhaled and squeezed the trigger.

The blow of the recoil came before he even heard the blast. The stock bashed his shoulder hard, shoving him back and almost knocking him off balance. The loud, bassy boom rolled through the area and an instant later there was a distant clank. The Cossacks were impressed.

"You weren't joking about this kick," William said, rubbing his shoulder. "Not a very quiet weapon, is it?" he added.

Makhno shook his head, smiling. "You'll definitely get only one shot to surprise them. Let's go take a look."

At the tank, William climbed onto the track to look for the hole and was surprised to find it in the right place on the side of the turret. The rifle was sighted in and accurate, despite the horrendous recoil. He could probably do better now that he knew what to expect. The hole was clean, about half an inch in diameter, with edges glazed and neatly rolled inward.

He knocked on the steel. "Not bad. This armor is about half of an inch thick."

Makhno examined the hole from the ground. He then walked around the tank to the other side. "It looks like you made it all the way through," he said from there.

William climbed to the other side to find a circular tear with a crown of jagged edges.

"Now, that is impressive," he said, touching the warm metal.

He hopped down and heaved the monster gun back on his shoulder, and they headed back to the wagons. He felt like a little boy carrying his father's rifle.

"So, what will we be shooting at with this?" he asked Makhno.

"Not so much *what* but *who*. I'll need you to neutralize the train's artillery. This train will have one or maybe two armored artillery wagons with gun turrets. These will probably be three-inch guns, but could be bigger. They can seriously hurt us during the attack."

"So, how do we stop them with this?"

"We break down the chain of command. Lucky for us, these trains are run like navy battleships, with very strict discipline and ranking. We can exploit that. Each artillery wagon can have twenty-five to thirty crew inside, and they all answer to the wagon's commanding officer. If we can take out this artillery commander, we will disrupt the whole wagon."

"How do we get to the commander?"

"Once the train is under attack, the artillery wagons will engage, which means each wagon commander will be in a very specific place – his command post. The command post has a small observation dome on the roof of the wagon, usually between the gun turrets. This observation dome gives him a good view of the battlefield. It will be armored, but that won't matter with this rifle. What matters is that his head will be squarely inside a metal bucket maybe two feet across. If you can hit that bucket, chances are good that you will take him out."

William had to admit that this was not a bad plan. At the front, he had seen the effect losing a commanding officer could have on the unit. He guessed it would be even worse in an armored train than in the trenches. These men would not expect to be vulnerable. Seeing their commander struck down inside their own wagon would certainly affect their fighting morale. There would be panic and fear. Would anyone else dare to climb into the observation post? They would now be blind and uncoordinated.

At the wagon, he put the rifle back in its crate and closed the lid.

"OK, and then what?" he said.

"If we can disrupt their artillery just long enough, this will give us a window to get close to the train. And if we can get close, we can get *these* inside." Makhno opened another crate and showed William rows of grey metal spheres about three inches in diameter with short brass tubes sticking out.

"Grenades?" he asked.

"Gas grenades; British," Makhno replied. "This gas is non-lethal, but it is extremely irritating to the eyes and the lungs. These trains are closed up for protection, and ventilation is very poor. If we can get these into the wagons, the battle will be over."

"How do we get them in?"

"There should be a few ventilation pipes on the roof, hatches, portholes – any small opening will work."

William picked up one of the grenades and tossed it in his hand. The pull-ring of the safety pin gleamed in the sun. "Do you suppose Reilly will appreciate the irony when a British gas grenade drops into his lap?"

*

At a collapsed wooden bridge, they crossed a shallow riverbed with sandy banks and a creek running through it. The sun was now high in the hazy sky, and Anna felt its relentless hot breath on her skin. The landscape was beginning to change. The yellow-green sea of grass that seemed boundless when they left Lugansk was now transitioning into low hills, vast groves and rocky outcrops and ravines.

She looked at her watch. She needed to stop looking so often. It was almost one. They could only estimate when the train would come through. Could be tonight. Could be tomorrow. All they could do was get there before it did. She was hoping they would have been there by now. What if they've already missed it? What then? They couldn't have. Because there is no way an armored train could have covered this distance so fast. And because there was no Plan B. This *was* her Plan B, or maybe even C – the last and only plan left to stop Reilly.

She glanced back. Egorov was sleeping in the wagon. Again. William and Makhno were riding a few paces ahead of her. They seemed to have become fast pals, bonded over guns, war, or whatever else young men found exciting. Last night, she slept in the same room as William, in the hut where Makhno had put them. She listened to his even breathing while she could not fall asleep. She thought of Sergei, of her life in Moscow, of Red Terror, of Masha and her parents, and of the terrible act Sergei had tasked her with.

She reached to check her watch again but stopped herself. Instead, she caught up to William and Makhno, who were absorbed in a conversation.

"... but isn't an *Anarchist State* a contradiction in terms?" William asked. "How can you have a government and be anarchists at the same time?"

"We only oppose a centralized government. We believe people can self-govern with local councils. And that's exactly what we want to do across the Ukraine once we chase out the Whites and the Germans."

"Do you think that can work?"

"It already does! In the Free Territory, we have over four million people living without the formal hierarchies of power – no ministries, no presidents, no governors or mayors. No political parties, no centralized government of any kind."

"But don't these people need a government?"

"What for? What do you think *is* the purpose of a central government?"

William opened his mouth to respond but evidently could not find a ready answer. Anna smiled to herself – this was a seemingly simple but surprisingly provocative question.

Makhno laughed lightheartedly. "OK, imagine you were *not* born in any country. Imagine you were just a person, living on your own off the land. What would possibly compel you to join with other people and let someone else govern you?"

William was still stumped, so Makhno proposed another angle: "OK, let's put it another way. How can we tell when your government is *not* doing a good job?"

"Well, I suppose when the people are hungry, homeless, unemployed, unhappy."

Makhno smiled. "If that's the measure, then there is not a single good government on this planet today. But realize that this is so by design. It can't be helped, given the constraints of the chosen system. Governments are constructs of power over people. All modern governments are rooted in tyranny, slavery, aggression and genocide."

William shook his head. "Maybe the old European governments are, but it does not have to be that way. Look at

America – it was designed from the beginning on the principles of democracy."

Makhno smiled. "But America is not a true democracy. It's a representative democracy which amounts to nothing more than indirect tyranny. Think about it – if your government was truly designed to represent the people, why are so many of your people today still poor, sick, and hungry? Why can't your women and colored people vote? Because even as young as your country is, your government is already corrupt. It is tainted by the will and influence of the richest one percent, while the majority has no real voice or influence. If the people in your country had any power, don't you think they would have already used it to improve their situation? But they can't because your system is too complex and rigged against them. A common working man will never be elected to be your president. America will never eradicate poverty and inequality because it was never designed to do that. All those levels of power have been built in from the start by those who crave power."

When Makhno spoke about the future of Ukraine, all traces of lightheartedness and tomfoolery vanished from his disposition. His discourse became passionate and reinforced with pragmatic conviction. She could see it in his eyes – the fire of unapologetic idealism, just as she did in Alexei's eyes. It did not matter if others called him naïve – she knew he was immune to cynicism.

"So, your answer is to have fewer levels of power in order to create a fairer society?" William was clearly finding this concept intriguing.

"Precisely. Less complexity means less opportunity for corruption and inequality. Governments are not natural constructs. They are complex, and complexity is not a natural state. Remember that tank rusting in the field back there? To create it, someone had expanded all that effort to mine the raw materials from the earth, process them into the metals necessary to build it, and then fill it with fuel, oil and armaments. And then it operated as was intended – it crawled, it killed, it enforced someone's power. But what does it always need in order to continue existing in this intended state?"

"Someone to maintain it?" Anna decided to join in.

"That's right! This machine exists in a temporary, fragile state – as soon as we leave it alone, nature begins to reclaim what we took from it. Paint starts to chip and peel, metal rusts, fuel begins to spoil. The whole thing breaks down into its raw materials and returns back to earth. The same is true of governments. They are unnatural constructs of power. As soon as people stop supporting them, they crumble and disintegrate, just like that tank. And what is left when social structures crumble?" He looked at them, his eyes squinting from the bright sun. "This –" he swept across the open steppe with his hand, "– the land and the people. *This* is our natural state. We don't want to replace it with new power structures. We want to harmonize with it. When this war is finally over, all I want is my family and a piece of land to farm. There is enough for everyone. That is what the Free Territory is all about."

"But don't you think power is inevitable?" Anna asked. "It does not matter what you call it. Take you, for example – aren't you in a position of power over these men under your command?"

He shook his head. "I am not. They elected me to defend their land, but I have no rank. This army is all volunteers, and anyone who does not want to be part of it is free to leave at any time. No one has power over others in the Free Territory. We elect local councils to coordinate some tasks for the community, but they are in no position of authority, and cannot force anyone to do anything they don't want to."

"So, basically you advocate for local councils, just like the Soviets in Russia?" William asked.

"Yes, except we believe a centralized government is necessary, at least in the beginning," she said. "Without it, I don't think the new Russia can survive."

"I think you could have, if you had wanted to from the beginning, but it may already be too late. Look at your papers: *Red Terror*? *Dictatorship of the proletariat*? Does that sound like a world everyone is free in?"

"Those are just temporary measures. The means to an end."

"Temporary?" He smiled. "You don't really believe it, do you? Power is never intended to be temporary, and it is never returned voluntarily. Once people have power, they rationalize why they have to keep it. They tell you they see *the big picture*, or that they are acting in the interests of the *greater good*. But all that is just a bunch of profoundly sounding horseshit!"

"Don't you believe in the greater good?" Anna raised an eyebrow.

"No! There is no such thing as greater good. There is just good, and there is just evil. *Greater good* is just a euphemism for evil," Makhno grinned. "People who believe in the greater good think they are justified to do terrible things for the right reasons. If they believed they could save a million people by killing just one child, they would do it."

"And you wouldn't? To save a million?"

"Hell no! Let the million die. A society that justifies killing children is not worth saving. In the end, *why* you do something does not matter. Only *what* you do matters."

He squinted into the distance and raised his binoculars. "And I do believe that is the railroad," he said.

Anna followed his gaze into the distance ahead. There, a thin silver thread shined, cutting through the hot, thick air like the edge of a blade.

THE IRON LEVIATHAN

When the railroad came into view, Makhno dispatched two scouts to ride ahead and provide advanced warning of the approaching train. He led the rest of the army north, following the tracks towards higher elevation and the jagged ridges of rocky plateaus as he searched for the most favorable point of ambush.

Anna was anxious – William could tell this by the frequent glances she cast up the tracks, probably expecting to see the scouts or the train appear at any moment. William could feel it too – the sleepy monotony of the long, sunbaked ride had evaporated, and the thought of the approaching battle quickened his pulse.

The landscape split into two levels, like a one-sided gorge, with the craggy wall of bluffs on the right and the low-rolling hills, hollows and groves of the steppe on the left. The railroad curved in a smooth, shining arc, disappearing around the rising rocky cliff. A small creek burbled leisurely on the steppe side of the tracks, playfully meandering through the contours of the terrain.

Makhno stopped where the broken side of the bluff rose about fifty feet high near the tracks.

"This is the spot," he said, surveying the landscape.

And from that moment on, his army launched into a whirlwind of preparation, with Makhno masterfully orchestrating the tasks and setting up the pieces in their right places on the stage where the battle was soon to play out. He directed a small crew of six Cossacks, armed with tools from one of the wagons, to begin pulling apart the rails in the spot he indicated. He sent the tachankas along with most of his army to the thick grove of trees about a hundred yards beyond the creek. Finally, he took the remaining platoon of around two dozen Cossacks and two supply wagons back about a quarter mile and then up the broken, rocky incline to the top of the bluffs.

Once there, above the railway, he placed his remaining pieces along the edge of the cliffs: two Maxim machine guns, William with the anti-tank gun, and a dozen Cossacks with rifles. He then took two men and a crate of dynamite farther up along the edge, eventually disappearing from view.

Leaving Egorov and Petro to discuss the particulars of the gas grenades at the wagon, William took the big rifle and a box of ammunition out of the crate and went to set up his sniper's nest. Beyond the rocky edge, the tracks below were only about fifty yards away. To his left, he could just see the spot where the Cossacks had disconnected the rails. And from that point of broken track, he had an uninterrupted line of sight of the railroad all the way to the right, where it curved out of sight behind the cliffs. The spiked feet dug deep into the shale under the weight of the rifle. He pivoted it from one end of the tracks to the other, getting accustomed to its mass and visualizing the wagons – their sizes and features – at the end of his sights. He placed a few boulders at the front of his position for additional cover, and, satisfied, pulled the rifle back out of sight.

The afternoon sun was beating down on the steppe. There, in the tall grass, the line of Makhno's cavalry was entering the grove.

He watched them vanish into the thicket one by one, and soon, the steppe and the forest looked undisturbed again. But on the bluff, the preparations were still underway around him as the machine gun crews were setting up and crates of weapons and ammunitions were being unloaded off the wagons.

His pulse quickened with anticipation and then receded. That same false, mocking expectation that used to haunt him in the trenches. Always waiting, with every breath. Waiting for orders, or for an enemy attack; waiting to charge or to take cover, to fire and be fired at; waiting for the next horror of blood, mangled intestines, torn apart brains and ripped off limbs. Waiting without any certainty. Who knew how long? Hours, maybe days. After a while, one numbed to it. Or went crazy.

The steppe below was peaceful. Every now and then, the wind rolled in waves through the grass. Soon, the train would roll through here, and everything would change. His mind tried to play through what would come next. From the very first shot and through the dozens of versions of what would follow, and all the possible moves of the chess pieces he could imagine.

"What do you think?" He did not hear Anna approach.

"About what?"

"This plan."

She peered into the open steppe beyond the edge. She lit a cigarette, took a drag and offered it to William. He took it and inhaled, feeling the familiar rush of nicotine surge through his body. Now he really felt like he was back in the trenches. He passed the cigarette back to her.

"It's as good a plan as we can have, considering what we are up against and what little we know. Do you not trust him?"

She shrugged. "Makhno is the master of partisan warfare. Some would say downright legendary. He is staking his own head on this, so I have to trust he knows what he is doing."

"Do you think he will honor the deal? What's to stop him from taking *all* of the gold?"

"Nothing except his word. But, regardless, what happens to

the gold does not matter, as long as it does not make it to the British or the Whites. I am here to stop Reilly and his plan. That's all that really matters."

She looked at him. Her blue eyes were even more luminous with the blue sky reflecting in them.

"Thank you," she said. "You did not have to do this, and I appreciate it."

He smiled. "You are welcome. I am glad to help, and this is certainly far more exciting than driving Robins around Petrograd. Although, after a day in the saddle, I must admit I do miss the old Rolls-Royce."

She smiled. "Yes, I do miss it too. That car has lived a remarkable life so far. I wonder what will happen to it next."

"Perhaps a local goat herder will find it?"

He could tell this thought amused her. And then, out of the corner of his eye, he saw a rider tear out from the grove, galloping through the steppe towards the bluffs.

"Is that one of the scouts?" he asked.

"That's impossible," she muttered. "That's much too early."

Makhno must have seen the rider as well – he returned from the far end of the bluff without the two Cossacks or the crate of dynamite. Anna and William walked over just as the rider made it to the top. His horse was breathing hard – its nostrils flaring, and its hair matted with sweat from the long, fast ride. The rider didn't bother dismounting.

"The train was leaving Golovtsy when we saw it half an hour ago," he said. "At the speed they were moving, they will be here in about twenty minutes."

"That's at least half a day early," Anna said. "Are you sure it's the right train?"

"Two artillery wagons each with two turrets. Three boxcars in the middle. Flatcars at the front and the back."

"Right train or not, it's coming this way," Makhno said, hoisting himself into his saddle.

"Are we ready for it?" Anna asked.

"We'll have to be," he said with a smile and turned his horse around, directing his men and wagons down the rocky slope into the steppe.

Egorov followed him, driving Petro's supply wagon. Seeing William, he shouted: "Good luck, Comrade American! We'll have many more things to drink to when this is over."

Anna climbed into her saddle. William put his hand on the neck of her horse. "You and Anton take care of yourselves down there," he said.

"You too," she said and gave him a reassuring smile. "I'll see you after."

*

Anna pulled back the slide of her Mauser. The sweet acidic scents of the weapon – iron, brass, lead and machine grease – mixed with the smells of the late-summer forest. And with the leaves rustling in the breeze, she had to only close her eyes to be transported back to being a girl again, hunting with her father. A perfect childhood memory that would never happen again. Nostalgia panged like heartache, like homesickness for a home that no longer existed. She wasn't that girl anymore. She considered all the steps that got her here – from Alexei's death to this grove in south-western Ukraine, waiting with an army of anarchists and a gun in her hand. *Did the past justify our actions?* Or did the future? She was less nervous about what was about to come than she was about what was supposed to follow. Attacking the armored train – even dying while trying – seemed easier than Sergei's order. Trotsky's order. It was an impossible choice, but maybe this was the cost of thinking strategically. Of seeing the big picture. Of winning the war and not just the battle. Who was she to know better? A rich, spoiled girl who had always thought she had a choice. But there was no decision to make here. Only an order to follow. She wondered if her parents and Masha had made it to Switzerland yet.

Egorov's giant hand reached down to her with three clips of Mauser rounds.

"You may need more than one bullet today."

She looked up at him. "How did you know?"

He laughed. "I picked it up one time, and thought it felt kind of light. Don't worry, I've been carrying extras for you."

She grimaced and took the clips. "We'll be in sad shape if it comes down to me and this pistol. You might as well start praying to that cross you hide around your neck." He wasn't the only one who knew secrets.

"Oh, trust me – I have been," he grinned and sat down next to her.

She leaned into his big, comfortable side and gazed to the distant bluff barely visible through the trees.

*

There was a charge in the air. William could practically smell it, like electricity before a storm. It was a different kind of anticipation. Not the daily fruitless anticipation that came with trench life and could wear a man down with doldrums over time. This was the opposite. This was the anticipation before a battle. It was a charge that carried with every click of the breech bolt, every clank of the ammunition belt, and every hushed prayer. And with each click and with each second that ticked down to that unstoppable certainty, this charge grew greater and more volatile. It built up, like the sum total of every soul's despair and resolution twisted together, added over and over again. Like a scream swallowed deep into the pits of a hundred stomachs, waiting to rip free with the first shot.

William swallowed down his own. The heavy round clanked into the breech, and the steel bolt locked it in the firing position. In the steppe, two dozen Cossacks rode out from the grove. Halfway to the railroad, they dismounted and made their horses lie down, completely disappearing from view in the tall grass. William appreciated the Cossacks' skill with making it look easy – he knew it took a lot of training and trust for the horses to do this.

And now they all lay in wait.

They did not have to wait long. A quiet whistle from someone on the bluff gave the signal. William cautiously nudged closer to see over the edge. In the distance, a group of riders emerged from around the bend, slowly materializing out of the hot haze over the tracks. It had begun. From this moment on, 150-some souls held their breath, counting each step as the raiding party entered the trap.

He tucked back in behind the edge, and time seemed to pass slowly again. For a while, he heard only the sounds of insects and the wind in the trees. But eventually, the wind carried to him snippets of voices and the knocking of hooves on the railroad ties. He made out two or three distinct conversations as the riders passed below him. In another 200 yards they would spot the disconnected rail.

He did not have to look down to know the train was coming. A cloud of white steam rose over the bluffs on the far right, billowing and growing closer. He peeked around the boulder to see the train appear in the distance, snaking slowly around the bend. The chugging and puffing grew closer, and he soon heard the heavy clanking of the iron wheels rolling over the rails. And then he felt it – the deep, slow rhythmic rumble penetrating the ground and everything around with its massive weight. The train grew louder and closer.

Any second now – he thought. Any second now, the raiding party will find the broken rail and signal to the train.

And then it happened – the steel brakes squealed, the steam hissed, and the tone of the engine wound down. They'd found it. But the train kept its screeching roll, laboring to slow down its immense weight. The iron wheels still pounded heavily on the rails. William peeked around the rocks – the train was now rolling past his position, gradually slowing down. At the front was a long flatcar with some supplies strapped down. Next, was a tall, boxy, windowless steel wagon topped with two snub-barreled gun turrets. Behind it tugged the armor-clad locomotive, spewing steam and squealing until it finally crept to a stop. The locomotive was followed with three long, armored boxcars with no windows – just the narrow black slits of viewports and rows of gun portholes along the green, riveted sides. And behind the boxcars was the second artillery wagon, also with two cannons, followed by the tail flatcar. The train was now stopped, and the porthole hatches in the boxcars began propping up and prickling with barrels of machine guns. The enemy was on alert.

Another dozen of the raiding party rode up from the back of the train towards the front. William backed away from the edge and gripped his rifle, prepared to move it into position. And then the ground rumbled again. An explosion blasted a cloud of rock and dust into the sky on his far right. He peeked to see an avalanche of large rocks and rubble slide onto the railway behind the train. Makhno's dynamite had cut off the train's retreat. The train was now cornered.

As if in slow motion, the machine gun crew to his right rolled their Maxim towards the edge and pointed it down. The first round of the long ra-tat-tat escaped from the thick barrel and raced towards the enemy cavalry on the ground. William took in a deep breath. Hell had just opened up, and there was no turning back.

In the steppe below, Makhno's Cossacks materialized from the tall grass and charged the enemy's forward raiding party. Now, there was machine-gun fire down there. They had awakened the iron beast. The turrets on top of the artillery wagons came to life and began slowly winding their way towards the bluffs. From the embrasures, the barrels of the machine guns moved around like the feelers of a mechanical insect, searching the surrounding landscape for prey.

He moved the heavy rifle into position, keeping the end of the barrel back from the edge to maintain some cover behind the boulders. He aligned his sights on the front artillery wagon. The iron notch at the end of his barrel fixed on a small angular cupola protruding from the roofline between the two turrets. He exhaled evenly, feeling his pulse beating in his thumb and his index finger as he pulled the trigger. The stock bashed the bruised spot on his shoulder and the two-ounce chunk of hardened steel hurled towards the target. The front turrets stopped turning.

Hit, he thought to himself, imagining the sheer horror unfolding in the cramped quarters of the wagon at this moment, as their commander tumbled down from the observation post with his head blown open. A heavy boom from the back of the train disrupted that thought.

The shell from the rear artillery wagon tore through the air and detonated into the side of the cliff to his right, blasting him with a shockwave of dense air, rock and dirt. When he looked up again, the whole edge of the cliff where the machine-gun crew used to be was gone, partly obliterated and partly having given way and crumbled down, taking the men and the gun down with it.

When his ears stopped ringing, he was returned to a world filled with gunfire. The long and short bursts of multiple machine guns were punctuated with the sporadic light pops of the rifles and the rumbling blasts of the cannons. Beyond the edge of the cliff, a cavalry battle was now raging at the front of the train, with what looked like a hundred riders and horses churning in one violent mass glimmering with slashes of sabers. Out from the grove, another group of Makhno's Cossacks was rushing in to provide reinforcements.

He reached for another round and noticed that his left arm was bleeding. Another boom from the rear artillery wagon made him look up. The round sailed above the steppe and exploded at the edge of the woods near Makhno's reinforcements. Even before the plume of the distant explosion had settled and the careening trees had crashed to the ground, the turrets were already moving to readjust. But he had already reloaded and was looking down his sights at the rear artillery commander's observation dome. The rifle kicked his shoulder again. He thought he could see the hole his bullet made in the metal.

He quickly reloaded and observed. For a few moments, the turrets stopped moving. Then the rear turret began realigning to his position. He hurriedly fired two shots into the side of the turret, where he imagined the gunnery crew would have been. The turret ceased moving, but in return, his position was showered with a hail of bullets from the machine guns.

One of the Cossacks close to him yanked back and dropped to the ground. William scooted over to him, but there was nothing he could do for him – there was a bullet hole in the Cossack's face and the back of his skull was completely gone. Bullets were whizzing around them, and the handful of Cossacks still remaining on top of the cliff were doing their best to keep the enemy engaged while trying to stay alive. The last Maxim gun continued to hammer out its angry beat somewhere on his right.

He made his way back to his position and checked his arm. His sleeve was cut by shrapnel, and his upper arm was bleeding profusely. He took off his jacket, tore off his shirt sleeve and used it to bandage the wound. He reloaded the rifle and took stock of the situation below the edge. The cavalry battle was drawing near the end, with the remains of the raiding party retreating closer to the center of the train, where their comrades inside could take more precise shots at the enemy. On top of the front flatcar, a figure was moving briskly towards the artillery wagon, with a bag across his shoulders and a pistol in his hand – in the midst of the all-out assault, Petro had managed to get onboard.

But he wasn't undetected for long. One of the hatches in the artillery wagon propped open and the muzzle of a machine gun pushed through, unleashing a burst of lead. Petro dropped and stretched out on the deck of the flatcar behind the cargo. William flung the rifle around and followed the line of the barrel inside the wagon with his sights, estimating the shooter's position. The rifle kicked his shoulder again, and the barrel of the machine gun jerked to the side and went silent. Petro jumped to his feet and made a dash toward the artillery wagon. Just then, a fiery arc jetted into the steppe from one of the boxcars and carved a long, slow, glowing line across Makhno's men.

Son of a bitch – they have a flamethrower! William cursed to himself. The tall, dry grass combusted into an all-consuming inferno. The blazing jet tracked back across, dousing more men, horses and the steppe with liquid fire. There were no agonizing screams. William had seen it at the front – the burning air would have incinerated those unfortunate men's lungs with their very first gasp.

Makhno's cavalry retreated hastily beyond the black smoke, chased by the enemy bullets. The front artillery wagon began firing again, sending exploding plumes of upturned earth into the midst of Makhno's men. William reloaded and shot again and again into its armored sides and turrets, trying to find and kill the invisible men inside who were still feeding shells into the cannons. In the steppe, the wave of fire was spreading. A burning horse galloped out of the flames, dragging its dead rider by the stirrup. The breeze carried the acrid scent of burning flesh and horsehair to the bluffs.

On the train, Petro had managed to scale the front of the artillery wagon and was now on the roof. He climbed on top of the first turret and tossed the steel ball of the gas grenade into the opening next to the barrel. Without waiting for the result, he moved towards the middle of the wagon and dropped another one into the ventilation pipe, and then the third one into the other turret.

The wagon fell silent. A few moments later, the reinforced door at the end of the wagon swung open and two dozen men hurriedly spilled out, pushing, stumbling, gasping and vomiting. Many collapsed to the ground on their own, while others were cut down by the Cossack bullets. Encouraged with the results, Petro jumped onto the locomotive. He hopped down into the coal tender and dropped two grenades, one after the other, into the machinist's compartment. Without hesitation, he proceeded to the top of the first boxcar.

Here, he encountered a vent pipe with a cap. As he struggled with it, first attempting to pull it off and then to knock it off with the handle of his revolver, he did not notice the roof hatch behind

305

him open. William fired, but it was too late – Petro spun around and fell. William fired again, sending the man with the revolver tumbling back into the hatch. Petro crawled towards the opening and dropped in three grenades, one after another. After that, he did not move.

The tattered remains of Makhno's cavalry had retreated into the woods. Despite the two wagons cleared out by Petro, the rest of the train was still fighting on. One of the turrets of the rear artillery wagon was breathing fire again, spewing shells into the grove. The two remaining boxcars were keeping the Cossacks on the bluff pinned down with their relentless, mechanical bursts of machine-gun fire. Petro was still not moving.

William barely had time to contemplate this unfavorable turn of events when a lone tachanka tore out from the woods. It burst through the ring of fire and flew across the steppe between the exploding shells and through the hail of oncoming bullets, making a beeline towards the head of the train. There were two riders in the tachanka. Squinting, William recognized the small figure in a black leather jacket driving the horses.

*

The tachanka bounced violently as it raced through the fields, and Anna found it easier to stand, dug in with a wide stance as she firmly gripped the reins. In the back seat, Egorov was holding on for dear life next to the machine gun. Up ahead, Petro was still lying on the roof of the armored boxcar – probably dead. On her left flank, the remainder of Makhno's Cossacks charged out of the woods to keep the enemy gunners busy, and the second tachanka carved a long arc to the rear of the train to tie up the remains of the raiding party and the dozens of soldiers from the wagons Petro had gassed. This was it. This was everything and everyone. If they failed now, it would all be over.

She did her best to maneuver around the exploding fountains of dirt and rock, trying not to think about where the next shell might strike. She needed to get to the bluff-facing side of the train, leaving Makhno to engage the enemy on the steppe side. They flew across the shallow creek at the front of the train and then up the small embankment of the tracks. She knew it was going to be a rough landing, but when they touched down on the other side of the tracks, instead of the ground, they hit a wall of detonated earth. The horses disappeared from view, and the reins were suddenly ripped from her hands. The tachanka flipped backwards, and the last thing she saw was the sky.

When she came to, she was lying on the ground, feeling scraped up and dazed. She tried to get up, but Egorov forcefully yanked her back down. A spray of bullets peppered the rocks overhead. They were behind a pile of large rocks at the base of the bluff. Twenty yards away was the wreckage of the tachanka, thrown back from the crater in the ground. The horses lay dead. Egorov must have pulled her into the rocks.

They were pinned down. The side of the train, so close and yet so far, towered like a fortress wall.

A spate of crumbled rock and shale rained from above. She looked up. William half-slid, half-jumped down the steep slope towards them, holding that oversized rifle in both hands. His arm was bandaged in a bloody rag.

"What are you doing here?" she said. "You'd be safer up top."

"Well, as you said, I can't say no to a damsel in distress," he grinned.

"And I am truly flattered," Egorov responded, putting his hand on his heart. "But I do need to get on that train. Can you do anything about that machine gun?"

William peeked out from behind the rocks, inviting a fresh hail of lead.

"God damn, you'd think they would have run out of bullets by now!?" Egorov cursed, ducking his head.

"He is in the second boxcar. I'll try to take him out," William said.

He grabbed his rifle and slipped back and over to a different position. The machine gun opened up again, tracing his movement with bullets chirping off the rocks. William placed the rifle in a space between rocks, aimed and shot into the dark opening of the embrasure. The machine gun stopped.

He reloaded to fire again, but Egorov was already on his feet, running towards the train. That's when the machine gun came back to life, and Egorov collapsed onto the ground but then hastily pulled himself behind the tachanka.

"Anton!!!" Anna screamed.

William fired again into the dark opening, reloaded, and fired once more. The machine gun was silent.

Egorov looked back and gave them a grin and a thumbs up. He jumped to his feet and ran the rest of the way to the train. William watched over him through the sights of the gun as Egorov climbed up the front of the artillery wagon and ran along its roof, hopping next onto the locomotive and then climbing onto the boxcar where Petro lay with the bag of grenades. William picked up his rifle and scrambled over the rocks back to Anna's position. Looking at her worried face, he smiled to reassure her, and just then noticed that the turret of the rear artillery wagon had turned, and the barrel of the cannon was now pointing straight at them. "Oh fuc..." he began to say, but it was already too late.

*

There was no more gunfire ringing in the steppe. Anton Egorov lay stretched out on the ground, his eyes gazing into the bright white clouds that slowly rolled and changed shape in the dizzying blue heights above. The singed ground smelled of smoke. Somewhere nearby, the creek burbled, and a soft breeze rustled in the trees. Anton Egorov was dead.

Anna held his heavy head in her lap. The front of his peasant's shirt, soaked with blood, was already beginning to dry at the edges under the hot Ukrainian sun, turning from dark red into rusty brown, caked with dust and ash.

She wanted to cry, but she couldn't. Seeing him dead had broken something inside her, and now sorrow flooded her. It was unrestrained and boundless – the old sorrow, and the new sorrow, and the sorrow yet to come. It was all so much that it made her numb, and she was unable to speak, or cry, or feel anything else except his warmth slowly fading in him. And that's how William found them. She had left him, unconscious, with a Cossack to be patched up at the supply wagon. She did not think he would be walking again so soon, but there he was – walking toward her with his head and his arm bandaged. And when he saw Egorov, his face sank. He carefully sat down beside them and put his hand on Anna's back.

She swallowed down the lump in her throat. "He finished it," she said. "He was torn up with bullets, but he did not stop until he dropped the last grenade."

He nodded without saying a word.

Makhno approached, looking battle-worn and grimy. He took off his hat. "You should come and take a look at this," he said.

Anna nodded. She closed Egorov's eyes with her hand and gently put his head on the ground. They followed Makhno down the length of the train, past the dusty iron wheels as his Cossacks were hustling about, moving cargo, horses and bodies.

"We did not find anyone named Reilly on board," he said.

"He may be using a false identity," she replied. "Were there any civilians?"

"Just one. But he was killed during the fighting."

She felt numb, and even the prospect of finding Reilly dead did not quicken her pulse. It was important, of course – she knew it in the back of her mind. But somehow it was so very distant and irrelevant at the same time.

Makhno stopped at the three bodies lined up on the ground next to the middle boxcar. Two were wearing White officer uniforms and the other a dark grey business suit. Anna examined the faces.

"It's not him."

"Are you sure?" Makhno handed her a bloodied imperial passport.

She studied the photo and then the face on the ground again.

"Gavrilov," she said. "He's one of Savinkov's lieutenants... Was." She put the passport in her pocket. "Reilly may be trying to pass for one of the Whites. I will need to check everyone who was on this train and question the commander."

"Very well. I'll have them lined up for you. The live and the dead ones."

She nodded.

"There is just one more small thing," Makhno rubbed his jaw. "How much gold did you say was on this train?"

"Twenty million. Why, is it not all here?"

"Oh, I think it is." Makhno motioned to one of his men to open the wagon.

The heavy barn door rolled open, revealing stacks of small wooden crates with the two-headed eagle imperial crest on each. The crates filled almost half of the boxcar.

"Is that all gold?" she asked.

"Every single crate. All 2,500 of them."

"This looks like more than twenty million."

He smirked. "Just a tad. How about two hundred million rubles worth?"

She sat down on the embankment next to the tracks.

"That's more than just a one-time order. This could bankroll the war for years," William said.

"As we agreed before, half of it is staying with my people," Makhno reminded. "How are you planning to take the rest to Moscow?"

Her gaze gravitated to Egorov's body on the side of the railroad a few wagons away. "Can you take us to Voronezh?" Her own voice sounded tired and distant. "We can move it from there."

Makhno nodded. "We can depart once the rock is cleared off the tracks."

He put on his hat. "I am sorry about your comrade. Including him, we lost sixty-three men today."

"How is Petro?" William asked.

"He was seriously wounded. I don't know if he will make it." Makhno studied the ground at his feet. "Now, let's go get a look at those prisoners."

Forty-seven dead bodies were lined up next to the tracks. They were laid out on their backs, shoulder to shoulder, their boots forming an uneven dusty black stripe extending alongside the train. Their faces – a bloodied, dirty, pale dotted line of final portraits against the battle-ravaged earth. They reminded her of those battalion photos taken before deployment. Like the one Victor had. Except this was not a battalion of clean, polished boys with their weapons, looking stoically into the lens. This was a battalion of ghosts. Gripped in death. So much death…

"These two are your artillery commanders," Makhno said to William, pointing at two officers on the ground, their heads covered up with bloodied army coats.

William looked away, but Anna pulled back the coats and forced herself to check what was left of their faces.

Reilly was not among the dead. He was also not among the ninety-some living, whom Makhno had lined up in tired, grimy ranks further down the track. She looked at every single face.

By the time she showed Reilly's photo to the train commander, Makhno's men had already taken a turn at interrogating him. His uniform torn, and his face beaten into a bloody mess, he examined the photo but denied ever seeing Reilly. He had dealt only with the man in the suit – Gavrilov, who was put on the train by General Alekseev himself to escort the gold to Baku.

She walked back to Makhno, who was smoking a cigarette, leaning on the side of the train. She shook her head. He nodded, put out his cigarette and climbed into the saddle. The Cossacks lined up with rifles behind the prisoners. Makhno nodded to his men, and the rifle bolts clicked. She turned away.

Shots rang out. When she looked again, only about a dozen men were lying on the ground. The ones still standing looked about nervously, or stared down, expecting more shots.

Makhno rode out in front of the ranks, his horse stepping wearily in the dust.

"Your highborn overlords are dead," he shouted, and the prisoners looked at their dead officers on the ground. "They lived, believing their aristocratic blood separated them from the working people. And today, they died by that principle. We don't take prisoners. Your wounded comrades, along with ours, will be taken to the hospital in Lugansk. And you – you now have a choice. You can leave unarmed and go home. Or you can join this volunteer people's army and help us liberate and protect this land, which will be your land."

Silence descended on the field. And then, one by one, a shout of *Hoorah!* rose up and grew to a hundred voices, as men ripped the emblems from their caps and threw them in the air. "For Makhno! For Free Territory!"

THE BIG PICTURE

William found Anna on the roof of the artillery wagon. He almost did not notice her sitting behind the turret and gazing ahead as the train rolled unhastily through the steppe. He climbed up the ladder, guarding his bandaged arm, and cautiously stood up on the sunbaked metal roof rocking gently underfoot. On the side of the wagon, Makhno's black skull and crossbones flag flapped lazily in the wind.

"May I join you?" he asked.

She looked up, squinting into the bright sky, and gave him a nod. He sat next to her, leaning against the warm metal of the turret. They sat silently for a while, feeling the sun and the breeze and listening to the sound of the wheels rolling and the flag flapping.

"The son of a bitch Reilly wasn't even on the train," she said finally, shaking her head.

"But you stopped his gold. Wasn't that your main objective?"

"Was it?" she pondered. "At *any* cost? At the cost of a good man dying on this roof? Is a wagon of gold worth a man's life?"

"Of course not. But he knowingly took this risk. And think of all the lives he saved. This gold would have bought a lot of weapons. He may have shortened this war."

"Is that what you wrote in those letters to the families of your dead comrades? Was it true every time? Did you believe it?"

He lowered his head, knowing she was right. There was never a way to rationalize the loss of someone close to you.

"I am sorry," she said and put her hand on his. "I should not have said that. It's just… this whole thing. It was all my idea. I brought him here. How do I live with that?"

"That does not make it your fault. It's this war; it's the enemy. We can't be held responsible for the situations we are put into!"

"Can't we?" She gazed ahead, where the rails were forever converging in the hazy distance.

"I think there is something terribly wrong with this world," she finally said.

He nodded, having himself considered that on a few occasions. "It's probably us…"

*

William was woken up by Anna. He opened his eyes and realized that it was dark outside and that the train was not moving. She told him it was time to go. He rolled out of his bunk and grabbed his rucksack. From the next boxcar, Makhno's men were already unloading hundreds of crates of gold onto the platform. He stared sleepily at the growing pile. Egorov's body was brought out on stretchers covered with an anarchist flag and placed on top of several crates. The horizon in the east was beginning to glow in smudged peach and pink watercolors.

Makhno stepped out onto the platform.

"Well, I guess this is goodbye, Commissar, or until we meet again," he said, extending his hand to Anna. "Thank you for everything you've done. Again, I am sorry about your friend."

"Thank you, Ataman," she said and shook his hand.

"And you, my Red Cross sharpshooter," Makhno turned to William. "I thank you for your skill and bravery in the battle. You are the first American to fight for the Free State. I hope you won't be the last." He unclipped his saber from the belt and handed it to William. "Please accept this as a token of gratitude from our people."

"It was an honor," William muttered, unprepared for ceremonial gift giving. He accepted the weighty blade with his good hand.

Makhno gave them a swaggerly salute, winked, smiled, and stepped aboard. The train hissed, puffed and pulled away.

Still waking up, William studied the black scabbard adorned with scrolling gold and silver leaf detail and the silver hawk's head with a gleaming ruby eye at the end of the handle. Anna sat on one of the crates and lit a cigarette.

"Where are your men?" he asked, looking around. "Weren't they supposed to meet us?"

"They are in Voronezh," she said.

"This is not Voronezh?" he asked, looking around and still rubbing the sleep out of his eyes.

She shook her head.

"How far are we from Voronezh?"

"About two hours."

"Why didn't we go to Voronezh?" He was beginning to feel like a child, asking question after question and still not understanding what was going on.

"It seems Makhno decided against going there. Don't worry, I have already called Voronezh from the station office, and they are sending another train."

He paced a few steps down the platform and then back to Anna: "So, all we have is your pistol and this sword to protect this pile of gold worth a hundred million rubles for the next two hours?" He cast a leery gaze at the sleepy village behind the station.

She shrugged and gave him a small smile. "Cigarette?" she said and offered him the pack.

*

In Moscow, autumn was beginning to claim the city. The sun was still warm, but the September wind was already playfully chasing the first yellow and red leaves down the cobblestones behind Lubyanka.

Anna tucked a loose strand of hair behind her ear. "I am sorry I could not get you another Rolls-Royce," she said.

William sized up the Red Cross panel truck pattering dutifully at the curb.

"This is more fitting, after all," he replied. "It will take some adjustment, but I think I will survive."

He had his dusty rucksack on his shoulder and Makhno's saber in his hand. His freshly shaved face beamed at her.

"Thank you for all you've done," she said. "And good luck in Petrograd with the Mission. Tell Robins I am sorry for returning you a bit the worse for wear."

"Thank you. And good luck to you, too. I hope you catch this Reilly. I don't know how long I will stay in Petrograd, but perhaps we will see each other again." He extended his hand.

"Perhaps we will." She shook his hand, lingering a bit in his warm, firm touch.

"I do have to tell you something, Captain Arden," she said, letting his hand go.

"What's that?"

"I think the infamous outlaw Billy the Kid would have been proud to rob trains with you."

His face spread in a grin. "Thank you." He put his hand clutching Makhno's saber over his heart. "And you should know something as well, Commissar Sokolova."

"And what is that?" She raised an eyebrow.

"You should know that all the famous world explorers can't hold a candle to you."

"And why is that?"

"Because all *they* did was find the worlds that were already there. They lacked the imagination and the guts to build a new and better one. I wish you the best of luck. I can't wait to see what you accomplish."

He raised his saber goodbye and hopped into the driver's seat. And when she heard the sound of his door closing shut, she suddenly felt alone. The transmission scraped, and the truck nudged into gear. He raised his hand, and she raised hers, and stood there, watching the truck roll down the street with a patter and disappear around the corner. The gears shifted once more and then the sound faded in the autumn air. She turned away and went inside.

Here, everything seemed the same. The same stairs and parquet hallways. The same rows of filing cabinets, the same gloomy courtyard, and, despite it being Sunday, the same cloud of cigarette smoke hanging just below the ceiling in the department.

And yet, nothing felt the same anymore. Everything felt strange and wrong. How could everything change so much in just five days? She slipped into Egorov's chair and could not hold back the cry. Emotions piled on, collapsing into her, burying her in the wreckage of this week. Of the last year. She never had the time to look back. There was always just one path forward. And always the next step to take. And each step felt right. And the cost was always acceptable. Until now.

She touched the papers on his desk. Everything was the way he left it, as if he were about to walk in, his giant frame looming in the doorway, just to stick his thumb in the strap of his suspenders and crack a joke. But he was gone.

And he wasn't the only one. She was not the same as she was when she left for Lugansk. That Anna Sokolova never came back. She thought of her as of another person now, with yet inexhausted grief. She knew exactly when she ceased to be. She had relived those moments a hundred times since yesterday. The shell exploded, and the blast wave slammed her like an invisible sledgehammer into the rock wall. When the cloud of dust thinned out, she saw William's body crumpled on the ground, covered with rubble. She pushed herself off the jagged rocks, and with her hands scraped and her legs shaking, stumbled toward him. He looked lifeless, but she grasped onto his coat and pulled his heavy body across the rubble, out of the line of fire. Her ears were ringing, and she did not hear the shots, but felt the hot sting graze her arm. She turned around to see a White soldier running towards them, his rifle raised. He was a young Russian boy, with wheat-colored hair and a thin cavalier mustache. His mouth was contorted with rage and terror, and there was hell erupting all around them. He was pulling back the bolt, to clear the spent cartridge and load the live one. The smooth, rounded handle of the Mauser slipped instinctively into her hand. He was raising his rifle again when she fired. She could not tell if her first bullet hit him – he still kept coming, and the end of his rifle was still rising towards them. She fired again and again, until he stumbled and fell, and the rifle rolled out of his hands.

She wiped her tears. What now? The last year had cost her everything and everyone she had. Her soul was heavy. She had nothing left to give, and yet she knew, if she were to stay, this job would demand more. She took off her gun belt and put it in her desk. It felt strange not to be weighed down by it. She had to go – she had been summoned to the fourth floor, and she had lingered long enough. She turned back in the doorway, to take one last glance at the office before turning out the lights.

Upstairs, Dzerzhinsky and Sergei hushed their conversation when she entered. Sergei's glance was long and penetrating, as if he were trying to read inside her head. He had suspicions, and he was right. But she did not care. She could not care less what the consequences would be. None of it mattered anymore.

"So, Reilly was never on the train?" The wrinkles in the corners of Dzerzhinsky's eyes were humorless today.

"We have no evidence to suggest that he was," she shook her head.

He scribbled in his notebook. "Any other leads on Reilly?"

"Not since September 2 in Petrograd. He could be in Samara or heading to Omsk with the rest of the gold. With his photo in all the papers, I don't think he would risk coming to Moscow or Petrograd."

He nodded and tapped his finger on his desk. "So, let me sum up this little operation you two have dreamed up and ran over the last month. As the result of your actions, the Cheka has eliminated a major domestic terrorist organization led by Savinkov, prevented a major weapons purchase by our enemies, and publicly uncovered a foreign government conspiracy against our state. Oh, and I forgot to mention the deposit of one hundred million in gold into our reserves. I'd say your little ruse has paid off beyond my wildest expectations."

He smiled at them now in earnest. "Did I miss anything? Are you two not pleased?"

She shook her head. "I am not pleased. We've lost a good man, and our two chief suspects – the masterminds behind Uritsky's murder and the attempt on Lenin – are still at large."

He nodded. "And I give you my word, the agency will not let up our search for them. Their day of reckoning will come. But in the meanwhile, you have given us something of immense value." He opened the thick file on his desk and paged through its contents. "In today's world, information can be more powerful than any weapon. This evidence of conspiracy gives us diplomatic leverage against the West. The disastrous publicity will make it harder for them to support the Whites. It will also show the workers of the world the true nature of their capitalist governments."

He closed the file. "I know this can't bring back Agent Egorov. But it will ensure his sacrifice wasn't in vain. He has saved many Russian lives, and he will receive a commendation. Does he have any next of kin?"

"Just his fiancé."

Dzerzhinsky made a note. "Was there anything else?"

Anna could feel Sergei seething with indignation next to her. His features were cold and hard, exasperated by her blatant indifference. She could have yielded and made an effort to assuage, but she had nothing left in her for him or for anyone else.

Sergei cleared his throat. "There is just the matter of Makhno. We still don't know why he decided not to proceed to Voronezh." He turned and fixed an interrogating gaze on her. "Is it possible someone tipped him off?"

Someone did, and that someone was sitting right here. But she reflected Sergei's gaze calmly.

"I was the only one who knew the plan. Makhno is clever. Maybe he suspected a trap, or maybe he had other plans all along."

Dzerzhinsky shrugged. "Well, it does not matter. I know Comrade Trotsky was disappointed, but perhaps Makhno can be of use to us as an ally, at least for the time being."

He stood up and stretched out his hand to Sergei over the desk. "You should be proud of having mentored such an excellent agent."

Sergei tightened his jaw and stood up to shake Dzerzhinsky's hand.

"Stay for a moment, Agent Sokolova, I'd like a word with you," Dzerzhinsky said as she rose up.

She settled back into the chair as Sergei walked out and closed the door. Dzerzhinsky had never before spoken with her alone. Was it something Sergei did or said? Maybe about their argument in Petrograd? The hairs on the back of her neck reflexively prickled up, anticipating another confrontation. Perhaps she was about to be excommunicated for not being a true believer. Right now, she would have been fine with that. Or maybe it would be worse.

Dzerzhinsky turned to the window and gazed at the Kremlin towers glimmering in the distance. Seconds stretched.

"You know, there is a reason the Cheka is not in the Kremlin," he finally said. "We could have been; there is plenty of space. But we are not, because we have a separate purpose. Their job is to look forward, and ours is to look around. Their job is to make sure our country has a future, and ours is to make sure we do our job so that they can do theirs. This may sound simple, but you know it is not. We are up against the best-funded and best-educated intelligence agencies of the world. We have plenty of people willing to pull the trigger for our cause, but we need more of those who can match wits with the enemy and outsmart them. Your whole approach to this operation – from infiltrating Lockhart's plot to convincing Makhno to ally with us showed intelligence, resourcefulness and creativity – everything our organization needs more of."

He studied her face. She was aware that she looked detached. "I know you are not a proponent of Red Terror. And that's OK. Not everyone is. You don't have to agree with everything the Cheka does. The Red Terror is our policy at the moment, and it will continue for now, until it runs its course. I don't want you to concern yourself with that anymore. I think it is beneath your talent. I want you to consider something entirely different."

He paused to make sure he had her attention. "As long as we have enemies outside of our borders, there will be more Reillys. Some may be on their way here as we speak. Others may already be here. Looking for more Savinkovs, funding more sabotage, assassinations and terrorism. But as long as we are reacting, we will always be a step behind them. What we need is to be several steps ahead. This is why I want you to form and lead our new department for counter-espionage. You can put together your own team and run it your way, reporting directly to me."

She swallowed. This was the farthest from what she was expecting to hear. "What about Sergei?"

"Comrade Zaverin will continue running the counter-terrorism department. Our domestic enemies will require his undivided attention for the perceivable future."

The wrinkles in the corners of his eyes smiled again. "You do want to catch Reilly, don't you? This is your chance. He and Savinkov are still alive and well. They will probably concoct another plan soon, if they haven't already."

He pulled out a small notebook from his desk drawer and slid it towards her.

"What is this?" She looked at the notebook and then back at Dzerzhinsky.

"This is Savinkov's diary. He fled abroad in a hurry and left it behind in one of his apartments. Maybe there is a lead there. If only there was someone to look into it. So, what do you say?"

ACCESSION

Blistering November wind was blowing sheets of snow in the headlights. Demidov drove with caution down the frozen road on the outskirts of Omsk, laboring to see anything up ahead. The headlights, try as they did to slash through the night, managed to illuminate only the blinding, endless stream of flurries coming at them. The storm was getting worse, and he was doing good just staying on the slippery road. Kolchak heard him exhale a sigh of relief when the faint glow of a house finally appeared up ahead, and he slowed down, trying to make out the barely visible driveway.

There were three other cars already at the front of the house. Demidov pulled up next to them, and the headlights carved out the snow-caked porch, the snow-frosted windows, and more endless snow blowing furiously across. He hurriedly got out and opened the rear door.

"Keep it running, Victor," Kolchak said, standing up the collar of his trench coat around his face. He walked to the door, his breath freezing in the icy wind and his boots crunching through the powdery snowdrifts.

Inside, three men were gathered at a table by the light of a kerosene lamp.

"Admiral! Thank God you made it!" Knox stood up to shake hands.

The other two faces at the table were all too familiar. On Knox's right was Semenov, looking fatter than the last time Kolchak saw him, and his eyes even more beady in this light. On Knox's left was the trim, cleanly-shaven Colonel Gaida – the commander of the Czechoslovak Legion. Kolchak held no affinity for either, and the fact that all three were now gathered in one place heightened his ill expectations of this meeting.

"Thank you for cutting short your time at the frontlines," Knox said. "I know this is not an ideal time."

"Why all the secrecy?" Kolchak asked, brushing the snow off his coat and his hat. He would have much rather met at the governor's mansion in Omsk.

"I am afraid there was no other way," Knox replied, inviting him to sit. "What we needed to discuss was both urgent and confidential."

Kolchak settled opposite of the trinity. The room was cold, and he kept his coat on. A small wood stove crackled reassuringly with fire in the corner, but he could still see his breath. From across the table, Semenov glared at him with his arms crossed.

"I am afraid we've reached a crisis point," Knox opened up. "The situation in Omsk has become untenable, and a change is needed. While you have been at the front, doing your promised part to fight the Reds, the All-Russian Provisional Government has failed to do theirs. They have not been able to establish themselves as a unified authority, and they have not been able to garner the trust and support of the Russian people – in Omsk or anywhere else. As you know, Colonel Gaida's troops provide protection all along the Trans-Siberian Railroad, and they are reporting disconcerting updates from across the region."

He turned to Gaida, giving him a cue to confirm.

Gaida nodded, lighting a cigarette. "There is no unified government; not in Omsk, and not in any of the other cities. It's a coalition at best, with each faction operating under its own command. My men are receiving constant complaints from the local population. There is wide-spread disorder, corruption and misconduct. Officers condone looting, profiteering and other petty crimes by their troops. Supplies and munitions are stolen from the depots. People's property, including livestock, is being taken away. There are almost daily public executions of suspected Bolsheviks. People are asking for laws regulating private property and land ownership, but the government has done nothing."

Kolchak nodded. He generally took any intelligence from the Czechoslovak Legion with a grain of salt. Foreign mercenaries were prone to exaggeration when it was to their advantage. However, in this case he knew the reports were accurate – he had heard as much himself.

Knox took over again: "Ataman Semenov is doing an admirable job of suppressing new Soviets from popping up in the area, but without a viable alternative from Omsk, this only enrages the peasants and the workers. It has now been an entire year since the Bolsheviks have taken power in Petrograd and Moscow. Yet, despite our best hopes, the provisional government in Omsk has been unable to bring about order and affect a reform that would appeal to the people. Vologodsky has failed to deliver on his promise. If he is allowed to continue, you will soon be facing a revolt behind your frontlines."

"And what is it you are proposing?" Kolchak asked.

"We need resolute leadership, not the fifteen-minister cabinet who can't agree on anything."

"Are you suggesting a coup?"

"A transition of power. Bloodless, if possible."

"Transition to what?"

"To a single ruler."

"An autocracy? You want me to betray the democratic

principles I pledged to defend, and instead support an autocrat?"

"Not betray – adapt. I fail to see another option. The current government is just too divided. Right now, what these people need is a strong, decisive leader. Someone who can be the face of the new government."

"And I am guessing you already have someone in mind as this supreme ruler?" Kolchak knew how Knox operated and could already see where this was going.

"Yes – you," Knox half-smiled.

"Absolutely not!"

"Think about it! Who better? You are already this government's supreme military commander. It only makes sense that you take the full reins of power as the supreme ruler. I think the Russian people would respond very positively."

"Sure, the Russian people had a supreme ruler just last year. And they worshiped him like a demigod. Need I remind you what happened to him? I think we should give the Provisional Government more time. It's been only two months."

Knox shook his head: "The time is running out."

"Why the rush all of a sudden?"

"The situation in Europe has changed. Germany is crumbling. Their soldiers are revolting. There is now talk about a possible armistice. If the war in Europe ends, it will become much more difficult to garner my government's support for our continued engagement here."

"So, why does it matter to the British, then? Wasn't your goal to get Russia to rejoin the war against Germany?"

"It was, but now there are also growing fears of domestic Bolshevism in England. The Reds are ramping up their propaganda in the West, and they are amassing an uncomfortable volume of sympathizers. Downing Street is keen to defeat Bolshevism, which means defeating it at the source in Russia. But if there is no viable solution in Omsk, the support for intervention will dwindle. We have an exceedingly small window of opportunity, Admiral. I have already vetted this with the Allied command. If you take charge, the Allies will recognize your government as legitimate – something the Bolsheviks will never accomplish. This will be the first significant victory towards the Russian reconstruction you desire."

Kolchak tried to consider his options but did not see many. It felt like drowning. He detested being manipulated, and he detested political machinations, and he also detested relying on foreigners. He was tired of feeling like a puppet dancing at the will of the British, and the Czechs, and the Cossacks, and the Japanese, but once again, what viable alternative did he have? Without the Allied support, the White movement would collapse.

Knox took his silence for consent, and Kolchak supposed that it was.

"So, if we were to do this, would the military support you?" Knox asked.

Kolchak nodded. "But the council is another story. Most of the ministers would turn over easily enough, but the SRs would never go for this. They are democrats. They had fought for decades to abolish the Romanov monarchy and they will fight this to their deaths."

"Then they will have to be neutralized," Knox said. "Get me a list of the SR leadership and anyone else you think would oppose the transition." He then turned to Semenov: "Ataman, can you ensure the men on the Admiral's list are detained for the duration of the transition of power, to avoid any unnecessary escalation?"

"It will be done," Semenov nodded.

"And what about the Czechoslovak divisions?" Kolchak turned to Gaida. "Where will your men stand in all this, Colonel?"

Gaida rubbed his smooth cheek. "Our men are growing weary of fighting another country's civil war, and they have even less desire to support the in-fighting between the anti-Bolshevik factions. Our arrangement is with the Allies. The best I can do is pledge that we will remain neutral in this affair and will not intervene."

"Then it is settled." Knox stood up. "Smile, Admiral," he said.

"Tomorrow you will be the sole legitimate ruler of the largest land in the world."

*

When tomorrow came, the storm had passed, and Omsk awakened to a clear, crisp winter morning. Virgin snow veiled everything, and with every slight movement of the air, the myriad of glittering flurries took to flight, fluttering carefree and sparkling in the boundless blue sky.

Kolchak had not slept. In the night, Semenov's men had raided the city, working down his list. Forty-seven names. Anyone likely to oppose him had been rounded up and taken out of the city. All forty-seven accounted for. Not harmed – he made sure of that – but simply removed.

In the early hours, dozens of Cossack checkpoints appeared. The city prickled up with bayonets and machine guns. The Cossacks secured government buildings, bridges, railroad stations, ports, telegraph and telephone stations, newspapers, and other locations of strategic significance. By the first light, squads of mounted Cossacks were patrolling the city to suppress any unrest, and two army battalions were setting up a reinforced perimeter around the governor's mansion. Not a single shot had been fired. A bloodless coup had rolled over the city like an invisible wave. Just forty-seven names – that's all it took. And now Russia was waking up to a new era.

There was no turning back now. No one to stop him. He considered why he had put Vologodsky's name on the list. The thought still hounded him now. Vologodsky would not have offered active resistance. The man had no army, no organization that would take to arms in his name. But he was popular. And Kolchak knew Vologodsky disliked him – he could sense it every time they spoke. He would disapprove, and people would listen. If not now, then later. It was prudent to just deal with it now. In the war of ideas, the enemies were many.

"Admiral, sir?" Demidov was looking at him, the pen hovering above the page.

"Yes, where was I?" Kolchak turned away from the window.

"Additionally, the military leaders shall now have the power and the authority…" Demidov read back.

"… *the power and the authority to make arrests of any political opponents of this government. They are further authorized to use any decisive measures necessary in order to stop subversive activity, including the use of military force.* Full stop," Kolchak finished. "Have this order dispatched to the entire military command," he said, putting on his overcoat. "I'll see you there."

This was it – the final bit, less than a mile away, under the high towers of the Uspensky cathedral. They said Tsarevich Nicholas had laid the first stone of its foundation as a young man, when he was passing through the city on the grand tour of his future empire. A trivial royal act that probably took him five minutes and yet had somehow imbued this cathedral with special significance. That was almost thirty years ago. But here it was now, the largest church of Siberia, standing before Kolchak in the wide, snow-covered field in the middle of Omsk. Under its crosses, Kolchak was now to be imbued with special significance. And Nicholas was dead.

A crowd had gathered, drawn in by the military band. Eight hundred of Kolchak's soldiers had already marched in and now flanked the low stage erected at the steps of the cathedral. Next, his generals and commanders took their places. Then the Allied command.

The crowd was still growing, now almost filling the field. The band stopped, and people hushed down. The grey-bearded Archbishop of Omsk climbed the steps to the stage in his black and gold vestments. This was Kolchak's cue. He turned his white horse and guided it down the snow-packed path towards the cathedral. Rising above him, the vast cupolas gleamed with golden crosses from the bright blue heavens. The air was silent, except for the snow creaking under each step of his horse.

He dismounted at the stage, ascended, and faced the crowd. The patriarch was at his side. Kolchak took a deep breath.

"Citizens of Omsk. Citizens of Russia."

His voice rang vibrant in the crisp air, reflecting from the cold stone walls and towers of the cathedral.

"The Provisional All-Russian Government has come to an end. The Council of Ministers has vested me, Admiral Alexander Kolchak, with all its power as the Supreme Ruler of All Russia and Commander-in-Chief of all Russian land and sea forces.

"I accept this responsibility at a difficult time, as our beloved country is in the throes of a bloody civil war, and our once-mighty empire has been torn apart by foes foreign and domestic. The fate of Russia hangs at the edge of an abyss, and I shall make it my mission to ensure we do not go over that edge. As your ruler, I have two chief aims. I will continue leading our fight to overthrow Bolshevism. But I will also dedicate myself to the establishment of law and order in this city and beyond, so that the Russian people can finally realize the high ideals of liberty they have been promised and denied for so long.

"But I cannot do this alone. My armies cannot do this alone. I call upon you, the citizens of Russia, to unite in the fight against Bolshevism. Help us root it out. Here, in Omsk, and everywhere else. If you stand with me, we will defeat it once and for all."

There were some cheers, whistles and applause from the crowd. He scanned his audience. Here he was now – before his people. And before the British, the French, the Czechs, the Americans, the Japanese, and the priest. Was God here, too? Was this his will? If it weren't, surely, he would have intervened by now.

He turned towards the archbishop, knelt down and bowed his head. The priest lifted a gold cross with both hands over him and began chanting.

"*O Lord our God, God of Power and Might, powerful in strength, strong in battle, You once gave miraculous strength to Your righteous child David, granting him victory over his enemy the blasphemer Goliath. Mercifully accept our humble prayer...*"

The golden cross was brought down to Kolchak's lips to kiss. From the corner of his eye, Kolchak saw the second priest ascend the stage with a vessel of holy water. Behind him were the walls of the cathedral. Kolchak wondered which stone Nicholas had placed. If it was really the first one, it must have been somewhere under the ground now, under all this weight. Just as Nicholas himself now was. Kolchak wondered what Nicholas was thinking about as he stood before the priest at his own coronation. What was he feeling? Did he have an epiphany? A divine revelation of his purpose? Of the plan?

The cold spray of holy water landed on his face.

"...*let your spirit be brave and let your heart be stronger and bring victory over your enemies, trusting in God, in the name of the Father, Son and Holy Spirit.*"

He looked up to see the priest make the sign of the cross above his head three times. The priest motioned him to rise.

And when the bells of the cathedral rang out loud in the bright winter skies, Kolchak arose.

WASHINGTON

"Just keep your mouth shut, unless he addresses you directly. Don't volunteer any information he does not ask for. He is already not a proponent of military intelligence; we don't need to give him a reason for more cuts."

William nodded, trying to keep up. The tall, lanky, uniformed man setting the pace with long strides was his boss, Colonel Van Deman. The colonel's taut, upright posture and graying hair of a career army man usually projected confidence, but right now all William sensed was his tenseness. Van Deman was on edge, and William supposed anyone would be, having been summoned and their operations 'poked into'. They walked briskly down the long, carpeted hallway. This place was a lot bigger than it seemed from the outside.

"Do you have any idea why he asked for me?" Van Deman's anxiety was beginning to rub off. He had been back for barely two days and felt underprepared.

"I received no additional information. But watch what you say about the Petrograd business – he has lunch with J. P. Morgan every week."

Two more turns deposited them in the reception area. They waited to be announced and then waited again before the secretary finally returned and led them in. William followed Van Deman through a white door and found himself in a vast oval-shaped room with olive-green walls. Here, behind a large desk, sat a slender man in a grey pinstripe suit. He pushed some papers to the side and stood up to greet them. The long face, familiar from the papers, was clean-shaven and sporting those trademark small frameless glasses.

"Mr. President," Van Deman said, "allow me to introduce Captain William Arden. Prior to joining us at the Military Intelligence Division in Washington, the captain has served under General Pershing in the G-2 Intelligence Division in France, where he was wounded in the line of duty."

William shook Woodrow Wilson's hand. The president's hand was cool and smooth, he noted to himself in an involuntary testament to Robins' tutelage.

"It is a pleasure to meet you, Captain," Wilson smiled warmly. "I've heard a lot of good things about you from the colonel, although he refused to tell me your name until just now." He cast a reproachful glance at Van Deman.

"We must do our best to protect our assets, Mr. President," Van Deman replied. "They prosper in obscurity."

Wilson gestured them to the chairs in front of his desk and settled back into his. He put his long fingers together and fixed his gaze on William.

"I wanted to talk to you personally, Captain Arden, as you have very recent, first-hand experience in Russia."

He waited for William to nod in acknowledgment: "Yes, Mr. President."

"How would you characterize the circumstances of your mission?"

"I positioned myself to be recruited by the American International Corporation, which sent me to Petrograd under the cover of an American Red Cross Mission."

"And how would you characterize your objective?"

"My objective was to determine whether certain American business interests were acting to subvert or compromise America's military operations in Russia."

"And by *certain American business interests*, you mean the AIC? You can be direct with me, Captain. I may work closely with Wall Street, but I am not so naïve as to confuse their interests with those of the American people."

"Yes, Mr. President – the American International Corporation and the affiliated banking, mining, manufacturing and transportation organizations."

Wilson nodded. "And this operation was unwittingly facilitated by your uncle who is a director at Chase National Bank in New York?"

"That is correct."

"And to the best of your knowledge, neither the AIC, nor Chase, nor the American Red Cross were aware that you were working for the Military Intelligence Office?"

"No, sir."

"And are they aware now?"

"I do not believe so, sir."

Wilson kept his steady gaze on William. "And so, Captain, were you able to reach a determination as a result of your mission?"

"Yes, Mr. President. I have found no evidence of direct efforts to compromise our military operations, but there is clearly a significant private funding campaign underway that is intended to counteract the Allied intervention. It would be naïve not to expect that this funding is being used by the Reds to finance their military efforts to fight the Whites and the Allied forces, including our own boys."

Wilson nodded casually, unsurprised. He pivoted in his chair. "Captain, as you know, today we live in a world that is much changed compared to the one in which you started your mission. The Armistice with Germany has just been signed. Next month, there will be a Senate Judiciary Committee hearing on Bolshevism and the increased Red propaganda in our nation. In two months, there will be a peace conference in Paris to finally conclude this war. I wish I could say world politics will become simpler now that the war is over, but that is just not the case. I am afraid the world will become even more polarized in some ways. And so, whereas ambiguity may have been acceptable and maybe even to our advantage in the past, now I will need certainty. So, please consider what I am about to ask you as especially important. I want your absolutely honest opinion."

Wilson paused and William nodded under his gaze.

"So, here is my question. Based on your observations, is it possible that Robins or others at the AIC are working for the Bolsheviks?"

This was a question which William himself had considered before. He shook his head. "I have seen no evidence of this, sir. While their work is most certainly contributing to the success of the Bolshevik state, I believe they are acting from purely opportunistic motives to the benefit of the American corporations."

Wilson leaned back in his chair. "I am relieved to hear this. Although, as a supporter of the American Red Cross, I am absolutely disheartened to learn that the noble mission of this organization has been debased with commercial purposes."

"I agree, sir," William offered. "And if there is any silver lining to this, it is that Mr. Robins has, despite his commercial motivations, managed to create the closest thing to a diplomatic channel with the Soviet leadership, and in the process has also built considerable good will towards America. This is something Ambassador Francis has apparently not been interested in doing. During my time in Russia, Robins had standing meetings with many members of the Central Soviet, including Trotsky, on a weekly basis. I am not aware of any other foreign agent – diplomatic or commercial – who has managed to attain this level of access to their leadership."

Wilson chuckled and shook his head. "Raymond Robins' audacity and people skills continue to astound me. Perhaps he would make a more capable ambassador than Francis. At least he had the presence of mind not to get tangled in that British conspiracy like some of the State Department fellows."

He contemplated for a moment. "Do you suppose the Reds stand a chance of winning the civil war? Everyone in Washington is telling me *no*."

"I think their victory is *very* possible, sir, but the sheer scale of their conflict makes it difficult to predict the outcome with certainty. If we consider our own American civil war, we can appreciate the intensity of convictions at play. But Russia also has a much larger territory and many more factions and sides in this conflict. By some counts, there have already been two million casualties in the first year alone, which is three times the losses in our entire civil war. And with continued foreign intervention, the conflict will only intensify and prolong with no end in sight. Given the size of their country, I believe it is likely the war will go on for several more years."

Wilson nodded and stood up, extending his hand to shake. "Thank you for your candor and for your service, Captain," he said with a smile.

William rose and shook his hand. "If I may ask, Mr. President, what do you anticipate being the outcome for Russia as the result of the Paris peace talks? In your *Fourteen Points for Peace* address, you had called for an end to imperialism and for allowing self-determination for nations. Does this mean you expect the intervention to end soon?"

Wilson's smile faded. "Captain, the unfortunate truth is that the Allies never took kindly to the principles I had expressed in the *Fourteen Points*. It appears I am an idealist in the company of wolves. As hopeful as I may be that America will herald the principles of self-determination, I fully anticipate the Paris Peace Conference will turn into the largest squabble over territories and reparations this world has ever seen. Unfortunately, the Soviets had signed a separate peace with Germany, so they will be excluded from the negotiations. And so, any actions or decisions towards Russia by the Allies will likely not be in the interests of Russia."

As he walked with Van Deman back from the Oval Office, William's thoughts carried him to Anna again. He had thought of her often since they had parted in Moscow two months ago. He wondered where she was and what she was doing. He hoped she was safe. He thought of the touch of her hand in his and wished more than anything to see her face again, and this time to pull her close to him and feel her heartbeat next to his. But she was on the other side of the world, and he did not know if he would ever see her again.

AGENT ST1

At 1:30 in the morning, the phone rang at No. 21 Queen Anne's Gate – a brick rowhouse on a sleepy blind street at the edge of St. James's Park in the heart of London. In the bedroom upstairs, a light came on. A balding, grey-haired man fumbled around for his glasses and sat up in bed.

The phone rang again. He cleared his throat and picked up the receiver.

"Yes?"

"Director Cumming?" A woman's voice.

"Yes."

"This is the office of Ambassador Howard in Stockholm."

"Yes?"

"We have a man here who claims to be an SIS agent. He is carrying a German passport in the name of George Bergman."

"Where is Scale?"

"Captain Scale is in Norway and cannot be reached at this time."

"Did this man show you anything?"

"Yes. He has a coded message hidden under the cork of a pill bottle. It looks like our code, but we cannot decode without Captain Scale. He says he is ST1."

Cumming straightened up. "Very well, put him on."

The phone line clicked and crackled.

"ST1?"

"Hello, Chief."

"Bloody hell, where have you been for the last two months? We've just about written you off as dead."

"It took me longer than anticipated to exfiltrate."

"That's hardly surprising, with your photo in all the papers. I must say, you've caused quite a stir at Whitehall. This is not how we prefer to operate."

"My apologies, Chief. The situation turned volatile. We have had a few setbacks, but believe me, we are back on track. I can update you on the next steps when I am back in London."

"Yes, yes. So, what do you need?"

"New papers. All I have left is this German passport, and it won't be of much help the rest of the way from here to England."

"I'll have the embassy take care of it."

"Thank you, Chief."

"Oh, and one more thing, ST1."

"Yes, Chief?"

"The Foreign Office is furious. It took them a month to get Lockhart freed. Had you succeeded, things may have been different. But as it stands, you have few allies left there. If I were you, I would prepare myself and expect that there will be an inquiry. For your sake, I hope whatever plan you still have in the works will be sufficient to appease them. Regardless, consider carefully the story you are going to tell about any involvement you may or may not have had in the events that transpired in Moscow and Petrograd."

THE LETTER

There was a letter on her desk. Anna saw it the moment she walked through the door. In the early morning light, it glowed softly like weathered bone from across the office. Her heart sank. This wasn't mail; mail did not get delivered here, to the secure room on Lubyanka's fourth floor. She came into the office early all the time – she liked to read the intelligence briefs before her team came in – and there had never been anything on her desk that she had not left there the night before.

She shook the snow off her coat and walked past the empty desks and past the wall pinned with photographs and notecards.

The envelope showed signs of a long journey in someone's pocket. It had been folded in half at some point and was now scarred with creases and worn at the edges. And yet it bore no name and no address, no postage stamps, and no other sign of its destination or origin. She turned it in her fingers with caution; it was thin. She tore it open and found a single folded page from a notebook. She knew that handwriting – the neat rows of rounded letters and evenly spaced words honed over the painstaking hours of practice and discipline at the Smolny academy.

> *My dearest Anna,*
> *It will likely be a surprise to you to find that we did not reach Switzerland. Papá, Mamá and I were taken off the train and detained by the Bolsheviks at the Finnish border. They said Papá has been giving money to the counter-revolutionaries. They put us on another train, but we do not know where to. A man came to see us at one of the stops and said he knew you and could get this letter to you. I am sorry I do not have time to write more.*
> *Find us, please.*
> *Love, Masha.*

For exclusive discounts on Matador titles,
sign up to our occasional newsletter at
troubador.co.uk/bookshop